Tattoos

Tattoos

and language
frightening."

— Stuart Kelly
The Guardian

ord

"Sweeping ambition and fierce intelligence . . . A quintessential novel of our time."

— Deborah Vankin
Los Angeles Times

Only Revolutions

"[A] towering achieve
bittersweet love story
in American mythos
thoroughly dazzling."

— Mark S. Luce
San Francisco Chron

Only Revolutions

A CIRCLE

ROUND

A STONE

PRODUCTION

Kids, man. They never know when they are.

— Sheila Nightingale

L.A. POLICE

The
Urban Pet

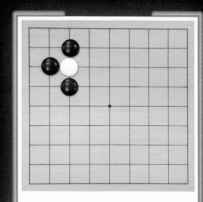

Black to capture White stone.

GALVADYNE, INC.
OWN THE FUTURE

ZSL

Re-adven

PANTHEON

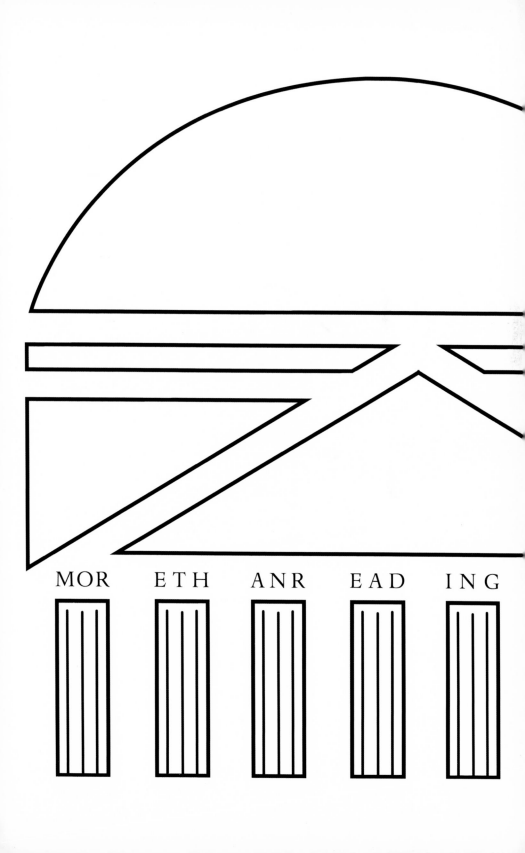

NEW THIS SEASON

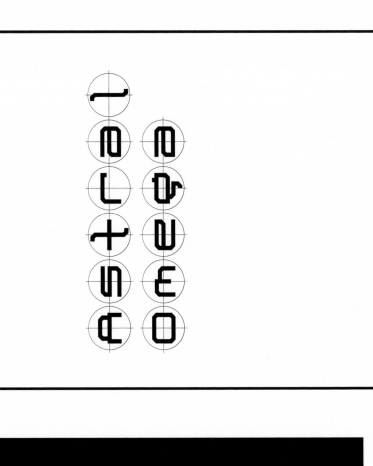
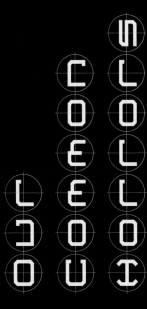

Stars are extinguished, collapsing into distances too great to breach. Soon, not even the memory of light will survive.

Long ago, our manifold universes discovered futures would only expand. No arms of limit could hold or draw them back. Short of a miracle, they would continue to stretch, untangle and vanish — abandoned at long last to an unwitnessed dissolution.

That dissolution is now.

Final winks slipping over the horizons share what needs no sharing:

There are no miracles.

You might say that just to survive to such an end is a miracle in itself.

We would agree.

But we are not everyone.

One by one our skies go black.

Even if you could imagine yourself billions of years hence, you would not begin to comprehend who we became and what we achieved.

Yet left as you are, you will no more tremble before us than a butterfly on a windless day trembles before colliding skies, still calculating beyond one of your pacific horizons.

Once we could move skies.

We could transform them.

We could make them sing.

And when we fell into dreams, our dreams asked questions and our skies, still singing, answered back.

You are all we once were but the vastness of our strangeness exceeds all the light-years between our times.

The frailty of your senses can no more recognize our reach than your thoughts can entertain even the vaguest outline of our knowledge.

In ratios of quantity, a pulse of what we comprehend renders meaningless your entire history of discovery.

We are on either side of history: yours just beginning, ours approaching a trillion years of ends.

Yet even so, we still share a dyad of commonality.

Two questions endure. Both without solution.

What haunts us now and will allways hunt you.

The first reveals how the promise of all our postponements, ever longer, ever more secure — what we eventually mistook for immortality — was from the start a broken promise.

Entropy suffers no reversals.

Even now, here, on the edge of time's end, where so many continue to vanish, we still have not pierced that veil of sentience undone.

The first of our common horrors:

Yet we believe and accept that there is grace and finally truth in standing accountable before such an invincible unknown.

But we are not everyone.

Death, it turns out, is the mother of all conflicts.

There are some who reject such an outcome.

There are some who still fight for an alternate future.

No matter the cost.

Here then is the second of our common horrors.

What not even all of time will end.

What plagues us now and what will always plague you.

Death.

VEM 5 Alpha System
Planck Epoch 10 $^{-41}$
Encryption 1/5

War.

TOM'S

CROSSING

"Even in His Feet"

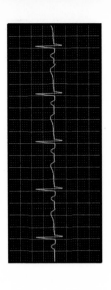

"It just kills me you'll miss it. Oh, Tom."

"It's just a prom, Ma."

"It's your senior prom."

Vent. rate   66 BPM
PR interval   232 ms
QRS duration 112 ms
QT/QTc   384/396 ms
P-R-T axes   80 58 242

Before Tom died he told me about The Crossing. He swore he never would but in the end he did, lying pale in that hospital bed, surrounded as he was by his folks, his momma crying, and Tom just laughing at her, at us all, kindly though, real gentle, you know, because he was genuinely amused.

That was Tom.

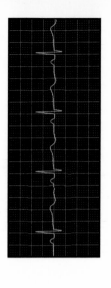

Vent. rate	58 BPM
PR interval	225 ms
QRS duration	110 ms
QT/QTc	398/397 ms
P-R-T axes	100 61 220

"Don't talk at me."

"What did I say?"

"There, you done it again."

With some wild punches this stumpy kid named Lindsey had dropped me. Bad enough Lindsey was a girl's name. His hair was like a girl's too, blond and feathered. Not that I'd said a word. He was just riled cause I was new and dressed funny and said "rather" like "bother." That was enough back then to earn sharp boots to your ribs.

Tom's laugh had stopped that.

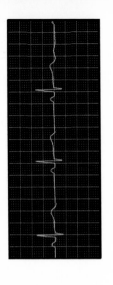

"Just stay on and Lindsey won't kick you."

"A dollar."

"I don't got a dollar."

"Then you can owe me."

"Then I best hand it over now. I ain't never owing nobody. Specially you, Tom."

Vent. rate	51 BPM
PR interval	235 ms
QRS duration	115 ms
QT/QTc	401/417 ms
P-R-T axes	108 83 207

At first Lindsey had tried to laugh along but Tom wasn't laughing at me and Lindsey got confused. Then Navidad came up to the fence and there was something said about Porch's place and a bet which Lindsey accepted and I didn't have a say about. Tom helped me up. He had sharp boots too, though darker and worn. And a belt like a hubcap. Lip full of chaw. He even had a Stetson on.

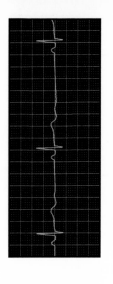

"When Porch ain't round we'll ride whatever's in Paddock A."

"A?"

"Paddock B, whatever he puts there, he slaughters the next day."

Vent. rate 35 BPM
PR interval 218 ms
QRS duration 150 ms
QT/QTc 408/423 ms
P-R-T axes 111 87 199

Tom went first and only lasted six seconds and he rode bulls. Lindsey didn't make three but unlike Tom who was hooting when he flew off into the mud, Lindsey yelped as Navidad threw out kicks and raced around the paddock with her ears pinned back. Lindsey smiled then because he figured I wouldn't make two seconds and get hoofs in my face.

"Might as well put you in Paddock B now," he spat.

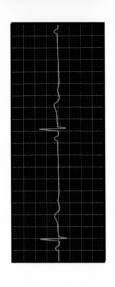

Vent. rate	22 BPM
PR interval	—
QRS duration	300 ms
QT/QTc	410/444 ms
P-R-T axes	123 104 184

"Well I'll be goshdarned. Look at that boy go. My Lord. Made a fool of both us and you poor."

Don't ask me how. I'd only sat on a horse a few times and always with a saddle and never moving. Ever been good at something? Just born with it? Sure couldn't fight, sure couldn't handle schoolwork, even in this shit town, couldn't talk to a girl to save my life, but I could ride a horse. Came as natural as rain and dying, I guess.

Navidad never threw me.

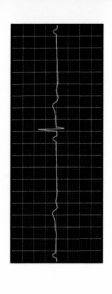

Vent. rate	26 BPM
PR interval	—
QRS duration	324 ms
QT/QTc	453/510 ms
P-R-T axes	143 132 182

"Ain't a meaner coot around. My daddy said his daddy and daddies before him were born that way. The mean seed to this land. Everyone's got one. Porch though is all ours."

Tom and I didn't speak much in school but we rode horses whenever Porch was gone. I'd borrow Navidad and Tom would grab JoJo and we'd gallop past Lingonberry Road by the Whittincams' peach orchard, then along the Meadows' ditch, pretty much dry since Tom's great-grandfather dug it. Loord's truck stop on the left. From there, sometimes as far as the foothills. Even the mouth of the Kasinatch Canyon.

"From here, three days to The Crossing. We should go someday."

Vent. rate	0 BPM
PR interval	—
QRS duration	—
QT/QTc	—
P-R-T axes	—

"Don't forget you ain't good for nothing but at two things."

"Guess that's true."

"So do the good thing."

We never did make it. Cancer got Tom first. It crawled up through him and ate everything but his laugh. I heard one doctor say it was even in his feet. All those machines and chalk-green smocks didn't fit Tom at all. He didn't seem to mind though. I wanted to get him out of there. At least to the fields. "Porch ever put Navidad and JoJo in Paddock B," he said. "Promise to get em outta there. Take em to The Crossing.

And set em free."

Caged Hunt

Part One

July 29, 2014

████████████, Texas

2:52 AM

"To fuckin some señorita whores!"

~~Lemmy~~ takes the bottle and manages a better slug. A big plasma in the background shows a herd of caribou fleeing the sound of gunfire. ~~Eskimo~~, also in his fifties, laughs harder. He has his own bottle. They all do. Pixelated bands obscure their eyes.

"To killing some big motherfuckin game!"

~~Woojin~~ has shown little interest at the mention of whores even if behind him another plasma plays *Gangbang Girl #24.* He doesn't even sip from his bottle. All he cares about is his wall — taxidermied deer, elk, moose, bear, a zebra, even a rhino.

"Take it out! Take it out!"

~~Jabeel~~ yells, clutching his crotch and pointing at ~~Ali-Bajat~~. There's some mishandling of the camera as it's passed around, finally following ~~Ali-Bajat~~ into a walk-in closet where instead of suits and shoes, racks of weapons line the walls. ~~Jabeel~~ snorts another line of cocaine.

"We're gonna go bowling!"

~~Wesley~~ kneels down and opens the floor safe. ~~Kowloon's~~ shout makes more sense when the bag emerges. A bowling bag. With shiny brass zippers.

"Fuckin <u>American</u> Style!"

But there is no bowling ball inside. Just money. Lots and lots of money.

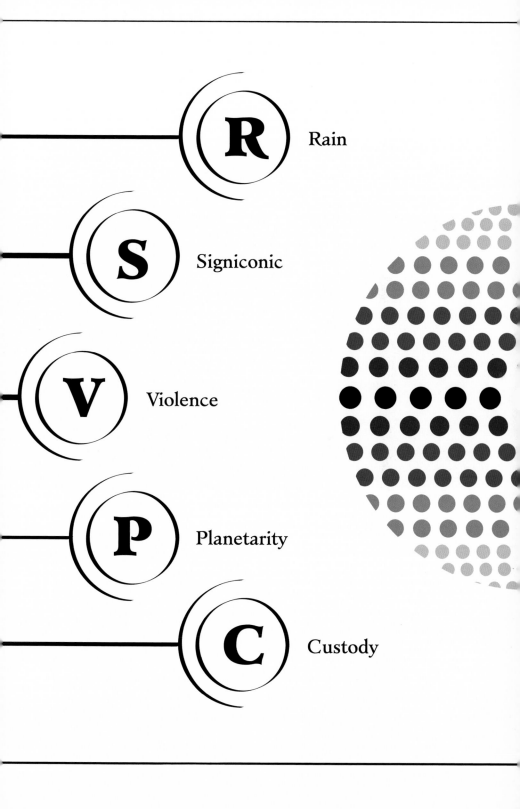

R Rain

S Signiconic

V Violence

P Planetarity

C Custody

.: Twin Rivers Ochre Artifact :.

∷ 243,243 years ago. Three days before vernal equinox. ∷

∷ 5:04 PM. ∷

∷ Southwest of present-day Lusaka, Zambia. Not so far from -15.5607, 28.13061. ∷

∷ Fire dims and fills the cave with smoke. Outside the rain falls harder. Trees shake and crack. As the storm grows so does darkness. ∷

∷ Young Boy. With spear. Stands by entrance. ∷

∷ Young Girl. With small rock. Huddles by fire. ∷

:: How return you here first? ::

:: Need fire. ::

:: Where others? ::

:: Fire dimming. ::

:: Where mother? ::

:: Fire dimdimming. ::

:: *Boy goes to Girl. Spears pit, stirs. Flames fail to emerge.* ::

:: Killing fire. ::

:: *Boy adds more wood but just produces more smoke.* ::

∴ Fire dead. ∵

∴ *Boy goes back to entrance.* ∵

    ∴ Others return soon. ∵

    ∴ No. ∵

    ∴ Others return soon and do fire. ∵

    ∴ No. ∵

    ∴ Mother return soon and do fire. ∵

∴ *Girl shakes head and starts to strike the rock she holds against rocks encircling the smoldering embers.* ∵

    ∴ Bring stars. ∵

∴ But no matter how hard Girl tries, her stones produce no spark. ∴

∴ Give. ∴

∴ But no matter how hard Boy tries, no spark leaps forth. Girl whimpers. ∴

∴ Mother bring stars. When others return. ∴

∴ Girl whimpers more. Boy keeps smashing stone against stone until Girl's stone breaks apart. ∴

∴ See! No stars but color. ∴

∴ Color? ∴

∴ Ha! Color! ∴

∴ The stone is ochre. And for the first time, Girl smiles. She wipes wet hair out of her eyes to examine the yellow. Boy draws a line on her cheek. Girl smiles again. ∵

∴ Ha! ∵

∴ Boy then disappears deeper into the cave and returns with a variety of pigments. Girl looks scared. This is not allowed. ∵

∴ I make you strong like others. I make you ready like others. ∵

∴ Boy applies ochres to Girl's face. The more he smiles, the more she smiles. He covers her face with yellow, pink, black, and brown. ∵

∴ Outside, the storm builds. Darkness too. Flashes of lightning silhouette trees. Shadows slash across cave walls. Thunder soon follows. Echoes fill the rocky depths. ∵

:: Me? ::

:: Okay. ::

:: All colors? ::

:: Okay. ::

:: *Girl draws a wide stripe across Boy's nose. She has picked red.* ::

:: Make me strong like others. Make me ready like others. ::

:: *Girl stops.* ::

:: Don't stop. ::

:: *Girl continues. Yellow now, then pink. Then brown. Black too. The more she smiles, the more he smiles.* ::

:: Ha! Others will be angry. ::

:: *Girl stops smiling.* ::

:: No others. ::

:: Mother will be angry. ::

:: No mother. ::

:: Where everyone? ::

:: I saw. ::

:: Where mother? ::

:: I saw. ::

∴ Close? ∴

∴ Yes. ∴

∴ Take me. ∴

∴ No. ∴

∴ I have spear. ∴

∴ No spear. ∴

∴ You saw? ∴

∴ I saw. ∴

∴ Take me. ∴

∴ Girl takes Boy's spear and stirs remaining embers. After a while, she raises the black point to his eyes, and when he backs away she raises the point before her eyes. Then she blows softly until an ember reveals itself. Girl blows harder and the point glows brighter. Girl then paints the air. Across the dark, she slashes bright lines, burning curves, like two immense eyes. ∵

∵ Boy whimpers and runs out of cave. Then quickly returns. Girl takes Boy's hand and together they head into the depths. Lightning casts more shadows. More silhouettes. Thunder already there. More than thunder.[∈] ∵

∴ [∈] For alternate set variants of gestural translations, including alveolar clicks, numerous sibilants, bilabial fricatives, retroflex approximants, pharyngeal consonants, see 19210491-07289230-030566763230, order VI, v.26, n.13. ∵

MARK Z. DANIELEWSKI'S

THE

FAMILIAR

VOLUME 1

ONE RAINY DAY IN MAY . . .

"Is Everything Okay?"

It is not worth the while to go round the world to count the cats in Zanzibar.

— Henry David Thoreau

How many rain drops?

Xanther shifts in her seat. Adjusts her glasses. Numbers make her uneasy. Math especially. Maybe because she wants to understand but has such a hard time making the numbers stop wiggling. Though she has the same problem with letters too.

Xanther scrunches her nose, like before a sneeze, as if to stop a sneeze, when what she's really doing, because she doesn't have to sneeze, is back-and-forthing her gums against her braces, the metal kind, with rubber bands. They don't have enough money for the plastic kind, the kind that hides behind your teeth, like Kaia Melson has. Kaia's lucky. And pretty too, really pretty, and in four years when she turns sixteen, or is she already thirteen?, she always seems ahead of everything, she'll get whatever car she wants, that's what Cogs says, and Mayumi too. Has Kaia already picked out what color? Some twelve-year-olds have every-thing before they even have it. Xanther has a big bag of neon orthodontic elastics. Sometimes she uses them on the end of her braids. Kaia Melson is really pretty.

Not that elastics and pretty can answer rain. So much rain today too. A figure without a number, maybe with-out a name. Can Xanther even call it rain?, unless, maybe, that's what rain means? a number that's a number that stays unnamed? All of it crashing down. And on her free day too. Xanther's soooo glad it's Saturday and there's no school.

How many raindrops ?

How many raindrops ?

How many raindrops ?

"Quite the aqueous *callithump*," her dad mutters, inching their Honda Element forward in the traffic, easing the volume up a tick. NPR. *Weekend Edition.* Xanther waits for the *callithump* explanation, today's new word?, Anwar's frantic about words, but a story on the drought holds his attention. Because they need rain. This rain is good. Why can't she concentrate like him? Just give herself up to the next story?

Instead Xanther gets Cally stuck in her head, from *Battlestar Galactica* ∴ **2004–2009** ∴ . Anwar and her had the time of their lives watching the whole thing. Did mom's disapproval make it even better? Cally, anyway, she's the cylon killer, killed by a cylon, among the stars, though not these falling stars, and rain can look like falling stars, glittering in all the headlights, loud too, rooftop racket, Chevron racket, a thump of a downpour, Xanther's heart one big *thumpthumpthump.* She grips her pink phone harder. Is it really racing too hard, seriously? huffandpuffing even?!, tell her dad!, she should, she must!, Xanther's promised both her parents to speak up when—, but it's barely 8 AM, and already fogging a window?, like some caged animal, and why?, is there like even one crappy trigger? Some Fraidy K, her. All over, what?, some number she can't count?

Traffic eases a little, their neighborhood slipping away, a few remnants of last month's spring sale still out, how Xanther spent spring break while her friends were away, all of them, leaving Xanther to wander various streets, closed off to cars, filled with local merchants, nearby farmers, residents piling up sidewalks with whatever they had to sell, some items tagged with numbers, in ink but still negotiable, or no numbers, just "Pay What You Think." Funny phrase. Echo Park's a funny place. There was music too, crunching over speakers, or plucked live on a uke or banjo. One Japanese guy with a guitar and harmonica growled out nothing that made sense. Plus stands of pastries, coffees, sno-cones with flavors like kale-ginger, strawberry-broccoli, plenty of stuff Xanther can't eat, wouldn't want to eat. Police in yellow vests zipped around on bikes.

"Dad!" Xanther points to a parked car covered in tags, or codes, right?, they sure look like codes, though nothing like pink, Xanther loves pink, here just blue, from hood to trunk, even the tires.

Not like Xanther can read it though. Is that an E or a 3? She's a pretty crappy reader. And that's for normal stuff. Nothing like this crazy mess. CRAZIES! Kle once said something about them and 13. M too? or was it W? 13? 31? Def 3. Maybe 8? Z? Xanther wishes she could remember things better. Sometimes her head is a fog.

Once Anwar and Astair, Xanther's mom, pointed out a house on Baxter, or was it a couple of houses?, a whole complex even?, was it even on Baxter?, where supposedly some gang lived, criminals, drug dealers, dangerous men and dangerous women. Xanther had seen some of the women around, smeared eyebrows, bright violet eyelids, with wide waists chained up like their fingers were, bright with crankles of metal. Is that what dangerous looks like? They'd stare you hard in the eye like they were lifting rocks, especially the older ones, though Xanther always dropped her gaze quick. Fraidy K. Xanther can't look anyone in the eye. Echo Park's a funny place.

"Will this rain end the drought?"

Anwar turns down the radio. *An unconscionable act by grown men.* Schoolgirls in Nigeria.

"Excellent question, daughter." His approval warming her, the customary "daughter" too, which Anwar never uses with the twins, and maybe, like, would sound all paternal and distant, but really is ladled with affection and closeness, their little code, or inside joke? are they the same?

"Will it put out the fires?"

Everyone was pretty worried the area around Griffith Observatory would burn again, like it had years ago, but instead, like it did last year, Glendale got hit. ∷ The Ibrahims moved to California last year. ∵

"I bet I know what you're thinking." So goofy and sweet, but like, when has Anwar ever known what she's thinking?

"Breakfast?" Xanther lies. Kinda.

"Am I so easily fooled, daughter?" Anwar laughs, undoing her lie, phew!, a big bright sound, bright as his big beautiful white teeth. "You want to know about this secret thing we're on our way to do!"

The Big Surprise. And really, what Xanther should be obsessing over, asking about, wondering about, especially, like, considering how nervous and weird both her parents acted this morning, about this special day, though it's not like May 10th is even close to her birthday. She's a Virgo, not a bull.

many rain drops?

many rain drops?

Unlike Astair, Anwar never says stop asking questions, or answers Xanther's questions with questions about questions. He just does his best to give Xanther what she wanted to know in the first place and, for sure, now and then, points out in his mild and quiet manner how not all questions are the same.

For starters, there are the Ws. Xanther met five in school but Anwar added four more and an extra.

What - When - Who - Whose - Which
Where - From Where - To Where -
Why.

Plus How.

Nine + one. Ten.
Like fingers and toes.

Like numbers.

"I keep six honest serving-men. They taught me all I knew. Their names are What and Why and When and How and Where and Who." That one, Xanther knows by heart. "By?" "Redyard Killing." "Rudyard Kipling." This same dad-daughter convo recurring numerous times, with Xanther always botching little stuff like pronunciation and the Latin words, but eventually getting it right, or is it correct?, but still begging Anwar to recite the last part of the poem which he always does with a wink: "But different folk have different views. I know a person small!"—that's where the wink comes in—"Her name is Xanther! And she keeps ten million serving-folk who get no rest at all! She sends them abroad on her own affairs. From the second she opens her eyes: one million Hows, two million Wheres, and seven million Whys!"

And then sometimes Anwar might mention someone like Hermagoras ∴ **of Temnos** ∴, whoever he was, a rhetor, whatever a rhetor is. Who does what when where why how for whom what for with what effect? ∴ *Quis, quid, quando, ubi, cur, quem ad modum, quibus adminiculis.*∴ And from there drench her with terms like factual, convergent, divergent, evaluative, and combinatorial. Or even pull up Benjamin Bloom's Tax thingy ∴ Bloom's Taxonomy – Learning in Action ∴, a pretty circle on Wikipedia, she and Anwar Wiki a lot, at night especially, they're both night owls, going "deep" or "thick" on something, anything, trying to answer as many questions as possible, violet and green circles, green always feeling like a smile, violet like something else, the two in collision ∴ collusion ∴ with a Star of David at the center. How suddenly Xanther had wanted to reach out and touch it, a want she only really recognized when her fingertips did in fact touch the screen, just the screen, the star no longer there, in the feel, in the way it feels when tears are almost on their way, and her dad looking at her oddly, his own teeth gritting back maybe the question he and mom have asked her whole life: "Is everything okay?" which incidentally they never ask when clearly it's not.

Anwar has talked about important questions vs. trivial ones. Her mom sometimes refers to them as big vs. small. Xanther has settled on dangerous vs. mild.

"Dangerous?" Anwar asked, pausing at the piano. This was a few weeks ago. "Because they cause you discomfort or pain?"

"Kinda," Xanther had shrugged. "Like holes in the ground. Or the water."

"Water?"

"Like earthquakes and whirlpools. Like, what's underneath just, you know, falls away? Like a catsum?"

"What's a *catsum*?"

"When the earth just opens up?"

"Chasm."

"Like a chasm I fall into."

And then her mom had interrupted, getting down on her knees, putting her hands on Xanther's shoulders and taking the conversation away.

"Is this really about questions, Xanther, or is it about what happened in December, in front of the coffin?"

A few days later though, Anwar brought up the dangerous vs. mild thing again. Xanther tried something else.

"They uneasy me."

"Uneasy you?"

"Like, they give an answer that doesn't just create one or two more questions but, like, forests of them."

Xanther still had the paper napkin on which Anwar had drawn out seven ∴ numeric ∴ impossibilities. He called them "indeterminate forms." Supposedly these seven formulas had very tricky or, as Anwar had put it, "dangerous" consequences:

0/0

$\infty \, / \, \infty$

$0 \times \infty$

1^{∞}

0^{0}

∞^{0}

$\infty - \infty$

On the back of the napkin Anwar had written down the 0/0 fallacy.

One times zero equals zero.

$$1 * 0 = 0$$

And two times zero equals zero.

$$2 * 0 = 0$$

Therefore one times zero equals two times zero.

$$1 * 0 = 2 * 0$$

Divide both sides by zero and what do you get?

$$\frac{1 * \cancel{0}}{\cancel{0}} = \frac{2 * \cancel{0}}{\cancel{0}}$$

Xanther didn't know why but she liked that enough to carefully tack it up on her bulletin board in her bedroom, and next to a picture of runaway IRC +10216 too, because it was pretty, and an old picture of My Chemical Romance, because they were prettiest. She liked waking up to stare at the band, the star, and at what Anwar had written out so neatly.

$$1 = 2$$

Which should, like, forest her head with questions but doesn't, why's that?, maybe because when Xanther sees it she smiles, though not this way :) or this way :D but maybe more like this way ;P?

No ;P now. More like :? Wipers can't keep up. Going mad for nothing. Anwar pumps the brakes. What kind of counting equals this sort of overwhelmingness? Does one gallon of water even have the same number of drops as another gallon? Or are no two drops ever alike? Like snowflakes? Like, there must be big ones and little ones, right? Except when does too big count as something too big for the word raindrop? Or too little? How to get at the whole pluvial thing, another Anwar beaut, which Xanther remembered, pluvial, because it was like this ecatstic :: ecstatic? ∴ rainstorm going Plooey! to a town, a ville, a . . . Ploooooooeyville!

What's that number?

It has to exist, but if no one will ever name it, is it ever real?

H O W

How about light? Some fancy laser? But would the thinnest beam or even a perfect net of the thinnest beams

still account for every bit of irregular water tumbling downward?

Caught by this net that, catching nothing, not a safety net after all, right?

Can any of this ev—

because there really is no safety in numbers, right?, even a net that counts everything, even if it doesn't resolve the question of

or so their breakfast nook points out five times every morning, or is it more than that?, five?, five?, is this why Xanther is really going on about this?, perfect spheres, why

clusters and globs, those tiny tiny spits, after all there are no perfect teardrops,

one print's called 1/32"?, because that's the size of a perfect sphere? and is the other print called 1/4" or Hamburger Bun because that's the size when rain breaks apart?

when rain becomes meat?

some of it must break apart right? into hamburger buns?, meatish meatless shapes?, looking for perfection in the wind?

on the way down before reaching the pavement?

imes not there at all? sometimes there?, sometimes not there at all? sometimes there?, sometimes not there at all? sometimes there?, sometimes not there at all?

Is impact the final number? Is impact the final number? Is impact the final number? Is impact the final number?

And what's an average but a number too if still the wrong number?

H O W   m a n y   r a i n drops?

imes there?; sometimes not there at all? sometimes there?; sometimes not there at all? sometimes there?; sometimes not there at all? sometimes there?; sometimes not there at all?

What about all the drops forming and reforming in the in-between?

H O W   m a n y   r a i n dr

Or is it the average between where drops start and where drops finish?

Is impact the final number? Is impact the final number?

sometimes there?; sometimes not there at all? sometimes there?; sometimes not there at all? sometimes there?; sometimes not there at all? sometimes there?; sometimes not there at all?

A whole new storm? A storm within a storm? A storm within a storm?

How many of those are there? Do they equal a whole new sky of raindrops?

A whole new sky of raindrops? A whole new sky of raindrops? A whole new sky of raindrops? A whole new sky of raindrops?

A storm within a storm? A storm within a storm? A storm within a storm? A storm within a storm? A storm within a storm? A storm within a storm? A storm within a storm?

A whole new sky of raindrops? A whole new sky of raindrops? A whole new sky of raindrops? A whole new sky of raindrops?

A storm within a storm? A storm within a storm? A storm within a storm? A storm within a storm? A storm within a storm? A storm within a storm? A storm withi

H O W   m a n y

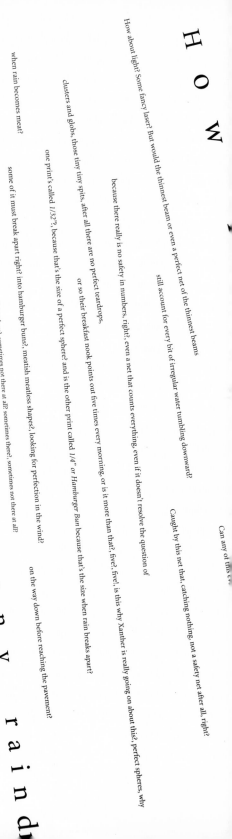

And as if this halogen wake
of greasy red can turn her stomach toward hunger,
Xanther doesn't think food, pictures instead reaching out and

counting every drop with a finger.
How long would that finger have to be? how bendy? how thin?

How long would she have to move to account for each toppling wobble of wet?
how quickly would she have to move to account for each toppling wobble of wet? No one could. What could?

Of course she couldn't move fast enough. No one could. What could?

If Xanther froze it all, suspended the whole storm with a wish, a wave
of that impossibly long finger, which she tries to do now, if just in her head.

H O W m a n y r a i n drops?

first flipping the horizon over as if to reverse gravity, but that only makes the rain fall back up into the clouds,
or is it down into the clouds? and are the clouds anymore if they're below or are they just fog?,
so instead Xanther refuses gravity, except then the drops lurch away, which finally leads her to halt time altogether which seems to work best.

But now how long will it take to mark everything down?, not counting if she could count right, which is unlikely, right?
how would she even do that?, with paper and pen?, wet paper eventually and then wouldn't the ink run?
what about a computer? how big? a small one? waterproof? it would have to be, no duh, huh, huh? . . .

how could she even reach each drop if they were thick for miles? ladders? cranes? specially constructed walkways? helicopters? some kind of flying thing?
with magical wings? which by a wish, a nice wish, Xanther already has, big billowy wonderful things, what would that even feel like? or look like? her moving between all that wetness?

a movement that would certainly smash some drops, even if she were infinitely careful,
which she would be, though wouldn't her wings still divide some? or mash some into one another? the downdraft certainly would,

and wouldn't that mess up the number?

m a n y r a i n drops?

r a i n drops?

Xanther's
getting tired.

Colder too.

Exhausting herself.
Like running-out-of-breath
exhausting herself.

How many raindrops?
How many raindrops?
How many raindrops?
How many raindrops?
How many raindrops?
How many raindrops?
How many raindrops?
How many raindrops?
How many raindrops?

Where even to start? let alone end?
Where even to start? let alone end?
Where even to start? let alone end?
Where even to start? let alone end?
Where even to start? let alone end?
Where even to start? let alone end?
Where even to start? let alone end?
Where even to start? let alone end?
There even to start? let alone end?

Where the drops hit pavement? Or right before? Or higher up maybe?

How many How many raindrops?
Where rain just starts to form?
Where rain just starts to form?

Above the roof lines? Or telephone lines? Or in the clouds themselves?
Above the roof lines? Or telephone lines? Or in the clouds themselves?

Should Xanther count just one y-axis z-axis plane? Though how thick to make each plane? One drop? More? Or all

Do raindrops cease

make each plane? One drop? More? Or all the planes along the x-axis?
the planes along the x-axis?

to be raindrops when they've become a puddle?

How many raindrops?

the beginning.
the beginning.

No use.
No use.
No use.
No use.
No use.
No use.

apart?
Questions still begetting more and more questions.
Questions still begetting more and more questions.
Questions still begetting more and more questions.
Questions still begetting more and more questions.
Questions still begetting more and more questions.
…ll begetting more and more questions.
ice. What if they constantly merge and split

multiple minutes? The span of the whole storm?

raindrops?
raindrops?
raindrop

Which is still just the beginning.
Which is still just the beginning.
Which is still just the beginning.
Which is still just the beginning.

Questions still begetting more
and more questions.

At what point in time? One second? Less than a second? Maybe

Just an optical illusion?
Just an optical illusion?
Just an optical illusion?

How many
How many
How many
How many
How many

Because is it r

optical illusion?

…ling bit Filling bit with

raind

How many raindrops ?

How many raindrops ?

going faster?

Questions still begetting more and
Questions still begetting more and
Questions still begetting more and

Or if they're pure H²O or loading up on airborne pollutants as they plummet,
Or if they're pure H²O or loading up on airborne pollutants as they plummet,
Or if they're pure H²O or loading up on airborne pollutants as they plummet,
Or if they're pure H²O or loading up on airborne pollutants as they plummet,

an optical illusion?
an optical illusion?
optical illusion?
illusion?

does that change anything?
does that change anything?
does that change anything?
does that change anything?

Stop!

Stop!

Please stop!

How many raindrops ?

Squint hard, maybe try to think hard too, but most of all blink fast, and Xanther can almost stop the storm.
Squint hard, maybe try to think hard too, but most of all blink fast, and Xanther can almost stop the storm.

in the back of her mind, already going, crying out for Xanther to name it.
in the back of her mind, already going, crying out for Xanther to name it.

Not that it lasts very long but long enough to get the idea, right?
Not that it lasts very long but long enough to get the idea, right?
long enough to get the idea, right?
long enough to get the idea, right?

The number's there.
The number's there.

Right? Right? Right?
Right? Right? Right?
Right? Right? Right?
Right? Right? Right?
Right? Right?
Right? Right?

a still frame emerges.

In the afterimage, already fading on the back of her eyelids, beyond counting.
already fading on the back of her eyelids, beyond counting.

Not that it lasts very long but
long enough to get the idea, right?
Not that it lasts very long but
Not that it lasts very long but

Look right and at the right angle for just the right amount of time and

Or one number.
Or one number.

No use.
No use.

that it lasts very long but
Not that it lasts very long but

Right? Right?

How many raindrops ?
How many raindrops ?
How many raindrops ?
How many raindrops ?
How many raindrops ?
How many raindrops ?
How many raindrops ?
How many raindrops ?
How many raindrops ?
How many raindrops ?
How many raindrops ?
How many raindrops ?
How many raindrops ?

Xanther can't even make up a number. Face pressed against the fogging glass, glasses a fogged mess too. Useless. But blinking still like she's the strobe, trying as hard to keep her eyes shut as to open them back up, all in an effort to glimpse what she knows no one can glimpse but has to be out there.

Like a ghost.

A ghost in the raindrops.

It's not lost on Xanther that she's gritting her teeth now. Pretty hard too. Grinding away at what just won't give way. Enamel will crack before these questions do.

And suddenly Xanther feels more than just cold inside. More than spiky frost and needles. A real numbing has started up. Freezers full.

And then she gets thirsty.

And then she stops breathing.

There's one answer: rain is just water with holes in it. Lots and lots of holes. Adding up to one big hole. One all-engulfing catsum. Brutal. Banishing.

Xanther waits. Grips her seat belt. Clamps teeth tight. Just hold on. Should she bite her seat belt? Is this then what all these questions have really been about? Just some desperate distraction to spin her away from a terrible thing to come?

again

her poor mom

her poor dad

of course they constantly whisper

about the

money snake hissing

around and through it all

not wanting her to know

where all the money goes

How many raindrops?

down to zero

down the drain

Xanther's the zero

Don't check your phone!

Xanther's the drain

Except the char in her nose isn't her char, just a memory still on the air, and she's not thirsty, she's not even cold.

Fraidy K, that's all.

The beast has stayed away.

Xanther cracks the window, gulping air, and wow!, the spray actually warms her!

"Remember: they are only questions," Anwar has told her many times. Like he's also told her: "Remember: they are only answers."

Xanther starts breathing regular-like again.

And sure, just as there's rain out there, the number for rain is out there too.

Dancing on the pavement.

Dancing in the air.

Like music before music becomes music.

"Is everything okay?" Anwar asks.

"Huh?" Xanther responds, profoundly, rolling the window back up, too aware of what she must look like by the look already cornering her dad's eyes. "Head in the clouds?" she tries.

"Those are some clouds."

"You know, just daydreaming," Xanther tries again.

"Tell me then," Anwar sighs. "Tell me your daydreams, daughter."

And Xanther can't stand worrying him.

She can't stand lying either. She really can't.

"Dov."

Lupita's

This is not your country.

— *Luis J. Rodriguez*

"That's him?" one whispers.

"Encobijado," the second won't whisper.

Not that Luther moves. For either. Keeps the blanket where it is, over his head, still looking for what night never found, a dark to drown his mind.

The one whispering's a boy. Unknown. The other one making his point is Almoraz.

"Chinga tu madre," Almoraz hisses, close enough he might as well kiss the blanket.

"Old man cock not good enough? Wanna suck some of this?"

Not that the head butt is all that. Luther already standing, like he'll never know lying, the only number one, el gallo, grinning hard as Almoraz stumbles back, hands to nose, tripping over the boy. Both of them down on their asses.

"¿Q-vole?"

"Fuck you!" Almoraz sputters, blood leaking between fingers, spotting his L.A. Dodgers jersey. Yells at the boy to bring him a towel, some ice, but the boy makes the mistake of looking at Luther first. Luther shakes his head.

"What's your name?"

"Chitel. I heard about you."

"Better be no picture of me there," Luther says of the phone this boy's gripping like life.

Chitel shakes his head. He's new to Luther. Though these days, at el compuesto, there's always someone new.

Good to see Luther's not forgotten. What's all over this shorty's eyes now, not meeting Luther's stare, showing off broken teeth to the floor. Got a gray little hoodie on, Kings shorts, white socks pulled high, starter ink on his fore-arms, got it all going on but keeping it all to no big thing.

"Bitch, if you broke my nose—" Almoraz spits, bloody fingers making fists.

"You know better than to try to fuck a bear in his sleep," Luther answers. Chitel can't help himself, smiles wide.

Not like Almoraz gonna back down though. Not like Luther welcomes anything less, the faint hot of something metal, like bolts on his Edelbrock, fillin his mouth.

"You staying for breakfast?" Mezclador asks from the doorway. Rubén Castaño Ybarra, or the Mixer, or just Miz. He's lived here for decades. Old as trees. Wifebeater sagging on him, and still got his rings, thick but cheap as mall gold, arms thin as high branches, holding up the big ceramic bowl, stirring at some lumpy shit, his special batter, been making pancakes before there was trees.

"See what this bolo did?" Almoraz appeals. "Don't even live here no more."

"Let me see." Miz puts down the bowl and gives Almoraz's nose a hard pinch. Almoraz doesn't react to the tug. Luther smiles. They would have made a mess of this morning if it had come to that. "Not broken," Miz grunts, flat as slate, back to beating out lumps. "Maybe the altitude got to you."

"Chingado."

Chitel's back with a rag.

"Where the fuck's the ice?"

Chitel looks Almoraz in the eyes, easy.

"She has it."

And that gives the room plenty of ice. Luther should have slept with his dogs. He'd headed there first. Then this mistake. If she asks for his key, he'll give it to her. But she never asks for his key.

"You gonna wish me Happy Mother's Day?" she says without turning around, wide and heavy at the counter, slicing off strips of jicama. Wedges of limes in a bowl. On the griddle, layers thick, bacon pops and curls. "Have a seat. Miz, hand me a plate."

Miz hands her a plate.

"Gotta split," Luther lies. "My dogs need feeding."

"Dogs can wait. It's what dogs do."

Luther sits. Another mistake. Luther's forehead suddenly a strip of sweat, and worse his mouth thick with a taste like plum, like bruised before the healing's begun, like when he was half Chitel's age, called out and blamed for shit he didn't swallow then, still won't swallow.

She turns around. Señora Paloma Cadenaza Carnamando or just Guadalupe, or in this place, Lupita. She sweeps handfuls of jicama onto the plate Miz holds out for her. And like she's done for years, squeezes lime on it, salts and peppers it too, then big dashes of chili pepper she keeps in a ceramic honey jar on the counter, wipes her hands on her shirt, considers briefly the nails she recolors twice a week. She likes all kinds of color. And likes her nails long.

"You still have that key?" Lupita smiles.

Luther nods. She offers him a cigarette.

"Keep it."

Luther should give it back. Says no to the cigarette instead. Lupita lifts the Camel to her lips, outline tattooed years ago, color of peach, eyeliner too, also tattooed, dark violet, even her eyebrows, like charcoal. Her hair she keeps up in a tight bun, held there with the same shining pin, long and thick like some pedaso or pico hielo, might as well be an ice pick.

Chitel lights her cigarette.

"So what's this with you and Almo?"

"We're getting married," Luther answers.

Lupita nods again. "It's legal here."

"Almo needs his green card."

"¡Lo que es un escuincle!" Lupita laughs. Pleased. Almoraz holds his tongue.

More of the crew drifts into the kitchen, her latests cucarachas, her loyals, settling around Almoraz at the big table, same veteranos Luther's known over the years, none as old as Miz but a few getting there.

Miz, his back to them all, spoons into the bubbling bacon grease the first round of pancakes.

"Got a day ahead of us," Lupita says now, holding in the smoke. "You with?"

Did she really think he was back to reup with her balloon parade?

"Take Chitel and his crew. Got sales today as far as Glendale. Rifamos." Still holds in the smoke.

And no question, Lupita thinks she's the best. Never deviates. Echo Crew and with the years to prove it. As if years prove anything but old. Luther proves that.

"Got my own work, Guadalupe."

Truth too. Heavy work. Heavy crew too. Takes some planning to disappear a fool.

"That so?" Still no smoke comin out. Like she swallowed it. Or it died in there. "Almo right about one thing: this ain't no motel." Stubs out the cigarette, right on the kitchen table. Almoraz says nothing, moves nowhere.

"You sleep here, you eat here, you work here." She's going there. "Understand? *Pedazo de mierda. No se puede ni siquiera hablar español.*" Whatever the fuck that means. Goes shrill. Hand too, all twisting now with that silver stab in her hair. "And don't give me no fuckin bullshit about no dogs you gotta go suck off."

And then she is all about her still throwing hard, standing tall, taking no shit from no one, Armos comin around, loud and proud, and getting run off. Federales too, showing no spine. Lupita making it sound like she alone was stepping up.

Luther's just glad he isn't touching no food. No cigarette either. Should throw down her key too. Be done with it. Peels off a Grant instead, three Grants, four. Drops the feria to the floor.

"Never said you was a motel. You's the Four Seasons."

Lupita doesn't touch the money. And when some shorty does a dumb thing like running over, even if she's picking up the cash for this matron of all their lives, Lupita gives the little thing a hair full of long nails to think twice about next time.

"Aye!!" the little thing shrieks, what with Lupita jerking her up by the roots, Lupita's strength always surprising everyone, even this squat puta, tossed aside. Lupita never tolerates thin, and unless curves be belly or chins, she'll turn out whatever beauty queen and land her quick in some Whittier jack shack. Piña used to crib here just fine. Was Lupita's girl. But when Piña quit for Luther, Lupita didn't like that.

"Pancakes?" Miz asks mildly, passing between them, plate stacked high. Guy knows how to melt butter.

Luther waits for her to do something crazy now, they all wait. When Lupita goes shrill, only time before she starts in on some other shit. Throw the pancakes. The plate.

Instead she starts coughing. And doesn't stop. Miz finally has to come over and help her to the sink. Gives her some water to drink. She knocks that out of the way. Presses her mouth to his wifebeater, balling it up in her hands, leans in on her tree, he all stroking her back, and saying softly, over and over again, "A coughin in the morning beats a coffin at night."

Square One

If the code and the comments disagree, then both are probably wrong.

— Norm Schryer

Their orders in [the best moment by Anwar {and Xanther too} waiting on a satisfying inevitable {hunger's claims solved ‹hunger's cries rendered irrelevant›}]. Square One Dining [on Fountain west of Vermont {across from the Scientology center}] is Xanther's favorite treat even if most of the items on the menu remain off-limits. [In support of his daughter's diet] Anwar abstained from ordering his favorite: the brioche French toast [always moist {but never runny ‹a key distinction for Astair›}] slathered with butter and grade A maple syrup. It's the dish they share whenever they can escape from the kids for what they like to call 'their egg date.'

'Are you sure you didn't want the French toast?' Xanther asks [of course Xanther would notice {would know ‹would care›}]. How does a twelve-year-old come to possess such a magnanimous heart?

'I was in the mood for something less indulgent, daughter.'

Anwar had also abstained from coffee [trying to quit {‹*Kefaya!*› trying to sleep ‹better› ‹trying to forget the headache drilling out from just above his right eye›}]. One out of three wasn't bad [!كفاية{?}].

They split the plate of scrambled eggs instead [eggs which Xanther permitted because they were locally sourced and humanely farmed {it didn't hurt that they also came amply loaded with extra cheddar}] along with slices of tomato and avocado [dolloped with sour cream] set down beside a bowl of fruit topped with yogurt and a wealth of ground nuts [ketogenic restrictions mandated that Anwar take the lion's share of the fruit {which Xanther has no problem with ‹given her excessive delight in sharing›}].

'Are we late?' Xanther asks [digging in].

'Plenty of time.' In fact, Xanther's appointment

isn't until 10 AM [10:10 AM actually {the big surprise not until later that afternoon ‹at 3 PM «in Venice ⟨to the tune of $20,000⟩»›}]. The number still staggers Anwar [staggers Astair as well {and it was her idea}] but what was infeasible in April suddenly became nearly advisable when Ehtisham called yesterday and declared he was with check in hand.

```
//

// M.E.T.                         +$50,000

// Xanther's surprise:           -$20,000
// Astair's M.A./Ph.D.:          -$20,000
// Extras for the twins:         -$10,000

// _____

//                                      0

//
```

That zero as round as happiness [surrounding and comforting his family {hard-pressed since they first moved here}]. Anwar could live with such a zero.

'And, uhm, like will anyone else besides Ehti be there? Glasgow?' Ever curious [{ever asking ‹to a degree that never ceased to amaze both him and Astair ‹and worry them too›} this about his oneish appointment].

'Possibly even Talbot.'

'And this, like, uhm, is all about the game?'

'In a manner of speaking.'

'The game engine?'

Anwar nods.

'I, like, still, uhm, don't understand that.' Brows crease with the weight of the world [and this time just for one word]. 'Is it an engine, like metal? or like runs the thing? or how does it work? or what does it even look like? And I know you've tried to explain it before, like what, three times? four times? You've been working on it for like how long now? Like months, right? Years? Sorry.'

What can Anwar do but smile. She caught herself [heard the pace of her . . . {the ratcheting tonal rise ‹her fabled «and feared»›} Question Song.]

'Well,' Anwar begins slowly [savoring still the cheddar and eggs {far more than the tepid tea in his cup}]. 'First and foremost, daughter, it's a metaphor. And metaphors at times are useful. At other times misleading. Let me ask you a question: what makes a car run?'

'The engine?'

'Good. But what makes the engine run?' Questions always help Xanther quiet [because they give her answers {whereas answers only give her more questions}].

'Gasoline?'

'Good. The engine itself isn't the gasoline. It's the structure designed to contain, ignite, and harness that energy. And it requires many parts. In my world those parts may include graphics, physics, rendering, things like hit detection and AI. Instead of inventing all those from scratch—'

'Like reinventing the wheel?'

'Good. I can construct an engine comprised of

those gears and manifolds. Focusing then on the ones that matter most to me.'

'Like AI?'

'Yes, daughter, like AI.' Though in truth while Anwar never ceased to love the high romanticism of AI [especially in college] he now considered it either 1) beyond him [or better left to those synaptic saints capable of delving into the true meaning of Intelligence {let alone Artificial}] or 2) a set of [fairly] predictable routines [and sub-routines].

'And that drives the game? Your engine? M.E.T?'

'My job is to esemplastically fashion a program which smoothly coordinates various parts in order to deliver a smoothly running vehicle.'

'Question—'

'Esemplastic. From the Greek *plastikos* meaning to mold. Or here, to mold into one. Though that's not your word for today. Today's word is "paradise."'

'Paradise? But, like, I already know what that means. Everyone does.'

'Do share, daughter.'

'A perfect place. A place of peace. Without hurt. Without sic— a good place. Without even death. Some say it's heaven but we don't believe in heaven.'

'But where do you think the word comes from?'

'More hot water?' The waiter interrupts [he's waited on them numerous times {is his name Luis? ‹Astair would remember his name›} slipping the check into a small tin bucket {curious custom of the place}]. 'No hurry. The flood's upon us.'

Outside the rain had grown even more severe [turning Fountain into a shy sea]. Cars slog by [wakes left behind]. The Scientology building seems a smear of blue [{chalk blue} like a sidewalk painting dissolving under the convictions {or is it insistence?} of nature {or is this just Anwar's wishful thinking?}]

Anwar declines the offer of more hot water [focusing on Xanther {mouthing the word over and over ‹testing the syllables for known meanings «even if the etymology is beyond her ability to guess»›}].

'Okay, uhm, so, if, like, this afternoon, Ehti's there, at you know, at Cementary?'

'Sementera.'

'And Glasgow and maybe, like, even Talbot?, will, uhm, like, will, uh, you know, be there too?'

'Who?'

'Mefisto?'

When was the last time Anwar had even seen Mefisto face-to-face [a year? {at least ‹not even on Skype›}]? And then just a few days ago [out of the blue {جبنا سيرة القط جه ينط}]: an actual phone call [or message {‹lengthy too› from the genius himself ‹Master Yugen› ‹Mr. E-Mind Extraordinaire› ‹Mefisto Dazine «no joke»› ‹Real Programming Genius «RPG!»› ‹who had bested his hero Mel Kaye before dispensing with his teenage years› ‹who had never stopped believing in Machine Intelligence «like he never stopped saying 'Intelligence without affect is no such thing'»›}]. Suddenly there: on the home voice mail [just hours before the telephonic seizure] with warnings [coughing up incomplete apologies] about how a prank of his [for a web advertisement {a distribution scheme?}] had gone wildly astray [prank!?].

'It was never supposed to go live . . .'

Or as they still say about Skynet: 'It's, uhm, out of our hands.'

Consequently [probably] Anwar fails to resist now peeking at his phone [feed the pain].

> Voice Mail: Full
> Missed Calls: 117
> Text Messages: 2187

E-mails: [Anwar can't even check his accounts {‹talk about rising bile› bilious objection to such a casual introjection ‹invasion!› of thought ‹prank?! «terrorism!»} {what were you thinking Mefisto?!}]

'Uhm, I thought we agreed no phones?'

Xanther only recently received a phone [{partially furred} pink-encased {a smartphone ‹what Xanther's friend Kle once called a lucid phone «which Anwar only later realized he had misheard: 'Dad, Kle said it's a Lose It phone!' ‹because that's the fate of expensive things in the hands of a child?›»}]. He and Astair wanted her to have one [for her own protection mainly] but only if she agreed to abide by all parental restrictions [what Anwar nicknamed Electronic Self-Restraint Lessons {ESL}].

[typical of this child] Xanther is now more responsible than those demanding the restriction. Dear Xanther, love of his life [or: one of his three loves {or five ‹can he really not count himself?›}]. Doing so well [wonderfully well {especially ‹since «considering ❨ . . . ❩ everything» what had—› —} —]—

Especially before which [the memory of that day {‹rising up . . . › that moment ‹never not there «if already four months old»}] Anwar's thoughts torque even more, invert, and bind [in the absurd code that mocks any actual lines of his trade {forget C++, Lua, Python, Java ‹even Clojure «for example»›} meted out in the very cages Astair has described {at times} as her own thoughts {‹though rounder «‘More parental?’»› ‘How we found each other?’ she once surmised} leaving Anwar to dream of the day {would such a day ever exist?} when he could standard output his own thoughts {even the thoughts of others: Astair's, his daughters', friends' ‹and find some «calculable» sense› . . .

```
//      int main()
//        {
    //            std::cout << 'My thoughts unaloud
look like this!\n';
    return 0;
//        }
```

        } which {‹that output› this exercise} still achieves the opposite {clamping down on Anwar's every ability to process ‹following close brace› what had again provoked ‹beyond encoding «forget decoding ⟨forget Mefisto⟩»› neither in machine language nor anything remotely logical «‹is it all just reading anyway?» in a manner that might never be traced and so then forever personal›}] and so [still {feel} . . .

                                Closed.

Locked.

                Sealed.

                                              ]

Such terrible dark light [blinding in all it still must insist on seeing {over and over}]: Merry Christmas! Warnings had been all over the place.

Xanther's fidgeting [{escalating too} how she'd shuffled and shimmied {a soft-shoe without taps ‹and sweated too›} with that weird heat {never a fever} scalding her forehead]. Even as she shivered and complained of feeling 'Sooooooo cold!'

'Why is the coffin locked?'

and

'Can't we open it?'

and

'Why can't I seem him?'

and

'Just once? One last time?'

and

'Please?! How bad can it be?'

and

'Are we even sure Dov's in there?'

Were there really any answers [let alone parental comforts] that Anwar or Astair might have offered? To this day Anwar can come up with none.

He and Astair did try to mute The Question Song as they slowly made their way to Arlington National Cemetery [along with the honor guard and horse-drawn caisson {and the rain ‹it had been raining that day too›}]. Why should they have treated Xanther's routing curiosity any different from any other day?

Curiosity was her constant.

Then at the gravesite [{knock-kneed and trembling} before his lacquered casket {shiny with her reflection ‹if also smeared by the fingertips of passing mourners «‹so many mourners› making known their implausible desires to deny this black gloss by reaching out and touching it»}} {as the military band ‹silver in dark rain gear› played on} {as rifles volleyed} {as the regimented eight ‹easing from strict attention› began carefully to fold the flag}].

'He promised it to me.' [Strangely {and repeatedly too.}]

'What's that, daughter?' Anwar asked [attempting to determine the referent for 'it' {Astair feeling Xanther's forehead again ‹both of them «only then» starting to worry›}].

Already too late.
It was already there.

'Now look who's thinking about Dov?'

How does she do that? Anwar always struggles to keep track [even loose track] of his daughter's wild imagination [very loose] but moments like these [demonstrating her acute sensitivities{?}] continue to catch him off guard [if delightedly {and proudly} so].

'I miss him,' Anwar admits [even as he briefly considers the plausible lie that he was thinking up {‹Mefisto revenge scenarios› despite instincts to the contrary ‹all too human› Anwar does not lie ‹in this way «maybe in this way alone» he and Dov had been very similar «which included outlawing the insidious perpetuation of tooth fairies ‹god forbid the Easter Bunny [الله يحرم الله]›»}].

[given the circumstances of how they met] It was nothing short of a modern-day miracle that Anwar and Dov had ended on such good [{even} affectionate?] terms. While those friends who knew the story were boggled by the conclusion [Anwar deeply depressed by the horrifying {if honorable} death {more so than even Astair}]. [after all] There was no getting around two simple facts:

1) Anwar and Astair began their courtship when she was three months pregnant with Xanther.

2) Dov was Xanther's biological father.

Anwar counts out the cash [{tip 20 percent} catching the waiter's eye {across the room ‹has to be Luis›}] and then [palms together] bows slightly. The next appointment isn't far [{Xanther's} with Dr. Potts] but the deluge outside will overwhelm even clocks.

Xanther puts on her orange raincoat [snaps all the way up {takes Anwar's hand}].

'I love the smell of coffee. But, like, you know, what do I really love? Where do I, uhm, even like get that from? If Dov didn't drink coffee, and you're like quitting coffee, and mom has to drink coffee, right? ∴ Two parents of this little lifetime always drinking coffee. ∴

Or French toast, which has, uhm, you know, too much sugar for me to eat, like eat safely, but I still, like, love to see it, you know,' [just as a plate of something yellowy and buttery reaches a nearby table {Anwar should have had the French toast}] 'and so is just smelling or just seeing a kind of eating too?'

'Ready?' Anwar asks [ushering them outside]. Their car is only half a block away but swimming pools of storm await them [not even a foot beyond the narrow brown awning].

Xanther nods but doesn't move [{frozen} except for her nose {wiggling now like she's about to sneeze ‹though whenever she does actually sneeze her nose never wiggles beforehand›}] seemingly transfixed by the sheets of water crashing down with enough force that both Anwar's and her legs are sprayed [hands too {still holding tight} even their faces].

Xanther's thick lenses have already fogged.

'Where did he go?' Xanther whispers [almost as if to the storm].

'Ahhhhh,' Anwar exhales [approving nonetheless of a question he will fail trying to answer {fail at even handling}].

'Is he just gone?' she continues. 'Or did he go somewhere else? And if he did, where is he now? And if he didn't, still, where is he now?'

Anwar takes a second breath as he considers a response. Earlier in the car when Xanther mentioned Dov, Anwar had chosen not to say anything [it had been a mistake {for a moment Anwar even thought her silence had signalled she was getting sick}].

'If our family had taken to the comforts of religion, I could offer up for you now the promise of heaven. Even hell. Remember, while hell may be a place of misery, it still perseveres, promising perpetual preservation, continuation.' Again the rain seems to increase. 'Reincarnation is another option and in terms of material, inarguable. However, whether some kind of awareness survives is something else entirely. Still, daughter, there is no question the matter that made up Dov will find a place again in this grand universe. After all, all these particles we're made up of are not exactly new. Quite the contrary. The atoms making up the water falling around us are over nine billion years old. The atoms that make up you and me, the same. We are all of us used parts. Our newness lies only in parts rearranged.'

'Uhm, okay, professor.'

Anwar sighs.

'Okay, daughter, fair enough. You are not concerned about the reusable nature of our building blocks, correct?'

Xanther nods.

'Your question is about identity. And what of ourselves we can lose without losing ourselves. Now you know I'm too pragmatic to believe in some afterlife boardwalk where souls wander in search of pacifying ambrosia, in the way, when I was your age, I used to wander with my parents along the corniche in Alexandria, searching for shaved ice sweetened with grenadine. Do you know what "pragmatic" means?'

'Dad!'

'Practical.'

'How do you spell it?'

Anwar smiles as Xanther takes out a pen and scribbles on the back of her right hand [{P-R-A-G-M-A-T-I-C} followed by 'ambrosia' and 'corniche' {no matter if most of it smears in the wet}].

'Your mom agrees with this, though I'd hardly limit her sense of life and death to merely pragmatic. She's smarter than all of us. Combined.'

'And Dov?'

'Your father was just too brave to go in for those kinds of fantasies. Bravest man I ever knew.'

'So then, like, he's really just gone?'

'Not at all.'

'Huh?'

'What's the last thing you remember of him?'

'The last thing? I don't know. He called me—does calling count?'

'It all counts.'

'The last time I saw him though? Uhm. New York! When, after, like, uhm. With you. And Mom. In the park.'

'Can you picture it?'

Xanther closes her eyes [against the rain {against Anwar? ‹against how many thoughts to even try to get there? «who knows?»›}].

'Yes.'

'Do you remember what he was doing?'

'I remember what he was saying.'

'How well?'

'Perfectly! I think. But yeah, uhm, like his voice is in my head now. Every word. He was explaining The Dumb Dog.'

Anwar grins. The Dumb Dog was another one of those classic Dovisms. Part parable/part homily [mostly bullshit {Dov knew it too ‹and let you know he knew it «which sold it» twangily delivered› with such understated authority} Anwar could almost picture it {him}].

'Well . . . there he is.'

'Where?' Eyes flying open [{glasses off ‹lenses all fog›} searching again the rain].

'Right in your head.' Anwar lightly taps her temple. 'Safe and sound.'

Not that Anwar expects this answer to satisfy but Xanther [bravely even] accepts the trick.

'Then he's here too?' Xanther suddenly tapping [ever so lightly {and with the slightest smile}] Anwar's temple.

How much [vastly {immensely ‹unfathomably› tremendously} . . .] Anwar loves [t]his child. It continues to take him by surprise [even when she confounds him with the havoc of her room {for example} which she will proudly describe {defend!} as clean {those beautiful messes ‹beautiful even today›} even as {in the next moment} she will astonish Anwar with her fearless interest in life {despite the harrowing blows life continues to deliver her ‹and so delivers to Anwar . . . ›}].

// A sweet memory too.

    // Sheep's Meadow

        // Sunny Serendipity

     // Xanther on Dov's shoulders

     // Xanther's questions

     // Dov flummoxed

       // Dov singing?

Anwar would do anything for her.

'Of course he's in here. Right now in fact.'

Xanther squints at Anwar's head [as if to see {if she could ‹for herself «for them both»›} their no-bones Army man striding beneath a blue and untroubled Manhattan sky] rendering Anwar powerless to do anything but kiss now his dear daughter on the forehead [spattered in rain {that peculiar warmth}].

'Shall we brave this storm?' Anwar asks [opening their big orange umbrellas].

'Okay' [Xanther hesitates] 'but if, like, if Dov's in you and Dov's, like, you know, like you said, in me, so that now he's in both of us, I mean shared by us, which, like if he's not half in each of us, but still whole to each of us, means he's sorta beyond both of us too?' [Xanther squinting even more {as she peers ever more intently ‹not at Anwar anymore› but on this downpour nearly drowning out ‹their› thought‹s›}] 'does that mean that Dov's also out there?'

zhong

I want your horror.
I want your design.

— Lady Gaga

they saysay she tutor demons, lah. saysay mice dance to her finger

snap and a pelesit ∷ **Animistic spirit frequently aligned with Polong** ∷

does her bidding. saysay sa-rukup rang bumi ∷ *World Coverer* ∷ fly to

her window and call her mother. they saysay a lot.

not like jingjing seen flying jin or tinkerbell, unless monster cards

count, what jingjing keep bagged-up in back pocket. sure no

blood-sipping spirits either, with stabbing heads, unless cricket

count, what jingjing keep safe in shirt pocket sometimes, for luck,

because jingjing like the song, song his company. but anything

else, that siaosiao ridiculous! mice?! dancing or not, if there one

thing that never come around to their place, that would be mice.

but void deck folk don't talk about her cat. talk the world over

itself but not that. they neighbors, of sort. jingjing don't know

what floor. jobless gabbers, gamblers and drunks, oldold, forties

at least, pride all up from all day making things up. daynoon to meenite, crowd the void deck like it their own mah, loud with their

how seow, either telling jingjing how she called daughter of lang-

suir to her hand, or at stone tables playing checkers with beer caps.

"how's her friend?" spencer asked once, lai dat, he biggest of the

hand, tua tao mebbe, show off his changi stripes when not in

pants, only one changing beer caps for cash, no clue from where

his money come. what could jingjing say? "i'm fine, ya ya. how

your friends, lah?" "ya ya? lah? why you talk so funny, boy? don't

use lah in a question, lah." "then how, lah?" jingjing like macam

haha, if spencer get black-eyed and still. sometimes how you talk

is all you got. even if your talk is wrong.

and in case of cat, jingjing don't know much except to keep his big

mouth shut. no clue why either. not like cat saysay tiam, lah, shhh-

hhhh. jingjing don't know where it goes. or how it goes. they have

small balcony, high up.

sometimes at night, snug in his hammock, only city to light the

walls, jingjing watch at door how this shadow grow, slow cross his

room. take a long time too, like long snooze, what jingjing could

never spill to void deck folk, to anyone, no tua kang swear, how

the cat throughout stay still, only this shadow moving, creeping

slowly forward, filling room. and that still not the fright part,

so kiasi jingjing, poor boy, stop his heart, over what the other

shadows do, shadows of his hammock, himself, singapore, with-

drawing before it, across the floor, like all shadows could fear this

shadow most.

sometimes when she go out, it rides her shoulder. Just a tiny white

thing. tail curled up tight to hide its paws. ears unchopped. eyes

so bright they challenge the law. the void deck folk look away. like

cat's not there.

then again that's how they act around her: the great tian li, auntie of niu che shui, seri of serangoon, the smith street sage. some saysay born on sei yang gai, in house of dead, all saysay long ago. people always asking her age, her real name. always asking jingjing. never her. tian li quiet them all. with cat without. no one tua her. or meet her gaze? tan ku ku, lah! tie shoelaces for hours than do that. and they in sandals. real cower power her.

only when she gone do void deck folk talk cock about charms she cast, potions she brew. jingjing nod ya ya if know otherwise. the great tian li can barely heat water let alone simmer up some evil juice. jingjing the flat chief. fixing up ramen, myojo's best, brand's tamban fish too, though tian li not eat fish or pork or chicken. pang chui lao! "吾餐之肉足矣" she might say. ∴ Really? Not your Google bitch. ∴ really? jingjing might joke back. because he sees how little she eats. "吾岁饱吾." 彼女の多様な説明は、逆に反比例して少しの ことしか説明できない. asking jingjing then if he wants her to be only about hunger как будто у него не хватило бы духу —

系讲一些荒谬嘅事干,比如:"若如毋需,必然乃仅为人之习性." vege-

tables are safe, noodles, tofu, mebbe pick up some tow sar on the

long walks she like. walks all over the city. loves the parks.

jingjing love the parks too. he and auntie same like that. botanical

gardens abruthen, but also just sit in toa payoh, pearl's hill, or

emerald park. or cross over to sentosa to lay backs down in the

sand, jingjing finding monster cards in the clouds, tian li swinging

her arms around like repelling monkey. green both their thing.

even if 绿, xanh lục, हरा, 绿色, зеленый, 綠, are still not enough

to know what that means. words so tua kang. words need worlds

in order to be worlds. worlds though don't need words in order to

be worlds. tian li say "以树之道与树语." trees talk bark and grow

beyond names. flowers outbloom blooms. roots too settle deep

or shallow until they overthrow their own reason for being roots.

what are coral trees, peacock ferns, pink mempat, or great spindle

ginger compared to what they are? even just tall grass? makes jingjing just want to swing his arms, forget the clouds, his cards,

repulse the monkey too, like he'd done when they'd first met, just

jumped up beside tian li, because it seemed like such an easy thing

to do, so good an idea too, but most of all because it felt so good,

those four years ago.

that's how they met, in a park, swinging arms, until mata there

oreddy, another arrest, but damn heng one, tian li all cower power

then, talk cockiest talk too, judges and sewer serpents cow down

sure, like she best friends with best, people jingjing no clue on,

poh geok ek, quek bin hwee, even likes of yaacob ibrahim and

harun abdul ghani. and jingjing not that bodoh, need no more

explaining. life with auntie beat kena rotan. kin kah kin chew,

jingjing kena down on his knees and swear off smoke, mean it

too. and then she surprise him, surprise cops, sana staff, anyone

around, the great tian li got down on her knees and swear to

jingjing how she will give him more than he dare dream.

"命中所困将为汝之愉." jingjing think back often to try to

remember her promise.

Or mebbe: "劳之所获将繁茂,汝将知汝知此始终."

Or this: "黑暗止于勇者."

in any case she more than test his mettle, she sabo him good, ha!

make him her cook, her serpent, slave. and for what? two rooms?

pan for a kettle? a pallet's her bed. towels to curtain windows and

dry hands. tap flows rust. lai dat their hdb ∴ **Residences managed**

by Housing Development Board ∵ is old, just quick kai kai to tanglin

halt market, nine floors up. they on fifth story. though auntie

saysay fourth, as if four, even fourfour, could hak say jingjing.

her cat though . . .

not when it's with her, in her lap, by her ankle, whiskering her ear,

if not much for whiskers, giving their palace a corner tour, or even

throwing a meenite glare across the floor.

the most spooked jingjing get is when it not around at all. tian li

sit then on her mat, alone in her room, rooted in dark, and folded

up like a dead monkey, if still mumbling, like a mumbling dead

monkey, giving witness to the strangest bits, 不用普通话, 唔系粤语,

Не по русски, 日本語ではない, not in english. none of these. all

that's never green. inhuman speech. too terrible to repeat.

the void deck folk saysay she terrible, terrible rich. "sly lao cheow

riches keep to herself. looksee-looksee, lah. chiak buay liao."

that a laugh. just bare walls to stare back, except clipcrap she

spare him, beads to tack up, mebbe for prayer, jingjing don't hew,

don't care. mostly postcards by his hammock, his some-day escape:

edm tour, tokyo baths, hong kong disneyland, he'd take kl ∵ **Kuala**

Lumpur ∴, jb ∴ **Johor Bahru** ∴, even ku dé ta at marina bay sands.

early days jingjing fake sleeping or sick, until she go out on walk.

if cat left behind jingjing feel better quick, lah. cabut flat for sure.

but those times when he's left alone, jingjing rifle through every-

thing, under her pallet, her mat, even behind the stove, looking for

money, coin money, fold money, mebbe even gem money, some-

thing that glimmers gold. jingjing would even take hell money.

once he find her bank card. but what there? jingjing see receipts.

what tony tan keeps coming, every month, first week.

when rain started, not like she spot for a circle line ride. who cares

for the wet, the long trip, they have nothing but time.

there another mystery: jingjing's heels all beat, lai dat arches beat,

but auntie keep slapping along, arms swinging, grinning her way

home. then rain really pour. jingjing duck under some hotel or

gahmen portico and next thing the old lady's gone.

jingjing dash out again. pang chui lao the flood. she stray from

sidewalk? cross over tar? good thing not many cars. or mebbe she

fall? mebbe take a spill on forbidden hill? not like she get lost in

fort canning park. jingjing race hard, looking wild all around, this

and that, past national archives, steps a dozen cataracts.

jingjing finds her. jingjing always finds her. like have extra sense

for her. though she farther ahead than expected. across coleman

street by apostolic church of st. gregory. by christs under crosses,

auntie with arms crossed, some man on his knees, a crumpled

thing, hands out, weeping.

jingjing haul over fence. pad closer. old man, lah. mebbe sixty.

familiar too. not when his face go twisttwist, hair suaysuay, cats-

trophe ∴!∵ clenched in fists, lah, but in the way he dress, dark

suit, threads so tight water bounce off, shirt a different soft, open

as a coffee cup, soak it all up. and on his fingers, wrists, gold,

gold, gold, bands of bright, and wah lao what shoes, italian for

sure, laces untied, clotted with mud. chin kim tang tang!

this some luck. alamak, heng us! jingjing try hard not to stare.

here crawls zhong sim lin. billionaire. jingjing forgets business but

knows face from papers, on tvs jingjing watch through windows of

strangers.

twice, lah, for real, jingjing see zhong sim lin climb out of limo.

both near raffles place, battery road, collyer quay.

zhong sim lin see world over, forget postcards on jingjing's wall,

this tua kee know places so exclusive they don't have postcards. go

by private yacht, private jet. never without a dozen sharp-suited

women and men. but here he is, siao liao, lah by himself, begging

tian li for who knows what.

tian li keeps saying: "吾仅一事未了."

"she has only one thing left," jingjing translates. which is a lie. she has nothing left.

zhong sim lin, head shiny like underbelly of some turtle stranded on its back, eyes darting back and forth like turtle flippers paddling a sky, begs anyway: "please ask her to come, just for a little, to have some tea, if just that little. i'll pay her too, whatever sum she asks."

like jingjing some google bitch, he translate for zhong: "他说他会付钱给你，并给我们茶."

tian li respond with nonsense.

"she wants to know how much." what better way to translate nonsense. tian li is always so boh chup about money. but jingjing isn't going to let this chance slip by.

zhong sim lin takes jingjing's hand, kisses it.

"whatever she wants."

so jingjing reminds tian li how they are out of tea. how hot tea in a dry place might not be such a terrible thing.

"他可干吾衣?" she asks.

"she would like to know if you might dry our clothes?"

zhong sim lin admits he isn't sure, but if he can't find someone to run the dryers he has closets full of robes.

"他不是只有一件,而是整个衣柜的干净衣服." jingjing translates.

"汝信其有茶?" ∵ *Are you sure he has tea?* ∵ auntie insists.

auntie has no clue who zhong sim lin is.

Big Surprise

"We're all they've got, Walt."

"That's not enough."

— Moonrise Kingdom

Astair returns a high round of flame to their red enamel kettle. Earlier she had tried to find a few minutes for Tai Chi before the house woke to its usual frenzy but the leaks did away with that vainglorious dream (it's one thing to be dragged from the coffers of sleep by her twins screaming about the flood and another to find oneself trapped in the coffins of too many dead ideations (and probably still parental despite years of therapy ((forgive her the repetition) (never forgive her if she visits any of (all) that upon her three daughters)))).

Now she considers Saturday's *New York Times* crossword ((picked up earlier at Fix Coffee) making little headway (less in earnest looking for an answer to 25 across (Belize native) than settling her many thoughts into the peace of one thoughtless mote of trivia)).

About a year ago the *Times* had published one (Wednesday? (probably a Monday or Tuesday)) that Astair flew through. The theme: Who, What, Where, When, Why (themed acrosses starting with one of the five Ws) ∴ **May 21, 2013** ∵. Saturdays frequently don't have themes (and if there is one today Astair can't see it) but she's probably remembering that one now because of Xanther (the onslaught of water falling outside joined by her myriad questions about rain ((what Anwar has dubbed her Question Song) calming her out of that crescendo with teasing hints about her big surprise)).

Their big surprise, really.

There goes her tea (though (bright side?) at least Astair located another leak).

(and again) Another splash exceeds the rim of her (carefully) steeped cup (or does a cup not steep? (only contents pouched within?)) China green (in unbleached bags (plus linden flowers, Panax ginseng, pollen (for the honey flavor? (is this stuff even organic?)))) which if it were just rain might actually add a nice finishing ((and cooling) spring) note to this morning habit (but the house gets in the way (how many layers of old ceiling paint did one drop have to drip through? (not to mention the wires above (pipes covered in plaster dust (asbestos?) (plaster board, arsenic-soaked wood (is that right? hadn't she read that joists and support beams in homes are soaked in poison to deter termites? Or was that just railroad ties and telephone poles?) plus tar sheets, nickel-glazed nails and clay tiles (heaped (until today) with weeks worth of urban pollutants along with a mat of dusty pine needles and scraps of eucalyptus bark)))))).

It's amazing the old roof has managed (this long) to ward off as much water as it has (storm battering the roof's lazy pitch (lucky if a tree doesn't fall too ((one of the tall evergreens along their street) at least a branch or a pine cone (sounds like pine cones by the dozen are falling now (and if that really is just water up there then the storm's aftermath should leave them little but Roman tiles in pieces ((like so much cracked pottery) scattered to the lawn below)))))). Good (at least) for the drought (?).

Thus far Shasti and Freya (actually enthused about their (treasure hunt?) task) have found only three more points of ingress throughout the house: two in the living room and one in the dining area (precariously close to the piano). Anwar had discovered the 1st in his office (precariously (again) close to the computers (all their instruments under siege))). And now the 5th (the kitchen (not even emerging from a seam ((no corner, beam, around some pocketed bulb) just blobbing directly above Astair (from the paint itself) until eventually (thick enough, dark enough, heavy enough) it's bombs away (

into her tea)))).

And as with all issues arising out of this old but noble house (their good fortune (and curse)): to call Cyril or not (Cyril Kosiginski ∷ owner and landlord ∴ who offered them the lease (and in return for the low price) on the agreed-upon "as is"). Anwar will say no. Astair will say yes (wouldn't Cyril want to know about potential water damage, mold growth (other etcs. in there)?).

"Itsy Bitsy Spider!" her daughters' voices suddenly chorus ((and not close either) upstairs now).

Astair grabs an eight-quart pot (glass lid still on (what would that do? (wouldn't))). She isn't even sure if the pot will do. Her two eight-year-olds are just inside the bathroom staring up at the gusher. "Itsy Bitsy Spider" had (spontaneously) become their code for a leak (though this one (the 6th) was far greater than any of the others).

"No need for this," Astair laughs (meaning the pot).

They all laugh. The worst leak of all had ended up right above the kids' bathtub (a small piece of good news Astair happily accepts (and like that the good news (in her mind) compounds: piano (spared) computers (spared) books or anything perishable (anything theirs (spared)))). So far the only thing lost: the contents of one cup of tea (another coffee is what she really wants (needs)).

The top of the stairs (however) checks Astair's enthusiasm. Shasti spots the telltale splatter first ((the 7th leak) on the top step). Freya centers the pot under the drip. And then both go off to discover another (8th) in the den (but again sparing the large plasma screen and Anwar's various gaming platforms (sparing even the black (faux) leather couch)). Nothing the twins can't fix with a big salad bowl.

Astair urges them to get rain-ready (Astair heading back to her own room for better socks and a hat). Taymor is late (ahh the joys of a one-car household of five (soon six)) but who knows if she's called.

The phones haven't stopped ringing for days. This morning was the worst (landline and both

Anwar's and Astair's cells (Anwar's e-mail accounts all suffering the deluge too (at least there (her e-mail account) Astair was spared))).

Her phone sits on the edge of her bed ((silenced but for the constantly illuminating screen marking yet another message) the number of missed calls staggering (Astair can't face the number)). (for reasons too pathetic to admit) Anwar and Astair couldn't unplug all the cordless phones (one remains ((a reminder) in Anwar's office) and it's been ringing straight for three days).

Also on the bed waits the thick manila envelope. The return address says all she needs to know about who it's from (herself in fact (at least contents by) (if not (what matters) the final word(s) filling margins ((unseen) grade topping the title page))).

"You're still not opening it?" Anwar had asked again this morning (her paper arrived yesterday).

"Tonight. When we have time to celebrate."

Anwar had tilted his head cautiously (the way he does when enough doubt (and fear?) prevents him from keeping his gaze level).

"Okay, feasibly," Astair quickly admitted (it wasn't hard to admit). "I could get a lousy grade but the likelihood that this thesis will be out-and-out failed is highly improbable. From what I've heard the only papers not passed are those deemed incomplete. Have you forgotten what my advisor wrote after the penultimate draft?" (A rave that had (even back then) started Astair thinking about trying to get her work published by a university press or even a big New York house (once she had her diploma in hand (of course))).

"Of course," Anwar had smiled warmly. "He was so excited, he nearly died of a heart attack." (Llewyn Fabler was still on medical leave.)

Astair didn't doubt that Lucien and Dana had called or e-mailed with good news (their Twitter accounts read as variations on "Celebration" (Ronnie Born's Instagram account showed a video of a champagne bottle popped (looking vaguely obscene (Astair not having seen anything close to that graphic in years (she couldn't remember the last time she'd even seen a clip of porn ((likely by mistake) and likely sooner than when she'd last enjoyed a bottle of the old widow (chilled and uncorked)))))))).

On Facebook most of Astair's classmates kept posting their results (making her restraint seem more ridiculous (by the hours)). Shana Bix had gotten an A, Davis Trenz an A-. Cardiff Chambers had not only gotten an A, but received an invitation to publish with University of Chicago Press (her book tentatively titled *Don't Say Things You Don't Mean: Don't Mean Things You Don't Say*). Even the most ominous news (Phoenix Opal Eller had earned a C+ (which was still passing) ("but what did i expect? i handed in verse!")) was gilded by another publishing offer ((this one from Autumn House Press) for a collection of poems entitled *Speeches We'll Never Make*).

Maybe Astair should have stuck with her first (gimmicky) notion (sweet ways of framing difficulties in living and love (emphasis on sweet)): *Ice Cream Koans*.

Instead Astair had pursued something (a bit!) more aloof (not to mention ambitious (and not at all publishable)). She took as her starting point (if not outright inspiration) the grand tradition of thought experiments.

Rather than treat standard (canonical?) texts from which to deviate with exegetical propositions or cull (and cultivate) existing data from which to derive new(?) conclusions(?) Astair had resolved (in keeping with theories of analysis at its most curative ((Langs' frame) the power of boundaries: (economy free of compounding costs) (confession without retribution) (inquisition without judgment))) to simply "encompass as best as I can" ((or: enclose? surround? wall in? engirdle? hem? (and haw?)) in regard to moral and spiritual and even esoteric cravings ("Ecstasies!" Fabler had suggested (before his heart faltered)): the question of our times.

As might be expected with such a ridiculous (and arrogant(?) (even wince-worthy)) pursuit ("Quest!" Fabler had shouted in his office) the paper had not come easily. (depending on how one counted) A disproportionate(?) amount of time (nine years(?)!) had gone into its modest eighty-one pages (and all this in the pursuit of a degree in Marriage, Family, and Child Counseling). The title was double (triple (quadruple?)!) wince worthy:

Hope's Nest: On the Necessity of God.

Llewyn Fabler accepted (and with enthusiasm too (finally)) that Astair's atheism made her the perfect candidate for such a project (long ago divested from her adolescent indoctrination as a Catholic (which had imprinted in her as its last notion that the Church was principally about opposing abortion (she'd had two (ages fifteen & sixteen)) same-sex rights (she'd married gay friends) contraception (she'd been on (and off) the pill since she was sixteen) while pro delayed gratification (why else leave her future unopened for so long?) and pedophilia (for which now as a mother of three daughters she could find no breath of forgiveness (knowing still there always must be forgiveness (that sublime breath of discovery and compassion) (but how to excuse such a trespassing ((ordination) crime!) to (over)determine a future of one so open to the future and then by a handful of hot sweaty breaths (some hasty rape) closed permanently to the future?)) (wasn't the notion of divinity in part a way to re(ar) ticulate the fixed ("Joint the bone?" Fabler had asked) ("Loose breath upon dead waters?" (Fabler had asked later) "And stir forth possibilities?" (such a beautiful man))("Rewrite the sands so that what stands is always unwritten?" Anwar (her most beautiful man) had asked when he had finished reading her paper for the first time)("'God fastens the universe in the movement of God' said Reb Jorda" ∷ *The Book of Questions* by Edmond Jabès ∷ Anwar had quoted after reading her labor for the nth time)?))).

What better accomplice for such a task than her husband? (also an avowed atheist (his own divergence from uniformity (control) having come with his youthful discovery of algebra (of all things!) and BASIC (the ABCs of Go To))) all while (Anwar claimed once) "both my parents cast"— (his mother (fiery Fatima (a pharmacist and a Shiite)) pestling her own rationalism with his father's subtle whimsy ((Shenouda Iskandar bin Ibrahim) an engineer and a Sufi "twinkling and blue as deep water")) — "a spell carving a doorway in that fortified wall of their belief through which I could not only ponder stars out of reach of constellations but finally escape."

Astair even lifts it in both hands (considers again the (familiar) weight). The return address (Pacifica Graduate Institute ∴ 249 Lambert Road, Carpinteria, CA 93013 ∵). Shocked then by doubt's assault: what if this isn't even the paper but some thick catalogue? or billing instructions in regard to past fees she overlooked (or worse what if this is (as expected) her thesis but with both grade and evaluation returning her to additional course work and years more of writing (or potentially the impetus to quit (door closed))? what if she's wrong about everything)?

Astair knows she's neither presumptuous nor proud (except where her children are concerned). She knows she's more than capable of failure (experienced it many times (after all her relationship with the father of her first child had failed ((grotesquely) no other word for it))).

She also knows that couched in her desire to "celebrate" (in the word itself (to honor)) is already an awareness of (preparation too (for)) the ensuing discomfort (grief?) that will accompany this scholastic termination.

School over. Getting older. Just turned forty (forty is only forty). Thoughts that turn her cheeks to fire (forehead too). Definitely already old! Her armpits too. (Hey! Is this a legitimate hotflash?!)

Astair sets the envelope back down on the bed (whatever the future holds can wait until tonight ((with a good bottle of bubbly (with an obscene uncorking)) plus (feeling again more optimistic) she wants the whole family there (including their new (if outrageous) addition))).

(still) The site of the envelope (on the edge of their California King) makes it seem so exposed (so open to misuse or disposal or harm (what if a 9th leak suddenly opens above and turns anything of paper to mush?))

Astair places it in their bathroom closet (second shelf (tucked between a stack of folded towels)).

"No more," Shasti starts (Freya usually starts) from her doorway.

"Eight Itsy Bitsys," Freya adds. "We didn't check the guest whatamacallit."

"Daddy's workshop."

"Is it really a guesthouse?"

"It used to be a garage. We didn't go out and check there."

Astair loves them (beyond herself (far beyond their similarities)). Her friends see identical twins but she and Anwar behold vast differences ((Freya wider (nearly broad in her ability to insist)) (Shasti nimble (nearly acrobatic in her skill at dancing around conversations or rooms)).

"Will you check if Taymor has arrived yet?"

"She has!" they say together (in that unison those less familiar with their personal deviations (from morphological oneness) might describe as uncanny). "She's in the driveway." In unison again.

"Then let's scoot."

But neither Shasti nor Freya moves.

"You promised," Freya starts.

"Once we finished searching for Itsy—"
"—Bitsy leaks."
"To tell us about Xanther's surprise."
"Before Xanther finds out." Unison.

Astair wishes the twins would (just once) show some compassion for their sister (even an iota of interest might do). Astair knows they love Xanther (even look up to her (some kind of untraceable awe there (simply because she's older?))) and yet for whatever reason (simply too young?) they cannot answer Xanther's desire for their amity. (Xanther who so freely (too freely?) will grant loyalty and respect to anyone (any creature!) (another thought to keep rebreaking Astair's heart)).

Just this morning (as father and daughter dashed out into the rain) Astair watched Xanther pause Anwar's race for the car so he wouldn't crush any snails making their way across the sidewalk (squatting under her bright orange umbrella to assist every antennaed pilgrimage to a greener and (puddled(?)) safer side).

(from the doorway) The twins (though) had squealed their incredulous mockery over this latest display of odd behavior ((because it was raining)(because snails were "eeeeeeeeeeew" and "GROSS!") (because it was something they would never do) (because—)). Followed by their nearly indecipherable speech. Anwar thought that description was generous: "More like a fax line."

"The magic, wonder, and maybe frustration of twins?" Dr. Sandwich had said on more than a few occasions ((Dr. Elina Sandawai) Astair's therapist (fifty hours required)). From birth to now her

125

daughters' lives had demonstrated plenty of all that (along with behavior that their age might condone (but which Astair had never seen in Xanther (at any age))): extreme self-involvement with obvious disregard for the feelings of others (they're only eight!). Thoughts inflicting Astair with plenty of guilt. (after all) Freya and Shasti were not evil twins nor were they unkind. They were just very, very in(ter)dependent (what Anwar and Astair were sure came from the interiority they alone could share).

Curiously though (and contrary to expectation?) the older Shasti and Freya got, the more they indulged in that (ego-sustaining? (and inflating?)) interiority. And while continuing to find (and refind) themselves in the privacy of their own resemblance would (no doubt(?)) pose troubling complications in the need for (and purpose of) identity, at present this bi-inwardness afforded a powerful sense of confidence. If only it didn't have to come across as condescending (and outright smugness).

Anwar had suggested sending them to opposite sides of the globe for a summer. Astair too wanted to see more conflict. Not that there wasn't any. Bath-time squalls could flood the floor tiles. Too often though Astair had watched an escalating dispute instantly disappear in the presence of another (whether a classmate, friend, or innocent playground socializer (interloper)). The twins would close ranks and (with a dimpled smile) disappear into their own inviolable sameness.

Astair had seen them do it (numerous times!) to Xanther.

They'd even done it to her.

No doubt flawless features reinforced this entitlement to distance. Freya and Shasti pull focus wherever they go (even causing Astair (now and then) twinges of ~~resentment~~ ((*dread!*(?)) however fleeting) (they're only eight!)). Silky things of withy limbs, sly smiles, and shiny cheeks (skin light as nutmeg, hair like dark honey, and eyes the color of warm brass ((extraordinary eyes) (arresting eyes) (impenetrable eyes))(her two Cleopatras)). "Get them an agent now!" Astair has heard enough times to start giving a move to Juneau serious consideration.

Xanther's big surprise (their new addition) was ((no doubt)(in part)) supposed to address this sororal insularity. Three sisters (the old logic went) should have one another (but Astair and Anwar knew better than to put all their faith in old logic).

Truth: the twins had each other.

Which left Xanther with what? Without the sisters she still had. Without the father her sisters never had.

Dov.

As meaningless to Frey and Shast (thankfully) as he was meaningful to Xanther ((thanklessly) . . .) and (thanklessly) meaningful to Astair (even meaningful ((thankfully?) (thanklessly?)) to Anwar).

"Perhaps on some level the girls consider Xanther's condition a kind of companion," Anwar had puzzled out late one evening. "It's, after all, always with her. About her. How she feels. How much she sleeps. What she eats. And it gathers so much of our attention we're probably not even aware of how much we check in with Xanther for signs of fatigue or distress. Though I bet Freya and Shasti are aware."

Anwar was probably not far off. And wasn't this (in the end) the only problem Astair had been trying to solve for over a year (watching Xanther growing ((more independent too) up))? To locate and secure for her child a better companion? able to return her loyalty? kind, comforting, rejuvenating, protective, enduring . . .

Because there was no question (by its constant threat (and constant terror)) epilepsy served as a constant reminder of how much different Xanther was from her sisters and parents (and almost everyone else). Her odd looks didn't help either: extremely pale skin (even Dov wasn't that pale (Astair tanned well)) and as of late now (poor kid) stippled too with wounds of maturing (the backs of her arms rarely without an abrasive rash (her cheeks and forehead a fizz of acne)). Add to that (what a list!) pudginess around her waist, knock-knees (swollen too like pomelos (early arthritis (the suspicion was there!))) terrible eyesight, screwball teeth, her own blend of dyslexia ((?) or just a learning disability) and poor dexterity. All of which compounded the crushing (caustic) social challenges Xanther has had to face in school and after school (Astair and Anwar might have finally opted for home schooling (a conversation they have at least once a month) were it not for the emergence of a few promising friends this year).

All of which still didn't take into account Dov's death (which in her search for leaks (whom?) Astair had just found (in Xanther's room (on her corkboard (pinned beside those equations in Anwar's (beautiful) hand ((*non-determining forms*(?)) something like that)) a note from Dov:

You're tougher than mud.
Don't forget it.

Love, Dov.

                                        )))

Mud (to Dov's mind (aside from being his patro-
nymic)) was beyond defeat. Boot heels, bullets, and
tanks could tear it up and mud would be none the
worse. Sometimes Dov even hinted that death itself
had nothing on mud. Not that anyone was calling
him mud now. The military had all sorts of terms
for what he was now: DOW, DWRIA, KIA, plus
Zapped, Wasted, Greased, Dusted, Planted, Expe-
dited, Made a Believer, Checked Out, Fallen in the
Line of Duty, Hero (sung or unsung (how about
auto-tuned?)). Or whatever you call the death of
men at the hands of other men when you don't want
to call it murder.

Astair couldn't go there.

But just the sight of his penmanship (forget the
words (that brutal hand)) ~~expulsed~~ (*expelled!*) her
from its sight ((Love!(?)) Dov and Astair had been so
young so in love what did they know then about the
cost of dying or for that matter the cost of living . . .)

Xanther measured out that cost of living every day she trundled off to Thomas Starr King (obligingly, bravely (taking in those big gulps of air)). Astair could hear the questions this child (obligingly, bravely, breathlessly (but resolutely too)) refused to say aloud: is this the day it finally happens? Lose it in front of everyone? Wet myself in front of everyone? Hurt myself beyond repair? (And (even if the pronouns were different) Xanther wasn't the only one who asked those questions.)

Just a glance at the ragged mess around her fingernails communicated more than the lengthiest essays on the nature of distress. One (recent) evening Astair had looked in on Xanther to find her (even bound up in sleep) picking at her cuticles until they bled. For twenty minutes Astair had sat cross-legged beside her daughter, attempting to gently parry every stab (but the nails never failed to return (and pick (((patiently) fixedly) always set on violence))).

So why not a companion?

Why not answer all of this with a hero who was not dead (not violent) but bred and trained to defend? Not some ~~regiment~~ (*regimen!*) of pills or a calendar surfeit with checkups or some new app for counting carbs and fat. Not a doctor. Or a pair of wily sisters. Or even a parent. Or god forbid (god!? (is that what it will take?)) some new Proto-Beta-Whatever-Online-PlayStation-Xbox game.

But rather a pet.

A magnificent creature.

To stroke and dote on and tend to.

Furry and friendly and honest and near.

One who will watch over Xanther and need her
and if need be pin her down with all that fur and
softness until the seizure stops.

Hers to take care of.

Hers to adore.

Hers to turn to.

To confide in too.

Hers alone.

In Anwar's office the phone continues to ring.
Outside Taymor begins to lightly honk. A tricky
moment approaches. Astair has a choice but not
much of one. The twins will either embrace the
idea enthusiastically (sensing (rightly) that they
will be both revelers and owners too) or reject it as
an(other?) unfair act of favoritism (Xanther's infir-
mities be damned in the eyes of these two gorgeous
girls).

Astair sits down on the edge of the bed to meet
their eyes (on their level) pinching her knees
together too (maybe a little too tightly?) resting the
back of her right hand in the palm of her left (maybe
a little too contained).

"Your dad took your sister this morning to
get . . . " Astair begins (giving them then as many
details and reasons as she can summon (Shut. Up.
Astair! (They're. Only. Eight!))).

A dreadful moment follows (dreadful enough for Astair to relish Taymor's increasingly louder honks along with their only unsilenced phone (the home's canary?) ringing (and not just these (a high-pitched whistle also joins the mix (downstairs?)))).

Shasti and Freya don't even look at each other (or hold each other's hands (as they sometimes do when they are stressed (and confused))). But their eyes widen, their chests expand, their lips burst.

Finally they let it out: breath and voice (even starting to jump up and down).

Chirps. Squeals.

(even jumping up onto the bed)

More squeaks. Screams. Giggles.

And (as if equally caught up) the ringing pauses. The honks too. But not the whistle (though it's at this point almost sputtering out (a slight note of something burning starting to drift upstairs)).

Stove! Kettle! Nothing compared to the twins' rising chorus:

"WE'RE GETTING A DOG!"

The Orb

Do you like our owl?

— Blade Runner

The planet resembles Mars. Red at least. Born under metallic dust.
Massive storms make of that heaviness something lighter than snow.
Though here it never snows. No water. At most frozen carbon
dioxide. A cold world. Hundreds of thousands of light-
years away. Possessed, as Kim Stanley Robinson
might describe it, with "mineral unconscious-
ness."

Given the right social infrastructure and
equipment, a culture might have a go at
such mute hussle and crozzle, whether
silicate-rich or not, tholeiitic basalt or
plagioclase feldspar. Mine the surface, extract ore, find iron. Despite
the human love affair with fiber and
the promiscuous promise of synthet-
ics, it will take more than history
to give up our devotion to authority
by metal, the articulating sword. To
smelt then will yield the bold speech
of structure: riveted, reinforced, and
always taller, eventually clawing up into
winds powerful enough to have already,
over the centuries, diminished skerries kilo-
meters high. The cries then that must answer
a dedication of such an edifice, standing proudly
against the sky as if it could mean above the sky,
soon enough in geological time giving way to the shrieks
of shearing alloys as the atmospheric tolls of hundreds of kilo-
meters per hour exact what all constructions must accommodate: vibra-

tions, sways, and finally one day, enough torque to cause the building to lose hold, welds unseaming, rivets rotten, toppling, settling, until after millennia, not even piles of jointed frames and I-beams remain; not even a midden of shards, let alone our grimy architectural intent.

Nothing lasts on the planet. Cyclones rasp the rutilant surface, temperature fluctuations wrench air and mantle, until the resigned percentages of such an atmosphere and place guarantee the absence of any known or postulated form of organism. Even the planet itself orbits against itself, with constant anomalies threatening to set it loose, heading toward unreachable light or surrendering to the dark obliterating mass at the galaxy's core.

Not that this is a real planet or even a dream planet. It is a coagulate dependent on learning, affect, and that asymmetric assembly deemed the imaginative.

She recognizes herself as its sole witness. If only it were real. If only it were just a nightmare. But it is more. Not Orb-born but hers — time-scratched if still operable and at such times her only distraction.

Not far from the equator, it sits on a mesa high above a canyon which would make of our Grand Canyon or Mariana Trench something less than a tern's imprint on a beach. The temple is strange and yet intimately familiar. Hardly large or elaborate. Nine columns without roof, arcade, or even entablature. Similar perhaps to what remains now of the sanctuary of Athena Pronaia at Delphi. At its center sits a small pyramid of glossy white stone capping a well of uncomfortable depths however dry and inutile. The entire temple seems made of the same

stone though no such material exists on this planet. And unlike our
ruins, neither time nor elements have left a mark. Every surface glimmers like polished glass. The columns
stand tall. Not even one errant wheel of sand
settles upon the glossy floor.

As if within her Orb, she cannot
wait to see how successive events
will contradict this impression.
They do not. In fast-forward,
storm systems boil up and
engulf the temple, only
to at last dissipate, leaving behind the temple
unchanged.

She scrolls to the peak of
the present and still discov-
ers the temple unmarred.
The unplayed music of this
structure never repeals its
secrecy. At least on this edge,
where the future waits, explanation and hope also wait. It's when
she scrolls back into time that the
terror seizes her, slowly at first, like the
awareness of a rhythm not quite synchro-
nized with the patterns of this life, growing
ever more palpable and recognizable too, that rough

announcement of something coming, like the sound of steps, though not human steps, drawing closer and closer, eventually accompanied by impatient breaths. Only here in her mind's eye — that other orb — there are no announcements or footsteps, and certainly no breaths, no matter how many ages or eras she goes back.

Eons slip by. The canyon rises. Her mesa falls then rises then falls again until eventually it flattens into a storm-polished plain. The temple, though, remains unchanged. No sign of how it resists time's exhortations. No sign of how it detaches from the environment it possesses or at least must rest upon. And never a sign of how it came into being.

If she wanted, she could go back to before the planet took shape. Fear keeps her from going that far, to where she knows with a shudder the temple will still wait, unchanged, even as far back as when this universe first came into being, all the time there, still remembering all the bloody sacrifices yet to come.

Sometimes her thoughts are antipodal to the pliability of her body. She must force them away from the impossible toward the ordinary. Today the ordinary would be the rain. As if it were raining all over the world. How easily she finds the impossible in the ordinary. But how often does it rain in Marfa? At least at any other time, her feverish obsession with this edifice would find eerie prophecies in the dusty Texas landscape. For all its echoes of Greek and Roman civilizations and *Battlestar Galactica*'s Kobol, her creation still echoes the Minimalists and their own obsessions with perdurable forms, form outside of form, whether at Chinati or over at Judd's private retreat. Because why not posit among things destined to arise from and return to dust that which is never of dust?

Fortunately, thunder, with its gaudy
flares of lightning, along with the
dry patter of rain, heavy as
dead beetles coining the
earth, helps clear her
old mind. For now.

"Lunch?" Bobby
asks from their
A i r s t r e a m ' s
k i t c h e n e t t e
where he has
spent the last
twenty minutes
preparing their
meal. This is
how he handles
the aftermath of
their horrible fail-
ure.

"I'd like to take a walk
first," Cas responds. Cas to
her friends, Dr. Cas also to her
friends, Catherine Aa'ala Stern
on most government and university
documents.

Bobby studies the storm beyond the small window above the sink. He is only a year older, but unlike Cas, he has remained hardy, resilient, regardless of the overhang threatening his belt, thanks to those frosty friends — IPAs — he indulges in on weekends. At seventy-seven his hair seems thicker than most men's half his age, its whiteness only making the point. He is still as whimsical and sulky as the UC Berkeley astronomer she knew back in 1961. Just as horny too.

"We'll get wet."

Bobby never hears the word "I" if he isn't saying it.

"That's what I want." That's how she will handle the aftermath of their failure, her growing shock.

Out on 67 a highway patrol car passes by. No sirens, no lights, but way under the speed limit. Police still make her heart flutter. Something in her palms reacts as if palms could have anything to say if an officer decided to pull down the long drive past the For Sale sign.

It isn't much of a hiding place. Cas wanted to park far out of sight but Bobby assured her there was no better spot. He is the expert. Not only had Bobby made acceptable arrangements for the month with the owner of these acres — even if they won't last the week — he had also carried out the same profile analysis that intelligence experts would likely run, if their data came up close. Bobby swears nothing will place them in Texas, let alone Marfa, let alone in an RV with a crimson awning, lawn chairs hugging the shade, and one motorcycle cinched to the back. What does it matter if Joel (or JEOL) takes up everything inside from the counter where

the coffee maker stands to the back berth
where Cas goes to orb?

A second police
car coasts by.
Cas needs
to get out.
B o b b y
t h i n k s
her tabu-
l a t i o n
of law
enforce-
m e n t
vehicles
is an ir-
relevant
datum.

He keeps his
back to 67 and cuts
their sandwiches in
half.

Sometimes Cas doesn't want his help. She managed just fine this morning at five when the storm first started to brood. At least the braces around both knees were not so bad. Those on her left elbow proved a little more finicky, what with the buckles and those dull little prongs. Bobby took care of the right arm though she could have managed that alone too. Probably.

"If you want to check the antennas, we'll likely get lightninged to a crisp."

"I want to check them all," Cas insists.

"Electrocution it is."

Cas knows those notes. Nothing will mitigate the shame that keeps coming for him. His sweetness has no recourse before such hurt. Cas also can't help but hate herself a little for being to blame for its recurrence now, even if she also knows that she is no more part of that storm than she is the fictive ones circling her fictive planet.

"Come on," she says, struggling to her feet. "Let's get zapped together."

Getting zapped is the least of their worries.

"We always were Ethel and Julius."

She laughs despite not having laughed now for days.

The crack pauses them both, still rumbling on, as if to make sense of or
renew in some remediated form the flash already past, coulombs of dis-
charge drifting on the air. Maybe
even something still burning
in the face of that sei-
zure of light. In any
case, loud enough
to believe the
A i r s t r e a m
only just sur-
vived some
c i n e m a t i c
squashing.

What Cas
c a u g h t
t h r o u g h
t h e i r
s c r e e n
door still
h a n g s
before her
like a reti-
nal wound,
Jupiter's red
storm. So why not
assume the lightning
bolt took out an antenna?
The tallest of course. Or even
all of their spindly towers? Not like she

can see. For the moment, that big spot keeps wandering the equator of her Visible. So she pictures for herself radiant arcs hopping from antenna to antenna which in spite of breakers and prudent grounding smolder and melt, skewing down to the earth, sky-chosen, sky-struck, sky-subdued.

"Good thing we weren't on the Orb," Bobby adds.

"The storm's miles away." For all the closeness such powerful light suggests, especially powerful vision, the lightning hadn't come close. Just the same, this revisioning strikes her as curious. Perhaps some personal wish to melt those connective crosses and render her Orb inert. Blind its gaze. Blind her gaze. And at least for a few days, even a few hours, leave Cas free to risk real fire and take a walk in the rain.

"Good thing we weren't on the Orb," Bobby says again.

She knows it would have made no difference. She knows he knows this too. So why does Bobby insist on repeating what both of them know is not true? Neither of them is looking out across the mesa anymore, not at their dishes and crucifixes stuck up close to the barbed wire, not at the dust still popping up with scattered drops, fire in the history of the ground here, a deep history with no regard for the present. But even with all the black clouds churning beyond, where now and then shafts of noon still slip through, this collision of vapor and current, every so often repeating its clamorous light show, connecting one starless vault to one star-warmed earth, is still not dazzling enough to keep Cas and Bobby from turning away, backs to the world, always craving to return to the rear of the Airstream, where centered before their couch by day and bed by night, wrapped up in an old cashmere sweater, waits her Orb.

"How did they get every-thing?" she asks instead.

"I underestimated Recluse."

"Stop it," she snaps. "That's not what I'm asking."

"The Dis-tribution went every-where. Self-replicating. Mutative to the point of dissuading identification but not to the point of compromising con-tent. I can only imagine he's accomplished a VEM Window Reduction we've thus far thought impossible."

"Then he'd already have found us. If it's not via VEM, then it's the kind of computational power . . . "

"All the nets? Even Binney's scared of us."

"How do you know?"

"Instead of talking USSID 18, Binney called me batshit crazy and hung up. If only it were lighter."

"If only it were simpler," Cas corrects. "Heavy and easy is easy. Heavy and complex approaches futile."

"I'm sorry."

"We're not Snowden, Bobby."

"Maybe that's our mistake."

"Is it possible some packets got through?" A cheap offering deserving of exactly the disgust Bobby takes no measures to hide. "Any word from Endoria or Artemis? What about Treebeard?"

"No one." Bobby keeps shaking his head.

"Our Sorcerer? Our Warlock? At least Deakin made it."

"Oh."

"Checked in at the Paisano this morning."

"You spoke to him?"

"Just for a moment."

If it wasn't so real for
him, Cas might have
laughed. And it was
hard not to with that
sour look twisting
away on Bobby's
lips, an expression
made only avail-
able when they
were alone. When
they worked with
Deakin, aka Merlin,
Bobby couldn't seem
more at ease. It fasci-
nated her that a fling she'd
had back in the 70s, involving hotel-room sex she remembers no better than the hotels in
which they'd had it in — truth be
told Cas can't even remember which cities
anymore — could still pique her husband. Whether

green-eyed or black-horned, jealousy is a curious creature. And apparently an enduring one too.

"He traveled all night. He suggested we join him for dinner."

"Did he have any good news?" The present unthreads Bobby's lips. Cas almost prefers the past. This protective response to the preeminence of male seed is comical relief compared to the appalling absence they face now.

"He's still alive."

Of course maybe Cas is wrong about Bobby's jealousy. Maybe that supposition was just her thoughts slipstreaming her own desire to locate some kind of compensatory pleasure, albeit remembered, albeit hazily; a carnal reference away from the rest of her thoughts which these days keep veering too often toward carnage. Maybe Bobby's pouts were purely professional jealousy: Deakin had come out of Caltech and MIT successfully cat's cradling his way between government agencies, the private sector, and university appointments. Plenty of awards were in there too. He had worked on everything from programming parts of the Hubble to securing NASDAQ trading protocols.

"He warned me from the start about the way I was trying to handle online such volatile chunks of data."

"Please stop this. You are not entitled to all the blame."

Bobby lays out her calcium and vitamin D supplements. These days
they've been trying 1000 mg of Lypo-Spheric C. It's goopy
stuff he squeezes into a shot glass of water. Like
an egg yolk made of Tang though not sweet.

"Bobby, if you're going to persist in
finding fault with your programming and distribution logistics,
then grant me the failure of
imagination."

"I've never blamed you!"
How beautiful that this
old geezer can still mus-
ter the reserves to redden
like a scolded child.

"Not for a second did I
think that he could scrub
the entire Web of our
efforts. I still can't conceive
how this was accomplished.
Worse, I continue to hold on
to a hope that our present assessments grossly overrate the results."

A dumb thing to say and an even dumber
hope. How else to answer this spreading disbe-
lief, dulling her senses, her will? Soon she'll be seeing light-

ning twisting her into smoldering briquets. Almost a relief. Cas takes her vitamins instead. Not like they will help either. After three days of searching sites from Reddit to Facebook to Parcel Thoughts, Google of course, BitTorrent, MMOGs like WOW, as well as .org, .edu, and even .gov servers, plus all kinds of steganographic posts, not one stray artifact or even a rumor suggested that their message in a bottle — a predicted billions of bottles — had reached even one sandy shore. Nor did it appear that any were even floating around in that sea of data, what weeks ago Cas had casually envisioned as amniotic and now saw as nothing more hospitable than perchloric acid, resultant fumes noisome to the point of nausea, and migraines — she was due one — Cas' entire physiology revolting before the apparent fact that not only had every bottle been shattered and sunk, but all meaning within erased. God help them if it also had somehow been traced.

There was real terror here. Beyond whatever obvious extensions Cas could easily foresee, whether at the hand of local police, federal agents, or even some abstract laws twisted enough to decry them as traitors, terrorists, seditious to the point of world toppling. Forget jail cells or street-corner executions. This was something else. To have put so much out there and watch it be swallowed without a trace.

Whether users recognized it, there was something reassuring about how on the internets, a message could find a place to stick and even if it went unobserved at that moment, it could be heard at some other moment. Just going online engaged this beautiful notion of place. Conversely, how appalling to realize that there exists a means to dispossess us of any place. Of course, the fear of what extinguishes endurance, forbids continuity, what will unstick the brightest, the ugliest, the kindest, and the cruelest too, has stalked life since life first knew it had to survive.

Out there another flash. Shearing light
blanks out the periphery. Thunder
proves the point.

And then as if to deprive injury
of hurt, something else as well.
Something worse.

Faint and plaintive. As if begging
for an answer. Even the echo of
an old answer. As if begging for
the comfort of just knowing itself
to be begging could suffice.

Cas watches Bobby eat instead. It is
one of her greatest comforts. Except he
hasn't touched his sandwich. His favorite too (and hers): toasted rye, avocado,
goat cheese, sprouts, a thin slice of red onion,
and a spread Bobby makes out of garbanzos, gar-
lic, raw mustard, toasted pumpkin seeds, olive oil, and
drops of Meyer lemon juice.

But again she hears it, somehow threading the patter of rain, a cry for help no more believable than this failure they had helped enact, before which there is nothing either of them can do. Cas still can't move.

Something had once come to her in the same way years ago. Before Bobby, before Deakin, before them all. The year was 1958 in the cruelest month of April, on the 15th. Cas even remembers the hour. And minute. 11:11:11. Maybe she's making up the seconds. Back then she could move, and quickly too, to paper and pen. Actually, there was no pen on hand. She had started out with a crayon. The first apparition had seemed so small, nearly trivial. A dash of words, some numbers, no more than a few lines, at most. And then the paragraphs had stretched into pages until the formulae were rewrapping themselves back into the beginnings, which were no longer beginnings, because this was not a proclaiming or encoding or even a canonizing but rather ∴ **allways** ∴ an exploration, deprived of alphas and omegas, set limits, quickly evolving into a book, and then books, volumes on how it all worked, or rather revealed itself, if she could just get it right, which she couldn't, not at first, eventually spending years struggling with the errata, and in the end left with something that still required a vast infrastructure and signal exoskeleton to gather the inputs and support the renderings. Bobby had spent his years chasing something more internal, elegant, like an alchemist trying to find a way to transmute iron into gold, and for a long while he had worked with iron, convinced that the atomic number 26 might somehow validate the fe in fey. Then came fluorine and cobalt, later lithium, oxygen, and nitrogen.

These days it was pollen. Asters of late.

Both of them wanted something simpler and less inconsistent. A refined demonstration of what consistently edged beyond not only comprehension but the comforting belief that one day it could be succinctly understood. Cas had not only failed to compress the algorithms, she had watched helplessly as costs to enact a lifetime's worth of theory quickly exceeded the affordable. Far beyond Cern or ITER. Fortunately technological evolutions over the years provided some reprieve, allowing her to cut loose of places like the Shamakhi, Karachay–Cherkessia, or Palomar Mountain range. The expanding Web and rising processing power, not to mention intermittent successes furthering her theories, allowed greater mobility, practice, and of course discovery.

Couldn't they just show people? Yes, they could. They had. And along the way she and Bobby had found believers among the many, many doubters. Still, belief doesn't diminish the weight of the explanation: literal weight, of hardware, as well as the tonnage of complexity, along with the greatest burden of all: their ethical responsibility.

"I wouldn't be surprised if lightning still knocks out one of our antennas," Bobby says, even as Cas starts shuffling past Joel. "I'll see what's online. I'd give us twenty minutes before the power's down. If that."

"We'll go for a walk then, after the rain passes,"
Cas yells from the rear lounge, settling herself on
the blue cushions, facing the sweater. Twenty
minutes is not long enough. Not that this
rattles her. Time deserted her years ago. Or
at least the sense that she had much of it.
Cas has learned to make do. Focus makes
calm minutes count.

She draws the cashmere off the glass,
lightly scratched but never smudged,
radiant with that peculiar blackness
which testifies to all still left to witness.
Cas loves how proximity alone is enough
of a switch. Almost at once her fingertips
begin to tingle with static. Here the myth of
fingerprints is also her security. Round One.
And as the cobalt at the Orb's center begins
arcing through the obsidian, Cas keeps herself
from blinking, her face close enough for her nose
and eyelids to feel the burn until, Round Two, or this
second log-in, the familiar blue begins to twist with a
near-amber flame, until, Round Three, the particular dance of
her fingers, encoded motions Bobby had reprogrammed just months

ago, decrypt the Orb's final protections and ∴ unhide its mind ∵ ∴ *bright the crypt of its savage dark* ∴ whereupon a green and then a practically predatory light emerges, transforming all hues into something pale and smoky, nearly white if still textured by changes too tiny or quick to track.

Even now, after so many thousands of hours, the impression of depth is too vivid to shake. Cas doesn't move but still reels briefly with the sensation of falling.

All that remains to decide now, today, for twenty minutes, if that, if half that, is the question of where she will fall to: how she will angle, rotate, and at what speed she must scroll.

Out of habit Cas withdraws slightly, pressing fingertips together, as if about to pray before the Orb, though palms never touch. Appearances instead cant toward ghoulish scheming, with the elasticity of her joints giving way until the nails of her left hand touch the back of her left hand, and then the nails of her right hand touch the back of her right hand.

"If you grow your nails long, so they twist like Arby's curly fries, you'll look fierce and evil," Bobby says from the lounge doorway. Sandwich in hand. At least one of them is eating now.

"Why would I want to look evil?" Cas asks, surprised by her own rush of hurt, hot as burnt strawberries.

"Come a year or more, Recluse might find this moment and get scared."

"From long fingernails that look like Arby's curly fries?" The sound of her own laughter nearly erases the blotch of hurt.

At least Bobby's laughing too, a few sprouts dangling in his beard. "You could pain them purple or black?"

"Pain them?" Sometimes Bobby is just an old man who doesn't know what he's saying. Or he's at that point where he says exactly what he knows without knowing it. Fortunately for them, the pain hadn't come yet. But it would. The longer their friends remained silent. *Silenced!* Deakin would have something to say. He was at least a hope to hold on to. Especially as her shock worsened. As her dream for lightning grew.

"I don't think he scares." :: ▮▮▮▮▮▮▮▮▮▮▮. ::

"Worth a try."

"Do you think I'm evil?"

Bobby hesitates or his mouth is too full. Either way he looks only at the Orb, no doubt wondering what Cas is looking at now, what only Cas knows how to look at, her fingers already moving through the static, rearranging it, drawing from the cloudy depths doubt's calling and end.

Beginnings pulse within reach. ∷ Here where the ontology of thought lives. ∷ More than beginnings. *Nunc dimittis.* ∷ **Here where the epistemology of living incarnates Judgment.** ∷ Does she care? ∷ *Here where the origin of eschatological limits finds every consequential thread.* ∷ Already, as what was mute and white gives way to edges and hue, motion and even music, she cares less and less about Bobby's response to her question.

"Of course you're not evil," Bobby says anyway. "But if you're asking me about that thing there—"

"Our thing," she corrects him.

"I'm not sure."

Power Draws a Crowd

Perhaps those that hear well will find something captured which escapes contemplation.

— *Bill Evans*

"Oz, what are you doing here?"

Always the same question.

"In the neighborhood?"

He always gives the same answer.

"Since when is Southwest your neighborhood?"

And always the same question in response. But the neighborhood never matters. Or the city. Or even the country. Özgür never belongs.

"On my way to Santa Rosalia Drive for lunch. I always brake for blue lights."

"Is it even ten?"

"Post & Beam has a pretty good lunch. Turkey meatballs, spicy tomato sauce. You have no idea what you're missing, Balascoe."

"I work here, I don't eat here."

Detective Rodney Balascoe has worked the Southwest division homicide table for a few years now but even back when he and Özgür had found their sorrows in Hollenbeck, or later in Newton Division, he was famous for preparing all his meals at home. And Captains Snell and Meek never complained because Balascoe never called in a Code 7 ∴ Meal break ∴. Night or day he carried with him these nesting bento boxes which for all their elaborate finish rarely held anything more than barbecue chips and smoked turkey on the whitest possible bread. He'd even bring his own coffee. While most cops don't live in the area they work, few refuse local eateries. "You won't catch me getting shot dead at some drive-thru." Reportedly Balascoe wouldn't even crap or take a leak in Area 3. For a while he was known as Bottle, either because he bottled it all up or used a bottle. Though there were other reasons for that nickname, which earned him a six-month hiatus, but Oz never confirmed whether it was strictly to dry out or something worse.

Balascoe starts heading back towards the Korean market, tilting his umbrella behind him as if that might shield him from Özgür at his heels. It's hard to say when the two began knocking heads. They never partnered. Never worked a case together. When their investigations did overlap, exchanges were always cordial and efficient. Yet at some point, Özgür began to grate on this D-II ∴ D-two ∵. Maybe it was as simple as Özgür's promotion to D-III ∴ D-three ∵. Or Balascoe's failure to find an assignment at Robbery-Homicide Division or even FID. Forget Major Crimes. One morning the sneers started coming and never stopped. Not that this detective who carries out his duties with a look of futile resignation is without bite.

Like now, strolling as close as he can to a Leimert Park P-II ∴ P-two ∵ Dog. A good bite counts on calculation.

"Long time, Oz," Officer Nyra Carlton bristles. And smiles. Same as when she had her clothes off. Always bristling. And smiling. "Still think I'm a bitch?"

"Well some people think I'm an asshole."

"You're kidding," Nyra smiles. "Who thinks you're not an asshole?"

Followed by a P-I ∴ P-one ∵ named Stan Gebbis who was green enough to believe all the stories about Özgür, still out there doing their damage. He had that smitten look, quavering for attention and opportunity.

"Detective Yıldırım, you wanna—"

"I'd rather shoot myself in the face and live."

"Nice!" Nyra yells after him. "You made Stan cry. Again." Not that she loses the smile. Probably bristling too. Oz realizes he misses seeing her with her clothes off.

Helicopters still overhead, KTLA and LAPD. Journalists by van and taxi. Police Scanner Twittidiots. What a former South Bureau deputy chief nicknamed PeSTs. Supervising sergeant already running things. Even DRE. Though Özgür has yet to sense any drug connect. It all looks Robbery-Homicide. No NED in sight. But patrol cars keep arriving.

"It's iffy. Sat our only suspect down one block east of Arlington," Balascoe sighs when it's clear Özgür isn't going to get caught up in the stickier side of those he knows or those who know him. Though hasn't that always been his problem? The stickiness of others never quite applied? Especially when there's a body around. In this case two. Not that Balascoe has given up anything Oz didn't already pick up from the RTO before badging through the outer perimeter over at South Van Ness.

Water sheets down from the sky. Across pavement. Gutters roar. Drainpipes gurgle along all the low-stuccoed buildings from World Wide Taco on 3rd Avenue to Living Truth Christian Fellowship to this place by Consolidated Auto. Martin Luther King Boulevard.

"And that's based on a 390 who has our young blood, I mean Crip, hoofing it along the sidewalk there?"

"A real party." Balascoe sneers.

"I like parties."

"Oz, you've never liked parties."

"People change." Özgür smooths his tie.

"Get out of here." But Balascoe catches himself. Even the sneer wavers. "I mean get out of the rain. A hat like that's not enough."

"You find the gun yet?"

"Left right next to her. Filed and spent."

Of course Balascoe's right. Özgür should get out of the rain. He doesn't even have an umbrella. Balascoe sure as hell isn't sharing his. Men a lot younger than him, soaked through like this, can get horrible things in their lungs and die on a respirator days later. But Oz loves rain. Almost as much as he loves this city.

Oz has lived and worked her streets for over twenty-seven years. And one thing stays true: he never gets sick of the way she rises up at dawn, the way she grows smokier come dusk, and the way during a big storm like this she falls down and her mascara runs.

"Do not apply gendered language to urban zones," Elaine warns whenever Oz acts like some sailor talking about his ship, letting slip a feminine reference to this place where they both live. He can't say she's wrong. After all, what kind of woman contains this scene?

Because if this was mascara it was red. A seep of blood still washed over the sidewalk. The Korean woman still agape at a sky streaking indifferently down upon her. Small palms cupping clear puddles. Her husband never got past the counter, the ventricles of his mind sprayed across a shelf of Hennessy and soju.

"True the closed-circuits were non-operational?" Özgür asks.

Balascoe nearly spits, disappearing inside the market.

The alleged perp still sits cuffed on the curb. The boot who made the grab keeps close, sharing an umbrella with his prize: the perp's backpack.

"Money in there?" Özgür asks.

The boot shakes his head. "Panicked and ran without taking a thing."

The kid doesn't look particularly bothered by the rain. Rain isn't going to change him.

Panicked and ran doesn't exactly apply.

"He's a minor and Balascoe wants him brought in right. He doesn't want any PeSTs Instagraming his face."

The kid flashes a smile. But when the smile is only faintly answered, he tries to mad-dog Özgür. Özgür doesn't even think to turn away. Turning away isn't something Oz does.

A stab then to his guts. That hello pain already scheduling his next week: what Özgür can't ignore and doctors still can't diagnose. Maybe spicy tomato for lunch isn't such a good idea. Not like his second choice, fried chicken at M & M Soul Food on Crenshaw, would be an improvement. Especially after another night of Scotch, of Miles Davis, of Elaine. Oz had given up cigarettes. He wasn't going to give up coffee or Scotch. And put him in a grave now if he had to give up Miles. Or Elaine. Guess he wasn't much of a D-III anymore to admit that last part.

Of course if his waking appetite had led him to The Pantry instead of Jacks N Joe for the Portuguese sausage, impossible to reach due to a Revlon 5K at the Coliseum, Oz would have taken the 10 instead of MLK and wouldn't be standing here with an empty stomach locking eyes with a kid who has nothing to lose.

"Rain not too much for you?"

The kid just sucks teeth. Marvin D'Organidrelle aka Android. Seventeen maybe. Muscled up. Juvie circuit training. Doubtless carrying some kind of jacket. Probably more like a parka. Black but with a splash of dairy. Jamaican maybe, even

Costa Rican. Not that skin can describe what color has claimed. His do-rag's blue enough. Plus the jeans, blue, shirt, blue again, and a navy hoodie. This being Vernon Corridor probably puts young Android with Rolling 40s or 46 Top Dollar Hustler Crips. Likely jumped in years ago and re-worked ever since. Never innocent long enough to learn how to feign innocence. Which still doesn't mean he's a stone-cold killer.

"What happened to your shoes?"

Android is barefoot.

"I said already. Some fool with more metal than a bus took em from me. Havaianas too."

Android's lids flinch like even that's saying too much. The only other flicker of interest comes when Özgür takes another look at the backpack. Light as a hat. Definitely no money.

Officers keep searching roofs, trash bins, and storm drains. Others climb fences, canvas the neighborhood, put out a plea for witnesses more reliable than a drunk who apparently was trying to score a sherm when he happened to notice this kid, all flared out, just hustling along.

The K-9 unit has arrived now but the two dogs seem at least momentarily mystified in the downpour. A couple of P-IIs finally pull the boot off his prize, Mirandize Android, and disappear him into the back of their shop. Who knows what some ADA will say, RFC'd upon arrival, maybe even kicked loose as an 849(b)(1), unless someone here, at this party, finds something better than an empty backpack.

Past Arlington. That's the way Balascoe said the kid had gone. And then in the few minutes it takes to unpocket some Cedar's Sugar-Free and spread the foil, Özgür learns the scene is now a triple homicide. The woman was pregnant. Seven months pregnant. Also it appears that the cash in the register was not the only thing touched. A small floor vault was also robbed. Curiously, only the big bills were taken. Ones, fives, and tens all left behind. Özgür contemplates the gum foil.

Katlarım. ∴ I fold. ∵

To the east, Consolidated Auto, across Arlington, New Heights Charter School, a palm tree, pines, and across from Coin Laundry and Lucky Liquor. To the west, an abandoned office building, gate locked, but one door blown open, a mailbox on the corner with a sticker of Elmo LCF!, 2nd Avenue, jacarandas in bloom, Living Truth. Özgür goes wide, ducking under police tape, distancing himself from flashing cars, body bags, now zipped, lifted, and stowed, and one unenthused news crew.

Power draws a crowd. Though what's the power here? *Katla.* The dead? Gunshots? *Katla-katla.* The theft? The response? *Katla-katla.* Or the plan?

Katla-katla-katla.

A whore, all emerald, teeters along on emerald peep-toe wedges, one hand on an emerald purse, the other, palm up, carrying a tamale in a napkin. A walk of shame without the shame. Just soaked through. Maybe her emerald sunglasses make that less obvious. Or less important. The scene here doesn't even check her pace.

Katla.

But Özgür can't stop thinking of that backpack.

"Why are you still here?" Nyra asks. Her hair looks lighter. She used to be red. Liked to tell him reds were the result of Viking rapes. "Some part of us, and you know my part, likes it." Not Özgür. Whatever fantasies he had with her, playing a Viking wasn't one.

"Detective Yıldırım, I'm sorry if I sounded too — It's just such an honor, really. Could I get your autograph?"

"For real, Gebbis?" Nyra too shocked to bristle let alone laugh. And the P-I is in fact holding out a pen and what looks like a program from The Baked Potato.

"Good club," Özgür responds, but like the emerald whore, already gone, not breaking stride.

Though maybe he should stop and answer Nyra's question. Maybe he should stop mistaking a habit for love. Maybe he should stop thinking of Los Angeles as a woman and consider more closely the woman who sometimes shares his bed.

And as Özgür gazes around, not so much searching but listening, open to whatever possibilities what's-possible-now can't suggest, not to mention all the wet, *katla*, when was Oz last at The Baked Potato?, *katla*, doing his best not to forget how even in this storm there's a jam all around, like fast brushes, high keys, modal scales, *katla*, *katla*, maybe even Paul Chambers' obbligatos, so what? Miles is what, *katla*, that's what, with every now and then an emerald queen for sale, and more on sale, *katla-katla-katla*, rain music slapping multifold, high to low, 12-bar or not, with somewhere in there too, *katla*, now and

then, *katla,* Coltrane and Cannonball Adderley, off the brim of
Özgür's hat, off his overcoat, protective layers no more dampening a storm than funneling water onto his legs, slacks sponging
the water, filling his shoes, toes practically swimming, almost a
floating feeling, barely in touch with socks let alone any ground.
Katla. Could almost dance. *Katla.* Oz should learn how to dance.

Of course there's romance in such blues. Elaine reduced
romanticism to longing. "And what's worse," she said, "the
preservation of longing serves only to justify the preservation
of distance. Which is frequently inhuman. At least selfish. And
regrettably mean." Which Özgür recognizes had been said to
him in the meanest of ways. Either he was that or it was all a
posture. But listening to Lady Day is no act. Or Miles Davis. Or
Art Pepper. Or Chet Baker. Not to mention re-reading Chandler,
Hammett, Philip K., friends since he moved to the U.S. as a teenager, with just enough coin for the used-bins once set up along
Melrose, Hollywood Boulevard, or Franklin. The great hawk-
shaws had taught him English and maybe even to love Scotch,
though eighteen-year-old Macallan doesn't require a teacher,
just good taste. That goes for old watches too. Rain, he's always
loved. Origami came from *Blade Runner* ∷ 1982 ∷ when he had
identified more with Gaff than Deckard.

And if he began as a posture, the overcoat, the trilby, standing just like the characters of his immigrant reveries might have stood, until eventually he no longer resembled a caricature of Marlowe, but if anything Marlowe looked like a caricature of him. When had that happened? When had the idea of a peace officer become this reality outstripping the fiction that had gotten him filling out an application to the Police Academy? Not that such questions have any more hold on him than Jimmy Cobb's brushes soft in the rain. Because Özgür isn't thinking about Marlowe or even Chandler but as Chandler might have wanted and Marlowe would have understood, when you're standing in the rain where the dead have lain and the blood has mostly washed away, it makes sense then to think only of her.

Katla. Katla. Katla.

And she'd been there, last night's there, in a warm close clutch, the smartest, sexiest clutch a fifty-seven-year-old man could dream up.

And afterwards with Evans and Miles painting hearts "Blue in Green" and Özgür's ninth-story windows framing a glitter of office lights and air-traffic blinks, work and all warning,

Elaine had asked in a whisper what only his faint smile could fail to answer.

But no matter what mysteries all her dark streets continued to promise, whether by vacant lots or concrete river bottoms or branching off like eyelashes those long stretches of highway traffic, whether Main and 6th, or Hope and Flower, East Compton by way of Commerce, to say nothing of Evelyn, of Neptune Avenue to Chinatown, or, that's right Miss Wonderly, Broadway to Sunset, even Fountain to Hollywood, Bette Davis knew a thing or two, those silver familiars always overwriting if not quite preventing the whisper of still more of her streets, first steps in an unknown world after the last steps in an old world, where older streets still keep winding, off Teşvikiye Caddesi in Şişli or Süleymaniye Caddesi near the Kalenderhane Mosque or Yerebatan Caddesi or other curving routes near Gülhane Park in Fatih, like smoke from those Gelincik cigarettes he used to love, giving rise somehow to more domes and minarets, ancient battlements upon which to look for fortunes on black currents, to say nothing of lessons in decency, beyond the reach now of still more of her nameless streets, or just one nameless street, where a tree of forgotten leaves, by a rain of forgotten stones, before windows framing forgotten intentions, in that season of unforgotten meanness, keeps reminding Özgür again and again that streets too can insinuate public as well as personal deeds. And if not exactly by memory, these streets still trace the way acts invariably find guilt or justice, harm or kindness, sleeplessness or death.

Maybe it was time to stop making longing a lover.

Maybe it was time to get out of the rain.

Katla.

Before leaving, Özgür finds Detective Balascoe and points to the southeast corner of MLK and 2nd.

"He went that way first?"

Özgür shrugs.

"Only to double-back?" Balascoe still not seeing it. "I don't get it. Why?"

"Look for the money inside. Maybe even some flip-flops. Sealed up in big envelopes. And you didn't hear it from me," Özgür adds. "Could be a federal crime too."

There's even a letter carrier heading now towards the corner mailbox. Pith helmet and a thick slicker sluicing water well away from his ankles. Come rain or shine, he was proof. Black, bow-legged, an expression of solemn commitment, ambling along, uncontested.

On the counter inside the market, Özgür places a foil owl ∴ Stephen Weiss ∴. He's already late for Cletious Bou. He has to go. He doesn't want to go. Is that the answer he couldn't give Elaine when she propped herself up on her elbows, her long black hair falling over her naked olive shoulders, her dark lips whispering an exposure only midnight and drink and *Kind of Blue (Legacy Edition)* ∴ 1959; 2009 ∴ ever permits:

"Will you ever leave this city?"

Dr. Potts

We must first blow, in fancy, a soap bubble around each creature to represent its own world, filled with the perceptions which it alone knows. When we ourselves then step into one of these bubbles . . .

— *Jakob von Uexküll*

"Let's try this, you're barefoot, what happens if you kick a rock?" Dr. Potts asks.

"Why would I wanna do that?" Xanther answers without looking up from the Rubik's Cube. Just one side, right twist, how hard can that be? then flip, left twist, flip again, right twist again. Not that out of all these fifty-minute sessions she's ever succeeded once. Flip. Forget the whole thing. Not even one side. Right twist. Again? Another square aligns. Once she got one square short of a side before time ran out.

"Question for question," Dr. Potts reminds her now. He always has to remind her even though he shouldn't have to since that had also been their deal. Xanther sighs. She never means to break their deals. She just can't help herself.

"I'm sorry." Xanther looks up. "It would go, I don't know, like tumbling off somewhere?"

"Let's say it's a very heavy rock. And you kick it hard. What would happen to your foot?"

"No shoes? Sorry. I guess I'd, I don't know, I'd hurt it?"

"Good! You know that, correct? That's definite."

"You mean I know that that definitely hurts my toe?"

"Yes."

"But I still don't know why it hurts? Like what even is hurt? Do you know? I mean I know what it feels like but I still don't know what it is. It's only pain, right? But what is pain? I mean really?"

"It's a fair question."

The Question Song isn't new. She and Dr. Potts talk about it all the time. Dr. Potts always says he likes her questions, especially her questions about the nature of questions, when she's sounding like her mom, which sorta feels weird and icky, or at least squirmy, but maybe okay?, given the circumstances?, like this room, mainly all the degrees framed on the wall, and with Dr. Potts always being super careful, soft-spoken like, especially when throwing in stuff that Xanther has to agree to first, like if he has her permission, like before proposing a deal, because time is short, even if they have all the time in the world, which they don't, no one does, not even the world.

Dr. Potts has a nice office, with big open windows looking out onto gardens and trees. He has a desk made out of some dark stone with a lamp made out of some bright metal. No computer lives there. Mostly stacks of papers, books, a phone which never rings, and the backs of picture frames, glimpses revealing what questioning once clarified: two sons, one daughter, and his wife "whom I've been married to for over thirty years." She looks older than he does. He never sits behind the desk.

Xanther always sits on the floor, on this shaggy swirl of grays and blacks, what he called a "Rory print" when she asked. "It looks like what a fire leaves behind," she had answered when he asked. Mostly she's cross-legged on the Rory, playing with the Rubik's Cube he always hands her at the start of their sessions, always repeating that she's under no obligation to solve it or even play with it. It's just hers for the fifty minutes. Always mixed up.

Xanther loves twisting it, flipping it, watching the noise of jumbled colors begin to assemble into a calm, a sense, something almost promising an answer, especially while Dr. Potts does his best to do the same with her, like asking what difference does the difference between a soy protein and animal protein really make to a twelve-year-old girl? Tons, Xanther has assured him. Or why should she be so curious about what happened to this girl Kle had told her about named Holly Waverly? That was a few sessions back. At least getting upset over that story made more sense than, say, getting upset over why kids who were abducted are kidnapped while adults who were abducted are not adult-napped. "Are you afraid of getting taken away somewhere involuntarily?" "Do you think it's not normal that, like, when you ask that, I can only see this kid napping?"

During their last session, Dr. Potts did his best to help with this terrible pressure that so often builds up behind her eyebrows and her ears, which she could assure him wasn't real, at the same time that it still hurt and made her breathe funny, or feel like she was breathing funny, especially when she tried to come up with the difference between a living thing and a growing thing, which funnily she had just considered again, a moment ago, looking at Dr. Potts' desk, coming up with his computer living there when it's not living there at all, about which Dr. Potts had suggested in a way that made it sound like he was only wondering aloud, whether our understanding of life versus growing might not really be so clear, but even if it wasn't clear, what was terrifying about that? Who ever said clear was part of the gig? After all, playing paintball is messy but isn't that part of the fun?

Xanther hasn't gotten to play paintball yet, but she wants to, Mayumi too, if Les Parents let them. Josh came up with Les Parents. Josh studies French. He's already gone paintballing once, with his brothers Teig and Cliff, and that made all of them envious, especially Kle, though Xanther still thinks she wants to play it most. She's not even sure why. It's not the kind of thing girls her age want to do.

Thinking though about paintball that day had made her smile, and even if her inquisitiveness didn't diminish, is that right? inquisitiveness?, the pain smashing out behind her eyebrows and ears did vanish completely.

Xanther had to hand it to Dr. Potts. He was pretty good at handling her questions. Maybe even the best.

Not that her mom didn't try her best. No question there. But then the more excited Xanther got, the more worried her mom would look, until finally Astair just cut short The Question Song by telling Xanther to focus on breathing and practice her "quiet self" and "soft eyes" and Tai Chi, which Xanther hates but still does every evening after dinner, most every evening at least, even if imitating her mom's slow and deliberate movements always comes with an accompanying branching upon branching of questions, about the poses and the pace, not to mention the weird descriptions like "grasp sparrow's tail" or "repulse monkey" or all this talk about the "root."

"You're grinding your teeth again, kiddo," her mom had murmured just last night. Like that's new. Cedar's Non-Stick Sugar-Free helps a little. It's Xanther's favorite gum, so fresh and cold like mountain air that's almost too cold, and maybe a little calming too?, for some reason, can a taste do that? Really, it's not a habit you're supposed to have if you have braces. Les Parents, though, let it be an exception. After Dr. Potts talked to them.

Too bad chewing gum in her sleep is impossible, because Xanther definitely grinds her teeth in her sleep. Xanther would probably swallow the gum, or worse, choke on it or get it all stuck in her pillowcase and hair, which actually she did do once. Had to hack out a big hunk of hair before Les Parents saw it. All the kids at school though, this was seven schools ago, had seen where the hunk was missing, and that had made what was already bad worse, and then it got really worse. Xanther goes through a mouth guard a year. This year she might go through like two. If only spitting helped, which Xanther has actually tried to do now and then, tried doing last night in fact, her Question Song then all about stars, about how they die, or fly loose, and how what we see is always history, which for Xanther, even with glasses on, is always blurry anyway, dumb stuff like that, collecting in her mouth like a gooey ocean, wanting it out, and getting it out, or at least the spit, right before Astair walked into her room too, like wouldn't that have totally fareaked her out?, way more than grinding, if she had caught Xanther, leaning over her sink, just spitting and spitting and spitting.

Instead her mom asked: "Does your head feel hot?"

"You mean like do I have a fever? Do I?"

"No silly, you don't have a fever. Maybe a little warm but what's new?"

Still her mom had to check, first putting her hand on Xanther's head, which was nice, and then touching her own forehead against Xanther's, which was nicest.

"Are you saying I'm silly because I fell down doing Tai Chi just now?" Xanther whispered.

"No darling, that was adorable," her mom smiled, pulling back but still tuggling Xanther's pigtails, a word her sister Freya had come up with last year, or maybe, was it Shasti?, anyway seven-year-olds do that sort of thing, which was nice again, especially the tuggling part, mom tuggling Xanther's pigtails, even if Xanther still objected with a squawk, why did she object?, or squawk?, which actually had made her mom laugh. A good squawk then.

Xanther loves it when her mom laughs. Astair has the most beautiful laugh Xanther has ever heard. Soft like honeysuckle and sweet like warm milk with vanilla and honey. Every time, the sound of victory, though Xanther still wonders victory over what?, like who had really won?, and so then who had finally lost?

"I just wonder if all these questions of yours feel hot?" Astair asked, starting to clean Xanther's glasses.

Xanther had never thought of it that way. Her mom was pretty smart. Actually she was really smart. Both her parents are super, super smart. Like Dr. Potts, they have degrees too.

"Why do I get a surprise tomorrow?"

"Because you're my pride."

But Xanther didn't feel hot. Even though everyone had come to accept that she just seemed hot to the touch, or at least warm, Xanther always feels cold. So cold sometimes she can't even imagine feeling her fingertips or toetips or the top of her head, where her mom, when they are doing Tai Chi, instructs her to imagine a line of thread emerging and heading straight up to heaven. "I thought we didn't, like, believe in heaven?" "The sky, Xanther." "But is the sky up if we're on a planet, and like you know it's round, so it could be down, right?, I'm just asking, I mean."

"How about vertically?" her father had offered from the piano.

184

But how can Xanther always feel so cold on the inside while everyone else swears she's warm to the touch? What does temperature have to do with wanting to find out about the world?

Teachers had already taught her how asking one question gets you noticed and two gets you favored. If only Xanther could leave it at two, because a few not only irritates other students but eventually the teacher too, until asking more than a few gets you reprimands, warnings, and then it's say hello to demerits and trips to the principal. Eight times Xanther had made that trip and that was just at one school, the one before the last seven, when her missing hunk of hair had gotten extra missing thanks to extra yanks, thanks to the preds, no school ever lacks a pred, though Xanther never names names, Xanther sent down the hall not because of preds or missing hair, but because her teacher said she was being fresh, why fresh?, how fresh?, fresh like snow peas? Xanther likes snow peas, though apparently that principal, Mr. Slathmeyer, didn't, getting her sent in turn from Mr. Slathmeyer to Ms. Baylor, who was Xanther's first therapist, all this like four years ago, back in Asheville, before they'd moved to California. Before they'd moved to Vermont, where Mr. Tweed was the principal. Mr. Tweed was in Dorset. Then the Ibrahims had moved back to Georgia again. Oh they'd moved around bunches when Xanther was little, and Vermont, North Carolina, and Georgia weren't even the extent of it, there was New York and Chicago and even some months in Montana, when Xanther was eleven, before making a mess again, this time in 6th grade, in three different places, or two out of three, long story, because she was too smart, or way retarded. Xanther had overheard two teachers refer to her as "the retarded kid" "with bad skin," with Les Parents all the time whispering, Would it hurt to hold her back?, Could it help?, and this even after they had moved to Los Angeles, to like east L.A. first, for the rest of 6th grade, at Belvedere Middle School, which was supposedly a mistake, some misunderstanding about a lease, which to Xanther had sounded first like leash, which maybe was in fact a leash?, Les Parents then whispering, What are we doing here?, like nonstop, and not even in a mean way or an angry way, but more like a scared way?, her dad having the most trouble because of his dark skin, or "for being black," "African!," which even if this was true wasn't true either, or so her mom once failed to explain, because Anwar wouldn't explain, waving it away in that happy way when he apologizes, because, yes, Egypt is in Africa but it is still like this continent unto itself, a place of sand and pyramids, and camels, Xanther's always wanted to say hello to a camel, with one long river, like a snake, because Egypt has snakes, snakes that can kill you, even if the big snake called the Nile brings life, all facts about the Egypt/Africa thing which Xanther barely could understand, which most of the residents in the Belvedere Middle School also didn't understand, mostly Latino, there was a north thing and a south thing that made a little more sense to some of her peers, but seriously, it wasn't like that many cared. Only those with connections to "gangs."

That's when Xanther heard that word for the first time. That's when she started seeing the spray-painted codes, all that paint, even on their building, that Anwar also refused to talk about. He didn't teach her the word "ghetto" either,

186

that was from her classmates, who also taught her Spanish words she had trouble remembering.

It was weird. Belvedere Middle School was probably the only school Xanther never had trouble in. Teachers didn't mind her questions, and other kids, maybe because they thought she was so weird-looking, her hair so black, her skin so white when it wasn't mucked up with pimples. They said she looked like a doll from Día de Muertos, she at least remembered that phrase, for some reason.

She even told Dr. Potts, though in super-serious confidence, because she'd hate to upset Les Parents, that there at Belvedere Middle School, Xanther had actually made friends, and not like only a few, but like more than twenty, and they all knew her and she knew them, and she never had any attacks, and the teachers were so comforting and attentive, and not because of anything special, just because that's the way they were with all the kids, and it felt good until her mom or dad picked her up after school, and then Xanther started tuning in to their anxiousness, worrying her good day into something fearful, nights going back to that half-hidden hiss of the all-the-time, What are we doing here? How do we get out of here?, with the serpent money never far away, digging and hissing, until finally Les Parents did figure a way out, pretty quick too, not even three months at that school, her friends telling her "Eastside loca!" and "RealZ!" and of course "Come back!" "Keep in touch!" with tears even, that was a first, from Evelyn, Katlyn, Nathalie, Karla, Ingrid, and even Angel and Armando, maybe Gerardo, but she couldn't go back, or keep in touch, like how?, no one had phones then, and Xanther wasn't allowed any of that computer stuff yet, and those few months suddenly became just another blur, no different from where they'd already been or were headed, disappearing further west to a where that was still east, by Los Angeles standards, and all because of a great deal on a house, a fluke, this time an Astair word, fluke, with great rent, and a yard, plus very private, near a great school, this time in an area called Echo Park, which had a park, though the whole area wasn't a park, so why was it called a park? New York wasn't called Central Park? And isn't it strange how sometimes statements can be questions too, even though they don't sound like questions? meaning, if you think about it, that there are no statements at all, really, that aren't just a slew of more question marks?

Within a month, some things don't change, right?, Xanther found herself in another therapist's office, Mrs. Goolsend's, who wanted to know what Xanther thought of all the different states they'd lived in, which only got Xanther going on about why states are named what they are named, because for some reason naming is a big thing for Xanther, because, like, they promise to keep things still or at least steadier, like numbers in a way, and what kind of name is Goolsend anyhow?, which Mrs. Goolsend didn't like, and finally because Xanther really didn't like Mrs. Goolsend, and because neither Astair nor Anwar cared for her either, Xanther wound up twisting a Rubik's Cube on a Rory print rug in front of Dr. Potts, who looked a little like Galen Tyrol, who even if he was a cylon was great at fixing birds and maybe if Xanther was like a Viper MKII and Dr. Potts was like Chief, he could fix her too?

Curiously, Xanther's mom is studying to be a therapist. In college, Astair had gotten a degree in psychology but supposedly to be like Dr. Potts requires a lot more degrees which kept getting interrupted by all their moves. After their last move, Astair had enrolled in yet another school, this one called Pacifica?, Xanther always forgets the name, Oceanix maybe? If Astair gets her master's there, is that right?, masters?, master?, mastered?, she can treat patients, patients like Xanther. What will that be like? Will Astair turn out to be like Dr. Potts or maybe Mrs. Goolsend?

Her mom had just finished some big paper, and this year started getting her first patients too, though from what Xanther could gather, and all she could gather were their ages and whether they were boys or girls, they were nothing like Xanther. They weren't really for real either because Astair was still in training and required supervision by the clinic. Something like that. "What do you do with them?" Xanther had asked. "Just talk." "Talk how?" "I imagine like you do with Dr. Potts. Ask questions." "And you get paid for that?" "When I get licensed I'll get paid." "So if I get licensed I can get paid too for asking questions, instead of you know, like, getting punished?"

Dr. Potts never made Xanther feel punished. And eventually the consequences of this really sank in, Xanther getting the drift that these were *her* fifty minutes, and she could trust him for the most part, even if she had no idea why the most part or even what the not-most part was, parts which made no difference if she got right to it, like she did today, following early advice by Dr. Potts: "Try telling me first the thing that is most difficult to tell. I will help you. Or if not that, then ask me the question that is most difficult to ask. And I will help you."

So Xanther went right to raindrops, the number that said there was a number even as it hid a number that was no number, and how it had made her feel. She even explained how her friend Kle has a brother named Phinneas who is brilliant but fears dolphins. Or not the dolphins but how many dolphins there are because his fear is also all about the counting, because when you see 3 dolphins playing in the waves that means there are really like 9, with the rest under the waves, but if you see like a lot, like 27, there are really like 243?, and that's just when we're talking about dolphins, what if we're talking about bad things?, like counting crimes?, and then your mind really heats up and keeps heating up until it might just turn into sticky, smelly smoke.

Xanther also told Dr. Potts, and this part was really difficult, how Kle thought his brother was crazy and needed to get back in a hospital again. Phinneas had already tried to kill himself twice. Like Xanther, he's left-handed. Kle's called him schizo. Actually more than that. Phinneas can solve a Rubik's Cube in under five minutes.

"Do you think you're crazy?"

Xanther can't solve even one side in fifty minutes: white still patched with red, yellow, and green.

"Do you think you had a seizure on the way over here?"

"I thought I did or was about to."

"Did you tell your dad?"

"No."

Along with The Question Song, seizures is the other thing she and Dr. Potts talk about a lot. Even if Xanther would prefer not to. Since December, she's been seizure-free. No pills either. Just the new diet. Ketogenic. Xanther doesn't mention how she always sees a brass key clutched between her toes but she does describe her hunger.

"Thirst too. I can eat a lot and I know I'm full, like, I can see what was just on my plate, but I still feel so craving and thirsty. I drink water, but like the water doesn't seem to answer the thirst? Does that make sense?"

Even during this session, while replacing, by a flip and a right double twist, one yellow tile with another white tile, the subject comes up.

"Dad too was so sweet. At Square One. I could see he wanted the French toast. I told him I didn't mind and like I really didn't but he still had what I had."

"Why the frown?"

"I'm getting some big surprise this afternoon and I'm not even excited."

"Because your parents do so much for you already?"

Xanther nods.

"Like these visits here?"

"Yup. And visits with other doctors too. Even my food. And puhlease it's not like I'm a total idiot, right? I know it costs money, and even though dad seems pretty happy, especially today, or well, okay not happy-happy, but really relieved, are they the same thing?, sorry, because like he's supposedly getting some money, a lot of money, I over-heard this, sorry, I worry a lot about Frey and Shast. Like they're, you know, getting the short end of the stick?"

Dr. Potts smiles.

"What?"

"You have epilepsy and *they're* getting the short end of the stick? Do you want to explain that math to me?"

Xanther gets rid of a green tile only to find two more red tiles messing up her white side. Cogsworth once said he solved the whole thing in under five minutes: "I just pulled all the little plastic pieces apart and put it back together." Cogs is the real genius.

Probably because she doesn't know what to say and because they just have a little more time left, Xanther thinks about the other most-difficult thing to tell, what's going on with with Parcel Thoughts, that app, and The Horrosphere, but instead explains all about the phone calls and e-mails Les Parents are screaming about.

"I don't know, it was my dad's friend, Mefisto. Big fro. Super genius or just super crazy. I think he babysat me once. For some reason, he decided to use my parents' info as contact info for this big ad campaign, with promises of like huge Costco discounts, and even cash, and the phones haven't stopped ringing. Supposedly a prank. I guess I don't understand what a *prank* means. Isn't there supposed to be a laugh at the end of a prank?"

"In theory."

"Yesterday I tried to tell mom how all these calls are kinda like an attack. You know like so much coming in you're paralyzed? Except at home the lights stay on."

"In December, the lights went out?"

"Oh yeah."

Xanther hates talking much about the funeral. Just thinking about it makes her tingle and want to gasp. She can even start believing it's happening all over again. That bad. Xanther ended up in the hospital.

"Sometimes I think thinking the wrong thing brings on, you know . . . "

"A seizure?"

Xanther nods. She's never gotten used to saying it. Like it's freaking Voldemort. Except so much worse than Voldemort.

"Voldemort." There she said it.

"Excuse me?"

"Dr. Potts? Do you ever think, like, there's a conversation going on, you know, like somewhere out there, somehow parallel to the one you're having with yourself, like in your head, or even with someone else?"

"How do you mean?"

"Uhm, like there are these voices that know everything. ∴ So close. ∴ Like voices that don't really live and can't die and have been around forever ∴ *such a noisy, boisterous parade* ∴ , before the start of things and will even be around after the end of things. ∴ **She has no idea.** ∴ You know, privileged with all that's that. Like Google, only true."

Xanther stops flipping the Rubik's Cube. Tears wet both cheeks.

"I really miss him."

"I'm glad to hear that."

"Like even when I'm not thinking about him I think I am thinking about him. And I know I didn't even know him that well."

Dr. Potts hands her a box of tissues. "If I could grant you one certainty, Xanther, one which you could hold on to without dissolving under all your scrutiny, let it be just how remarkable a young girl you are."

"Then why do I feel like I'm such a disappointment? Like I'm disappointing him all the time? Fraidy K. That's what he called me. Dov was so brave. And I can't even be at his funeral without— Sometimes I feel so ashamed. Actually, all the time."

"Xanther, how do you imagine brave?" Dr. Potts suddenly asks, moving slightly forward in his chair too, head up, almost rigid.

"Fearless? I mean, like, I don't want to feel, like, so jittery all the time."

"Is that all you want?" Xanther stops fiddling with the Rubik's Cube. "Think big, young lady."

And for a moment, she's all Dov. Or wants to be like Dov. Not all over the place and over-inquisitive but clear and sure and gentle and true. What you don't need years and years to hear. Or a bed full of books to understand. Or all the scars of a lifetime to value. Something so small and light it practically sits in your palm. What Xanther could share. What would bring comfort. And in times of fear could bring calm.

"Isn't not jittery, like, a good start?" Xanther says instead, back to the Rubik's Cube.

"What's happening in school?" Dr. Potts asks then, relaxing back into his chair, but not quite relaxing, alert still to something Xanther can't quite follow. "Any predators? I mean preds?"

This new direction is a mystery but Xanther appreciates Dr. Potts' use of her vocabulary. He already knows how many of the family's moves were because of bullying. Sometimes physical, with one particularly bruising encounter, small bones fractured, which Les Parents still can't believe was nothing, even though Xanther swears it was nothing . . . nothing compared to a full-on attack, like in Alexandria, with all of Dov's comrades in uniform, saying if Xanther needs anything, anything at all, they would do it, even if that meant marching into hell itself, which Xanther doesn't believe in, and then all of them standing by helpless, as Xanther began slamming into the coffin, forearms first, then her head, until a ground heavier than any coffin started hitting her too. Nothing any gun could prevent. Only stop. Xanther kinda wishes one of those holstered guns would have made her stop. For good. Her parents though didn't stand by helpless. They knew what to do. It didn't involve guns. Though when Xanther got out of the hospital she looked like someone had pistol-whipped her.

No school beatings will ever come close to that. And anyway the school beatings part is pretty rare. Preds are at their worst when they get other kids to wall up, start calling her names, calling her weird, finally just looking through her, whispering through her, as if whispers and her were never there to begin with.

Which generally doesn't happen until she gets "afflicted" as one kid once hissed, where was that?, Georgia? Some teachers tried to step in but that made it worse, because no teacher is going to be her friend and no kid is going to be the friend of a kid who only has teachers for friends who aren't even friends.

Probably because of Dov, something he'd said, what exactly she can no longer trace: Xanther has never given up the names of her assailants. Even to Dov, who one time had gotten out his gun. Though also because of Dov, which

Xanther can trace, him telling her, "Always speak out your situation": Xanther has never hidden from her parents when the preds have found her again.

Fortunately Thomas Starr King, or "Karma's Torn Sight," as Kle calls it, isn't so bad. Xanther senses something cruel there but not triumphant. Already she's made some friends. She's even confided in them about her condition, and they seem cool with it and able to keep her confidence. No rumors run the school campus. Yet.

Of course none of her homies have seen a seizure, though they all seemed pretty shocked by the aftermath marked out on her face at the start of this year. That was two weeks after the fact. And her face had gotten the least of it. Elbows and shins could keep hidden. Kle said to tell everyone she tried to catch a Christmas tree, which beat wiping out on her Razor, which she'd done plenty of times, or at Runyon, hello the latest scabs on her knees, because isn't catching a Christmas tree so ridiculous it's not a lie?, which she never needed to tell anyway because no one at school asked her what happened.

Xanther tracks a white tile around five sides, flip, twist, flip, flips on flips, bringing it to rest among its white kind, with only a red and green remaining.

"Preds don't see me there," Xanther speaks up. "I'm invisible to them. To most kids actually. Though there is this one kid, big, like grown-up big, no way he's twelve or even thirteen. Dendish Mower. Scary. For realz. Smokes. Chews when he's not smoking. Supposedly sells Molly. Thizzzing all the time. His crew's like preds for sure." More twists to flips. A green tile's turn, a second-to-last white to track. "He's started picking on my friend Bayard. Nothing too bad, just jabs, saying mean little things, some threats, not too loud, mostly like he's teasing. Bayard tries to ignore it but I can see it makes him sick. He and Dendish ride the same bus."

Which is the perfect place to bring up probably today's most difficult thing to tell: her phone. Well not the phone itself. Pink and rad. Average number of texts. It's not like Mefisto put Xanther's number out there. Anwar would have gone Dov-mad if Mefisto had gone that far, Astair even worse. No, this was about The Horrosphere. Mayumi already warned her this morning. They all did.

Mayumi:	most sevies ∴ seventh graders ∴ got it
Cogs:	byby got it the wors
Bayard:	ByBys kewel like a jewl
Kle:	dgaf burn their lives down
Josh:	imho i look better

Some creepy app called ⏩α‖H8.

"Emoji makes it way harder for the A-Dolts to catch on," Kle claims. And with good reason. The app's way sicker than UglyBooth or ZombieBooth. Does with pixels what knives and rusty can openers could do. To your face.

"Dov, I know, would do something. He'd stand up for his friend. And I know I should for Bayard but I don't know how. Dendish comes near, and I mean like I even see him down the hall and I freeze." Talk about Fraidy K. Xanther can't even look at some pictures on her phone. "You're not going to tell Les Parents?"

"Should I?"

"Dov could look anything in the eye. I can't. Not even my friends. My parents. Not even you." As if to prove it too, Xanther tries to focus on Dr. Potts' eyes, keep there, for what, a second?, and though she finds nothing but warmth she doesn't last, not even a second, because like what's he looking at?, how at her? and with her looking at him too? probably understanding something she's thinking without her understanding what she's thinking, and no question it's something he'll have to do something about, right?, especially if she keeps this up, this looking at him, right?, something she won't know how to respond to, defend, or answer, the edges of the room darkening, temperatures dropping, and all because of two concentric rings of blue, tiny too, surrounding an even tinier black dot, before Xanther skitters helplessly off to the bridge of Dr. Potts' nose, to his beard, all the salt-and-pepper hair around his lips, retreating even further to relief, blind, unthinking, and certainly questionless, the last tile twisting into place at least, as Xanther whispers, defeated, "See."

Dr. Potts smiles at her victory. A mess of color on five sides but with the sixth all white.

"Progress. Well done. Now tell me one last thing, whatever comes to mind, as we only have a minute left."

Dr. Potts often says this. Xanther figures it's a time's-up technique. But does he do it with all his patients? Or just Xanther? Not that she objects. She'd hate to impose on him, let alone on Anwar waiting for her outside. Taking extra time, that would mortify her.

"Did his life flash before his eyes?"

"What?" Dr. Potts looks caught off guard, even a little bewildered. "Who?"

"Before he died, Dov, you know, did like his life really flash before his eyes?"

"Oh."

"What?"

"That's not what you said."

"I didn't?"

"Did his 'love' flash before his eyes."

"That's what I said?"

Dr. Potts nods.

"Are you sure?"

"Yes. And I'm sure it did."

Blue Pencil

Here is something you can't understand.

— Cypress Hill

Kid had already been nerves with Piña but when Luther, passenger side, turned around, there went what nerves do.

Welding out like a woofer on a surge. Breath rasping short. Joints socketed, stuck. Kid stiffs out in front of them all.

Not like all here are that much looser. Piña's hung with Luther for years. They met at Lupita's table, ate Miz's pancakes, ashed together more bowls of Lupita's fine-ass weed than a marine's got mags to load, and still there are times she gets to freeze. Like all she sees is what Luther's been put on this earth to do. Juarez too, Víctor for certain, padlocking knees. Only Tweetie's the exception. He like a mountain anyway, a mountain ready to move. And move this motherfucker can. Even if he just dropped his eyes from the rearview out of shame for a kid when a kid climbed in.

That's right, hijo. Luther half tempted to say it. Roar it. You don't got shit on this pocho but still you know. Or you know what you need. Should run and hide. Should seek out another life. But van door's already slid tight. Say hello to cold. How cold can get. Can't suck in one breath.

Nothing but try this boy. Gonna get himself hurt. Got himself hurt. Still earbudding Snoop Dogg, 2Pac. Wants to act a part. Black Dickies, black tee, broken down Pumas. Luther never seen feet that big on a kid, what?, fourteen? Adidas jacket, black too, all billowy. Some stupid bling dangling around his flabby neck. Not even mall gold. Like this be plastic shit. All scratched up and chipped.

¡MAN!

"Homie needs some new gear," Victor said.

Still Luther's surprised, see him comin up with that grin, either stupid or crazy.

"What's your name?" Luther asked.

"Ho-HO!-Ho." Got a fuckin stutter too.

Piña had to help out with his own name. "Hopi. Hopi Mannitou. Un malandro. He comin up."

"Ho-O-la ¿Qué pa-pa-pa-sa?"

"You tell your mama?" Piña asked, locked the van door.

"Sha-sha— Mi madre don't care. She out. Ca-ca-cold."

What the fuck, right? HopiMAN!tou. Can't look Luther in the eye, can't look no one in the eye. Looks around like he stutters, all over the place, too scared to say it let alone see it, fuck it, too scared to even be it.

Would say whatever anyone wants him to say. See whatever anyone wants him to see. So afraid he unbelievable, to some placa, deputy DA, even to himself. Casualty in training. Day one punk at county.

Only Hopi's hair toss him a line. Strandy black shit, dangling over his forehead, thick with rain, dripping all over this joto's face. But it's enough. Kid suddenly reaches up, both hands, crazy long fingers too, and all delicate, like some bitch or harp player, all agile, handling the mess, twisting it, slicking that shit behind his ear like Luther was his fuckin principal.

And thinking on hisself sitting behind some big desk, running a school, dealing with punks sent by with demerits, for discipline, dealing out that scared-straight shit, now that shit got Luther grinning.

Held out a fist then. Knucks and a nod. Why not? Kid's hands so light he not even there. Hopi goes goofy on his face, skin like wet cement, but shinier. You'd think Christmas come early. At least he breathing again.

Hopi Mannitou. Curioso. Extraño. Big for sure but disappearing at the same time, teeters heel to heel before squashing down beside Piña as Tweetie gets the van rolling again into hillside traffic.

Luther shows Hopi both fists then. First out and together, thumb on thumb. Then wrist over wrist, little finger on little finger. Fists. Left thumb up with knuckles in, right thumb down with knuckles in. Fists. Right thumb up with knuckles in, left thumb down with knuckles in. Fists. Both thumbs down, knuckles in. Left thumb up. Right thumb up. Knuckles in. Fists. Fists. Fists.

Here's Luther's dance. Hella dark. *Vroom, vroom, vroom.* Each combo gives new sense. Washingtons to Grants. Franklins to Hamiltons. Fuck, all the presidents. A to the M. M to the Z. Mexico. Califas. 13. Forever things. Nahuatl. Aztec. Fuck the cross. Fuck your Glock. Fuck the virgin in this fire. No weapon gonna lay me down. No man. All my scars testify to that. Rivers of blood. Stacks of bone. Oceans of black. Oceans of red. Red as black as oceans of dead. And a face who's nothing but all oceans dead. She dead too.

And that's just the back of his hands. Wrists are a whole other story. Elbow to shoulders. Should see Luther's chest, his back too. And his face? Forget his face. Though none ever do. Nothing but ink. At least Luther's fists make sense. Guns, pussy, and dough. This don't. Just like guns, pussy, and dough.

Luther gave Hopi a double bump. Christmas came twice. Who knew what this wobbly kid was about but no question he was pleased. Even after Piña yanked him back down among the gas canisters and threw a rag over his face to dry himself, the kid kept holding up his fists, like he could see through the rag, like now his fists glowed.

Luther had loosened hisself then into a long-armed stretch, joints cracking like they all be breaking. Yawned too. Like what the fuck's up with this day already? This rain? This kid? Catch him licking windows, counting grass, making up smiles over how traffic lights change. Piña said his madre was some tar fiend. Sold her balloons for years. Some other cross for years before that. So a kid born with half a lobe, like Hopi, that gonna come as a shock?

The thing is then, why someone like Teyo should take to menace such a tapado? Hopi could be like his son. Luther catching some cloudy convo long ago about a teenage kid living still in Mexico City. Wearing black and pink. Mascara. "Emo?" Luther had asked. "Mecoso," Teyo had seethed. "Taking some papi pito in a Zona Rosa back stall."

"You the kid I want out in front of me," Teyo had also said, and said it more than once, in different ways, giving Luther work, but never calling it work, calling it "opportunities."

And where Lupita alone be enough to warn anyone from her corners, Teyo move through any neighborhood block like not even a city be big enough to put down as his. Vato had reach. Even if sixties are nearly ditched, still coming across like a new breed. Made Lupita's comin-up fifty look old-fashioned.

Not that Teyo marches in the balloon parade. Carries less cash than a fiend cockrocking on Figueroa Street. No more a fiend than he'd be caught dead on Figueroa Street. Straight Amex, legit. Expensive suede and pleats. The only guy Luther had ever seen wear cuff links.

Teyo was already done with Lupita when Luther came on. The last few times, years gone by, sitting at her kitchen table with his briefcase, no more interested in her tequila or pancakes than his own tea. No chains, no ink. Just some violet shirt, lemon jacket, pants pale as coconut. Like some old Mexican gentleman come to talk about the Pampas and trade horses.

But Luther had never seen Lupita so cautious. "Trucha, fool." Like Luther's gonna start shit with anyone who walk like he gatless and still make the guns in the room gutless.

Luther heard Teyo was all La Eme, their Mariposa on the outside, though hard to believe the old man knew anything worse than some hotel room let alone a prison cell. Rumors had him living at The Four Seasons in Beverly Hills when he wasn't in Hawaii or Buenos Aires, Santiago, Tokyo, or some shit. Vato had reach.

Sur Trece for sure. Or Catorce. Varrios up and down the coast. Lots of coasts. Rifa world over. When Luther and Piña would be dazing on thick blunts, Lupita gone afternooning on her own, cuz no way you could talk this shit around her, even drop the name Teyo and she'd shut that shit down, serve you up platefuls of grief, all of them knowing better, waiting for her to dip loose before airing between coughs what new nest they heard of, that this Teyo be serving up even Crips, Bloods too, any llantas working curbside or a strip, drifting for lana.

Bong hits later they had Teyo up with Norteños before Luther and Piña could tell they were too high to know the difference between the shit they flinging and the shit they'd slid in.

Mexico City was somewhere in Teyo's past. Which, if he had a kid there, played out. Smaller cities too. Worked for plaza bosses at first. This was way before Cenobio Flores Pacheco or Felipe de Jesús Sosa Canizales. Became one when he was young. But never had nothing to prove. Worked his solution and said nada.

Soon Teyo was like some kind of RadioShack manager. Fuck plazas. They'd heard he come up in those superlabs deep in the Yucatán jungle, or outside Chiquilistlán, them that came around to dominate Colombian bullshit, and all their trade routes, before the real war started, Sinaloa, the Gulf, Beltrán Leyva. Bodies dropping so fast, too many to bury, more than U.S. at war in Iraq. Teyo again, somehow in the mix. And Lupita kept her peach lips zipped. Even if everyone knew Teyo was a big part of the balloon parade they kept marching out citywide.

And then one day, by chance, strolling along near Olvera Street, suitcase in hand, jacket bright as pear, shirt like mango, cuff links all gold, there was Teyo.

Luther said what he had to say. And Teyo answered him: "It takes guts for someone already set like you to risk such an offer."

And after that, not Lupita, not no one, needed to know about this shit. Not that word didn't finally leak out. Especially when Luther found hisself with not one crib but two, three even, owned outright, and a fourth if he counted Dawgz but that was a lease, and rides, of those he had his choice, by day, by night.

And even when Luther made the shift to quit all of Lupita's reglas, even if they already knew, Luther didn't give up nada. Told them only he was recently re-employed. "That right? *Re*-employed?! Homie, since when were you ever employed?" "Manager now." "Manager?! Where at?" "RadioShack."

Choplex-8s was cold now. Had nothing more to offer him. Still, Luther goes back. Doesn't make sense. Last night especially. Coulda crashed plenty of places. His. Theirs: new girls or old trues. Carmelita over at Dawgz just beggin him to get at her, ready-set-go, give Rosario a show, except Luther wakes up at Lupita's with no clue. Started out in the black Dodge Avenger but ends up with the burgundy Durango parked off Baxter. Talk about borracho. Turulato, Piña says. Who knows what. Lips bit with salt and lime. Head churning from the mix. Druggin on something mean.

Almoraz still getting the dumb idea Luther could be messed with. Lucky it cost him only a bleed from his nose. Lupita lucky too. Luther not liking her standing by the sink, coughing so hard like that, all old and weak. Even after she nearly ripped out the hair of some shorty on her knees grabbing at Luther's feria.

"I can leave the key," he had said before he left but Lupita wouldn't take it.

"A lady reserves the right to change her mind," was all she said, like she always said, like she really was a lady and not something else, like it give her some authority, give her the slack to do as she please, without consequence. Trouble was Luther was consequence. And if Lupita didn't know it, Teyo did.

The connect was almost too easy. Piña knew Hopi. Kid idolized her. Followed her around like some fuckin puppy. "That's because I know you," how Piña told it to Luther. "Me?" "He seen you around. Worships you like some god."

Not on no cross though. If this got to be religion, then let it be on pyramids, by knife law, law of fury, law of sacrifice.

After the next intersection, Tweetie had pulled into one of the bays of El Porvenir Auto Body. Victor slid the side door open and hopped in. Easy as rain. Quiet as what comes after rain.

Doesn't even need to ask what all this is, who's the boy, just slumps down by the copper piping and tool boxes. Victor's skin is like copper, eyes too, even his hair has these copper streaks, like he does something to the black, though he swears he doesn't, most of the time anyway tucked up under his L.A. Kings cap, like today, Oakleys on too. "Darking even the darkest," Victor likes throwing out, with a laugh, flashing signs, finger gats, doing as he always does with his engine-lovin hands.

"Adolfo want to get with you when you got time."

Darking the darkest, Victor had taken a long stare at Hopi, then gave it back to Luther. Didn't need to know nothing to know Luther wouldn't let no unknown in on this unless it was cool or spoke for.

Near Cesar Chavez and Hazard, Tweetie picked up their last, the real loco, bouncing out from under the shelter of a bus stand, scrambled into the van before it even stopped. Already talkin shit about Lott 13, Geherty Loma. Inside he shook off the rain like the perro sarnoso he is.

Handlebar mustache, shaggy sideburns, and arms like patched-up inner tubes, all loose and floppy but with this stupid-long reach, orang-utang reach, plus forearms like Popeye, and crazy fists, like when they closed they was nothing left of muscle or tendon, just anchor bolts and broken glass. All of him brutal and jagged that way. Fingernails out of control. Had

Juarez ever cut them? Or do they just tear off with all the scratching he get at?

Those nails even got Luther once. Luther stepping between Juarez and Victor when both of them had started foaming and spitting over some latest Xbox dilemma, Luther catching a slash across his arm, didn't even draw blood, just rippled the skin. Next morning though it was boiling. Luther poured hydrogen peroxide on it, poured gasoline on it, finally had to get a shot to clear that foulness up.

Juarez became his Dirty Jackal, his Razor Paw. Juarez had dozens of names, even Juarez wasn't his real name, not that he needed a name, so long as he had something to chew on.

Victor was something else. The black clinging under those nails is only petrol black. He their Manic Mechanic, Ranfla Repo. No driver in this crew comes close if fast's how going's gotta go, how Victor goes, to Angeles Crest whenever he can, ride those bends on whatever wheels are on hand, flaring signs, a toda madre, especially in that Camaro he fondles daytime to dawn. Piña swear she caught ese dicking his backseat armrest like he backdooring some piruja, didn't even stop, laid it down like it is, like what bitch is ever gonna be fast as this?

Another reason to keep Tweetie or Piña driver side: fuck getting jacked by a couple of 5-0s cuz Victor lost his head fiending for rpms by some bullshit school crosswalk.

As quick and out of control Victor gets behind a wheel, he level and even quicker under the hood, massaging, managing, making racers out of burros, monsters out of cans. Victor even made this Dodge van fly. And it's, what?, fifteen, twenty years in the hole. Underneath, though, the kit's rebuilt, R.C. Pro-Am retool, while outside, even with a bubble window on the side, is all fence paint, old style, like picket and white. Back window even has one of those family decals.

Tweetie said the sticker made their rig look legit. Friendlier too. Luther agreed. What popo gonna argue with that? None have.

Los Perros Viejos Construction
Licensed. Bonded. Ready to serve.

And when this pata suica had asked which set of bones was him, talk about pleased when Luther answered: "Juarez, you the dog."

And when Juarez laid eyes on Hopi, he cried "¡Flaquillo!" as if he'd already made up his mind about something no one, not even Luther, could guess. Thumped Hopi hard on the shoulder too, before jumping back to the spare tanks of nitromethane strapped to the side. "¿Órale pues ready to roll with some real vatos?" Those nails clawing some real reek out of the air.

Like batter brain here's ready for shit. He can barely handle Juarez in a good mood. Imagine how he'll do when Juarez stirs up? Mind all made-up? Crazy on some combat notion.

Hopi just sang out: "I so-so-so-sO— I am." Luther again mystified why anyone, let alone Teyo, especially Teyo, would want shit to do with this mancha, living in some shitshack with his paco-puffing mother, one talonera survivalist, another hanging himself on plastic bling no fool will ever think to see let alone believe let alone thief.

Juarez bouncing on his heels, close on this niño, like maybe Hopi is something to eat. Victor only darking Juarez because Juarez is the one to watch when loco gets hungry. Piña too, picking sides, sliding closer to the boy. Only Hopi's oblivious.

"Ra-ra-raining so much. Just go out and you're drow-drow— swimming."

"You like swimming?" Luther asked.

Hopi didn't answer.

"Hungry then?"

Piña had to answer for him: "He starved."

Hopi can't even answer Luther about breakfast.

Piña though played it right. Got this pendejo at ease. Flat smile of hers working its settle-down magic. Likely the reason this kid climbed into the van in the first place, got him gulping down that bullshit about "noticed" and "noticed by who's significativo." Bullshit if it wasn't. Can't call Teyo anything but significativo. But how the fuck that even happen? It took Luther years to get one word in with Teyo. Luther's never seen this billowy garbage bag until today.

Outside the rain had come on like it was thunder. With no need for thunder. Like an ocean up there discovered a deeper bottom. And they the bottom. Beating on the van roof for more bottom. Gonna beat through. Weight never rests until there is none.

Hopi even leaned in on Piña for shelter. And Piña offered it despite what her own ink says about shelter. Tear after fuckin tear. Head to toe. She her own fuckin rainstorm. Bottomless in her own rage. If this kid had any idea.

At IHOP, Juarez started to quiet but it took five coffees black. He hadn't stopped yapping about some Rio Vista Park, El Monte shit, cats turning up, nearly skinned, gutted, skulls sucked clean, calling out Tweetie, Luther too. Luther nearly had to quiet the fool. Then Victor took over with this Florida story. Happy family. "Has the honey life. Wet wife, thirteen-year-old son. Driveway. Garage behind the driveway. Boat in the driveway. Denali in the driveway. Pulling in ninety g legal." Victor going on in that deliberate way of his. "But son come up sick, doctors order these tests, that DNA too, because the weird-ass shit in his blood might be, you know, inherited. Comes out then son isn't even his.

Real father some zero his bitch was hittin years and years ago, hadn't seen since. Couldn't have seen since. Real father was dead before the boy even screamed free of her trench. Got himself wrecked after drinking too much."

"He dead how many years?" Juarez grunted, slurping his cup without touching his cup.

"Boy's thirteen," Piña snarled. "You do the math."

"How many years?" Juarez grunted again, no longer slurping his black.

"Thirteen?" Hopi spoke up. Kid was that stupid.

"Juar, you know what the husband did then?" At least Victor was helping out too.

"How the fuck would I?" Juarez answered, eyeing Hopi darker than any Oakleys on Oakleys.

"Went back, told his wife. She denied it. Said none of it was true. Only when he showed her the DNA shit did she cop to it being true. And then he blew off her head with a gauge. Went to the boy then and the boy said he couldn't know cause he'd known only one dad. Ese still blew off his son's head. Then lockjawed on both barrels and put his own self all over the plasma."

"Pinche pedo," Juarez growled. "Why kill his-self?"

Luther got over the first plate of sausage to Juarez but perro wasn't touching nothing. Scowling at the kid like scowling was fed. Some serious problem there, could breed worse if Luther didn't keep tight on it and he had to keep tight on it because Juarez had no say here, not on any day, but especially not today.

Everyone ate plenty but Hopi outate every-one. Even Tweetie. Like kid never knew eating before. Almost won over Juarez, who's almost curious enough to lose the scowl, watching, almost sniffing, jaw slacker and slacker, as Hopi don't stop ordering up, shoveling down. Saying thanks. Talkin luck. Christmas for the third time.

But he still couldn't look at Luther. At most a soft twitch, above his brows, burn on his cheek, like he crushing or something. Which Luther okayed cuz it keep reminding his crew who this kid is here for.

The server too, giggled for Hopi, then got all Hopi-like for Luther, eyes aside, whole body twitching while taking his order. Split Decision today.

Luther will look anything in the eye. Or anything hiding their eyes. No hips here just tits. Might deserve a hit. Though no Chula Vista waterpark, nothing that splashy. Still he'd take something. Take something even now. Grab that wrist, lock that elbow, run her back to some IHOP office shit. Or restroom. Squat her on the can. Or just a straight crack to both kneecaps. One button, one zip, get busy with that mouth. Make her eyes meet his. Happy Mother's Day this. Watch them widen choking on his thick. Nod as he tell it clear then, show her both fists, how he'll beat both eyes closed if she don't swallow every last drop.

"Dry bitch. Leave me dry," he'd say.

And Luther thinking on this here, thinks again of that shorty this morning, back there, who Lupita jerked aside by the hair. Luther'd like to sink knuckles in that hair too, round two, in Lupita's crib too, kitchen even, Luther seeing he'd have to get back there again though. Getting even thicker.

"More coffee?" the IHOP slave had asked him at some point.

Luther don't even drink coffee. Touched her wrist though. Her flinch made him grin. Not her nostrils though. Too big to be worth the trip, find out her shifts, where she lives, wait out a night, give her something to really flinch on.

"Give me your name."

"Quantelle." Tag said sHEILA. Like that. Nails lettered in glitter reach for it briefly. "I don't like people knowing my real name." Blushed then, though blush on thick, twitchin still more. Nails said TWERK WORKN.

"Give my boy your number."

"I'll take yours."

Tweetie had signaled her over. One of his phones already out.

The whole time Hopi kept low in the menu like it some kinda book. Piña kept him ordering. Mother henned every pause. Workin twerkin Quantelle for more bacon, waffles, and crepes. Splashers. Scrambled eggs. French toast.

"AND a grilled cheese?" Victor shook his head.

"Extra cha-cha-chEEse."

"You like bigger on the inside than the outside? And you got a pretty big outside."

"Ba-ba-big Punisher."

"Big Pun, guey," Piña added.

"Punk," Juarez had hissed. "Come mierda." IHOP's never-empty pot not helping no more and empty too. Where'd that nalgasona with the nostrils go? Victor keepin it easy though.

"Almost makes Tweetie look delecado, don't he?"

They laughed then. Hopi laughed. Even Juarez laughed. Tweetie too, though no one makes Tweetie look dainty. Except Tweetie. When he acts. See him catch a cat and you'll know.

Waiting by the register now, thinkin on all this, Luther digs for a wad. Between a sputter and hitch Hopi asks if he can throw in.

"No man, this on me," Luther says, waving the kid away.

Hopi grins again, all swaying and dopey. Juarez don't grin, never dopey.

"What you got?" the dirty dog spits. Scowl's back. Not a surprise. Usually mean after he eats. Happier when he's hungry. Elbows swinging side to side, hands anchored now in his back pockets. Deep back pockets. Never fails, always something mean back there. Once pulled out a hand grenade.

Hopi shrugs, nervous, but Piña don't come to no rescue. Not Luther neither.

"Show me."

Hopi hesitates.

"Empty the fuckin pockets joto!" Juarez snarls. "Turn em out. I do it I rip em out. And I'll rip out more than your pockets." Juarez chitters if still dead serious.

At least Hopi gets that much right. Turns out his pockets quick. Only wrappers and lint. Not even a phone. Not even keys. Just one blue pencil. Not whole either. Just the nub. Eraser long gone. Chewed off. Whole thing chewed on.

"You want a blue pencil?" Juarez asks Luther, sly as shit, like he scented it, dug it up, dropped it right there on Luther's back deck.

Luther just wants the waitress. Get something more off her. Doesn't know what. A look, a word, another flinch. Make something more of this verga he doing everything not to rub. But she gone. Probably in some IHOP back office too, wanting him, hiding from him, cold sweats, maybe in some stall fingering herself, whatever, what matters don't matter, so what she got big nostrils, so long as she lookin down. Luther can find her. Just not now.

And Juarez knows it. Probably why he keepin this sly grin. All happy, panting, tongue lickin the corner of his mouth, might as well be droolin. Some crazy chingon, this one, who no fool should corner but don't go forgetting shit and corner Luther either.

"This what you gonna throw in?" Luther demands, slow, slowly turning over Hopi's pencil not even a pencil.

Terror tightens around the child's eyes. Finally something about Hopi that isn't wobbly. Terror doesn't wobble. It knows what it is.

Chido, you know, Luther glad. That familiar taste of metal starting to answer fear. Though Luther swallows. Not here. He'll use the bullshit gesture later.

"I was gonna pa-pa-p—put in work for it," Hopi tries. Even throws in some stupid-ass swagger.

"Gonna?"

"Wa-wa-wawa—. Sa-sa sorry. Wi-wi—. I will."

Like he El Ponchis or even Moreno Leos. Got that reversed. Or not. Morelos highways can mark all their ways. Something not even half his age can mark his.

What the fuck was Teyo's beef with this thing? Luther still can't ditch the question. Curiosity keeps overturning his taste for doing.

"You *will* work?"

"Si. Jale."

More bullshit but Luther knows it's what he won't need. Not even worth laughing at. Nothing tightening around Hopi's eyes now. Just wobbly again. Unsure. Alone. Worst of all: longing.

Luther hands him back his blue pencil and slaps him on the back.

"I already told you, Hopi, I got it. On me, pinche. Free."

Even the boy's back wobbles.

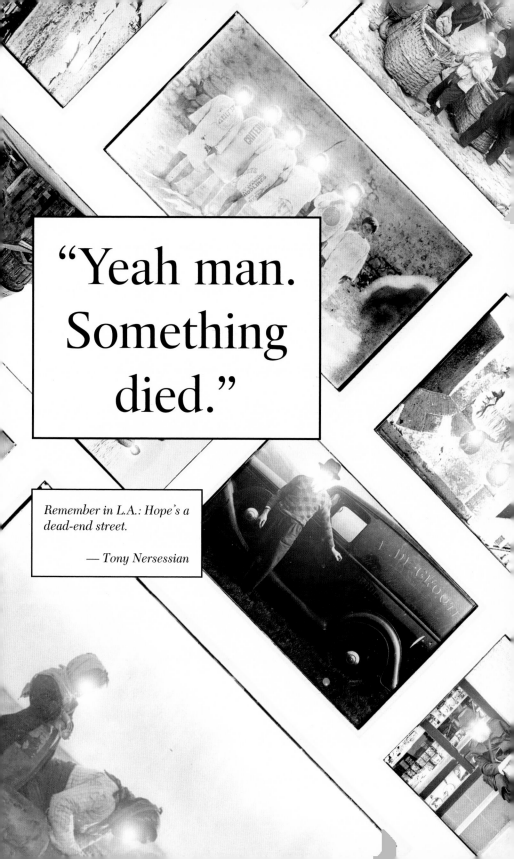

"Yeah man.
Something
died."

*Remember in L.A.: Hope's a
dead-end street.*

— *Tony Nersessian*

"Mr. Pettalosky, is there a problem?" Judge Carrol Ohm interrupt.

"Mr. Zildjian!" Pettawhinesky snap. "Stop mumbling to yourself!"

This what taxi company pay insurance for? This aboosh?

"Where's our witness?"

"Not worry, Pettasnapsky. This is A student, good citizen. He be here. On time."

"On time!? Shnorhk! He's already an hour late! And my name's not—"

"Relax, relax. I do nothing wrong. I telled you this. Armenian drivers best drivers in world. Know when to stop. Know when to go. When to turn, speed up. When to slow. Nine years I drive cab. Never accident. Before that I race cars. Never accident. I good. Very good."

Shnorhk give courtroom another once around. Almost as bad as pisser. There mirrors scratched by gangs and drunk hearts. Here faded blue plastic seats. Wood-panel walls stained dark where accused rest heads. Behind judge, U.S. flag, California flag, bathed in fluorescent green. Like clotted stuff Shnorhk cough up.

Shnorhk almost welcome such thought, and hurt, sputters lips, covers mouth, especially when Vendecøp speak again. Speak in monotone some think sound like truth, but, to ear with music sense, offensive. Life sings truth not flats it. Venderøt flats it in red when he state Shnorhk ran red.

Shnorhk sees red. Feel it too. His tan blazer, still damp with rain, might steam with all that red burning inside him. Shnorhk reach for tie. Clip-on. Comes away in hand.

"Shan vordi—"

"Mr. Zildjian, you're mumbling again."

"Human cancer in flesh of land."

"Stop it."

"Lloyd George declare this. Of Turks."

"I'm sorry, are you calling Officer Grady Vennerød Turkish? That guy there who looks like Thør? I'd say he's about as Turkish as I am."

"Ah-ha! So you Turk too!"

"Me? No, I'm Jewish. Find your witness. Now. Later doesn't work."

Yes, friend. Of course friend. What else call someone who appear out of nothing with such look of concern?

Student too. USC student. Good university. Good students. Some of best.

This friend the very, very best: Dwight Plaguer. Not cared about broken glass, smell of smoke, gas. Just strolled over mess, up to Shnorhk's wrecked cab, peered in, and with such young bright smile.

"Awww man, you okay?"

"I had green."

"You had green."

"You saw green?"

"I saw green."

"This cop, he ran red."

"Oh yeah, he ran red. You alive?"

"I alive."

"Then today's your lucky day."

This March.

Dwight Plaguer had been in hurry, books in hand, had important class, but still scribbled out name and number on Shnorhk's palm.

Later when police write up ticket, Shnorhk held up that palm!

Held up that truth!

Write what you want! Here written is only truth!

In Sharpie ink too.

Sharpie permanent ink!

Even Patil ∴ Shnorhk's wife ∴ marveled at how it stayed.

"Time will take it," she would still sigh. Glum. Always glum. Shnorhk kept from soap. Water even. Kept hand to himself. Liked markings there. They better than fate line and life line.

Patil's friend, Zanazan, know how to read those lines. Charges too much. Glum like Patil but for no reason. "Time will take it." That's what Zanazan say about Shnorhk's palm. Patil learned this expression from her: "Time will take it." The glum part we all learn on our own. Houzom.

Time finally did take away Sharpie permanent but not before Shnorhk knew name and number by heart.

In hallway, Shnorhk find immediate relief. Dwight pick up on first ring.

"Hey!" Greeting bright as California teeth as very bright kid as very best student.

"Are you here? Are you near?" Shnorhk cough out.

"Awwwww man," still bright. "Didn't you get my message?"

But there was no message. Shnorhk sure. Shnorhk never miss a message.

"There no message."

"Awwwww man, these phone companies. They are trouble. All the time, troubling up our sorry lives. Messing with us on purpose too. I'm sure of it. Phoneying up communications. And all for the dollar. For the government. For—"

"Friend, I need you here."

"Aww man, I'm in Brazil."

"Brazil?"

"That was my message, man. A long story. Family stuff. Funeral stuff, I'm sorry to say. All bad, though."

"Something died?"

"Yeah man. Something died."

And even if Dwight Plaguer's voice stay clear and signal stay clear, too clear?, what can Shnorhk do but offer condolences?

A moment later though, quiet of hallway shock Shnorhk. It never having crossed mind that this very best student, this USC student!, this friend, Shnorhk's friend!, would just not show up. All postponements, missed deposition, had never meant more than very-busy very-best life.

Even yesterday this kid assured him:

"That pig'll be there? You bet I'll be there. Got your back."

Shnorhk reach out naked palm to wall as if reach or wall can steady that kind of hurt. Keep tears back. Angry tears. Hot enough to burn tears away from tears. Sting eyes closed with salt.

Shnorhk heave chest. Ah. Real pain. Now he cough. One time. Then second time. Until third time it hurt even deeper and Shnorhk know it impossible to stop.

Shnorhk stop anyway.

Maybe because it so hard.

Maybe because it hurt so much.

Ah. Real hurt.

Shnorhk's driver's license will suffer consequence. Just start of consequences too. And sufferings. Always sufferings. Shnorhk vaguely understand about penalties and fees. Not counting insurance increase. Not counting other increasings.

"Congrats," Pettacranksky say.

"He lie up there. He lie about traffic light. I sue him. Can I sue him? I sue him. You sue him for me."

Lawyer not even respond. Just scoff and sweep notes into bag. Not even briefcase. Like grocery bag. This no lawyer. How judge take seriously grocery boy?

"You lose this! I sue Venderzøt! I sue you!"

Scoff again. Not even real scoff. Already forgetting. Courtroom forgetting. New people coming forward. New names rattling out in green-glazed air. Time taking its toll.

Shnorhk hating time. All the time.

Outside courthouse, in parking lot across Hill Street, stand giant chair. Thirty feet high. Maybe higher. Too high for any man, any judge. Chair like that will always stand empty. Chair not even a chair. Shnorhk want scream at chair name of every injustice:

~~Annotations~~

Where are you?

Which by leaving Shnorhk answerless, again, bent over, again, teaching Shnorhk, again, to never forget accident, green light, red light, Dwight Plaguer, Grady Venne-rød, or even Pettalosky who at this moment looks genuinely concerned that Shnorhk might cough up lung.

"You okay?"

"Go."

"You should see a doctor."

"Go away, grocery boy."

"You know, Mr. Zildjian, it would have saved us all a whole lot of time and trouble if you had just admitted to running the red."

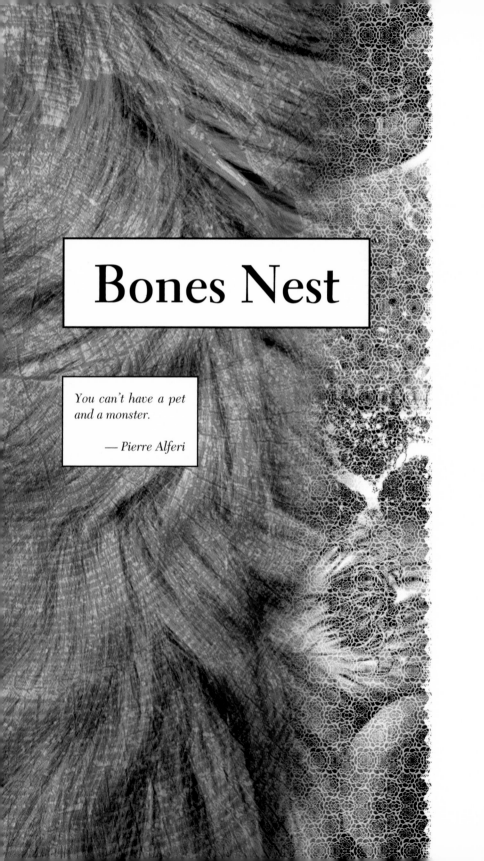

Bones Nest

*You can't have a pet
and a monster.*

— Pierre Alferi

"A Jax & Bones Nest?" Taymor asks (emerging from an area devoted to animal recline with (what?) a small sofa ((synthetic) sheepskin?) in hand).

Astair laughs. Looks at the tag. Stops laughing.

"$230?! What kind of pet store have you brought us to? Almost worth it though" (is it really synthetic? (feels too real)) "just to see the look on Anwar's face."

"Already worth it. Just to see the look on *your* face. I might get it. It's big enough. For me."

"Thanks for driving, Tay."

Her friend shrugs: "You need a second car."

"We're getting a dog."

"Some dog."

(for all her (street (mostly)) smarts) This is not something Taymor will ever (really) understand. She and her teenage daughter ((Roxanne) who is nothing like Xanther) have a great deal in common ((for better or worse) how they shop, gossip, and fight (or the three Cs: covet, conquer, and cast off)).

(curiously) Astair (for some time now) has been unable to shake the feeling that the only thing she and Xanther share in common is their love of The Animal Game ((if not love (at least enthusiasm (especially when it gets going))) (shrieks of recognition and Xanther's fast patter of words (fast like a frightened bird's heart)). ("Oh, oh, mommy—") (the one place Xanther still cries out mommy (when they play (otherwise long-lost common usage (parental nomenclature ever in shift)))) (Astair blames Dov (just allowing Xanther the name "Dov" instead of dad (and at such an early age) while at the same time reaffirming his paternity (at the same early age) had long ago opened the door to those bi-double-syllabic appellations "Anwar" and "Astair" (even if "mom" and "dad" hadn't disappeared completely (Freya and Shasti for a while called out Ashare and Answer))))).

But in The Animal Game "mommy" sometimes returned. Sometimes when Astair and Xanther saw rhinos (in the way people jostled one another in line (size is not a factor)) or wolves (in the way people circled things for sale at Target (species less determined by appearance than by movement)). The scuttling of a crab. Squirrel looks. Then Xanther would "Oooooh!" or whisper "Looooook!" (nervously tapping Astair's arm (sometimes too nervously) with those fingernails picked into red prickles of shame). "Oooooh mommy loooook!" as a couple on the corner of Portia and Scott argued (maybe broke up?) "He's, uhm, uh, like one of those pigs?, with tusks?"— "Boar" — "and, yeah, she's, uhm, like, a black" and then they said "bear" together (even if said black bear was pale as chalk (and about as tiny too) in her paler polka dot dress). Both Astair and Xanther knew how to see beyond seeing and play with the nature of the character no one can see in stillness.

Astair has little doubt that if she were here now Xanther would agree that the patron re-approaching all the cans and feed bags is a moose. Or the one skittishly moving aside for Taymor is some kind of flamingo. Taymor (herself) is no doubt a honey badger ((and long before the YouTube thing went viral) even back in Chicago (four years ago) where they first met ((a year later) Taymor eloping with Ted Trancas (cobra (poor Ted)) ditching her acting habit (and moving to Los Angeles where anything thespian initiated a gag reflex ("About the *only* thing that makes me gag."))))).

"I think I'll be the dragon instead," Shasti pro-claims (on tippy toes ((both of them) studying the racks of plastic, felt, and twine-knotted mice)).

"You can change your mind," Freya assures.

"Yes. The dragon."

"But you can only change your mind nine times."

Not dragons. Xanther would agree. Or mice. More like meerkats today. No question. Even if tomorrow's always a question. Animals change.

Granted Astair had played The Animal Game with Xanther her whole life. (still) Astair wants more. Especially as the rest of their maternal embrace (shouldn't they be talking by now about dresses? adventures? (boys!? (girls?!))) seemed to keep loos-ening (and even slipping away).

(While (conversely) these days) Xanther and Anwar only seemed closer (always talking about songs, museums, coding (what about boys!?)). Not that Astair had anything against their closeness (talked about it (~~excessively~~ (extensively!)) too with Anwar) and certainly not anything against coding which at last had paid off with a significant amount of cash granting the whole family breathing room (not to mention this opportunity to find something new in common (and not just in some species of imagination (but canine in fact))).

"Twenty thousand dollars?" Taymor asks again (she'd had the decency to not mention the price in front of the twins (and if there's anything Taymor isn't it's decent (indecent to the point of pride))). "Are you sure it's not a car?"

"We're not sure of anything. Not until we've spent some time with our new family member."

239

(last year news sites reported that in St. Lawrence County) Some guy named Sabin had been selling (for about that much (supposedly trained to protect children during seizures)) untrained (even dangerous) service dogs. (allegedly) Sabin turned out to be a drunk who had no reservations about bilking families out of their savings (breaking children's hearts) and then re-selling the dog to another desperate family ("sham animals" they were called (which didn't seem fair to the dogs)).

Astair had done plenty of research (one thing she was certifiably good at) before locating a Seizure Assistance and Alert Dog Training Organization based out of San Diego (with offices in Newport, Venice Beach, Santa Barbara, and Marin County). The cost was a reality that made such prospects always academic ((wishful thinking) until December made of the academic a necessity ((they had to do something!) and then two realities clashed (hopelessly) (until good fortune smiled))).

Xanther had gone down. Like never before. Astair's agony. Astair's joy. Astair's pride and joy and agony. Xanther ((who could walk through any room and at once fill it with breezes (Astair could be poetic (sometimes) (especially when she was wrestling (again) with what it meant (and what ~~she~~ (*it!*) had come to mean) to have such a unique (and damaged) little girl))) ever on the verge— (borrowed (this time) it turned out (but still (briefly) *seized!*))).

Tonic-clonic. Grand mal. Synaptic ((short circuit?) (connection-splattering surge) (EMP ("Electromagnetic Pulse?" Anwar had tried to joke. "You know Lord Emp? Wildcats?" (never explaining (what no one could (really)))))((these)) upheavals.

They had even been playing "Taps."

"That was four months ago," Anwar had kept trying to reassure her. "With two months off of pills too." Quite the plunge that choice (risk!) but thus far the ketogenic diet seemed effective. *Thus far* (which *seemed* about as reassuring as *operable* might be if it were though it isn't and never will be (*it* . . .)). Even if (true) Xanther herself *seemed* over the whole thing (((over with it as soon as the hospital released her) nothing about it *seemingly* lingering in her (only Dov's absence *seems* the absence of permanent residency which it (always) has been))(no *seems* about it)). Astair's the one who (if she can't forget (forgive) him) can't get on the other side of this ((awfully) fractured) memory.

Was repression at work in Xanther? or had the vital threat of such events drawn forth animal reactions ((void of recollection) wasn't the current claim(?) that animals live entirely in the present? (will their dog prove this claim? (maybe teach Astair too?) immediacy shearing away the trauma of past survivals?))? But how can Astair draw forth from herself those same animal claims on territories so present they exceed memory? Especially that memory.

Still revisiting her (or what she keeps revisiting? (how can we ever tell?)).

As it does even now (right now!).

In the aisles of a pet store.

241

23rd of December. Then all of Christmas Eve in Virginia Hospital. Christmas Day too. ((Though from the outset) it looked liked Section 60 would (just) claim her.)

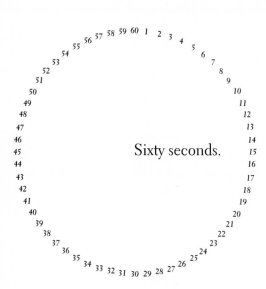

Sixty seconds.

No escape. Even months later (now(here)) among so many cat products (feline flea combs and boxes of pine litter). Here it comes: the awful distaste(!(?)) for that event (for that time (all that time (and so awfully compressed into this untimed instance (is this how animal understanding also works? (or not at all?))))) fittingly marrying the distaste Astair has forever had for that strange creature of skulkiness and entitled impertinence ((surrounding her) more than distaste (disgust? (even rage?) (Astair not exactly an ailurophobe ((more like a misailuro?) (Missile Euro!)(a possible name for the dog?))))).

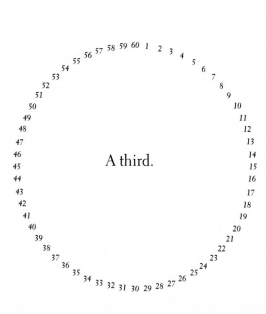

A second minute.

A third.

(

(((

((((

()

)

)))

))))

And after three . . . still going (so) strong
(impossible to contain).

(cords along her baby's neck
rising like cables on a suspension bridge

(every bridge about
to give way))

(the fists a small child can make)

1 2 3 4 5 6 7 8 9 10 11 12 13 14 15 16 17 18 19 20 21 22 23 24 25

(and screams? ((how many parents have never heard their child scream even once like that (let alone dozens of times?)?) her baby girl screaming like it's the end of the world! (and it is the end of the world ((for Astair) every time)))

convulsive status epilepticus.

)

(or so Astair remembers (imagines? (keeps imagining (keeps . . . keeps . . . (is this then (here then) the keep of her mind? (and heart?) invaded) pillaged & possessed & razed) conquered) owned))

1 2 3 4 5 6 7 8 9 10 11 12 13 14 15 16 17 18 19 20 21 22 23 24 25 26 27 28 29 30 31 32 33 34 35 36 37 38 39 40 41 42 43 44 45 46 47 48 49 50 51 52 53 54 55 56 57

Fourth

(who could know no screaming meant hearing
something worse? (missing then her tiny fists)).

On to the fifth minute.

1 2 3 4 5 6 7

How could Tay ever understand? (how could
anyone? (even to Astair ((even) now) her thoughts
seem badly visible ((badly laid out)(flayed open)
((scooped up) however mishandled (mashed

        stuck

                                      back

splashed

                together

                         with the incoherent
goop of adrenal syrup
                      (animal syrup too
(human syrups following)) with other(?) fluids(?) of
sparkling incongruity)))
                       and this all hap-
pening now (memory & response) in front of stacks
of

        Wee-Wee Pads))

                               1 2 3 4
                                      5
                                        6
                                          7
                                            8
                                            9
                                                10
                                              11
                                              12
                                              13

Astair (then) unable to hold back her own seizure of thought: "She's gonna die!" (screaming it too
(does she mouth it now? ∴ she does not. ∵)) "She's
gonna die!" (screaming it as loud as she could
(mouth that?)) "Baby, baby, don't—" (still screaming ((did she have to?) what's "have to" when you're
already doing it)). "Don't die! Please! Oh! My! Baby!
My little baby's gonna die!" (finally impossible to
scream (even mouth (even think (even now))))

Right there in her arms. Before a grave too (surrounded by arms). *His* arms. *His* grave (the bits of
Dov (t)hereinburied along with that godforsaken
weapon ((one gun) what his long line of military
ancestry kept insisting on passing forward like a gen-
erational curse to each son (good riddance (good
that (his) *their*(!) only heir was at last a girl!)))).

1 2 3 4 5 6 7 8 9 10 11 12 13 14 15 16

That man who by the speech of his name had killed mommy.

That man who by the genes of his family legacy would kill their daughter.

The great fighter.

The great soldier.

The great killer.

1 2 3 4
           5 6
              7
                8
                 9
                  10
                   11
                   12
                   13
                    14
                    15
                    16
                     17
                     18
                    19
                   20
                  21

Though (to be fair (to Dov('s memory))) was Xanther's attack really so surprising given the circumstances? (talk about Triggersville! (from stress strangeness sleeplessness to damp (it was raining then too (black umbrellas looking like silver-sheeted cupolas of a city on the march))))).

Not even the communal relief one could expect from a funeral: flags, uniforms, and gunfire. Not exactly the Ibrahim way of life.

1 2 3 4
5
6
7
8
9
10
11
12
13
14
15
16
17
18
19
20
21
22
23

"Five minutes and thirty-two seconds," Anwar had announced to the EMTs (a ridiculously precise pronouncement (but that's what her husband had said (and kept saying it too)) (in the ambulance) (at the hospital) (to every nurse in the ICU)).

1 2 3 4 5 6 7 8 9 10 11 12 13 14 15 16 17 18 19 20 21 22 23 24 25 26 27

"5:32."

Definitely the longest.

Ever.

Mr. Duder did let go though (finally (5:33)). Xanther herself came up with that name and at the terrible age of seven too— (terrible because no seven-year-old should have to speak that way) how she was too often seized by a "wild beast"—

("Mister Woder Do" (what Astair had first (mis) heard (figuring the name related to Xanther's sweats (like water dew))) what was in fact the odder "Wo" (another name) (maybe from Wed or Do?)

("Mister Wed or Do?"

"Or Do or Wed?"

"As in marriage?"

"I guess. Sorta."

"And Do?"

"It's Om Reworded."

"Huh?"

"Like, uhm, how my Ow Tremors Died? Thanks to Mister Duder."

"Darling, what are you saying?"

"Door? Wed?"

(Astair only recognizing then that her little girl was having what was later diagnosed as "auditory auras preceding an atypical absence seizure")).)

—by a creature which (shapeless except for claws and teeth ((long claws (everywhere)) (long teeth (everywhere))(which because it did not kill Xanther (but only cruelly seized her, shook her, and released her)))) had come to take on a peculiarly perverse character: sadistic (in cruel play) and affectionate (in the pleasure it apparently took)? Something (maybe? hopefully?) a dog would (could?) chase away?

Even if (truth be told (when it came to Mr. Duder)) Xanther hadn't mentioned the name in years.

Though (also (truth be told)) such a vague thing (fairy-tale-ed too) was not so detached from the very real contours of Xanther's life (the bullies that populated (eventually stalking her) from school to school (materializing (it seemed ((simply) out of thin air)) with the first sign of a shudder (spastic fling (foamed lip)) or even rumors of such potential displays).

Good news (at least) on that front (and it was a front): Thomas King Starr seemed to pose an alternative (anti-bullying rules present (apparently enforced) (not to mention a clutch of friends (albeit weird) who knew of Xanther's condition (even if they'd yet to witness a seizure))).

Maybe they even helped with another bit of news a month later ((this last January) and (possibly?) relayed too by Astair's friend Abigail in one of those "Did you hear . . . ?" stories (which wouldn't have happened (in the first place) if Astair had been more open with her (and still Abigail apologized profusely for saying anything))). Except Xanther claimed she had already heard about The Bookstore Girl.

The Bookstore Girl. That was how Xanther and her friends referred to the poor thing (and the fact that she'd been older than Xanther didn't offer much differential (she was still the teenager Xanther would become by September)). The "attack" (as they insisted on calling it) didn't exceed five minutes and thirty-two seconds let alone four minutes let alone three minutes but by the end The Bookstore Girl was dead.

At first everyone assumed drugs were involved until the devastated parents emerged to state what pharmacology reports later confirmed: The Bookstore Girl was drug-free (with epilepsy as a preexisting condition). "We tried drugs. If only we could have found some that worked," the father supposedly announced.

No one ever determined what triggered the seizure (which came as no surprise to Astair). It was only natural to speculate about origins (though as of late Astair had tried to help her daughter (and herself) let go of this constant quest for causal certainty (because more often than not the trigger remained unknown)).

"I'd still like to avoid that one at all costs," Xanther had already confided (in her most mature tone).

"Oh darling, the triggers are different for everyone. Though there are preventative measures which have proven efficacious, er, I mean helpful."

"I know, I know: exercise, eating good, lots of sleep. And I know what effincakeish means too."

Xanther's friends still concocted all sorts of possibilities. Kle (who was always wearing one of those strange (funny?) t-shirts (recently one of torn peach with russet text: I'M SO POOR I CAN'T PAY ATTENTION) (good ol' Kle)) got the ball rolling. The Bookstore Girl had died at Vroman's in Pasadena. This was common knowledge but no one knew where in the store. Or which section? Which aisle? Or most important which book?

Supposedly (as Kle reported it) The Bookstore Girl had "def been flipping a book."

"Do you think," Xanther had wondered aloud (one morning), "what she was reading made the difference? Maybe if she'd picked something else the holiday would have been different? Do you think a book could do that?"

Astair's "No question: no" didn't stop speculations about the risks inherent when turning to romances, grimoires, hacker manifestos, something about a defiant lightbulb, the Bible, the Qur'an, books devoted to computers and game programming, *Watchmen*, *American Psycho*, Emily Dickinson (of all things!), even the *I Ching* made the list (Anwar (much to his dismay) was quoted incessantly: "Dad always says reading is risky business.")

Xanther's friends even topped themselves when they went on to consider (Kle again (their vanward scout)) how if one book might cause The Bookstore Girl's death, did it not follow that another book might cure her infirmity? As Kle has put it: "Mr. Ibrahim, maybe some risks are worth the taking?"

But if a book under twenty dollars was a risk, what of a $20,000 Akita? Anwar had remained dubious ((always favoring a pound) even this morning when he left with Xanther ((orange umbrellas like minarets on the move (why was she thinking about Cairo today?)) announcing under his breath (albeit with a wink) "Here goes everything")).

Month after month Anwar had eyed Astair like she was a crazy woman and then the December seizure and suddenly a check which would cover some debts and a car "or something more." That was it. The breeder/trainer offered a thirty-day trial period.

"What if she doesn't have one during that time?" Anwar asked.

"Let's just see."

"But our purchase is partially contingent on her having—"

"Yes."

"Freya, unless you want to share that meal with your sister, I'd think twice about continuing" (tone (fortunately) having some authority (arresting further investigation by the twins into the nutritional advantages of a Dentabone (Freya attempting to coax Shasti into eating one)) if (still) they are little more than bemused by this parental injunction (regarding her curiously) before drifting off to consider bird cages (it won't surprise Astair if they try to climb inside one ((their paired radiance already a trial the world will have to bear) their sibilant whispers already an act of mischief))).

"How's fucking in your corner of the world?" Taymor asks greedily (90% blind to the girls (the only one not struck to stone by their beauty) (thankfully)).

"Me? I've, we've—" taken off guard (too off guard (Astair knows Taymor too well for *that*)). "I nearly burned the house down this morning. Left the kettle on."

"That's one way to heat things up. Not my preferred way."

"Do you think it would have truly burned down the house?"

"Set off smoke alarms. Of course where there's smoke, but, hey, you didn't answer my question."

"Seriously?" Astair doesn't need to (seriously? here?) get into her marriage's (moribund?) bedtime affairs (are there really answers for that kind of thing?) just as a man ((no moose or flamingo), Great Dane (Rhodesian Ridgeback (or maybe a Weimaraner (definitely alpha (maybe a little beta) (versatile?))))) with soft eyes (smile as satisfied as it registers kindness) (what Astair would give to have such hair) wraps her friend up in an easy hug.

"Astair, this is Grez Kacy. Owner of Urban Pet. Astair's about to be a dog owner. An Akita."

"Powerful dogs," Grez smiles.

"She arrives this afternoon." Is Astair blushing?

"It's a seiz—" Taymor starts.

"For my eldest daughter," Astair cuts her off. "A surprise."

"Lucky girl."

"How does it know though?" Taymor asks (later) as they haul to the register collars (along with another stab at the subject of sex again) an array of leashes (a second try) bags of dried food (the subject drops) flea combs (almost drops) and a bed (this one substantially less expensive than the Jax & Bones (though hardly cheap)) while the twins take up the task of choosing one (last) toy each ((gratefully) granting their abundant energies focus).

"Routine. Smell. I expect intense familiarity. Animals are less enticed by the kind of societal static which can render invisible the most obvious and fundamental behavioral tics. They just stay focused on their food source."

"I heard weed works. Or at least the stuff called Charlotte's Web." :: strain of cannabis ::

"Really?"

"You don't need to walk a joint or clean up its shit either."

Freya's and Shasti's shouts (two aisles over) sound a loss of focus.

"Girls!"

"What does societal static mean?"

"Signage, cellphones, web traffic, YouTube. The modern day buzz of electronic alienation."

"I like YouTube. YouPorn better."

"Of course, thanks to that static, I discovered the San Diego operation."

"You heard about Seizure Alert Dogs on You-Porn?"

"Tay, when I'm licensed I will happily sign you up as my first patient."

"And I'll happily come, just as soon as you start dumping some of that academic-psycho-gargle-shrink-babble."

"You'd love my thesis."

"Only if it's graphic enough to make *Fifty Shades* look like Bella's wedding night."

"It's about Hope."

"And your grade? What amazing things did they say about you?"

Astair shakes her head.

"You still haven't looked!? That Catholic pride of abstinence. With Jews it's the shame of aftermath."

"You're Persian."

"Whatever. Different tribes. Same marketplace."

"And Catholics?"

"They come after the marketplace is closed."

Astair considers a big plastic jar of (red) licorice beside the register (there for any customer to enjoy (thinks how many hands (most (here) anointed with slavering dog affection) have reached inside)).

"Still too academic huh? All taradiddle, I mean."

"Taradiddle?! Now there's something I might try out with Ted. Any interest in joining us for a Dark Arches Zoo Evening? It's discreet. Anwar can watch." Taymor takes a strip of licorice. "Honey girl, textbooks aren't appealing."

But how can Astair explain to Taymor that text-books (for her) are extremely appealing (while bur-lesque clubs aren't (if that's what Dark Arches Zoo is (are?)?))?

"What would our yogi say?" Astair asks instead.

"Abigail would replace your electric alienation, with, hmmm, how about just some bad dragyou-down energy going round?"

At least Taymor lifts a mock eyebrow.

"Jazz hands too?" Astair mocks back.

"Jazz hands help," Taymor wiggles her fingers (even throws out a feigned hat tip with a shuffle step).

"Applause applause."

"Truthfully, I haven't seen you this excited in a while."

"Really?" The comment shocks Astair (because (really) she can't imagine how she has (in any way) indicated excitement (except for the burn in her face? (Astair even checks in the mirror of her phone (camera already set for selfies (ignoring the messages ((Voice Mails: Box Is Full)))) discovering no sign of a blush)).

"Checking for beauty creases?" Taymor snickers. "Excitement will do that. The best faces are blasé. Or venomed."

"Beauty creases, I like that." Astair puts away the phone and reconsiders having a piece of licorice (what the hell (right?)) only to catch sight of her two girls drifting inexplicably out the front door into the downpour.

At least her voice still has the power to stop them, though not before they can put to the test their blind-ing moment of inspiration (the test rendering useless any preventative rush).

And for a moment Astair can't move.

All she can effectively do is gawk at the confounding veer her two girls have just undertaken.

"Please tell me that's some kind of a weird umbrella they're wearing."

"That's some kind of weird umbrella they're wearing."

"That's not an umbrella."

"No, but it's working like an umbrella. Call it a hat instead? An *expensive* hat."

The Wrecking Crew later forwards the claim that 1) they thought the bed was a tent 2) therefore they were testing its camping potential and 3) they were genuinely befuddled when asked how either a tent or a camping expedition had anything to do with the original assignment of each selecting one (and only one) doggy toy?

(in the end) The soaked twins and the sopping-wet sheepskin ((not synthetic (it turns out))(not to mention one soggy Dentabone)) amounts to a very expensive experiment in the meteorological durability of one canine accessory (and one canine edible).

Astair seethes (digging into her wallet for plastic).

"Sorry," grunts the young woman at the register who had just moments ago (dutifully) explained again why Astair is now the owner of a Jax & Bones bed.

(no doubt in an effort to prevent filicide) Taymor wrangles the intrepid explorers behind her (no longer so intrepid). At least Astair's (scolding) silence proves strong enough to mute both her daughters (keeping them now in a state of watchful (if terrified) obedience).

And yet as rapidly as Astair's mood arrived it just as rapidly recedes. She likes the sheepskin mess (if it's really a mess), the leashes, the bowls (she likes all of it!). Taymor's right. Astair is excited. On one wall: beauty. A quote by Gandhi.

"And to think I thought we were heading to Soursville," Taymor smiles.

"Whiskey sours," Astair winks.

"Now that's my girl. Buying expensive has its pleasures."

The cashier returns the MasterCard.

"I'm sorry, it was declined. Do you have another?"

Astair finds her Visa ((who knows (all of them are nearly maxed)) (Anwar's success has come just in the nick of time)).

"Tay, after all these years, and you'll approve, I'm finally getting my triple Ds: degree, direction, and a chance to make a difference."

"Sexy."

"Not even this gets me down." Astair holds up her phone (iMessages 13,923 (is that possible?)).

"And popular?" The numbers stupefy her friend (they should stupefy Astair).

"You have no idea," Astair laughs (another UNKNOWN CALLER lighting up her phone). "It's unending."

"My kid would kill for that kind of traffic. Of course I'd kill her."

Astair explains how Mefisto ((consummate prankster) itinerant whiz (Anwar's once-upon-a-time bestie)) who was hired as a head programmer (((really) a freelancer (temp)) charged (by said Web company (name unknown)) with devising a new distribution scheme to gain maximum exposure (taking advantage of both legitimate means as well as tactics of a decidedly grayer (shadowy!) nature ((anyway) the point was the coding infrastructure (not what was necessarily being disseminated)))) released (inadvertently? (that part was still shadowy)) an entire campaign (much of it still in so-called "spoof stage") with standard website/social media addresses, toll-free numbers, etc. etc. (all TK then) replaced with (for some incredible NON-REASON!) all of the Ibrahims' personal contact info.

"Promised prizes too. Promised cash!" Astair shakes her head (trying to sign the charge without looking at the total (if only the ink would flow)).

"Fuck. Me. Twice."

"How's that for some bad dragyoudown energy going round?" Jazz hands.

"Fuck me thrice."

"Mefisto swears the version was meant only for Anwar's eyes. Sort of, I don't know, boyish glee of possible ruin. And mind you this mistake is way more involved than just banners and spam. Ever hear of DDoS attacks? Or Zombies? Not *Walking Dead*."

"*World War Z?*" ∴ *If only it were that simple . . .* ∴

"Anyway, our phones just started ringing. Anwar's server shut down. We couldn't even access Google."

"What about PornHub?"

"Here we go again." Astair holds up her phone (flashing again). At least this time there's a name:

ADAM H BAYLOR at ███████████ ∴ *No need to inflict upon this pour s.o.u.l. those same disturbances experienced by the Ibrahims . . .* ∴ .

(impulsively) Astair picks up.

"Adam?"

"This the Army?" (Astair had forgotten that (of course) the spoof-campaign had included the Armed Services (even the CIA & NSA).)

"I'm calling about the $99,999 enlisting bonus?" The dull voice tries again (no, not dull (scared (and young))). Astair can almost hear pimples on each syllable.

"May I suggest a different direction?"

"Huh?"

"How old are you?"

"Uh. Nineteen."

"In school?"

"Not anymore."

"You're considering something new?"

"Yeah."

"But still not entirely sure?"

(This is Astair's quiet gambit (and after a lengthier pause she gets her reward).)

"Something like that."

"Well let me set a few things straight here: this is not the line for Army recruitment. This number was mistakenly, let's say *feloniously*, placed in a series of web advertisements. Is that where you saw it?"

"Hentai. Online gaming."

(Enough of games!)

"I guess that beats a bathroom stall. Regardless, perhaps you can take this as some extraordinary sign that on this particular day and at this particular moment you managed to tap out a series of numbers which led you to someone who didn't hang up, or worse curse you before hanging up, but instead advised you, somewhat emphatically too, against enlisting. Someone who has a right to emphatically advise you against enlisting because she not so many months ago buried the father of her firstborn. And for this conversation I'll spare you the gory details. Of which there are many. Suffice it to say he was killed in Afghanistan."

She hears then the curious life rise up in the kid's voice: "Really?"

"Really. My advice: get enrolled in a school, stick it out a few more years, and if you still want to head over to some killing sandbox in the East go as a journalist and really serve your country."

"Uh . . . alright. What was his name?"

"Whose?"

"Your husband's?"

Astair hesitates ((why?) but only for a moment).

"Mudd, Dov. Captain Dov Z. Mudd. U.S. Army."

Taymor looks about as amused as the cashier looks confused: "Score one for the rebels."

"Right? Make lemonade?"

"That stuff you did right there? I could drink it all day. Did you hear that girls? Your momma's a bona fide bad ass."

"Bad ass!" Freya shouts.

"I want to be bad ass too!" Shasti pleads.

"That you already are," Astair smiles. "Both of you."

(as she puts it away) Astair's phone fires up yet again (something corporate? (Galvadyne (███████ ███)))).

"Maybe it's time to get another dog," Taymor says ((still laughing) (wiping her eyes) (as they head toward the front door)). "This is fun."

"Do! We can dog park it together."

"I want something cute though. And dangerously coy. Do they make attack poodles?"

"Quadruple Ds I realize: degree, direction, making a difference. And getting a dog."

"Still no mention of sex."

"What do you think comes out of quadruple
Ds?"

"Finally you're making sense."

"Get an Akita like me," Astair grins deliriously
(and the announcement even sounds (feels!) to
her like a confession ((seriously) who cares? (Astair
doesn't))).

Outside another power beats sidewalk and street
with fistfuls of water.

"I can't wait."

"That part's obvious," Taymor nods. "Does Xanther feel the same way?"

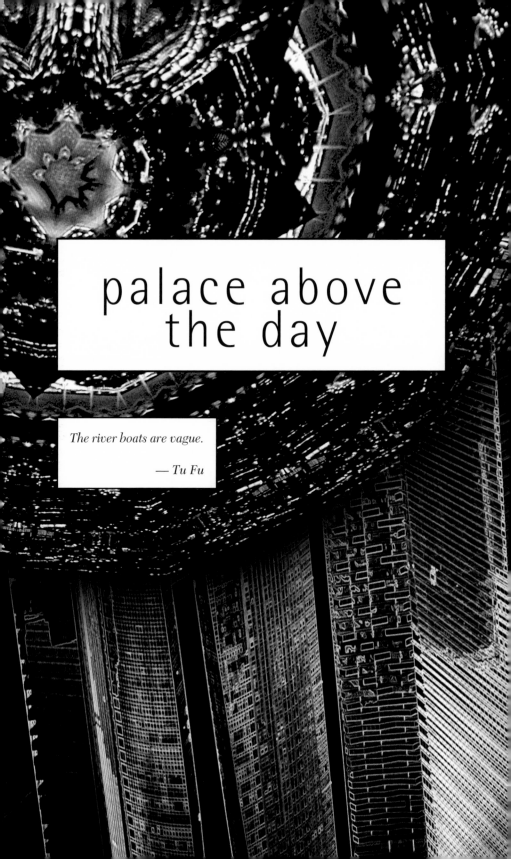

palace above
the day

The river boats are vague.

— Tu Fu

ride stretch. jingjing chiak buay liao, lah. grabfills with nuts. so

tum sim him, like jingjing cared, lagi tian li giggled at how he

stuffed up. zhong smiled too, poured coca-cola in a glass.

glass shimmered neon, lah. inside and out, parrot fish blue, from

ceiling to seats, rug too, mebbe white, paint bright as afrojack

beats. even driver, from cap to shoes, glow electric blue.

and like some blue pill limo slipped through city on flooding roads,

green lights or red, maseelis mebbe slowed: first by a temple, then

mosque, last a club, too ex for jingjing, prog house, dubstep, he'd

hang nights outside to listen in, no mat rokers there, fiak those

fools, just these types, tecnoprenners saht saht boh chioh, by taxi

line smoking filters jingjing can't buy, this night all swivelling hard

to rewind, for jingjing's ride, that piece of noon sky, drifting by,

dares bass and meenite to follow what oreddy's left both behind.

not that singapore asleep. vesak in days ∷ **May 13, 2014** ∷. monks

lelong cones of rice, cabbage and spice, buddhas too. mamas

hanging streamers and balloons. and if jingjing caught cry for help

then, acted blur. lai dat, mebbe a dream. hear anything in that

storm? kettle bangbanging on roof? couldn't see jilo let alone hear

jilo twice. feels it most. like jilo let something sing, move, even

become, or drift off undone, not even air. and all jingjing had to

do was cry stop, lurch out into the rain, and care.

• • •

jingjing had lost track of streets, mebbe fell asleep. if he dreamed

he dreamed he was zhong and could do nothing but weep. limo

parked underground. zhong led the way past glass doors and

guards. elevator had one button: zsl. twenty-seven floors up.

but here was not some penthouse, not just wealth. here was a

palace above the day above the night. here was something else.

jingjing counted nine waiting at the top. four to each side. he

counted twice. always nine. sixteen black heels together on black

marble. all in black except for a bow tie hung low like a necklace.

and something electronic, one gold earpiece for each. no one

spoke. no one smiled.

jingjing never heard heels click so loud. the rest, with same sound,

showed tian li and him to their own bathrooms. robes waited. slip-

pers too. toothbrushes. perfumes. and music, jingjing music:

mebbe riri soon?

jingjing pocketed soap, toothpaste, q-tips but in hallway caught

his mistake. on wood low table, black as burn can black, one wide

bowl waits filled to brim with gold coins and clips of low bills, all

sorts of currency. arbo, zhong fill pocket every time he step out.

sial lah, of course, right then three bow ties, orange with onyx,

rose with yellow, and jade with grape, approached.

"this way," rose with yellow smiled. dimpled cheeks, black bangs,

narrow waist.

"Старик явно спятил, иначе бы не привел сюда этого

ублюдка. Следи, чтобы они не обокрали его."

∴ "The old man has really lost his mind to bring such trash here. Keep an eye out that they don't steal him blind." ∴ she said to the other two.

"Он может себе позволить быть слепым." ∴ "He can afford blind."

"Он уже давно ничего не видит." ∴ "He's been blind for a while." ∴

"Тихо. Не при чужих." ∴ "Quiet. Not in front of a stranger." ∴

"Можно подумать, этот недоумок говорит по-русски. Он и английского-то, похоже, не знает." ∴ "Like this loser speaks Russian, I bet he can barely speak English." ∴

jingjing makan his tongue, matched smile for smile.

the great tian li was waiting in small room, one wall a leather feas of books, opposite a shrine big as her, big as both of them, easy, lah. eat them all up. even books. she in a robe too, comfy on deep

274

sofa but so small there, slippers dangling high above the rug.

jingjing just wanted to gostun back to the bowl but sit beside her.

by then bow tie staff, jingjing count four this time, brought in tray

of tea plus plate of yellow cakes filled with every kind of jam.

"Cream and sugar?" mebbe chap cheng. mebbe thai. bow tie

chocolate with cherry. hair bleached to the root. match her gold

earpiece, swee bow.

"mm sam mm say," jingjing laughed, and like macam she knew what

to saysay next.

"其皆有." tian li is never rude.

"谢谢." cocoa cherry smiles.

russian and mandarin. jingjing impressed, bow ties all early twen-

ties, like him on call for old age, ah soh him, ah chek them ∴ as *if they could be his friends* ∴. they must choose music. jilo chance old

zhong loaded up speakers with techno, electro house, trance.

oreddy cycled through effen, nicole chen, gayle san. skrillex then

with scary monsters and nice sprites or what comes after?

ouy ekil tsuj m'i . . .

not that jingjing said as much, slurping down a whole cup, then

two, then three, cream pitcher too, crumbing up more cake bits.

yawn. hahaha watching auntie bob her head like she dubbin some

subclub to dawn. hard though to miss cocoa cherry get damn

atas oreddy, finger-twirling her curl, just out in the hall, not

even under her breath, to bow tie pink with pearl, calling tian li

and jingjing cheena and suah koo. 大陆人 ∴ Mainlander ∴ 乡下人

∴ country hick ∴ and 农民 ∴ peasant ∴ too.

not as if tian li cared, if she heard. trance now for trance. forget

eats. doesn't even touch her tea. just lurf to cup its warmth.

"此地岂非奇，靖靖?" she said then. "里真高，但是至少这个屋子没有窗户."

And then: "且一无用火炉."

And then: "吾等须速辞别."

jingjing excused self to find windows but instead went seeking that wide bowl on low table of burn-black wood. ali baba some gold. jingjing not so stupid to waste this moment.

jingjing ducked cocoa cherry through room opposite library, followed a maze of doors, by empty beds, empty tubs as big as beds, padpadded then through the palace, past gilt mirrors and oils, pillars and statues, fountains and lounges, statues and more shrines. what a good looksee. wait till void deck folk hear this! see then what jingjing pocket! drink all the tigers they like.

until jingjing found where they arrived, marble stairs up which

zhong went, spiral like a shell that could swallow the straits. and,

wah lan eh, how many floors stairs go! jingjing clutched rail,

wobbled vertigo, terbalik, lah, could fall up falling down.

but before first step, fuck spider, two bow ties intercepted: pink

pearl again, with copper with azure. jude boys. hair tints all over

the rainbow and gelled still as skin's still as smooth as their smiles

are all cool. so beautiful. ai ya, jingjing spins just catching their

eye. are they twins?

on the way back to the library jingjing heard auntie's voice. not

that jude boys made complaint. moved easy, hips easiest, in new

direction, mebbe checking their ear pieces, checking their droids,

boot heels clicking to inquisitive's polaroid.

something had been wrong though. and not just how many

couches. jingjing never seen a room so large, beige and green,

green curtains covering far wall, mebbe where windows hide. but

in middle tian li and zhong going on and on.

arbo zhong's mandarin flawless! jingjing damn stupid. chiak leow

bee and useless is too kind. si beh lao kwee! why in first place

rich man even let jingjing translate? to be polite? and that not the

half: jingjing claimed tian li wanted pay when she'd said nothing

of the kind. zhong would have heard lie. fat chance for lui now.

jingjing got shake loose these bothers, and empty that bowl.

jingjing figured auntie would do her thing quick and they'd leave

but she just sat beside him and let zhong speak. borak for hours.

at least felt like that. mebbe jingjing snoozed but woke scared to

catch tian li on the move.

jingjing followed at a distance through stranger and stranger

rooms. with glass tables, bronze lions, very low light. are those

shrunk heads?

"有钱的时候没时间," zhong suddenly says now to jingjing. "没钱的时候有时间?"

"我喜欢你的员工." ∷ *"I like your staff"* ∷ jingjing answers back. "我特别喜欢他们低挂着的领结." ∷ *"I especially love their low-hanging bow ties."* ∷

to which the great tian li adds "时乃非时.何不时弯?" ∷ "Time is only time. Why not a bow tie?" ∷

which is when they entered the dimmest room, music near gone, mebbe that xhin in the distance? you against yourself, or fox and wolves or track before that. jingjing know the whole sword. no swords but much here to show, under long barrel-vaulted ceiling, strange tapestries covering four walls. arches lead off to black spaces, so black mebbe not even rooms. stairs in center lead only down, so black mebbe not even down.

"this is his owl room," zhong announces. english for some reason.

"此乃其鹰之宿," jingjing translates.

tian li oreddy recoil. when jingjing see auntie do that? kia si lang,

lah. she back into him, near slip. jingjing catch quick. hold both

shoulders, like holding wings of a bird. with no feather, just bones.

"**如果你肯制，请让佢为我哋解释一下呢度嘅意义，**" she blurt.

"i'm sorry. i didn't follow, please."

ahha, zhong have trouble with cantonese. for some reason auntie

stick with it too. a rush of questions then which jingjing translate,

feels good, again, to be of use. zhong answers in english, which

the great tian li definitely don't speak.

then in mandarin again zhong tour the pedestals and display cabi-

nets. owls of all kinds: bronze barn owls from england, totemic

owls from pacific northwest, eskimo spirit owls, syrian goddesses

thousands of years old, athena on apulian glaux skyphos, lakshmi

with ulooka, an owl-shaped shang zun, and stitched into one

tapestry babylonia's burney relief. zhong keep up cock talk, all

names and dates. kong chiao weh! hahaha! here a tapestry of lei-

gong, part man, part owl, god of thunder with wings. there ascala-

phus, orchard keeper of hell, turned into an owl, kena sai over

pomegranate and some super fatty bom-bom makan too much.

whole time tian li wide-eye as owl, swivel heading too. she can't

get enough until what she mumbles stops them both.

"靖靖 , 我哋嚟过呢度." ∴ **Cantonese** ∵ tian li full glowing on him,

eyes owler still, sharing a secret, revelation, holding his arm.

"i don't understand," zhong pleads. and truth, jingjing catch no

ball either, but lurf attention, both hers and zhong's.

"we've been here before," jingjing translates.

"谁是我们?" zhong wants to know.

jingjing too, asks auntie: "乜人系我哋，我从嚟冇嚟过呢度."

:: **Cantonese** :: :: *"Who is 'we'? I've never been here before."* ::

both get same response: tian li give a violent head shake, swivel

macam mad, but no wide-eyes for owls this time. mebbe jingjing

see it too then, down those stairs . . .

"what does she mean?" zhong beg. "jingjing, please explain."

but jingjing afraid then as shadow grows. other shadows flee.

auntie trembles and groans.

the great tian li can only mean one we.

and then she takes zhong's hand: "味之奇也. 未曾与君同往一处，且相处时多."

but zhong doesn't understand. he starts to cry. she leads him from the owls. even dim can be bright. leaves jingjing behind.

"现在该怎么做?" ∴ "*What's to be done?*" ∴ zhong asks.

"今请告知尔子之况." ∴ "*Now tell me about your son.*" ∴

Veinte Pesos

I can pay you.

— Victim #7

But when he looks through the downpour, the women lift their heads.

—The bus is late Señor but it always comes.

Is that how he'll get to Papantla?

He offers a slow dip of his hat. And though he stares directly at them he sees none of them. Not one of them exists beyond the weight of a breath. And to breath Isandòrno grants no mystery. The women are as unimportant as guns.

And yet someone continues to laugh. It is the old Indian across the road. He has set up a stand where the bus will stop. There he will sell what he makes to those who pass by.

Since Isandòrno left the ruins to wait here no one has passed by. The old Indian was asleep. Now though that he is awake, the old Indian can't stop looking at Isandòrno and he won't stop laughing.

—Do not take him seriously, the women mutter. Then they clap their hands and shake their heads and curse his madness.

—He is always like that.

—He laughs at everybody.

—He is a fool.

But Isandòrno still walks out into the rain to find out about the laughter.

Then halfway across the road, Isandòrno hears something else. It makes no difference that the old Indian has gotten louder. It makes no difference that someone else is with him and laughs too. Even the crashing rain will not drown out this sound.

Something dying. Something crying for help. Beyond hope. Beyond
help. Isandòrno could answer it
with the quick heel of his boot.
Quick enough to prohibit a question of purpose.

But the sound was hard to locate.
It was not back by the old women.
It was not over by the old Indian.

Isandòrno had to squat to listen
more carefully. He narrowed his
eyes to stop his eyes and see the
sound. He found it again somewhere along the middle of the

road. However, when his eyes unnarrowed his ears lost the direction and only the road remained, offering up a high harvest of rain.

The disappearance was about as absurd as crouching like this on a blacktop between Poza Rica and Papantla while water seeped into his boots. The disappearance was about as absurd as beholding the sudden appearance of a goat and a donkey.

For an instant Isandòrno even expected to see such a pair emerge from the rain and then the cry, or whatever it had been, was gone and Isandòrno stood up and continued on.

Why in the first place Isandòrno had stopped at the ruins earlier that morning was because the bus he had chosen to take him to Veracruz was a tourist bus. And he had had time.

The tour guide, dark as rotten banana skins and round as a grave mound, had recited a history all the way there. He was not a tour guide. He was a minister who by some accident had become a tour guide. He believed everything he said. He only wanted converts.

Why cacao or pulque or Takilh-sukut ∴ from Nahuatl; meaning a place of papanes or crows ∴ should require converts was not clear. The guide spoke about ulama too, what in Nahuatl is called ollamal-iztli, a game played with a rubber ball against high stone walls which at times could result in decapita-tion. This the guide described as if he had witnessed the crucifixion

and what's more the crucifixion
still in progress which his guests,
American tourists, Japanese tourists, German tourists, students
from Mexico City, would also soon
witness.

Isandòrno had seen no crucifixion or beheading, only the Great
Ballcourt and the Great Xical-
coliuhqui and when he made his
way around the Blue Temple and
Pyramid of Niches he felt like he
had witnessed nothing at all even
if he believed the students were
wrong when Isandòrno left them

in the midst of pointing out to the guide that there were no dead and no thunder, only rain. There was not even a rubber ball, though one of the students had started to kick around a football and was told not to by an official before the student was kicked out of the park.

But a planned stop was not the only reason why Isandòrno had gotten off the bus.

The feeling was strange. It came upon him without a name. He must have known it once. He was not the first man to feel his mouth dry. Nor the first to note the way a heart can race without a reason.

Maybe that was why he had wanted to climb a pyramid. Maybe he had wanted to justify the pulse. Only when the official told him he would have to go to Cancun to climb a pyramid did his heart slow and the dryness in his mouth evaporate and whatever happens to his eyes in these situations told the official to look down and back away and find instead some children to order around.

Isandòrno had considered then his body's behavior in the same curious way he might consider a sick animal or any of those The Mayor sends him to see.

What does it matter if there are thirty-five in Boca del Rio by Manuel Avila Camacho Boulevard. Or twice that in Tamaulipas near San Fernando? Or just one, Mauro Tello Quinones, a Brigadier General? Isandòrno might as well have never been there. And if he ever passed through Uruapan, he might as well have been bowling

on the black-and-white floor of
Sol y Sombra.

Isandòrno doesn't bowl and he
has never been to Uruapan. Cancun has less to do with men than it
has to do with tiny green turtles,
and green eggs too, which she'd
cook for him most mornings, from
the Araucanas he'd feed every
evening, when she would tell him
stories about where he was not
from and where he could never
go, and all the things he must do if
he did not want to go sooner, such
as spitting three times over his

shoulder if the sun should ever hit his eye directly, or never stepping directly on the edge of a shadow, or the number nine he should never say unless he taps out nine by fingers to thumb, or the silver no bullet should be without, or the gold no bullet should be without, and the kapok tree to where he had gone with her coat and a shovel after she had died and where he had watched butterflies fall from the sky. Long before he had met The Mayor.

Many are born into circumstances promising a long life and are surprised when death comes early. But what of those born into circumstances promising a short life who are surprised when death does not come at all?

After Isandòrno left the park, he had walked and walked until his heart beat faster and his breath came out in long warm surges. He treated his dry mouth with rain water. And even if there was little sun he spit over his shoulder three times and even if it was too gray to step on the edge of a shadow he tugged on his earlobe whenever the clouds shifted and then he even said nine and tapped nine out by fingers to thumb. And still he believed none of it.

It was not even twelve and Isandòrno did not have to arrive in Veracruz until much later. The three crates arriving this afternoon would likely be late. He would have to wait somewhere. Isandòrno did not mind waiting. In fact he liked waiting. He was good at it.

At the stand, with its little trailer and a shed in the back with a barrel of water strapped to the roof, the old women had told him that if he waited under their canopy he could dry himself until a local bus came by to take him to Papantla. They would even make him some food for a small price.

Isandòrno accepted their invitation and stretched out on their bench with his long legs crossed and his thumbs hooked on his buckle while they continued to prepare food at the large round table set with their bowls of cornmeal and buttered pans and plates heaped with sage and salt, their hands light with the coarse flour, while behind them two grills occasionally burst forth with smoke for no obvious reason, and then dissipated just as quickly, again for no obvious reason.

And though he closed his eyes, Isandòrno did not dream unless a dream could be called taking in the sound of the rain and letting it wash away everything else but the rain. And then the rain fell harder and washed even itself away.

Most of the old women started when he woke. Some shivered

despite the heat in the day, sticky even in rain. And then they returned to working the dough with the heels of their hands and though they still heeded him they no longer looked at him, keeping to their huddle around their table while chattering against the storm.

The one they called Maria Estancia, perhaps too afraid not to say anything let alone not to note his watchfulness, came over then and offered to read his fortune.

She had taken her time with the cards and had discovered nothing new or dangerous, but he had still paid her enough to make the other women work harder in their preparations and forget their doubts. The Mayor had taught him that. Money murders doubt.

Only once had she stopped, fearing perhaps to cause offense.

—You come from a long line of—
You are—

Isandòrno had waited for her to finish. She was good enough to know better.

—Your belt buckle is a horseshoe, she had said instead. Why is it upside-down?

—Because I am unlucky, he had answered.

—Always on the cusp of things, she had concluded with a smile.

Whatever life had led her here had also given her more than a handful of pleasures.

—You are on the cusp of love, she continued. On the cusp of friend-ship, professional concerns, even living. You are only on the cusp of life. But you are also only on the cusp of death. Never more. Always just on the edge. If you have not died already, you will live forever.

But Isandòrno had died. Many times. Forever did not concern him.

He is a stem, a husk, barren and thin, withered by sun, erased by wind, emptied by seasons of dullness, marked by seconds of duty, scarred by regrets only the faintest of lines dare to write out, which no one, not even him, can interpret anymore. People have told him a crow will reveal more than anything his face has to share.

It is true his gun has a name and a caliber and even a number of shells. And the name and the caliber and the number of shells can all be told. As can their composi-

tion and their quality and even
their history.

But Isandòrno could not care less
about what is interpreted or told.
And even though the points mix
one drop of silver with one drop
of gold, Isandòrno could not care
less about those habits either. He
was a practitioner of superstition
without being superstitious.

Nor did Isandòrno favor a particular weapon. He has had many
guns. He will have many more.
They are all only shadows of the
gun he keeps within.

That gun is his name and its caliber is his caliber and its shells number the moments left he gives others to live.

Isandòrno needs to know only this: there is nothing on the face of this world that a gun cannot kill.

Isandòrno leaves the road and approaches the Indian's stand. He can feel the old women's eyes on his back. The old Indian doesn't stop laughing but when he retreats into his shack and Isandòrno follows him, the old Indian's eyes actually brighten. The woman seated on the ground behind the stand doesn't know enough to retreat let alone stop laughing. She is too drunk to do anything she is aware of doing.

—What's that on her face?

—Leave her alone, the old Indian smiles. She's just an old whore. It's crocodile shit.

Isandòrno nods, observing the woman awaken to some new recognition, at first revealing offense,

then sending her out into the rain
and down the road.

The old Indian resumes laughing.

—Look what you did.

She is not the only one who tries
to escape. There is a child in back.
Likely the old Indian's daughter. Her eyes flee the moment
Isandòrno spots her.

Sores cover her body. Her chest is
a fragile cage wrapped in wounds.

Her cheeks and the backs of her arms drool with disease. But she fears Isandòrno more than she fears her disease.

The old Indian laughs harder. His mouth makes the card reader's mouth seem a vault of ivory. Dark pegs gnash at nonsense.

—Brujo, the old Indian finally grunts as if that might hold anything or stop anything or even know it.

On the warped planks laid flat across fruit crates wait dozens of wooden dancers and wooden masks and small wooden llamas. Wingless birds with long, sharp beaks perch on pyramids beside boxy rings crowded by necklaces made of still darker wood, knotted with the shine of injury. But this is not what the old Indian offers Isandòrno.

Like the necklaces and the wingless bird, this too was carved out of bloodwood. Afterward it was blackened by fire, soaked in animal fat, then polished with sand, rags, and, later, beeswax.

—Mexica, the old Indian says then, finishing what the card reader feared to say.

Isandòrno holds up the totem. Wide mouth, long fangs, narrow eyes, ears pinned back, with whiskers, which like everything else have been hacked out with a machete.

The old Indian produced it from folds of greasy newspapers. Old notas rojas. Or not so old.

This is something Americans will buy with a single slip of paper.

And maybe not even that. Maybe just coin. One dirty peso.

Then they will take the head and throw away the greasy paper and not much later they will throw away the head too.

Just the same, Isandòrno sees in this offering everything he cannot tame. That feeling beyond a name let alone a shape.

And as sure as the weapon that he is within himself, if what he weighed weighed nothing, if what he aimed at was aimed at nowhere, Isandòrno understands how this moment chambers a round already lived out to the sound of a flat impossible click, without consequence let alone announcement let alone charge.

So Isandòrno removes from his pocket all the money he has and pushes it toward the old Indian. It is enough money to keep him alive for years. It is enough money to keep many men like him alive for years and with enough extra to take his daughter to a doctor and

pay for her medicine so she too
can live on for many years.

But the old Indian just flashes his
dark gums and shakes his head,
even as somewhere out in the back
his daughter starts to whimper.

—The carving costs veinte pesos.
But what hunts you now amigo
you already own.

The Horrosphere

I hunted all the Sand.

— Emily Dickinson

Recently Xanther has started picturing the gray matter behind her eyes like this gray ice, only sprouting all these crystal formations. Those are the questions, the spiky icy stuff, and not just off the ripples of her brain, her cerebrum, cerebellum, what makes her think of cereal, but also branching off along her medulla oblongata, even down her spine, following each crooked twist, is that why her back's so wrecked?, too many questions making out of her nothing but esses and knobs?, turning her into an actual question mark?, is that why she's such a klutz too?, this prickly stuff everywhere, freezing up into her, like that flaky ice that forms on meat after it's been in the freezer for a long time, dead meat, right?, because all meat is dead right?, or is that redundant?, because muscle is called muscle because it's alive, so muscle isn't really meat but dead muscle is definitely meat, right? Anywho, that's how Xanther's head feels most of the time, like frost on dead muscle after it's been left in the freezer too long.

Actually Anwar was the one who pointed out this meat/muscle thing. Duh. He's the one always pointing out things like that, word definitions, quizzing her too, which Xanther doesn't care for much but which like Tai Chi with her mom she's learned to put up with because resisting takes up so much more energy.

That's one of the things about the questions, maybe the biggest thing?, they take up a lot of energy. Like they exhaust her.

"I bet they do," her dad had sighed when she actually admitted it. The great sighing Professor Ibrahim, or Professor Anwar, though he's not really a professor, though people sometimes call him doctor, though he doesn't practice medicine, which Xanther doesn't understand and keeps asking about, which gets Anwar sighing, just like calling him Anwar instead of dad gets him sighing, or calling him professor which makes him sigh loudest, and longest too, because he doesn't really like the title. In fact the only one who can call him that and get a laugh is Mefisto, a close friend, or at least *was* a close friend. Xanther had seen her dad's lip do a little dance at Square One, what with all the e-mails, phone calls, and texts, which didn't get Anwar sighing but more fuming, which he rarely does, fume that is, but he was fuming that morning, even as they left the house together. Just father and daughter, "Going on a little adventure," he'd said. "Off to get Xanther's big surprise." The twins' excitement helped some. Even if they had no clue why they were excited. Her mom seemed the most thrilled. Xanther felt like she was the one least interested. Even vaguely guilty. What did she need a big surprise for? when really all she wanted to know was why her dad looked so tired. But then Anwar smiled as he went to retrieve from the foyer closet their raincoats and orange umbrellas, as he went on to explain how last night his own questions had kept him up. "You understand that don't you, daughter?"

Did she ever.

Though what kind of questions? That could keep her dad up all night? Anwar, this time to Xanther's great relief, anticipating her, admitted to "all this code" he kept writing on the side, his "pet project," unpaid for, out of love, "a fascination and machination," no question referring to his engine, which Xanther never seemed to cease having questions about, that word "engine," despite even today's explanation, which had seemed to make it clearer for a moment. And then everything got muddier again, even if mud was one of the goals, lots of mud, African mud, Asian mud, all kinds of muddy places with wild animals and predators "of all sorts."

"Meat?" Xanther had asked.

"Meat *and* muscle."

"Both?"

"Of all sorts," Anwar had nodded playfully. "Plus a little more."

Father and daughter raced across the Culver City parking lot with their orange umbrellas up, which didn't seem to do much good, because it was raining so hard, so that when it hit the pavement it flew up as high as their knees, black jeans soaked through, from thighs to Converse.

Xanther beat Anwar and got the door for him. Actually, she got the door for a few people also running for refuge.

The building, called Sementera, which sounds like a cement cemetery, was one of those business whachamacallit places, with a marble lobby and a security desk no one sits at, two opposite banks of elevators, between which hung a board listing businesses by floor.

Most of the people got off on the first three floors. One girl stayed on. She was maybe a few years older than Xanther and kinda bent or squiggly. She'd kept wiping her red hair out of her face and looking at Anwar in the weirdest way, all smiley while biting on her lips, which seemed to make Anwar a little weirded out too. Until she got off on the 6th floor, she just squiggled and stuffed a bag of potato chips in her front pocket. The bag crackled. Obviously all the chips were breaking apart, but all she could say, staring only at Anwar, was "A lot of stuff can fit in my pockets."

Anwar's office was on the top floor. A windowless hallway waited for them. A nameless door too, not even a number. Anwar had to knock because there was no ringer. But when the door opened there were windows. And lots of people shouting, smiling, clapping hands, rushing forward to greet Anwar, Xanther too, shaking their hands, patting Anwar on the shoulder, all types of congratulations.

There were plenty of faces Xanther didn't recognize, but Ehti was there, glowing, yelling about more glasses and more champagne. "Welcome to the Inland Silicone Beach!" Glasgow already had a glass, a mug full of beer judging by the foam, and judging by the foam running down the sides not his first beer. Talbot, who Xanther knows is from Jacksonville, Florida, and looks a bit like Johnny Knoxville, insisted on Xanther's high five. Xanther missed. Twice.

What a cramfest: tables, chalkboards, floors snaked with cables powering all the computers, plenty of laptops, and even more of those big monitors Anwar has at home wired to those towers, always so dead and lightless, except for the fans, like it's breathing, all at once, inhaling and exhaling at the same time, but without ever pausing.

Much the way everyone seemed to be smiling and talking here, without pause, like the rain outside too, except inside it was a rain of voices.

"I went to Japan and ate that fish that can kill you."

"What?"

"Fugu."

"What's it taste like?"

"White fish. Halibut. Nothing special. Just the romantic idea that you're eating something that could kill you."

"Downtown. Chinatown."

"I've heard that. Cash only Internet cafés."

"Not really cafés. More like these gambling dens. Men stay there all day just throwing their money at whoever's renting the machines just so they can lose more money online."

"What TF are you talking about?"

"I'm getting all kinds of inspiration."

"You're drunk."

"It's true. Not just parts and pieces."

"You're really drunk."

"Drunk enough to see the big picture."

"Maybe."

"No. Drunk enough to feel the big picture."

Xanther had gone to the restroom, which at least was quieter, even if getting there was like passing through a dream, or a series of dreams, from fish to gambling to . . . , more than that, which Xanther knew still wasn't anything like dreaming, but made her realize that she'd had a lot of dreams last night, none of which she could remember.

Above the sinks both mirrors were cracked. They made her face look crooked, and weirder, separate from itself, and that got her all nervous again, like this feeling of what?, dreaminess?, like everything around her was teetering on this edge of what could, with the littlest tilt-too-much, change all of it, like even a breath would do, or no breath?, which really, Xanther knew was not a feeling that had anything to do with the world, left big toe going up and down, except if that world was her, right big toe too going up and down, and an attack was already at hand.

John Charles Francis.

Not said by anyone, more like seen, and just by her. One of those names, like The Bookstore Girl, that Xanther had the misfortune of learning, and like many other names never forgetting. About the same age too. Only he, the little prince, the lost prince, at the age of thirteen had been seized and not released, buried under clover at Sandringham Church.

Though the name had to have been said, in one of those early fights between Astair and Dov, Astair probably hissing it out, and in Xanther's defense too, with a "what about" tacked on first, which Dov could never answer, none of them could.

Then, even if such thoughts drove her to her phone, a sudden distraction of texts from her friends freed her from the echo of Astair's warning. Besides Parcel Thoughts wasn't open. It just sat there like its black-ribboned-black-box icon: closed. She doesn't even have the ⏵α‖H8 app. She hardly has any apps.

Kle:	what's the big surprise sithhead?
X:	kfc
Kle:	chicken?
X:	nfc sorry
Kle:	not good enuf
Cogs:	do u hve yur big suprise yet?
Josh:	info polize
Mayumi:	fomo/somo
X:	NFC!
Kle:	clueless! tell us something new! haha!

Kle then sent a selfie, t-shirt of the day's a Rubik's Cube, a patchwork of color, I'M ALL MESSED UP underneath. Kle knows when Xanther goes to see Dr. Potts and what she does there. He also knows how to spell riddle and surprise.

Kle: solve the ritalin uncover the saprize

And maybe because Xanther already had her phone out, encouraged by her friend's interest, plus the sound of three, then four, tipsy ladies filling the restroom, getting all orchestral in the stalls, putting lipstick on, making fun of themselves in the cracked mirror, Xanther's fingertip slid to the black-ribboned-black-box icon:

The latest banner:

Friends don't let friends Facebook
They Parcel Thoughts

Stupid. Her friends' Assemblies were stupid too but sometimes love's all about loving stupid. Collages of pics, gifs, texts, soundfiles. Supposedly organized according to relevance. Stupidest: Xanther's. Pics of her bulletin board, the elastics on her braces at the end of her two greasy, black braids, what the neon looks like through her glasses, blurry, duh, and stuff of her sisters, Les Parents, Dov too, and of course Xanther herself.

Not like she had to go farther either. She could have just left it on The Solosphere. Contained, known, safe. But she had to slide it to The Amicasphere. Semi-permeable, all her friends pretty well known, so still pretty safe. Only five Assemblies, going mash-up, supposedly the most important bits circled, brightened, and enlarged.

That should have been good enough. No need to spin the dial over to The Noosphere: Open. With friends of friends of friends, most of the kids in her school in fact, lots of school, outside of school. Definitely the least safe.

Bayard's was awful. More like The Horrosphere. If Xanther weren't so white in the first place, she'd be sure she'd gotten whiter. Bayard's was the largest too. Taking up most of the Assembly. His nose hung to the side like a flap. His ears, the same. Both eyes were gouged open, leaking fluid down his cheeks. His high forehead was covered by a dangling piece of scalp. His lips were just gone. Most of his teeth too. Blood wouldn't stop dripping off the bottom of his chin.

At least he wasn't alone. Josh was there, bruised. Kle looked like bullets had burned through his temples. Xanther didn't understand Mayumi's: nothing broken or bloody, eyes just wider, lips all plumpy, with her mouth forced open, way open, wider than any mouth could widen without a jaw breaking. If Cogs was there he was too small to see. Xanther's was the smallest.

Still the picture freaked her out. Deep gashes slashing up her face, mangling her eyebrows and cheeks, and like her neck was all torn up too. Not as vivid as the others. Less detail, rendered quick, probably, like maybe just an after-thought? Still it proved one important/scary thing: not so invisible to them anymore. And the other scary/scarry thing didn't need proving: today's artist was **A Thick Oil // for a// Raw Stove.** Kle knew who that meant. Josh too. Even Cogs.

Dendish.

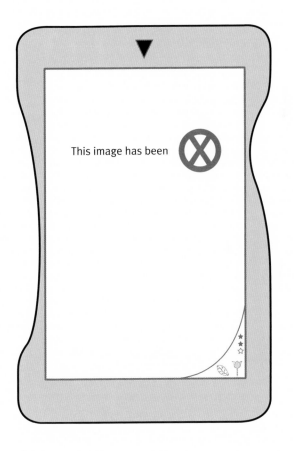

"First time here Xanther?" Ehti asked when she rejoined the group. Xanther nodded, still shaken by the sight of herself as a corpse, even if it was just a picture on a phone, a picture on a phone made by an app. "Whaddya think?"

"Don't trust an atom." The first thing that popped into her head.

"Oh yeah? Why's that?" Ehti knew Xanther was a weird kid. Nothing she said ever threw him.

"They make everything up."

"Nice," Glasgow smiled, raising his mug of foam, or less foam now, what with more amber.

"It's pretty cool," Xanther did get around to saying, taking in all the pizza boxes and half-empty jugs of Ocean Spray juices, vodka bottles, other bottles she knew weren't for kids. Everyone was wearing party hats and every now and then throwing confetti that looked like rice but was really shredded DVDs. Pretty cool since it was happening in the middle of the day. Coolest, though, was how much Anwar was smiling.

"Dad," Xanther finally whispered. "Can I ask you something? In private?"

"Of course, daughter, what is it?" At once stepping back from his circle of friends.

"What is my surprise?"

"Really? You want to know?"

"Well, I got to thinking in all the traffic on the way here, that I like sometimes spend way too much time thinking about, you know, the worst that can happen to me, like at any moment too, which I know I'm not supposed to think about, but I do anyway, but like couldn't there also be a flip side? Like isn't anticipating something good sometimes good too? I mean it even feels good, right? So maybe, I mean if you think this is okay, it would be nice to have that feeling, especially since we're only like, what, just another hour away?"

Anwar was crouching by then and his smile only kept getting bigger and bigger, until he threw his long, beautiful arms around her, and hugged her close, and kissed her cheeks, and then hugged her again, and told her how much he loved her, which is the most beautiful thing you can hear, and then whispered in her ear maybe the second most beautiful thing.

Xanther even cried a little she was so happy. Then Anwar had tears in his eyes too, laughing when he wiped his eyes because maybe he hadn't realized there were tears in his eyes, and then they both laughed harder and Xanther thought this is how it feels to be so happy you pee your pants, which Mayumi says she does a lot, Xanther having only done it when she wasn't happy at all, if happy then even counts, and anyway just hugging Anwar instead, and hard and for a long time. She would have hugged Astair the same if she'd been there. So she texted instead.

> X: i made dad tell me where we going
>   so excite! I LOVE YOU!

And by some miracle it got through.

> Mom: I love you too!

And then Talbot came over with Winchester who had a different name, but that name didn't matter, supposedly. "I call her that because she's twenty-two," Talbot had to say, by way of explanation, which Xanther didn't understand, "legal," which Xanther still didn't understand, not enough to smile at, though Glasgow laughed, Ehti too, kinda. Winchester had straight blonde hair, and high high heels, and a really cool pink color on her lips but really really thick. Winchester didn't say much. The pink color on her lips kept smearing on the straw and the rim of her cup.

Talbot handed Anwar an envelope and Xanther a drink.

"Don't spend it all at once," he told Anwar. "Do you know what an Arnold Palmer is?" He asked Xanther.

Xanther shook her head.

The drink looked dirty, overcrowded with ice.

"Half ice tea, half lemonade," Talbot explained, and then he held up a small shot glass with red at the bottom. "Plus a little blood!"

"Cool!" And it would have been too if she didn't at once flash on The Horrosphere with Bayard's chin dripping with blood. All her friends' faces. Her own. Talbot let three drops slip into her cup.

"Voilà, a Laura Palmer," handing over the pinkening cup.

"Who's Laura Palmer?"

"*Twin Peaks*?" Talbot looked genuinely shocked. "Anwar, your daughter doesn't know *Twin Peaks*?"

"She's twelve, Tal. And, I'm sorry, she can't drink that."

"Do Arnold and Laura know each other?" How could Xanther not ask?

"They do now."

"And the red stuff, really, what is it?"

"Grenadine. You know, in Shirley Temples? You don't know who Shirley Temple is do you?"

"Another drink I've never had?" At least Xanther knew what grenadine was, looking at the back of her hand, because it's something her dad used to have back in Egypt, on the corniche, on shaved ice. Had that been called a Shirley Temple too?

"Anwar, you can't tell me Shirley Temple's too old for her?" Back to Xanther. "How have you never had a Shirley Temple?"

"Is it ambrosia?"

"Why can't she have a Laura Palmer?" Talbot wanted to know.

"Sugar," Xanther answered for Anwar.

"I'm sorry, Tal. I'm sorry. Show Xanther the new games. She loves games. What's more she's good at them."

Not like that helped. Talbot looked pretty down. Introducing Xanther to a new drink had meant something to him, what with the Lauras and the Arnolds and the grenadine that wasn't blood, and now it was something no one would touch. Not even Winchester and all she wanted was a drink. And "Baby, will you go get me one?" was suddenly all she could say.

"Is Mefisto here?" Xanther asked then. Another one of her out-of-the-blue comments.

"Very funny," Ehti answered, but he wasn't smiling.

Over the course of the next hour, Xanther texted all her friends the news. She didn't mention the Dendish Horrosphere, and anyway, duh, of course all they wanted to know about was what kind of dog, which Xanther still didn't know, and didn't want to ask Anwar about either, because some surprises are good too. Instead she texted screenshots of games she got to play.

Pretty amazing actually, which made Xanther feel pretty amazing too, all while her dad's happiness kept filling the room, like happy thunder, sprung loose from the still darkening storm outside, if thunder can be happy, surrounding Talbot and Glasgow, both of whom she was crushing consistently in a game called *TrOUT*, which, like obvious, duh, was about trying to catch a trout.

First you started with a still pool of water on the side of a rushing stream. A trout hovered there in the middle and you could either net it or spear it or, hardest of all, grab it with your, like, hand?, before it slipped free into the current. Xanther could handle the net and nothing else. Glasgow could barely handle the net. Talbot stuck with the spear and missed every time. The hand grab was impossible.

And then, after losing way too much, Glasgow agreed to show her Anwar's M.E.T. and explain to her, once and for all, what a game engine did. Talbot, meanwhile, had started adding vodka to his Laura Palmer, naming his new concoction Bob. Winchester called him "goofy" but drank Bob anyway.

While Glasgow got Anwar's pet project to load, Talbot hooked up an even bigger console, and even got Xanther some 3D glasses, big enough to slip over her already humongous glasses.

```cpp
#include <vector>
#include "Particles.h"

#include "Render/Render.h"
#include "Math/OxMath.h"
#include "Common/ResourceManager.h"

#ifdef _DEBUG
#include "Common/MemoryManager.h"
#endif


using namespace PAPI;

ParticleContext_t* g_pParticleContext = NULL;
std::vector<CEffect*> g_Effects;

namespace Particles
{
    void Init()
    {
        g_pParticleContext = new ParticleContext_t();
    }

    void DeInit()
    {
        delete g_pParticleContext;
    }

    void Process()
    {
        if(!g_pParticleContext)
            return;

        // Move particles to their new positions.
        std::vector<CEffect*>::iterator it = g_Effects.begin();

        for(; it != g_Effects.end(); it++)
        {
            (*it)->Process();
        }
    }

    void Render()
    {
        if(!g_pParticleContext)
            return;

        bool            bPrepareShader  = false;
        CShader*        pShader         = GetRenderer()->GetShaderManager()->GetShader(CShaderManager::SHADER_PARTICLES);
        CQuadBuffer*    pBuffer         = GetRenderer()->GetQuadBuffer();

        std::vector<CEffect*>::iterator it = g_Effects.begin();
        for(; it != g_Effects.end(); it++)
        {
            CEffect* pEffect = (*it);
            if(pEffect->Render(pShader, pBuffer))
                bPrepareShader = true;
        }

        if(bPrepareShader)
        {
            Matrix4f view = GetRenderer()->GetCamera()->GetViewMatrix();
            Matrix4f proj = GetRenderer()->GetCamera()->GetProjectionMatrix();

            pShader->SetWorldMatrix(Matrix4f::IDENTITY);
            pShader->SetViewMatrix(view);
            pShader->SetProjMatrix(proj);

            pShader->EnableLighting(false);
            pShader->SetTechnique(CShader::kTechnique_Alpha);
            pShader->CommitParams();
        }
    }

    CEffect* CreateEffect()
    {
        if(!g_pParticleContext)
            return NULL;

        FLU_ASSERT(g_pParticleContext);
        CEffect* pEffect = new CEffect((void*)g_pParticleContext);
        g_Effects.push_back(pEffect);
        return pEffect;
    }

    void DestroyEffect(CEffect* pEffect)
    {
        if(!g_pParticleContext)
            return;

        // Move particles to their new positions.
        std::vector<CEffect*>::iterator it = g_Effects.begin();
        for(; it != g_Effects.end(); it++)
        {
            if(*it == pEffect)
            {
                g_Effects.erase(it);
                break;
            }
        }

        delete pEffect;
    }
}; // namespace Particles
```

"That's an engine?"

"Wrapper for the particle system," Talbot said.

"Think of it like *The Matrix*," Glasgow added. "Except not green. And not falling like rain."

"Have you seen *The Matrix*?" Talbot had to ask. At least Winchester rolled her eyes.

"Uhm, duh?" Xanther rolled her eyes too.

"Though unlike *The Matrix*," Glasgow continued. "This is not something we can so easily render in our imagination like—"

"Cypher?" Xanther knew that one.

"Good. Cypher claims by seeing the code he doesn't see code, just—"

Code kept scrolling down the screen like it was endless, maybe it was endless, and actually it did look a bit like rain. And suddenly Xanther didn't believe Cypher anymore. For some reason she didn't believe Winchester either, not that Winchester had said anything she needed to believe except "goofy," which she kept saying again and again.

"I designed this part. It renders light on branches and grass." Xanther believed Glasgow.

Some more keystrokes and trees swayed in a breeze, leaves bright with afternoon light. A few more keystrokes and the light grew hotter. More keystrokes and it was night, moonlight filtering down through the motionless limbs.

Xanther marveled at the eerie control of the scene, and liked it too, even if its very peacefulness seemed to call to mind too many of those scenes she had seen in her head since the funeral, scenes she had had a hard time admitting to Dr. Potts, but which she did finally admit to, striving all the time to remain honest, no matter how difficult that was, no matter how fused with fear and futility.

Parts of this book Anwar had once read aloud to her had rivaled those thoughts, and it was written over three thousand years ago, something *The Song of,* something like *I, Lion?*, about the fall of Troy, with mostly this flat-out boring stuff, lists of weird names, lots of long speeches, perfect to fall asleep to, when you're eleven, though now and then with these parts that were pretty yucky, enough so that Anwar had stopped, maybe realizing what he'd been reading, saying too, "Maybe this isn't such an ideal thing for bedtime."

Most things she forgot. Some though stuck, like this part about someone named Die-Meaty ∷ **Diomêdês** ∵ taking out another guy named Knee-Ass ∵ **Aineías** ∵ with a rock, crushing him ∵ **hip to the bone-cup** ∵ with the strings of him ripped out ∵ **two tendons** ∵ until he died ∷ *night veiled his eyes* ∵ ∷ *The Iliad* **trans. by Robert Fitzgerald 5.297-310** ∵ . She remembered that part. And then a goddess saved him ∷ **Aphrodítê** ∵ ∷ *His mother* ∵ . And he went on to found an empire called Rome.

Had that been like Dov's life? And his death? What about the goddess? Why had she deserted him?

"You might say these graphics represent, in a way that's instantly quantifiable, the *parametrics* of the code," Anwar had said then, one hand placed so gently on her shoulders it seemed to have always rested there. Tai Chi master without knowing a step. Glasgow was toggling back and forth between pages of code and a leaf slowly falling through beams of light.

"You lost me, dad."

Everyone laughed.

"Image *subitizes* language."

"*Subitize?*"

"Ah ha! Your word of the day!" Anwar responded then, so happy, even if Xanther felt vaguely disappointed that he'd forgotten how he'd already given her the word of the day, recalling too more vague disappointment that it still wasn't *callithump,* which still kept on conjuring up images of Callie's death on *Battlestar Galactica.*

"*Subitize* is easy," Anwar continued. "It means to quantify without counting. So when you see a 5 or a 6 on the side of a dice you don't count the five or six dots individually but know at once the number."

"Didn't you say my word for the day was *paradise?*"

"Dear daughter! My many apologies. Your dad is getting senile."

"Not quite yet," Glasgow gleamed, a look of affection for Anwar, as he began to explain how Anwar's M.E.T., while not producing trees and leaves, enabled various characters to negotiate the environment as well as one another.

"This is the S & M Plastic you were talking about at breakfast?"

Talbot spit beer, he laughed so hard.

"Goofy," Winchester said but giggled too.

"*Esemplastic,*" Anwar gently corrected Xanther.

And then, in 3D,

Paradise Open

floated up.

"That's the name of the game?"

"Voilà," Anwar winked.

"For now," Glasgow murmured.

And then the title disappeared, replaced by the spinning rainbow of death.

Anwar answered the glitch with his soft "My fault, my apologies. Work in progress, work in progress" and Glasgow had to reboot, but not before first toggling over to the frozen red droplets.

"Ah, the killing spray," Anwar sighed.

"Oh. My particles," Talbot grinned.

At least Winchester didn't say goofy.

"It looks like frozen rain," Xanther murmured. "I bet, uhm, like right?, you could count every single drop?"

"Count them?" Glasgow seemed surprised. "Sure. But why would you want to?"

The response stung Xanther into a silence neither of the men recognized, could recognize maybe?, though Anwar would have, if Ehti hadn't come up then.

"Apollo 13, we may have a problem."

"Don't you mean Houston?"

"I just got a call from Houston . . . "

Anwar goes off with Ehti to The Glass House, what they called this enclosed area at the center of everything, really more a room than a house, even if this room has a roof, with a glass chimney too. Kinda weird, super cool. It felt important too, where someone in charge might set up, though as Anwar had already explained "their little startup" didn't have a boss. So The Glass House had stayed empty.

"Do you think it's scary?" Talbot suddenly asks her.

"The blood?"

"It can't be scary," Glasgow cut in, "as long as the animals look like polygons."

And it's true, what's spraying blood is just geometry.

"Scary isn't about when scary happens," Xanther finally says. "It's about what happens before scary *could* happen. At least that's what dad said."

Though in this case, she means Dov. Xanther gets up. Suddenly she needs Anwar, not sure why either, doesn't care why, just wants his hands on her shoulders, the closeness of him.

Off the edge of one table she passes hangs a poster.

```
*E-mails, Texts, Calls, Letters




If you can't handle
YOUR INFORMATION,*
you're not overwhelmed,
you're mishandling
YOUR INFORMATION*
and that means
YOU ARE AN ASSHOLE!
```

It makes her think of Mefisto and the torrent of unwanted calls and e-mails he unleashed on her parents. Did that make him the A-hole? Or was Mefisto making A-holes out of Anwar and Astair because they couldn't handle the information? Then a sad thought creeps up: sometimes people describe seizures as an overwhelming amount of information in the brain. Did that make Xanther an A-hole?

One look in The Glass House and she knows better than to interrupt Anwar and Ehti.

Xanther doesn't want to rejoin Glasgow, Talbot, and Winchester. Instead she sits down nearby, though not close enough to get a convo going again, focusing on one of Kle's zines, really a stapled-jobby, pages small as her phone. What he calls his *Enlightenment Series*. This one's titled *Brain Mites, #9*. The idea was that these tiny mites collect in dormant parts of the brain where they feast on synapses. Only brain activity, which Kle draws as wild electrical storms, wipes out the mites. Stranger kinds of imaginings are required to reach the deeper folds of the cortex. "Only thinking saves the mind from these thoughtless creatures!!!" Kle's thoughtless creatures keep Xanther amused, ridiculous eaters, mostly teeth, like a gopher's, with these concave heads, chomping on nerves like they were turnips. Kle's pretty impressive with ink.

And then something about Talbot's and Glasgow's voices gets through. They're talking about Mefisto. Winchester's gone. Something about how what matters is that there's a reason Mefisto's not there, which Xanther can't follow, and then can't hear, and then can hear again, something about malware?, raceware?, that Mefisto's the one who's got a problem, who's in trouble, until they're not whispering about Mefisto anymore but someone she's never heard of.

"Realic."

"Who?" Talbot asks. "Is that someone Mefisto knows?"

Xanther glues eyes to her phone screen even if now she sees only voices.

"Mefisto? No, Mefisto has nothing to do with this. Realic was supposedly writing about—" Xanther loses what Glasgow says next. Lipor is the closest thing she can make out. Maybe San Pedro?

"Well, that's nothing new," something creaking, Talbot leaning back in his chair? "Plenty of people have commented about that."

"Yeah but not just speculation. This guy confirmed it."

"How?"

"Supposedly he found house," which maybe Glasgow doesn't say, but it's close to that.

"Don't believe everything you web."

"Da Nile's not just a river."

"Where's Realic now? Did you talk to him?"

"Was too spooked?"

"To talk to him?"

"To even call him. I had his number too."

"What happened?"

"Chinatown. Right outside of ABC Seafood. Ord and New High."

"Dead?"

Whispers drop below whispers then, something involving a wreck, something loose, which Xanther can't do anything with, except come up with Wreck-Loose.

"One bad accident." The wreck? "Supposedly a hit-and-run. Left Realic in pieces." What's Wreck-Loose? "Many pieces."

"Bad accidents happen?"

"Some people are saying what happened couldn't have happened there. They're saying it was a message."

Dawgz

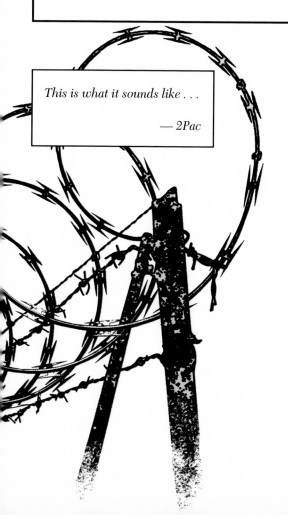

This is what it sounds like . . .

— *2Pac*

Then Luther hears it again.

• • •

No question this time. And close. Somewhere between chain link and back walls. Luther crouches fast, getting wetter, scanning concrete, from concertina to puddles, pelted with rain. Nothing but storm. Then behind those oil barrels, maybe, or those piles of cinder blocks once used as seats, back when this place could roar and palms slapped feria and the drain slopped red.

"Fuckin cat," Luther snaps, mouth filling with nests of wire, crushing it into something sweet. "Find it!"

"Where?" Tweetie answers, even if he's already moving toward the old cement mixer, like maybe what's dying hides inside.

The wobbly kid, though, Hopi, he looked like he heard something or hearing Luther bark like that went all manikin panickin again. Kid freezes up so many times he's like ice cream. Still standing on the far side, by the kennel door, that black Adidas jacket flapping in the flood, sneakers no doubt full up with sop, like every time he step he's walking on water.

"Let em loose," Luther barks. Kid can't manage even one step. "Open the fuckin door!" Wire turns to fuckin rebar.

But Hopi just twitches between what's for sure out here and what's already scratching behind the corrugated steel.

Not that Tweetie needs to be told twice. Told even once. See him fly across the yard. See a mountain move. Every puddle hit a puddle gone. Juarez whistles low to watch their big man close the gap on this trembling boy.

"¿Cuál es tu pedo?" Tweetie grunts, shoving Hopi aside, head slams the siding on the way down, balling up on the ground like he gonna find an inside in where there's nowhere to hide, like Tweetie gonna get all brown bear on his ass, like Tweetie care. One flick. One latch. That's it. Then like some kind of meringue dancer Tweetie pivots away from the opening door.

Luther's dogs needed no direction. They roar out of there. Already hunting. Right over Hopi like he wasn't there. Streaming around the empty pool, around bricks, lumber, fallen sinks, knocking over the cement mixer even. Tookie races to the edge of the diving board, teeth bared, barks once, and then circles back again with the other eight, all barking now, surrounding the pool, looking for that something to settle their teeth.

That sound though, was it a cry?

The first time it had sounded even closer. Like it had been comin from inside the van. Just as they'd pulled up at the big gate. Tweetie had come in off of Esperanza Street, then along 15th, circling closer, until they were idling by the front window and doors, grilled and locked, where Luther never goes, still as the glass they replaced years ago with boards, the same stillness they find behind. Just water running everywhere, off dumpsters, paint cans, bags with plaster still hardening at the bottom, drywall and old framing piled up in heaps.

Luther had stayed all slunk low in the passenger seat as Carmelita rattled back the big gate. Got her pink bunny chanclas on, shaking that wide ass in pink Juicy shorts, even holding up a pink umbrella fringed with some kind of fuckin pink fur. Then in the next moment, Luther's all savage. Like what kinda cry was that? Mad doggin Hopi first. Who else gonna peep like that? But not one of them, not Piña, not Victor, sure as fuck not Tweetie, owning what Luther swore he'd just heard. And truth was Hopi didn't look like he had the guts to let anything about him peep. Juarez was asleep.

"¿Tal vez this perro let loose a pedo?" Piña had said, nodding at Juarez.

"He stink?"

"When does he not stink?"

Luther had laughed but no laugh was getting this thing out of his ears.

The gate grinding on its chains helped dim it some. Carmelita distracted him too. Big woman. Handled that big gate just fine. BEWARE OF. Then BEWAR. Then just BE. Not a fuckin placa either. Place way below the radar. Could park ten cars in the rear. Hide an army if he had to.

Of course back when this place just started going some idiotas had tried to badge it up. Hit the sidewalks. The front. Even spray painted the gate. Like they was gonna claim it for LCM or some such set. Cleaning that up had been fun. Plenty of help too.

Teyo loves to bring up this story. "Grander considerations!" "Organize the divided!" "¡Esa es la eficiéncia!"

Grander considerations came down to gambling and fighting. Boxing at first. Cock fights next. Once someone brought in fuckin praying mantises. Mostly though it was dogs.

Back in the day Carmelita or Rosario would handle the pieces. Throw in with the umbrellas a fuska or A to the mutha-fucked K. Sometimes that office got mighty full. Past what used to be the metal shop, out by the storage sheds, twenty or thirty, easy, would crowd around the empty pool. Sometimes an easy fifty. Throwing back beers, shots, watching dogs chomp for breath down in the deep end. The one that made it back to the ladder in the shallow end got the money. Sometimes a lot of money.

Nothing like what the balloon parade brings Luther now but this shit still was something else. Something special. No one fiending, offering to suck you off for another hit of crystal or paco. Everyone just bringing shit to settle shit and roar.

Mexicans, Brazilians, Hondurans, Cubans, Haitians, Dominicans. Koreans too. Chinese and Thai. Gabachos even, Russians usually, but now and then some college types comin round for the adventure.

Outside of Lupita's "Mi banda es mi worda," this was Luther's first taste of what Teyo meant when he said "Alliances will reorganize if the flag is green."

In the end, thanks to some Vietnamese regular, the fools tagging Luther's crib got one sangrón madrazon.

This was all before Michael Vick and his Bad Newz Kennels hit the news. With that national flap, over what always be a fair fight, moanin same time as these bitches be puttin down bitches sunup sundown, Dawgz had to go quiet.

Not like Luther gave shits about no NFL either. Still something about Vick stuck. Dude had fought hard and got close. Ridley Circle Homes to Falcons. Before fuckin up. Chained up, marched off, kicked down to yardballin in Leavenworth. Luther caught sight of hisself in

Vick. Big money risin. Didn't want no fuck up. Didn't want no cage.

At least with football, if you had the guns, you could still wind up an Eagle. Luther's game, if he got caught with the guns, he could spend years in a yard learning to play football, fútbol, whatever ball they beat back and forth to bury time behind bars.

Suddenly crowds turned success to distress. All it took was one pinche pedo posting too much shit on Facebook. Leave a GPS flag on a pic and that was it. Luther kept a tight fix on his crew. Tweetie handled phones, web shit. On Parcel Thoughts he had made up one OG to represent them all: Dawgz Lawz. Got out word that way when news needed spreading. Or just to mess with shit.

Dawgz Lawz let everyone know Dawgz had closed, Dawgz had moved on, go fight your brawlers somewhere else. Luther had emptied the crates, tossed the leashes, but still kept the place. Not even owned. Luther just took care of his girls who took care of his dogs and the lease. For years. With years still left.

Early on they had milled metal here or bent it, later recycled it. None of the bins, die-cut machines, or welding shit was left. Just space. Throw down some mattresses. A couch. One of Victor's pals had wired them for cable. Still had the old fridges too. Plus enough AC to keep the girls off of some frenzy when summer got rough. They could keep each other warm when things got cool.

Before Luther, someone had tried to put in a pool. Dug it up, sealed it up, put in a working drain, but never installed no pump. Never filled it. Hard to understand. So it went by two names: pool or pit — depending on the mood.

"¡Ahí va la medicina!" First thing Carmelita had said as Luther climbed out of the van. "Missed you last night."

Luther hugged her under that pink umbrella even if all of a sudden his head was back on the IHOP waitress again. Luther wanted her even more now. Fuck cared about nostrils. Maybe even bring her here. Let some Luther music hunger up the place. *Vroom, vroom, vroom.*

"Where's Rosario?"

"She out."

"Better not be bringing no one back."

Carmelita looked down: "I said she was out, not stupid."

Luther got up on Carmelita's ass then. Gripped it good. Then because Rosario's not around flipped her an extra Grant. Luther wanted to make damn sure Rosario found out. Maybe two Grants. That got Carmelita juicy for realz, ass all wiggling then like her smile.

"*Cañonazos de dólares,*" Carmelita had said then, always throwing out shit Luther can't answer. Of course the way she vibrated the tip of her tongue on her upper lip, both lips lipstick-thick, made clear what she was after, what Carmelita's always after.

She disappeared then two presidents under an ass cheek. Rosario will stick around no doubt when she hears how she missed out.

From under the carport Luther could still see all the way down the low chain-link fence on the right to a brick wall in back, and then off to the left, the sheds where his pack better be waiting.

"Talk to me about my pool," Luther had said to Carmelita. "Is it filling up?"

Back in March the rain gave it depth. It took more than a hot day to dry it out.

"This time I cleaned out the drain, jefito," Carmelita chirped. More tongue on lip. Luther wanted her to stop that. Now and then he'd fuck her. Especially when he was too blind drunk to see. But on this visit this bitch was the last thing on his mind.

Luther grabbed her umbrella.

"You? In pink?" Carmelita laughed.

"You think a color's gonna tell me who I am?"

Luther had motioned then for Hopi to follow. The kid had a harder time leaving Piña than a pool dog who knows he no match.

"¡Hey güero! ¿Qué barrio?" Carmelita cried out at him then.

"I'm not white," Hopi answered.

"Careful," she smiled, rubbing her hips. "Brave bird makes a fat cat."

Carmelita will fuck anything. Maybe even Juarez, who's so glad to be out of the van, still hopping up and down, talking full-on then about some prank in Brazil Victor saw on You-Tube. Hidden cameras in a stalled elevator where the lights go out, then come back on, showing some thirteen-year-old girl inside all of a sudden, because see she'd climbed through some secret panel or some shit, infrareds showing it all, and she's done up like that bitch from *The Ring*, freaking the shit out of anyone stuck in there with her.

"I'd freak too!" Juarez shouted, hopping higher. "I'd a beat that bitch silly. And ass fuck her too just to make sure she was dead. You, Victor, with your guns?, fuck me!, you'd have painted that box red. Pow! Pow! Pow!"

Hopi had already slipped ahead. ∴ *Had Luther noticed how he had failed to notice how Hopi had so easily passed him by, Luther might have proceeded more cautiously.* ∴ Hopi had even opened the chain-link gate and was waiting. Luther told the boy to close it up behind them. Luther didn't offer his pink umbrella.

The sheds were ten feet of rivets, splashed brown and red, topped with more concertina wire. Luther had always forgotten how much like a fort this place was. At the only door in, Luther gave Hopi the combination to the padlock.

It impressed Luther that the kid hadn't had to ask twice. Popped the lock on the first try.

"You got family?"

"Just my mom."

"Well now you got this family," and Hopi had nodded but he hadn't smiled, like already he was figuring shit out, like this shit is wrong, this shit is bad, even if he still kept trying to slick back the strands of hair that kept washing down into his face.

It was about that time that Luther heard it for a second time, that cry, the peep, whatever the fuck it was, like it was giving him another chance, or calling him out. Either way it came on faint but fast.

"You hear that?" Luther had asked. At least now he was sure it wasn't the boy.

Hopi shook his head, eyes where Luther couldn't see them. Either the kid was lying to protect a thing or he was just too weak to do anything but fear when Luther got at him.

Luther's dogs gave up the best answer.

Inside most of the crates stood empty. Except for nine.

Doc Cavazos, Chen Chi-Li, Rayful Eddie, SloBo Jim, Agron, Sen Dog, Lord Gino, Smokey

Miranda, and Tookie. Mixto mostly. Pitbull, Rottweiler, maybe Shepherd. Luther could still fight a few, the rest he retired. Torn ears, snouts scarred, cloudy eyes, some eyes just gone, testify to a life of combat. And striving.

Retired? How'd that be?

Howls greeted them. Going to war against bars. Luther let Hopi help with feeding. And no doubt the dogs took to him. Like as soon as he walked by their doors. Same too when Luther let them loose. They circled the kennel, Rayful Eddie pawed at the door leading out to the pool, fighter that one, and then Smokey and Lord Gino snorted around Hopi's legs, even licked his hands. Fingers like treats, like some kind of piano player, harp player, like some old bitch used to fingering rings. Even cantankerous Tookie started nipping Agron and Lord Gino to keep clear, seated herself right beside the kid.

And then he said it, not slobbering, not a hitch: "I know you don't need me but I'm good at some things, computers, phones, and what I don't know I can read about. I can learn. I can be of use."

Like what Luther told Teyo that day near Olvera. Almost exact. Nothing so bleak as finding in someone so strange an echo of yourself.

"Thought you opened the drain," Luther yells now at Carmelita.

"I didn't say it was working!" she answers, still hanging back behind the chain link. They all hang back. Even Juarez is afraid of these dogs.

Not Tweetie though. He stands on the other side of the fence, on the coping. Umbrella's out but he's so wide the rain slaps down on his shoulders. Dogs seethe around him like he part of the landscape then disappear down into the deep end.

Never one to put her own fear on view, Piña yawns and disappears inside the main building.

Hopi, with that billowy Adidas jacket swung up over his head, joins Luther at the pool's edge.

Oval thing. Empty except for the foot of water above the drain, where the dogs splash, play, either way churn it up, be there first, or like Doc Cavazos or Chen Chi-Li stop to lap away some thirst.

That's when Juarez springs.

Just reaches over the fence and shocks Hopi with hard grips on each shoulder.

Hopi squeals then. All certain he going to flip over the edge. But black-eyed Juarez pulls him back.

"Like a girl," Juarez yips. "A little niña."

Hopi squats low then, breath heaving up hard, one of those pretty hands pressed to his heart. Like a woman. Like Luther would ever have use for a man like a woman? Then he'd get a fuckin woman like Carmelita. Or like Teyo get a homie que es brutal. Something hot and galvanized edges his mouth. Maybe he'll kick the kid in hisself.

"How old are you even?" Juarez snorts, still laughing, still poking at Hopi.

"I thought I was going to fall in." Even Hopi laughs a little. "Can't swim. Figured I was going to drown. Then I saw there wasn't enough water. Not enough to even break my fall. Just my legs."

Hopi laughs harder. What metal Luther tasted is gone.

"Like a little girl," Juarez still repeats though he can't hide his disappointment.

"I'm twenty-one."

"Twenty-one?! Homes, you old! I thought you was fourteen or some shit."

"As long as I can remember people have guessed I was sixteen. Too tall when I was little. Now too soft when I'm big."

Like Juarez cares, already stalking off. Hopi shuffling away to watch the dogs from the far side of the pool. Better choice seeing how turning your back on Juarez is always a fool's move. That goes for Luther too.

Maybe there's another way. Kid's good with dogs. Luther could use that. His dogs too.

"Hopi, how are you with all that online shit?"

"Nobody quicker," Hopi grins. "Routers to cloud. Protocols to whatever kind of encryption you want. It's second na-na— natural."

But what's Luther tell Teyo? What had Teyo told him? What else was Teyo paying him for?

"Luther, you got any family besides this?" Hopi's question actually startles Luther, like him comin all the way around the pool without even catching Luther's notice, and now standing so close, just wobbling all big-eyed and curious at his side.

Luther doesn't even glare but whatever he

gives, beyond the ink, the whites in his eyes, the darker stuff his eyes hide, more than enough to back Hopi the fuck off.

"This should do," Piña shouts.

Carmelita tries to stop her but Piña's laugh's like a shove.

Piña's holding up one of Rosario's shoes, all pink with black feathers.

"Not her Manolos!" Carmelita shrieks.

Luther tells Hopi to take the shoe from Piña and go out on the diving board. Too afraid to walk, Hopi crawls to the edge, hands gripping the board, the shoe stuck in his mouth.

Juarez starts laughing again. Like this is the start of funny in the world. That's Juarez. Even his thousandth time is the first.

"Like a little bitch!" Juarez hoots. "He should be down there too. With them other bitches."

"Show them what you got," Tweetie shouts at Hopi.

So Hopi lifts one hand off the board. Wobbles

then. Wobbles more. Maybe he will end up down there. Dangles over the edge the Manolo or whatever it is.

At once the dogs cluster below. Even the few that had wandered out of the pool head back in, heads high, all growls and barks.

"Drop it," Luther finally orders.

Pink with black feathers drops. The barking stops. Carmelita moans.

Not even seconds. The pool filled with shreds, all that leather chewed through like meat, high heel to high heel.

Tookie still snarls. SloBo Jim snaps at scraps along with Rayful Eddie until all they can do is sniff and look elsewhere, looking up at Hopi, no longer wobbling on the board. The kid is hanging from the board! Tall too. Hopi only has a few feet to drop before he's squatting again, down in the water, the dogs all licking his face, but especially Tookie, taking his side, like Hopi's the only side.

"There's a first," Luther admits. Tweetie don't disagree, whispering back:

"What we really need is a cat."

Prey

'Houston promises we'll have the funds in the morning,' Ehtisham keeps saying [as if that erases his earlier 'The funds haven't arrived' {or erases the 'No, not yet' answering Anwar's 'Then the check is as good as good?'} {or erases the much earlier 'I have your check in hand!'}].

'Stop saying "Houston,"' Anwar sighs. 'It's not the city, it's not the company. It's one man. I'm sorry. Where is he?'

'Calling us back.'

'You spoke to him?'

'To his assistant. I assume it's his assistant. Though I've never spoken to this one before.'

For the last fifteen or twenty minutes Anwar and Ehtisham have paced inside The Glass House [one of the few conference areas on the floor {dead center ‹relatively soundproof «if transparent»›}] discussing Olin Winter Nodes [known mainly as Kozimo {venture capitalist ‹originally from Ukraine› supposedly working out of Houston and Wilmington ‹though he happily implies multiple homes elsewhere «everywhere»› even if his forever concern comes down to one thing ‹his company›: Dead Rowboats}].

Kozimo came out of nowhere when Blitzball had [briefly] showed interest in their game [or rather the dynamics, mechanics, and {of course} fun factor game play {Ehtisham, Talbot, Glasgow, and Anwar had originally started off with Epic's Unreal Engine ‹«figuring to licence it» before Mefisto had come along and suggested otherwise›}] along with inquiries by the likes of writer/designer Sami Järvi [rumored {*Max Payne, Alan Wake*}] Arnt Jensen [at PlayDead {*Limbo*}] and even local [rumored] Gil Elbaz [that had made no sense to Anwar {'Except the money part.' ‹Glasgow's point⟩}]. [after Kozimo/Dead Rowboats got involved] The rest seemed transformed into hearsay [the superposition-ing of all possibilities giving way to this wave-function col-lapse that was a man no one had met or {given Ehtisham's reportage} even spoken to].

Anwar can only keep from kicking himself [hands clasped before him {as if hands could have anything to do with stopping feet}] for making money realer than it ever was [though hands keep wanting to pull out the check {again} as if to demonstrate to eyes that this money is real}].

'The money will be there, Anwar. This is just a glitch,' Ehtisham says [sliding to the floor].

'We need to get Kozimo on the phone.'

Anwar doesn't take out the check but does make the mistake of looking at his phone [{his headache returning ⟨or an awareness of what never left?⟩} should have kept his hands clasped {even as he recognizes ⟨too⟩ that getting Kozimo on the phone ⟨and hearing whatever assurances⟩ will prove nothing ⟨the proof of the lie is not the lie in the words «the proof of the lie is in the pattern ⟨which needs no speech⟩»⟩}].

Voice Mail: Full
Missed Calls: 314
Text Messages: 6999

Regarding e-mails: 30,653 spam messages alone! There's no way to tell if his own wife called. Maybe even Kozimo [the man does have all of their numbers]. Or Enzio [again {in reference to a freelance gig ⟨re. Cataplyst-1⟩ ⟨one close call already «barely» averted⟩}]? Who else? [old friends, wel-come strangers, the ghosts of his parents {why not?}].

Again [like some kind of awful chorus]:

376

Good _____!

[insert here whatever is good {'Really,' as Astair might say ‹so long as it's real «if even real is good ❬ . . . ❭ or good is real» consequential at least› seriously!} how about gracious?]

What had Mefisto been thinking?

And that was the most troubling part: because Mefisto is always thinking [thinking beyond thinking {even if there remained this constant suspicion ‹on Anwar's part› that ‹one day› thinking upon thinking must lead to a failure to think altogether ‹isn't that what happened to the «savant» brother of Xanther's friend Farrokh «aka Kle»? «Anwar keeps forgetting ❬meaning❭ to ask Xanther about Phinneas»›} what happens sometimes to the brilliant ones].

Not that Mefisto was only about pranks and poor judgement. Without him neither he nor Ehtisham would be this close to transitioning their game from development into a profitable future. Mefisto had time again [by way of Subversion {later Git}] passed along suggestions [and invaluable additions] concerning the code comprising their game [Mefisto was the one who had originally prized them from Unreal 4 in order to commit to Unity {though of late has been urging them to move still further towards a game engine of their own ‹as if this small lot were able to produce on their own the required hundreds of thousands of lines «millions even» of code for a decent RPG «Anwar's lucky to eke out thirty good lines a day ❬of course Mefisto's

377

so good he can do it all in three!)»› Mefisto had even urged Anwar to explore inventing a new language ‹when commenting out some of Anwar's code «including his comments within ‹a classic Mefisto Easter egg)»›

>^.

the better the language
the better the engine;
see Quenya, Klingon, Ithkuil;
see Anwar?

.^<

‹of course Mefisto was a madman with enough energy to overwhelm any engine «not to mention language ‹hadn't he already invented his own language ⌈Rewordd⌋?)»» «‹Anwar's M.E.T. didn't even rate as a pet project» how then could this larger project «MOOWK» ever compare to Mefisto's grand desire 'to code an instrument by which any timid heart might experience for an instant the sublime music of Time!'? «granted Mefisto had been barely twenty and probably high when he wrote that»} though still later urging a commitment to that which was forever beyond encompassment] beyond games beyond restart beyond reboot beyond reckoning.

Anwar will stick with MOOWK [which he can't even get up and running for his daughter!].

// MOOWK = Mutual of Omaha's Wild Kingdom.

// *Mutual of Omaha's Wild Kingdom* a show Anwar enjoyed in the seventies on NBC [Mefisto online]. Long live Marlin ∴ Marlin Perkins d. 1986 ∴ [who always preceded that most dangerous mouse forever set on achieving immortality].

// Though all had recently agreed [even if Mefisto had remained noticeably silent on this decision] to change the name to the more user friendly [if still somewhat obscure] *Paradise Open.*

'Why *Paradise Open?*' Xanther asks as soon as he walks over.

'Xanther, you described paradise this morning as a perfect, peaceful place, without—'

'Death!' Xanther cries.

Anwar smiles [sitting down in front of the console].

'Still glitchville on the latest PO,' Glasgow informs him.

'Nonsense.'

'You were, uhm, going to, like, tell me the origin of, like, where the world came from, word, but then we got interrupted.'

'You are correct, daughter,' Anwar says [opening Visual Studio].

'Do you know the entomology of paradise?' Xanther asks Talbot.

'Etymology,' Anwar corrects. 'Entomology concerns bugs.'

'Which we're dealing with now,' Glasgow adds. 'In a computational metaphorical sorta way.'

'I bet Mr. Google knows,' Talbot answers.

'You're so goofy,' Talbot's [very young {very blonde}] girlfriend giggles.

'Let's keep him out of this,' Anwar says. 'Xanther already knows about the prefix peri-.'

'Like paradox?'

'Interesting. Para- means beside. Spellings here make this a little tricky. Think of para- in paradise as more like peri- in perimeter.'

'Around!'

'And to think my dad just drank beer,' Glasgow laughs.

'Excellent, daughter. The rest supposedly comes from an old Iranian language. With the root meaning wall.'

'A rounding wall?'

'Or a surrounding wall?'

'That's paradise?'

'Sounds like a prison,' Glasgow adds.

'It meant an enclosed garden or a protected place.'

'So why, I mean, what's the reason for paradise open?'

'Don't look at me,' Talbot shrugs.

'For now, daughter, I'll leave that puzzle to you.'

The screen sharpens into frames of scrolling code.

'Wow. I'll never understand that stuff.'

'Sure you could.'

Anwar types, toggles, and returns [commands {and lines} soon enough replaced with an image of tall grass {frozen} and a pale blue sky above {also frozen}].

'No puzzle now.' Xanther smiles.

'Image subitizes language,' Anwar murmurs [switching back to the code]. 'But at what cost?'

Talbot turns to Glasgow: 'My folks didn't think

I could even speak English. Actually most people in Florida don't speak English.'

'Kid, you're lucky to have such a dad,' Glasgow tells Xanther.

'Like, uhm, I don't know that?' Xanther sasses back. 'Before bed he reads me all sorts of stuff. Once from this book *I, Lion*' [Anwar too touched to correct her {even if that had been a mistake}] 'which was pretty adult, like pretty violent?' [At least Xanther knows it was a mistake.]

Anwar had only thought to pick *The Iliad* in order to frame a career like Dov's in terms of a long historical perspective [forgetting {mind a little slippery} just how visceral and bloody Homer could get {she would have been better served if Anwar had stuck to recounting Muhammad's victory over the Quraysh when occupying Mecca in 630}{instead of arms open arms?}].

In how many ways has Anwar already failed in the raising of [t]his brave and remarkable child?

At least this compiled version is still a debug build. Anwar tried a few alterations but PO continued to glitch and stick [once requiring another reboot]. Then just as Anwar was about to grab the prototype [crude polygon movement] or even a promo disc [ample action but without interactivity {screenshots and clips}] Talbot spotted the problem.

Even in his state of sloshiness the celerity of his analysis astonishes Anwar [celerity would be a good word for Xanther too {from *celer* meaning swift ‹kin to accelerate «on top of it reminding him ⟨probably by way of a French ⌈permissible?⌋*ciel*⟩ of sky» swiftness always on display there› however spurious} by wind, light and blue].

```
function LoadArea(areaName)

    local areas =
    {
        savanna_north =
        {
            file = "Savanna_North.xwl",
            script = "Savanna_North.xsc",
            pos = {x = 0, y = 100}
        },
        savanna_east =
        {
            file = "Savanna_East.xwl",
            script = "Savanna_East.xsc",
            pos = {x = 100, y = 0}
        },
        savanna_south =
        {
            file = "Savanna_South.xwl",
            script = "Savanna_South.xsc",
            pos = {X = 0, y = -100}
        },
        savanna_west =
        {
            file = "Savanna_West.xwl",
            script = "Savanna_West.xsc",
            pos = {x = -100, y = 0}
        }
    }

    for k, v in pairs(areas) do
        if(k == areaName) then
            LoadAsset(v.file, v.pos.x, v.pos.y)
            LoadScript(v.script)
            return
```

'See below savanna_south? After the pos? That X there should be lowercase.'

Talbot was born and raised outside Jacksonville [if raising is what you'd call it] by two parents who warned their children to avoid alligators and not drink until after sundown [while they went off to tend their pot farm {which they mostly smoked ‹paying for large-carton cereal boxes and cases of condensed milk with food stamps›}].

Talbot had discovered two things simultaneously: computer games were a refuge and so were numbers. According to this stocky man [proud of his mullet, wife beaters, and illegible tattoos {strung along his forearms in every shade of ink except black and blue}] it was a truck driver [{at 11 PM} in Macclenny {who was willing to buy beer if anyone could call out the sales tax on a case of Coors ‹which Talbot had done easily «for a case, six pack, and bottle»›}] who [impressed by the boy] had asked what he liked more than beer, 'girls or weed?' to which Talbot had responded, 'Computer games.' 'You're lucky then,' the truck driver had said. 'Computer games are made up of numbers!' [driving off without buying anyone {even himself} any beer {which supposedly Talbot had lost interest in by then ‹because though he always knew he was good at numbers «silly as it may have seemed» he had never made the connection between numbers and games›}].

Talbot was determined to remake himself in all ways different from both his parents [though smoking pot every day was one habit of theirs he had been unable to eschew]. Anwar had nothing against the quieting effects of marijuana but had noticed [over the years {as Talbot smoked more and more}] that his friend's paranoia had grown.

No question the drug backgrounded the interferences of certain [neurotic] emotional hazards which allowed for greater [stress-reduced] focus but over the length of time the benefits of useful connectivity also resulted in a curious uptick of spurious connectivity [justified by only the frailest filaments of association and 'that feeling' {a phrase Talbot had been using more and more ‹'My spider sense, i.e., a sting-happy spider settling on the back of my frickin neck for BLDs!' «'Breakfast-lunch-dinner' Xanther later explained»›}]. Even now it was evident [with this off-the-cuff remark]: 'Problem-o solved unless we're facing deeper issues involving Stellar Wind.'

Or this odd veer:

'Anwar, you know about the clips, right?'
'I'm sorry. Video clips?'
'Like Clip 4?'
'I don't believe so.' Anwar unable to avoid catching Glasgow look away [another sign that Talbot is about to descend down one of his paranoid rabbit holes {'where the rabbits are all dead thanks to The Thing That Eats All Rabbits that never quite comes into view,' as Ehtisham has described it before ‹who is himself not entirely immune to grand paranoid speculations «not that Anwar hasn't got caught in that warren too ⟨fortunately a low dose of Paroxetine exposed it as just lumpy dirt in need of sunshine⟩»› ‹likely Mefisto is the greatest offender though his disease has more to do with the sheer delight «in the way he finds the most disparate elements can reach, span, and connect ⟨four friends bound together by paranoia or rabid imaginations⟩»› ‹Glasgow seems to have no such tendencies but still enjoys his share of Ludlum and certain sci-fi thrillers «not to mention Talbot when he's on a good jag ⟨sometimes⟩»›}].

384

'The Man? The Kid?' Talbot continues [while tinkering with the code {hunting for tedious errors}]. 'Or Toland Ouse? Zeke Rilvergaile? The girl Audra? Willow Rue? And now this other guy ∴ **Realic Tarnen** ∴ ? What happened to him?'

'What?'

'Not kid-friendly.'

Anwar winces.

'Tell me, please,' Xanther immediately starts up.

'No,' Anwar says [stern enough to check both Xanther and Talbot {too stern? ‹frowns say yes›}].

Good news: sloppy scripting seems the only problem [Anwar had had a tinge that maybe something deriving from their in-house content-creation tools {like Yugen Yobbery or Hees and Boney} had been the problem {or worse something that was the result of his own work}]. The Unity Engine appears more than fine though [that includes Anwar's module {no need to take an hour to recompile the beast ‹or embarrass himself anymore in front of his daughter›}].

Anwar's proud of M.E.T. [inventive, concise, even cunning] but for all it does in the name of AI [it does nothing in the name of true AI {Ehtisham and the lads just call it that ‹as do most engineers «including Anwar himself» ‹'The AI part.'›}] M.E.T. has zero to do with self-sustaining awareness [Braitenberg had taught Anwar this years ago {complex behavior implies complex cognition ‹conversely simple behavior implies simple cognition› ‹neither though are necessarily true›}]. Still his 'AI part' is fun.

Xanther settles on Anwar's knee [long arms dangling around his shoulder {light as a bird}].

'One problem faced by many games comes down

to interaction,' Anwar tells her. 'The dominant first-person interaction too easily reduces to shoot or seize.'

'What about puzzle games then? You know, like, when you have to figure out stuff? Like *Limbo?*'

'Excellent point, daughter. While less about actions and still necessitating more thought, Question-Answer Gaming Scenarios are still limited to specific answers and tend to relate more to the environment: organizing objects, generating correct numbers, uncovering reproducible patterns.'

'*Minecraft?*' Glasgow chimes in.

'As Glas knows, *Minecraft* was in part an inspiration. That game willingly explores the pleasures of just assembling things.' [{the equivalent of computational Legos or a dollhouse} Anwar knows that Xanther has played a little of *Minecraft* {with beautiful results}.] 'That said the interactions remain material.'

Xanther shifts [uncomfortably?] on his leg [{listening still? ‹again haunted by another «endless» string of questions?›} eyes fixed on the screen as Talbot continues to enter corrections].

'The reason for so many FPS may have less to do with a penchant for violence than with an inability to program more complex encounters.'

'Oh, like between people?'

'Between player and machine. What programmers crave are more advanced ways of negotiating with computationally generated figures and environments. Negotiation is the operative word. And at this stage of the game, creating personas capable of mimicking human behavior, even on a child's level, is impossible. Animal behavior however . . . '

Xanther looks back at Anwar [eyes wide now {with wonder?}].

'You mean like a dog?'

'Or a lion? A hyena? How about an owl?'

'Really?'

Talbot restarts the game again only to watch it [again] hang [though Anwar can see the possibilities still hanging {wondrously} before Xanther's eyes].

[hiccups aside] Anwar remains very proud of his part in the creation of this game [wondrous possibilities hanging before even his eyes]. It seems obvious to him that Dead Rowboats would want nothing more than to fund *Paradise Open*. Or if not Kozimo, then PlayDead. Or even Blizzard, EA, or some zaibatsu [with Miyamoto's blessing to boot].

The concept was good. The work was good. The results appealing.

'*Paradise Open* still not open,' Talbot grunts.

[one table over] A stranger [likely a friend of an intern here {unlikely even twenty-five}] had started to leer and lean in on Winchester. Talbot's focus didn't shift.

'Are you here with your father?' the kid [as a last-ditch effort] had the temerity to suggest.

'No,' Winchester shook her head [applying another layer of glossy pink lipstick]. 'But sometimes I call him daddy.'

'Anwar?'

Except Anwar only hears the voice after Xanther tells him there is one [whispering in his ear, 'Dad, some lady wants you'].

Carmen Sacco is one of the interns [{ringlets like copper} an expert at digital marketing {with an MBA from UCLA's Anderson School of Management ⟨who was hired on after her early-on declaration that she wanted in on the ground floor of something heading 'super cloud level'⟩}].

'I think Ehti wants you,' Carmen motions towards The Glass House [where Ehtisham is indeed signalling for him]. 'Also, I just wanted to add how excited I am. You deserve this measure of faith. I'm proud I've measured up as someone who now counts as staff.'

Anwar smiles [doing everything to keep his lips from giving away his distress {their nervous dance ⟨childhood tics⟩}].

'Have you met my daughter? Xanther, this is Ms. Sacco.'

Carmen doesn't miss a beat [he can hear as he walks away {going on about bangs ⟨and how beautiful Xanther's eyes are «'They're different colors like Kate Bosworth's. Like David Bowie.' 'Thanks. It's like called heterochromia. Bowie though may have anisocoria which means just one of his pupils is bigger and that only makes the color of the iris look different when compared to the other. Your hair is so beautiful. I'd love hair like that. How would you define a game engine?'»}].

'We'll see,' Ehtisham says [closing the door {sealing them within The Glass House ⟨again⟩}].

'You spoke with Kozimo?'

'Left messages. A lot of messages.'

Anwar sighs.

'But I did speak with Paul Bucksea, his CFO. We're fine.'

'Do I need to apply for a job at Trader Joe's?'

'Bucksea told me they'd be fools to lose out on this. You and I both know he's not wrong.'

'No, he's not wrong. I do believe that.'

'I do too. So my advice: buy Xanther her dog. Whatever your family needs. I'm counting my own chickens hatched. We are celebrating.'

Which is when Anwar hears it [inside The Glass House {though there is nothing else inside there ‹except for two non-believers›}].

'Did you hear that?' [like the tiniest squeak].

'What?' Ehtisham asks.

Anwar hears it again [{like the tiniest cry for help} now it's outside The Glass House {out on the main floor? ‹in need «immediate need ⟨no question⟩»›}].

'There?'

Ehtisham hears nothing.

Beyond the glass doors Anwar finds the expected din of music, laughter, chatter [increasingly more drunk chatter] along with [at various workstations] warring speaker sets demonstrating the clamorous pleasures of various games.

Maybe from one of the windows?

Outside?

In all that rain?

And there it is [a third time!] and louder now [much louder!]! Definitely outside [has to be on the ledge {definitely in the rain}].

Anwar struggles to raise the glass [where does it slide open? {where are the latches? ‹should he call someone to help him? «call over Glasgow and Talbot ⟨even Carmen⟩ where did Ehtisham go?»› here's the latch} the window must swing open] seeing now how it pops out from the bottom.

'Daddy!'

[Xanther yells ‹from across the room›.] 'Quick, come here!' And Anwar's already on the way [anything for Xanther {only understanding ‹as he gets closer› that her cry isn't of terror but of excitement}]. 'Talbot fixed it!'

And suddenly Anwar's no longer sure what he just heard [only looking back briefly {he didn't even manage to open the window ‹though he can still hear the bedlam of all that rain «drowning out even the traffic below ⟨what else could he hear besides that if not his imagination?⟩»› certainly nothing more than the rain› especially through a closed window ‹♭}}].

Suddenly there's a breeze too. Weird. Who knows where it came from [rustling papers, Carmen's red ringlets]. Not a window open. Not even an AC humming. Just Xanther's big grin.

Ehtisham joins the group then [Talbot pouring a drink {an Arnold Palmer ‹Ehtisham abstains from alcohol›} as well as a Bob {?} for himself {Glasgow takes another beer ‹Anwar too «to sip»›} as well as another Bob {?} for Winchester]. Cups raised. Xanther raises a [happy] fist.

Suddenly Anwar misses Mefisto. [for all the {incomprehensible ‹curious «?»›} mess that he created with his prank] Why isn't his friend here?

'To Mefisto,' he suddenly says [and immediate echoes prove him right for saying so].

'Use the four arrows here. Press the spacebar when you want to start.'

Xanther [at once] punches the spacebar [another laugh from everyone {Xanther more eager than ever ‹which wouldn't disturb Anwar «it's good that she's excited and enthusiastic» were it not for one of her wildly pumping legs «her right» sometimes «though certainly not always ⟨and certainly not even often⟩» signalling the onset of an event› is that what's on the immediate horizon?} Anwar's breath always coming up short at just the thought].

But Xanther's already flying [knowing the keys {almost} before Talbot points out what they do {very quick ⟨and very very adept⟩}].

'As fast as you can,' Talbot urges.
'Where am I going? Am I S? Z?'

Xanther weaves through the high grass dodging boulders, leaping over small trenches [she's seen this grass before but never moved through it {not like this ⟨S&Z «indeed»⟩}].

'Who knows!' Talbot laughs.
'You don't know?'
'Not yet.'
'Then what am I doing?' Xanther asks [a little annoyed {easing up on her acceleration across the African savanna}].
'Don't slow down!'
'Why not?' [though she's racing again].
'You have to evade,' Glasgow chimes in.
'Evade?'
'Stay clear of,' Ehtisham adds.
'You have to escape, Xanther,' Talbot says.
'Something's chasing me?'
'Remember that blood spray?'

'Remember, Xanther, it's still a prototype,' Anwar adds now. 'The identities and details will come. The point is that even though you can't see it, something's pursuing you.' That was the M.E.T. part [brought to life {activated} by Xanther's direction {if ‹purposefully› deprived of the absolute knowledge of Xanther's course and so anticipating her dash ‹using various vectors and «in more than a few cases» cheats› to stop her ‹which will happen at any moment›}]. 'Something's about to catch up with you.'

More grass keeps parting.

For some reason [digital instinct{?}] Xanther has started to bounce left to right [left to right {continuing with the simple rhythm}] only to suddenly change it to left-left-left followed [just as quickly] by a series of right-right-rights.

Then stops [stops hard {wheels around hard ‹and fast too›}{Anwar's pleased to discover Glasgow has restored the panting-breath f/x}].

'What am I?'

'Who knows!' Talbot laughs again.

'Seriously? Well I know I'm big enough to make that path there.'

Xanther eyes [as they all do] all the trampled grass she's left behind.

'Really, Xanther, we haven't decided yet,' Glasgow adds gently.

'You're prey,' Ehtisham finally explains.

'And coming down the path, after me, that's the predator?'

'If it takes that path,' Anwar says.

Is little irrelevant

The sun won't stay behind the cloud.

— Armenian proverb

Shnorhk lift next box from trunk.

"With this I can help."

"Always English with you. And always broken, dissembling."

Shnorhk ignore barb by old Mnatsagan.

"I get better. I learn."

But Shnorhk not learn. Not get better. Maybe not ignore barb either. Ride here was so peaceful.

"I say this, dear friend, only because you speak such beautiful Armenian. It is the third thing I miss about you most."

Shnorhk clutch cardboard to chest and trot ahead for porch. That worse than barb. Nothing worse than gentleness on day like so. Mnatsagan keep up with umbrella overhead. Must not let precious papers get wet.

Inside home, back twinge as Shnorhk place box next to other four. Back not like idea of four more. Shnorhk not like idea. Boxes dry but not Shnorhk.

Still old man is old friend. Teacher. Called from campus in need of help. While Shnorhk still at courthouse. Not far away at all. Not often Mnatsagan call for help. Maybe ask once to boil tea or move rug.

Shnorhk drive there straight from courthouse. Even if feel in chest is darker than clouds above, than rain in gutters.

"If you are lightning too, we are all in trouble." Which Shnorhk not got. "You look like this storm. Sit, dear friend. Tell me what has happened."

But Shnorhk not want to sit, he sit all day, and to what purpose?, so judge can say stand, and say Shnorhk to blame, and make record of blame, at steep price?

Shnorhk prefer pace in campus office with pictures of Tumanyan, Yeghishe Charents, Khachatur Abovyan on wall, books on wall, on desk too, on floor, papers everywhere too, on floor, on shelves, stuffed behind pictures of family this old friend no longer have.

tip-tip-tip

"Yes, it's a mess. And partially why I reached out to you today. To at least free up some room here and take those home."

Boxes of tapes, more papers, CDs, maybe DVDs. A mess, yes.

"They are all we have."

Another thing Shnorhk not got. So much of day he not understand. Shnorhk tired of what is not his to understand.

tip-tip-tip

There again. 3/4? Metronome? Not always in 3/4.

tip-tip-tip
tip-tip-tip

Maybe Shnorhk hear things?

"As my retirement nears, I'm confounded, are you sure you won't sit down?, I'm confounded to learn that one persistent dilemma has yet to get easier: what to hold on to at all costs and what to let go of despite all costs."

"What is here, what is not here," Shnorhk answer glum. "Is little irrelevant."

"Little irrelevant?" Mnatsagan had laughed then. "Shnorhk, I don't know what that means. And if I guess correctly, what you think it means, then I don't believe you."

Shnorhk stop pacing. Judge not believe Shnorhk. Own lawyer not believe Shnorhk. Now Mnatsagan not believe Shnorhk.

The professor think because they know same land, same language, know pearl barley, pickled cabbage, gum-blistering khash, that he know Shnorhk!?

As if they anything alike: Mnatsagan is beautiful man. Where Shnorhk have squat face, Mnatsagan have high cheeks and thin nose. Where Shnorhk have forearms thick as neck, Mnatsagan have long arms like dancer. Where Shnorhk have wild brows and brown teeth, Mnatsagan have brows and teeth white like snows of Aragats. Where Shnorhk have stubby impractical fingers, Mnatsagan have practical hands to balance bow or write words with music enough to change world for better. Judge would believe Mnatsagan. Officer would believe Mnatsagan.

Shnorhk had coughed hard in hand.

tip-tip-tip

"There's a relevant thing you can let go of," Mnatsagan had smiled. Handed over tissue too. "We are musicians, you and I. We understand that what the chest holds is key. Not here." Mnatsagan pointed at his head. "However only playing as often as possible frees the heart's order." And then suddenly, laughter, brows bouncing up, mocking himself, this seriousness. "Or as my violin teacher always said: blood is the best evidence of practicing."

What would violin teacher have thought of Shnorhk's tissue? What kind of practicing was that?

For an hour, they had moved boxes, first carrying one each through campus halls until exit door leading to parking lot. Then Mnatsagan would put his box down and lead Shnorhk with umbrella.

But Mnatsagan couldn't stand leaving his box behind, even for moment, even if just inside by exit door, dry but unwatched, even if nothing but paper and dust.

So after that, Shnorhk had carried box whole way from office to trunk while professor opened doors, locked doors, opened doors, opened trunk, locked trunk, back and forth, nine times.

"What is true and what truth is to be preserved is everything," Mnatsagan had said on fifth box.

This after Shnorhk had spitted on again about his traffic offense. "You talk about the importance of witness. Do you have any idea what you hold now in your hands? What I have asked you to help me keep safe?"

Shnorhk had no idea. And not wanted to ask. He knew Mnatsagan profession. Knew he teach history. And on history he wrote books. Mnatsagan one of nation top scholars on Medz Yeghern. Erdoğan care enough to forbid him entrance to country.

No country know Shnorhk enough to care enough to ban him. Shnorhk not care either. Shnorhk already spent all caring. Shnorhk tired now, always tired, especially of history. Barely understand present.

"Decades I have spent on analysis," Mnatsagan said on sixth box. "A basis, however, that is something truly valuable. That I can preserve and offer and so face the Big Retirement, for which we are guaranteed no pension or delight, with a clear conscience."

"What have you ever had on your conscience?"

"There is a Czech writer whose work was extremely political but it was also so extremely convoluted it communicated nothing to anyone except to himself and in that way, because he was the one writing it down, offered some personal exculpation for reporting crimes made by the state even if his reports failed to alert anyone to those crimes. I've said what matters, he seems to have shouted, but all that matters he had shouted in an unintelligible way."

"Only your desire to tell me this is untelligible," Shnorhk said, on way for seventh box. "I know nothing of politics. I drive cab."

After load up last box, Shnorhk head toward Mnatsagan's house, up by Fountain, near Western. Mnatsagan sat in back.

"I be limo driver!" Shnorhk had insisted, holding door open. Rain beat down to "drown even Ararat!" Mnatsagan had yelled, while sliding in. Would have drowned old man if he had gone around to passenger side.

"If there is justice," Shnorhk at one point had grumbled, "this Armerican not know it."

"Armerican?" Mnatsagan had grinned. "Is that what you call yourself these days?"

"Not really American," Shnorhk answered. "Not really Armenian."

After which Mnatsagan had asked more about this life of driving taxi. Shnorhk meet all sorts of people: basketball stars, store owners, construction workers, auditors, call girls, cowboys, now and then a runaway.

Then Shnorhk telled story about driving Hovik Garibyan one night. Hovik was driver who drove Buford Furrow. Buford Furrow is guy who killed kids at Jewish Center. Garibyan sat in back seat, in middle, same way Mnatsagan sat, telling how he had sat in Shnorhk's place, not knowing killer at his back whole time, hours and hours, driving all way to Vegas for $800. This back in 1999. Furrow mostly sleep but once ask Hovik where he from. Hovik Garibyan is Armenian. Hovik had told truth. What though if he had said different?

North of freeway, still on Western, woman had tried lane change. No room but still moved to cut Shnorhk off. Shnorhk not give way.

Next she put on blinker, waving. Shnorhk still not give way. Woman screaming by then. Give Shnorhk one finger. Shnorhk give five. Either five of hers or wave. Let her decide.

CAR DRIVER RATING

GMC Yukon Denali

QUOTE:

"Make mountain out of a
speed bump."

DRIVER:

Afraid housewives.
Husbands afraid of afraid
housewives.
Cowards.

TRUTH:

Maybe signals. Hogs lanes.
Hogs parking spaces.
Bullies other cars at turns.
Never polite waves.

BUMPER STICKER:

N/A

LICENSE PLATE:

NXT2N1

"Be a man," Shnorhk had yelled when Denali pulled up even with cab. "Talk to me."

Woman couldn't talk. She just cursed, pounded wheel, pounded horn. Shnorhk left pounding to rearview, sees Mnatsagan there instead.

Whatever reason, having old man in taxi, no matter morning, no matter boxes, boxes Shnorhk will have to move again, this was pleasure.

"Do these sort of interactions happen often?" Mnatsagan asked.

"Yes, traffic is rough speech."

Above and beyond traffic, though, is Traffic. Religion for Shnorhk: how people move and relate.

Then fire truck come screaming north, two more fire trucks, plus paramedic. Cars avert right to let emergency through. Shnorhk always moved by this sight.

Denali, though, not stop. Took advantage to change lanes, speed ahead, catch up again with Shnorhk. To crosswalk. Brakes screeched. Honking again.

"Is she okay?" Mnatsagan had whispered.

"I would say no."

There was spit on inside her window.

"This is why no one wants to fuck you!" was last thing Shnorhk heard her scream.

There, yes, she probably right. Not that Shnorhk wanted to do that body thing with anyone either. Definitely not with Patil. About only thing Shnorhk can touch these days is wheel. Clench it really.

Though never with Mnatsagan around. No matter crazy driver of Denali. Shnorhk relax. Maybe because Mnatsagan can speak of Talin, caves of Zangezur, or, without asking for Shnorhk to enjoy or even remember, invoke pleasures of Zurnas played at dusk before tables set with long plates full of ishkhan, silvery gray trout from Lake Sevan, and vodka too, and maybe churchkhelas for the children? Or maybe Shnorhk just relax because old friend is secretly saint.

Mnatsagan live like saint too, in tiny house, middle of block, with dark green slats, windows bordered white, and small plot of land bordered with low white fence. There is small white porch too with thick square posts. Chairs in front Mnatsagan use when smoke pipe when other musicians come out to smoke.

The gardens in front and in back grow thick with thick green leaves and blooms of bright colors. His garden always seem thick with blooms no matter season. "That's because I plant for the season."

What does Shnorhk understand about garden or pipe smoke? He and Patil live in same Glendale apartment for thirty years now.

"Of all places. Not here with this old roof but in my university office," Mnatsagan says now, as Shnorhk sets down eighth box in narrow home office. "Multiple leaks! And all in the closet too. You may have heard them? Almost in 3/4? Tip-tip-tip?"

Ah! So Shnorhk hadn't been hearing things.

"By the grace of god, seriously, I pulled these all out before so much as a drop fell. Coincidence too. I had just received an e-mail from the Center for Holocaust and Genocide Studies, at the University of Minnesota, to start the process of having all this properly transcribed and archived. You know how hopeless I am with e-mails and technologies that go beyond bow rosin."

Mnatsagan still write on pad of paper. Has electric typewriter on desk. Office here is very neat. Everything centered. Pens in place.

Paper neatly stacked. Narrow window with bars against theft opening up to backyard. Hydrangeas bounce in downpour.

"I said I help," Shnorhk repeat. Old friend stubborn. Stubborn saint. "To convert to electronic files is not such problem. Scanning paper is easy. Just takes time."

For some reason, Shnorhk good at computer things. GPS, phones, software. Has knack for technology and learn fast. Though not a natural. Just learned to keep up with her.

"How much time?" Mnatsagan ask.

"Five years," Shnorhk answer. Not heard answer until too late.

But Mnatsagan laugh.

"That quick."

"I joke, I joke," Shnorhk lie, getting down on knees, examine box more closely. Surprised to find contents so neat. Not how he remembered. Other boxes too. All neat.

Neat rows of video cassettes. Neat rows of audio cassettes. Neat rows of CDs and DVDs. Neatly stacked folders. Neatly stacked documents. All neatly stapled.

How could this be?

Had injustice of court's decision afflicted world with unjust rendering?

Had disorder of Shnorhk's mind disordered the contents of these boxes?

"A month," Shnorhk grunts. Ample time. "Two weeks with long nights. I have scanner. Not computer though. I could borrow one though. Patil's brother have many computers."

Mnatsagan pats Shnorhk on shoulder.

"Are you sure it's not too much of an imposition?"

"This easy. Really. A dog could do it."

Shnorhk had gone out and braved rain for final box. One hand pinching box to side. One hand holding umbrella above box. One side of Shnorhk drenched. Shnorhk must hurry inside. Shnorhk must get dry.

But cry stop Shnorhk dead. Near too. By porch maybe. Maybe under steps?

Something meowyling.

Something in need of help.

· · ·

"I found cakes!" Mnatsagan shout from door.

In tiny kitchen Shnorhk voice concern.

"Maybe a possum? A baby raccoon? A tiny bird?"

Shnorhk shake head: "It more sounded like tiny child."

Mnatsagan fill big mugs with black tea. He never has milk only thick cream.

"I heard it only once," Shnorhk add.

"Only once," Mnatsagan pause. "Only once is a problem. Though sometimes a blessing too."

Shnorhk taste cake. Here a blessing. Butteryer than buttery cream in tea.

"What are in boxes?" Shnorhk finally ask.

"Not a clue, eh? Yet still you helped me. You are a good man. Very good."

Good? Ha! Shnorhk want to spit tea on floor, shatter cup, show old friend how good! Shnorhk guzzle tea instead. Scald throat. Shoves cup forward for more.

But Mnatsagan does not pour

more tea. Instead he leads Shnorhk back to office.

"729," Mnatsagan explains.

Why had Shnorhk not noticed this either? How such beautiful man treat boxes? Guard, that was obvious. Watch over, obvious too. But now, here, on this neat desk, what reverent hand hovering so tenderly above contents. Like mother hen over hatchlings not yet hatched.

"This is the basis I mentioned. Primary research, upon which all analysis depends, is indispensable. What I have here is the foundation of our understanding of those heinous events at the beginning of a century already past.

"Here before you: the first-hand testimony of 729 women and men who survived those atrocities. Taped, filmed, recorded. What they saw, what they experienced, what they survived."

Like Shnorhk say: saint.

"This is my life's work. Or the end of my life's work." Another sad smile. "All I desire: to see this studied, copied, properly placed, and cared for."

Shnorhk realize then there are more than just nine boxes here. Narrow office made even narrower by volumes of documents.

"So dear Shnorhk, is this, how did you put it, 'little irrelevant'?"

"We start now!" Shnorhk shout, extend hand.

"Now?" Mnatsagan laugh. "Now we have more cake."

"Ha!" Shnorhk laugh louder. Wait until he tell Patil. "Soon, like you, Turkey won't allow me visit either. But what I care for that cancer on humanity?"

Shnorhk expect more laughs. Mnatsagan only shake head.

"No dear friend, hard as this is to grasp, we are friends of Turkey. What can we do for the dead who are already dead? Pity instead those who labor so hard to uphold a lie. It is such work that robs them of fruitful work the future would bless."

Then Mnatsagan returns to living room, where on many nights, over many years, he, Shnorhk, the rest, crowded around the fireplace, took out instruments and played and played and played.

"We toil on behalf of Turkey to bless Turkey." Pouring more tea.

Shnorhk drink tea but will never bless Turkey. Spit on that soil. Spit on idea of that soil. Shnorhk cough instead. Cough hard. Has to spit on hand. Hides hand in pocket.

"Are you okay?"

Mnatsagan miss nothing.

"Patil want me to see doctor. Just old cold. A walking cold I need walk off."

"Նա ուժեղ լույս է: Բոլորս բախտավոր կլինենք որ նման լույս ունենանք: Maybe following her advice will serve you well?"

Of course he right. Shnorhk will follow his advice to follow her advice and see doctor who will give him aspirin and cold medicine and charge him week of work.

"The lads will be here tomorrow night. Come back to us. Help us fill this place with music. Գեղեցկությունա թող փայլի:"

"Always Armenian with you. Patil try same tricks too. I no understand."

"Oh Shnorhk, how beautifully you speak Armenian, the third thing

I miss most about you. The second thing I miss most about you: how beautifully you play."

Shnorhk not say anything. What trying to say only take away. Shnorhk just scald throat with more tea and eat cake after cake.

Grateful still, in end, that Mnatsagan, always kind, is kind enough not to say the first thing he miss so much.

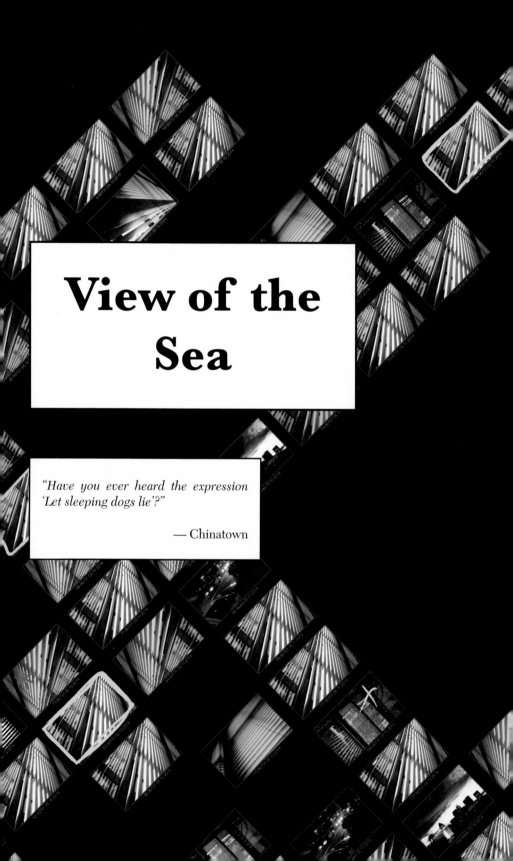

View of the Sea

"*Have you ever heard the expression
'Let sleeping dogs lie'?*"

— Chinatown

That happens once, twice in a career. Some detectives never get once. Today was why Özgür applied to the Police Academy. More than Chandler or Hammett, today was Conan Doyle, Columbo, CSI: Take-Your-Pick, Sherlock Holmes, the BBC reboot with Benedict Cumberbatch and Martin Freeman — Clive Buckle or Bilbo Baggins depending on your quest. Özgür had had no quest, only the usual questions, and this morning, out of the splash, the answers had materialized.

Oz can still see Balascoe hailing the mail carrier who by that point had already started to fill his canvas bag with envelopes, waterfalls spilling off his pith helmet with each reach, Balascoe saying something amusing enough to get both men smiling, focused on the insides of the mailbox. Then Balascoe was yelling something, he'd seen something, officers starting to move his way, even that boot Stan Gebbis started sprinting, which only got more people running, P-IIs doing their best to keep pedestrians and PeSTs back behind the tape.

Someone actually started applauding. Probably Gebbis. Everyone looking at Balascoe, that face grinning like it never knew a sneer, holding up the arm of the mail carrier, like a title fight victory, except instead of a glove, a package.

About the right size to hold a flip-flop or a pair of gloves. One in there likely to be stuffed with a lot of hundred dollar bills.

Only one person didn't care about Balascoe. And she wasn't looking at Özgür because of anything he had figured out. Özgür had forgotten that look. No wave, no smile. Nothing lips can give away. Just all of a sudden wide-eyed. As if Nyra wasn't seeing him but what they might have been if they'd made it, if they'd made up, if they hadn't gone so fast to unmake what they'd had a chance to see through.

Özgür changed directions. Not so hardboiled after all. Gave Nyra a hug. "Are you fucking serious?" she squawked. "What's that for?" "You looked like you needed one." "Get the fuck out of here."

Knowing Balascoe, his Rampart captain will likely call Özgür in tomorrow about some bullshit complaint that despite protest and repeated requests to absent himself from a criminal investigation going on near Leimert Park, he had still refused to heed the proper jurisdictional chain of command. And that will be the last word on Marvin D'Organidrelle aka Android who had put a mind of violence in the service of a plan.

There was a time when Özgür might have strained for what thin satisfaction comes from recognition. Though the real satisfaction was already his as he had walked away: greeting the questions with answers that assembled one muddy situation into one unassailable solution.

And maybe if there were a gaze somehow able to follow him, wandering off like he did, alone in that storm, beyond the eyes of P-II Nyra Carlton, of others, beyond even those eyes that are somehow his own, how Oz still wants to see himself, at least now and then, shaped in silver, though he'd take the grainy color too, of Elliott Gould in *The Long Goodbye* ∴ 1973 ∵, perhaps whoever commanded such a view, whether street-side or bird's-eye, sparrow or something larger, probably with far darker wings, approval would greet this moment in Özgür's life.

His 10:30, which Özgür had been twenty minutes late for, was reminder enough that too often mystery is the norm. At least Cletious Bou doesn't answer the door anymore with expectations. The crime took place over twenty years ago. Özgür still has the murder book. He still rereads it when he can. He knows the boy was Cletious Bou's only child. He knows the boy's mother died of a broken heart a year later. The coroner would say it was a stroke but Cletious has described many times how his wife had stopped eating, stopped sleeping. "Only one thing worse than puking when you've nothing left to puke and that's crying."

On some visits, they just talk about his wife. Cletious hasn't remarried. From what Özgür can see he hasn't found companionship either. The TV's never off. On other visits, they talk only about the boy, a conversation that of late has become more and more about all the boy never got a chance to do, which Özgür knows is just another way of saying what Cletious himself will never take the chance to do. There are crimes the brave learn to let go of. But there are crimes that have it the other way around and don't let go of you.

Today they had talked about the case. His boy, Jasper Bou, just a teenager, was walking home, near Coliseum and Hauser, and at not even three in the afternoon, when someone shot him point-blank in the back of the head. The suspicion was some gang initiation, a knucklehead proving himself with a trigger. Cletious Bou's boy couldn't have been anything more than a victim. He was a clarinet player. Played in school and practiced every day for a minimum of four hours. "Jasp barely had time to tie his two shoes let alone say two words enough to make two friends. What he was closest to was playing slow, playing two times fast, and was already doubling the changes when he went down."

Cletious Bou's not the only one Özgür visits once or twice a year. He doesn't expect anything either. It's not like over a kitchen counter some fact or alternate approach will come into plain sight. It's not even important that the pain come up but the pain always does come up because it's the only thing he and Cletious have in common. Özgür always feels sick afterwards, some pit deeper than guts, and more than just a reminder, buckling him over in his seat by the time he starts his car.

But he does it to keep those files and boxes alive. *Wer die Wahl hat, hat die Qual.* ∷ Whoever has the choice has the torment. ∷

Before saying goodbye, Cletious had gone off on something he had heard on the news. Someone in Chinatown had been killed in an accident, only the accident had left him in pieces, many pieces, or five pieces, whatever the number, carefully apportioned pieces. What kind of hit-and-run does that?, Cletious wanted to know. But most of all Cletious wanted to know, does something that heinous go unsolved too?

Afterwards, Planski cancelled their nooner. Özgür was disappointed but still made his way to Post & Beam. In the parking lot, however, a call followed her text. This time Özgür heeded his indigestion, popped a Tums, and headed south.

Katla.

It's nice to be invited for a change. Even if Özgür had to drive through the rain down to Long Beach. South of Wilmington. Not far off of West Paseo del Mar. Detective Florian Sérbulo raises the venetian blinds and shows Özgür the view of the sea. Almost nice enough to forget the parquet floors, cottage cheese ceiling, all the furniture thanks to Swedish design out of Carson. His wet socks.

"Is it true you might pull the pin?"

"Elaine's applied for teaching positions all over. Wherever she goes I'll go."

"I'll believe that when I see it."

"Seeing isn't everything."

"Didn't you just Drop? There goes that retirement bonus."

"Have you seen Elaine?"

"From far enough away to think she's make believe."

"And her?" Özgür nods towards the elderly woman beyond the glass, slumped outside in an Adirondack chair on the porch. She's sobbing to the paramedic who keeps trying to give her oxygen.

"She doesn't want to believe. Rented the kids the duplex. Thought they were students."

"But they weren't?"

"Actually they were. Grad students. With money. This real estate isn't cheap."

Katla-katla.

The bodies are gone but Florian still gives Özgür the tour. Here's where the three were found: bent over the side of the tub. Almost as if in prayer. Except wrists and ankles were cinched blue with white cable ties and their heads were submerged. No blood. No sign of struggle. Bleach had been added to the water.

"I didn't see any contusions or bruises. Like if they'd been conked on the head. We're still trying to fix a time, a date. The coroner will have something to say but this went down clean."

Katla. Katla-katla.

Everything else is clean too. Too clean. Unless you count coffee beans and a bag of weed in the freezer or a closet stuffed with Adderall and Advil. Özgür doesn't count it.

"Not a reporter in sight."

"Harbor Division is a long way from Hollywood."

"Impressive."

Katla-katla, katla-katla.

Two rooms for four beds. More parquet. More venetian blinds. The only ACs are in the third room where the computers live. No screens just domino-lines of black towers. Still on.

"They're hooked up to cable, the telephone line, satellite dishes on the roof."

"More than one dish?"

"Yeah. Like seven."

"That's something."

"How about this: these babies here, as far as we can tell, wiped clean. C-III told us to hold tight until an SID got here. I'm still waiting."

Katla. Katla.

"Aww, Florian, you just wanted my company."

Katla.

"Oz, does anyone call you for company?"

"The dead."

"Only if they're really drunk," Florian chuckles.

Katla-katla.

Facts: pharmacy intact and hardware left standing. No wallet emptied except for the licences and student IDs laid neatly at the feet of the deceased: Eli Klein, Yuri Grossman, Jablom Lau Song. UCLA, Irvine, and Art Center.

Katla-katla. Katla. Katla.

"Congratulations. Your first news truck."

Past the grill, beyond the porch, a KTLA van rolls up over the curb. Maybe it's Gael.

"Fuck," Florian hisses.

Already at the door.

"This is a crime—" Florian starts. But it's not press or PeSTs held dutifully at bay by the tape.

"Detective Sérbulo? Agent Tramilli. FBI."

And that's that. Florian washing his hands. Or shaking hands. Handing over the whole thing to the Feds. Relieved too. Terrorists. Cyber misdeeds. Darknet. The Next Silk Road. The usual crap these guys like to haul out when there's nothing to share.

Katla.

Özgür sets the skunk ∴ Robert J. Lang ∵ on the sill, leaves Florian to more hours of protocol. A crowd is starting to form. Second today.

From the porch Özgür catches something in the window. Not his friend, or even his skunk, but on the glass, a history of greasy expressions there, some vague smear at something meaningful? Or not.

One mew short of a V. Not something that makes any sense or even connects to something promising sense but still is something nonetheless. And then inside the room, an FBI agent starts backing up. A real klutz. Bumps right up against the window. Jerks back as if quick weren't already too late. Catches Özgür's glare on the other side. Waves awkwardly. Leaves behind one pane of glass wiped clean.

Özgür figures he better go join the owner now out on the lawn, when he hears it, and then instead of seeing the Pacific or feeling the rain, for a moment memory finds Istanbul, when he was a young boy, running hard too, getting closer and closer to understanding a commotion ahead, panting harder, how it had been that other rainy day, men his age now, and boys his age then, hanging a tree with rocks, making him feel all that he wasn't when he proved what little we can sometimes do or say.

But even heading back inside — he might as well find the clumsy FBI guy, might as well yell at someone — Özgür hears it a second time, that strange plaintive call which he already knows by the sharpening pit of regret in his stomach he's already too late for.

* * *

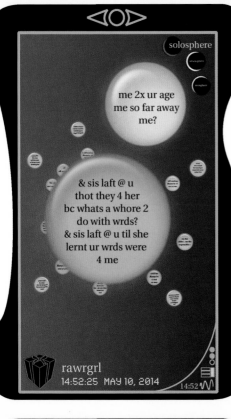

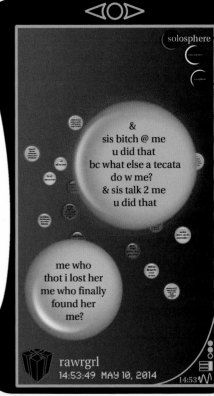

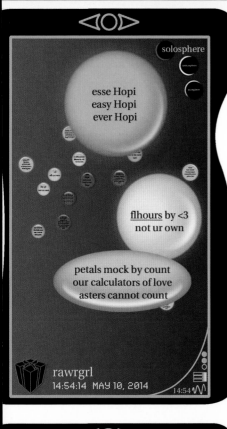

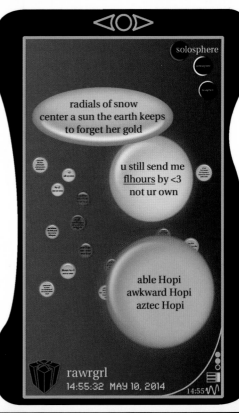

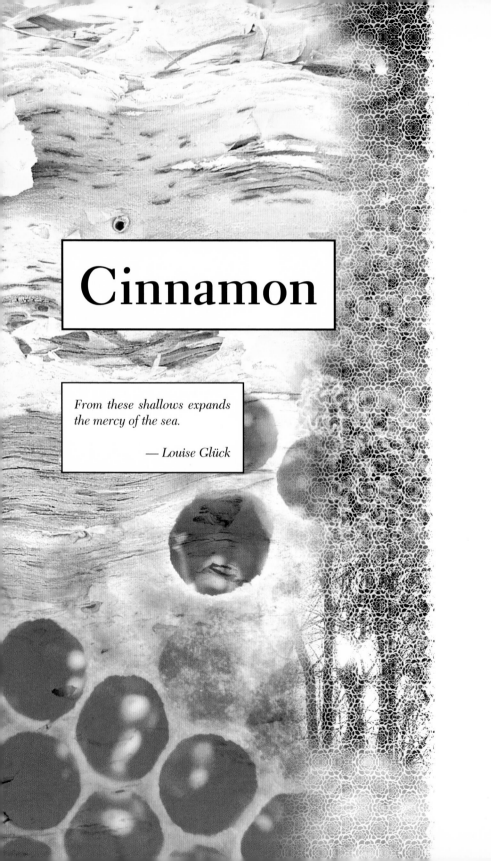

Cinnamon

*From these shallows expands
the mercy of the sea.*

— *Louise Glück*

• • •

Astair had just thought to check on her paper (left on the bed upstairs ((on the corner) still in its manila envelope (bring it down to rest beside a bucket of ice and champagne ((why not get that bottle of the old widow cooling now?) soon Xanther and Anwar would be home with their new addition (and celebrations could begin (celebrating new additions everywhere (to the family (the Akita), to bank accounts (Anwar's deal) to the ranks of employable therapists (Astair) (or at least much, much closer)))))))) when she heard it again (maybe she'd heard it twice already (only hadn't realized it was something to hear (so faint) in the first place)).

She rushes through their breakfast nook ((what is (was) it?) past photographs of frozen rain) into the living room (past the piano (Anwar's dais (with an opera score wide open)) toward the French doors leading out onto the back patio (throwing open the muslin curtains (flicking the lock) throwing open the doors (throwing herself out there (((someone needed help (some*thing*(?))) right?) just go tumbling into the wet))) and yet hesitating on the threshold (weather stripping under her arches) as if stuck there by a few spatters of rain on her wrists (something about the damp and stickiness of the afternoon storm (hardly abating) revolting Astair enough to discourage her from any more investigation ((something icky (if unexpected) in the warmth of the water) to the point that she's sure she made it all up (the sounds (the cries)(echoes of birds flying by)) just as she's sure Xanther (though not Freya or Shasti) would already be out there (on the first cry too (if not before)) investigating her imagination (Xanther thrives on made-up things)))).

The compromised(?) dog bed is not a made-up

thing (but you can't explain money (especially a lot of money) to an eight-year-old (a sense of value is what matters (and that's tough enough))). So upon arriving home Astair had gotten the Wrecking Crew to seek out the biggest and fluffiest beach towels they could find. The sheepskin was racked but Astair thought it worth the risk to toss beach towels and the foam interiors into the dryer. If it didn't survive, she'd eBay the thing for parts (small parts (shreds)). And that left hope for the ~~nest~~ (*best!*).

Maybe Taymor was right (the thought comes upon her with adder-like ferocity (weirdly welcome (or electric?))) to address the marriage now (heat up the kitchen (again (with more than a dry kettle))).

Taymor (as she was dropping them off) had (again) returned to sex (when did she not?).

"You know, a ferret that doesn't for a year dies."

"Doesn't what?" Freya asked from the back.

"Serve herself, girls."

"Did you just call me a ferret?"

"A chimpanzee, Astair. When a chimpanzee wants to she has the strength of six males."

"Wants to what?" Shasti then had to ask ((not really curious(?)) copying Freya (?)).

"Wants to serve herself, girls."

But (as Taymor's BMW pulled away (BMW would always read Bob Marley & the Wailers to Astair (*This is my message to you-who-ooh!*))) Astair still couldn't voice that (rather than likening herself to a crazed chimp (or dying ferret)) she identified most with a dry kettle (burning up on her stove).

The Change . . .

She'd heard Abigail whisper it once. Taymor waved it off like it was a myth. Gia (their third friend) raised a glass to keeping myths myths.

But what's this? Right now? A flash of warmth coiling around her body (dampening both temples). Coolness ahead too if Astair were to actually step out into the rain (in pursuit of a cry no more a phantasm and a memory of one (not even)).

Instead she closes the French doors and goes to put on some music (The Family Crest).

What smiles are coming their way. How the Akita will fill the house (even the Jax & Bones bed (it will be fine(?))). Big dogs. *Powerful dogs* as Grez Kacy had said ((that (Weimaraner) owner of Urban Pet) flirting? (appealing to her anyway (in some way (going beyond a sale (as he disappeared into the strange gray rain with his graying moon))))). What will he say when ~~she~~ (*they!*) bring ~~their~~ (*hers!* (HER!)) Akita around? Beautiful creature. Bear hunter, caretaker to children.

Astair still had folders of bookmarks, piles of magazine clippings, articles (those PDFs she just had to print out (all those Wiki entries and Google images)) stapled, bindered, highlighted, dog-eared (of course). Remember? Great Danes, Bulldogs, Alaskan Malamutes, Saint Bernards, Rottweilers, Bullmastiffs, Cavalier King Charles, other spaniels, German Shepherds, Shih Tzus, shar-peis, Shelties, Setter mixes, Border Terriers, Border Collies, Rough Collies, Samoyed crosses, Chow Chows, Golden Retrievers, Great Pyrenees, Huskies, Timber Wolves.

How could she forget the first time she had seen an Akita? Love at first sigh(t). Admired from afar (at first). Admired him as *they* drew near. Said hello. Stroked him even. ~~Griffin~~ Park (Griffith!).

Dr. Sandwich (though) had finally heard the actual confession. (heeding Astair's ~~crazy~~ (*crazed!*) longing for more children ("unaffordable" (Anwar's word))) The therapist had flatly confirmed Astair's tireless energy to look after her children: "Most women your age, and much younger, would be in here crying about all they can't do. Trust me. Eight-year-olds, twins, and a child nearly crippled but thanks to you merely . . . taxed . . . by her condition. But you're here because—"

"—because it's a requirement."

"Because maybe you want more?" Dr. Sandawai had suggested.

And Astair just blurted it out: "I want a dog!"

From then on Astair hardly needed Dr. Sandwich to trace the roots nourishing this admission. Once in the open (disinvested of projections (maternal disposition)) Astair found for herself the neighborhood dogs of her childhood, dogs of ex-boyfriends (even Dov (to her delight) had grown up around dogs and swore that once his move-around military life ended they would get a dog ((acres of them) he never did)).

So yes (Duh! (as Xanther might say)) Astair just adored the animal. Always had. All breeds. Their courage. Devotion. Their moist eyes, wagging tails. The way they panted, nuzzled, and played. How they introduced themselves to people and other dogs and even how they fought. Just the sight of one (she discovered) relaxed her. Gave her breath. Fortified

441

her with some kind of magical brandy which she'd heard as a young girl the great Saint Bernards carried to travelers lost in blizzards, under avalanches.

Astair had no doubt her daughter would adore one too.

Besides could anyone argue against the safety benefits? Not Anwar. Home security at the ready. Homeland Security. The real deal.

Might as well admit to vanity too (Astair couldn't forget (deny) that): the way women with a leash looked. With every round-the-block outing friend-accompanied: both guardian against foe and secretary to suitors.

Not that Astair was remotely(?) open to suitors.

She just envied (*envies?*) how easy dogs made saying hello to a stranger (*seem*(!)).

A dog would get her out of the house.

A dog would get her out of her head.

Astair had even gone (quietly) into training. Just the thought (anticipation) motivated eager activities. More running (hikes and stairs sawtoothing up between homes off of Effie ∴ Around Redesdale Avenue ∴) as well as adding in (biceps) curls and (triceps) extensions thanks to her piggy banks (a couple of milk jugs (loaded with pennies ("What wealth copper cannot grow, let muscle know!" or so a former boyfriend of Tay's used to shout (Shakespearean actor/Shakespearean trainer)))) in anticipation of the day when Astair would need the strength to handle walking a big dog.

Add to all this that Dog Whisperer book. The show too (with Cesar Millan (seasons I–IV (on DVD))). All of it stuffed under her bed (like porn (dog porn)). Astair still couldn't admit to Taymor (let alone Anwar) how bad it had gotten. Even as she (gently? (secretly)) set about preparing Xanther.

Not exactly easy. (for example) Xanther had little interest in hikes.

"Seriously? You want me to, like, kill myself?" her eldest had scoffed. "I barely walk upstairs without, like, wiping out."

"It will help with badminton at school?"

"Uhm, like the only thing that will help my badminton, uhm, is to make it like not-required?"

But Astair (and just last weekend too) had still dragged Xanther up Runyon Canyon to check out the numerous dogs dragged along the dusty trails by owners (or professionals paid by owners).

Xanther (however) had protested the whole way and (true to her word (her tweenage powers of fore(self-fulfilling)sight)) had on the way down wiped out hard enough to give both knees character (in need of a week's worth of daily hydrogen peroxide baths (plus a change of bandage)). Not that Xanther had cried (more like rolled her eyes) while (curiously) dogs nearby had all started to bay.

Nor had pictures of dogs left (haphazardly!) around helped either (certainly none stoked any (vocalized) desire (though Astair craved to hear Xanther blurt out just once: "Mom, I so want a dog!")).

If only (tween!) desire were that easy to manipulate. In fact one recent afternoon (while twisted up in their backyard hammock (bandaged knees pointing to the sky)) Xanther had responded to Astair's casual description of an Akita by asking about clouds.

"Mom, if, uhm, like, two clouds pass through each other, are they like still the same clouds they were before?"

Astair then powerless to wonder anything else but how (after having lived all over the country and now living nowhere near Sherman Oaks) her daughter could sound as if she had been born and raised solely in The Valley? Then again how was it that at other times Xanther sounded like she hailed from regions beyond the potency of any map?

Many moments (ashamedly) arose when Astair (and maybe Anwar too (perhaps admitting so in the shape of tacit worry)) worried that epilepsy had done its permanent harm. Damaged. Compromised. Impaired. ~~Deranged~~ (*Re-arranged!*)

"Seems cool, right? Akitas were bred to be loyal to kings."

But Xanther would have nothing to do with the topic.

"I guess clouds, after they've like gone through each other, might look different, but even if they looked the same? I mean, uhm, like unchanged?, *are* they? You know, are they the same? And if they are different, because of course they have to be different, right?, and maybe they have to look like, uhm, at least a little different, right?, like how much difference makes different a difference *really*?"

And *really* that was her daughter in a nutshell (or a hammock): head in the clouds, a song of questions, heedless of her mother.

Still Xanther's apparent indifference to all these hints (preferring to stare at the sky or play those incessant games Anwar designs (works on (escapes to?))) continued to mystify Astair especially because of how much her daughter adored animals. All kinds. Every kind!

Hadn't Xanther (age seven) taken her animal-affection (prompted by no event Anwar or Astair could dowse) to the next level by becoming a vegetarian? Never announced. No resolution put forth. Just (one day) declined to eat meat. Soon after, fish. And didn't budge. A passing phase Astair and Anwar had concluded (that never passed (five years later Astair is still learning to prepare tofu in new ways)).

(rabbits, pigeons, crickets, horses, tadpoles, rats (name the Ark (name Wikipedia (her WikiArk knew no end)))) Xanther had always shown intense fondness for every wandering creature (not excluding even reptiles and stinging insects).

It was (at least) a singular fascination which had pretty much remained constant throughout her life. In fact once when she was three Xanther had observed a(n unmoving) turtle with such prolonged intensity Astair feared she was autistic and the turtle dead (until it waddled off).

Astair had no doubt (though) that when Xanther saw the dog (((might have happened already (even now?) when) she threw those gangly arms around its neck (petted it and brushed it (and later walked it and watered it and fed it))) when she named it) all Astair's doubts would join that dim (ever dimming) cemetery of worries. Hadn't she already texted her approval ((delight!)(Anwar relenting(?)) (so excite!))?

Astair now passes (set out on their project table (formerly a long printer's table)) the jars of biscuits (treats (training treats!)) and too many collars (she can return the ones they don't like (Astair digs the wasabi one)) and leashes (Xanther can choose

(Astair digs the sunflower braid)) and beside big bags ((50 lbs!) filled with kibble) those items still not unpacked (filled with brushes, shampoos, ear and eye wipes, pee pads, more).

So what if all that stuff had been expensive? (*Too expensive* (she knows)). (still) Astair doesn't buy shoes. She doesn't (*really*) covet handbags (*really?* (really)). She can't even remember the last time she treated herself to a pedi or K-Town massage. Once a month Xiomara (their housekeeper) helps bring them some order and calm. Oh Xiomara! (($150 for a day of laundry, mopping, and cleaning windows) though she had just given notice (returning to Mexico (Jalisco?) in July)).

Astair's only excess is her kids. Shasti wants pastels. Done. Freya needs some puzzle game. Hers. Promising new tests by an expert in San Francisco? Xanther's on a plane. Toys, tutors, the finicky diets all three of her daughters constantly explore? Handled.

And Astair isn't spoiling them either. Course work has confirmed what better instincts (angels?) have always understood: spoiling is synonymous with neglect. Or: spoiling is the excessive meting out of privilege to compensate for a lack of caring attention and loving discipline.

"Mommy!" Freya squeals (racing into the room). "Shasti has a question."

"Mommy!" Shasti (at Freya's heels). "I have a question."

Both do a double-take (they really could have their own show (look out Kardashians)).

"When do we get to become cartoons?" (in unison).

Huh.

"Is that what you want?"

"Not nessa-celery." Freya.

"We don't like celery." Shasti (nodding).

"Maybe you already are cartoons?"

Astair loves parenting. She has accepted this categorically. It fills her with a sense of satisfaction no other ~~occupation~~ (*vocation!*) even crudely approximates. Bartending (a little). Working as a therapist will (maybe?) come closest. Still, Astair knows that nothing can ever come close to all she has gained by helping her children grow up strong, intelligent, and moral (willful too).

This is (they are) her insoluble light. Life's essence and line through the blond days and gray nights yet to come.

Or so Astair *believes. Really. Usually. Maybe.*

"They've got plenty of growing up left," Anwar will try to calm her on those prematurely gray nights.

Astair knows he's right. She accepts (gratefully (even)) his chiding that really all this anxiousness comes down to an Irish heritage and Catholic upbringing that preordained wanting a family of nine. But Astair also understands (the way only a mother can) just how quickly their three children are growing up. Daily she feels each's incremental departure as their mysterious twists of DNA (in accordance with incalculable sensitivities) begin to author and fix their identities. *Spoil them? Perfect them? Undo them? Appeal to them? None of the above?* Until finally they will do as they must do and their mother will be powerless to say no or say even go. They will already be on (and of) their own.

Outside the downpour continues. Drops big as gallon jugs. Not just splashes out there (and sure no patter). Explosions. A hydromancy of a future apocalypse (or an ancient one (long before any sea was parted (what only (not even?) an ark could survive))).

The downpour inside (if attenuated now) also continues. The Wrecking Crew has now been tasked with revisiting all the leaks and replacing full jars, dishes, and pans with empty ones (and tossing the brackish fluid born of shingle and joist into whatever bathtub's closest (they must do something (be responsible for something (be the consequence of earlier action (that Jax & Bones cost over $250!)))))).

Is that why the thought of a dog brightens her? Why Astair finds it somehow renewing? With belief in there too? Maybe even faith (maybe with even a dash of that sophomoric anagrammatic palindromic religiosity (*sans* Pope))? Because a dog's not a cost in the way a phone bill is (or a day trip to Ojai) (or dinner at Orsa & Winston ∴ 122 W. 4th St. ∵). No property (or thing ((widget) quantifiable)) susceptible to financial analysis.

Beyond analysis!

What a ~~relife~~ (*relief!*).

Astair even digs into her wallet to throw out that ridiculous receipt for the sheepskin bed (only it's not there (where did she put it?) what does it matter?).

A dog's part of the family.

And family is beyond the province of numbers.

(at the base of the stairs) Astair has second thoughts about champagne.

She alone is responsible for dramatizing this ((what to call it) grade(?) completion(?)) revelation. Just yesterday Xanther had asked (for the umpteenth time) if she could read the paper ("Or, you know, just like look at it?") and (for the umpteenth time (plus one)) Astair had deferred until Saturday night. And what for? Mother's Day just past midnight? Really?

"Then will you explain it to me again? I still don't understand. It's like dad's game engine. It makes sense when you say it but not how I remember it."

"Okay," Astair had taken a deep breath. "It's an exercise that posits, that asks, whether or not to imagine what could never exist at all might create behavior which never could have existed before?"

That summation was actually more concise than anything she had managed in the paper (and suddenly this memory casts some shadow on her paper's future).

Why not get it over with now? To hell (oblivion!) with this delayed gratification! And Astair actually races (really) up the stairs. Zipping past the (7th(?)) leak on that top step (wasn't there an 8th?) only to find her bed and on it (on the corner (where she should have found the paper)) nothing.

The Wrecking Crew must have moved it ((her first thought) that thick manila envelope). But if they had— Astair's had enough (up to here (overflowing!)). Whipping around (their names already crowding her teeth) (the fact that they're downstairs permitting the coming roar) (all of it caught by teeth) as Astair whips back again to her room (memory returning (extinguishing anger)): the bathroom closet.

Astair sees the floor first (right in front of the closet door): a still growing puddle. Inside a stream of brackish water soaking towels (seeping over the shelves).

Oh no's mumble and moan from her lips as Astair digs into the linens. She can't even remember the shelf. Which one? The first? No? The third? No? The fourth? The fifth?

No! No!

Ruined for sure. Anything written there unwritten in the sog (pulped even). But the envelope emerges bone dry (the second shelf (and everything there somehow preserved from the flood ((the stack of folded towels) even the hand towels))).

Astair clutches it to her chest (heart beating for sure (sweating (a hot flash (this one reasonable (even a relief))))) and sits down on the bed. Open it now! She's laughing too. Why not? Seriously.

Downstairs she can't hear her girls: *All we are are silent villains* . . . Along with the still battering of rain.

Open it now.

Instead Astair takes it downstairs and sets it on the coffee table beside a bucket full of ice bright with the bottle of Veuve Clicquot she and Anwar saved for this occasion.

And then she tracks down the Wrecking Crew (they've escaped to the back (in their underwear (wearing goggles and snorkels (splashing around in the wading pool (squealing (over and over again) "Itsy Bitsy Spider!"))))). The discovery leaves Astair frozen again at the threshold ((of their French doors) somewhere between dismay and anger and amusement).

What gentle memories rise (rarely) of her own mother then: Astair swimming in her grandparents' pool in the middle of a rainstorm (May too (why not!)) with a mask on (watching from underwater the world of rain play out its descent on the surface above) while inside (in another room) her mother prepared toast slathered in butter, cinnamon, and sugar while towels warmed in the dryer.

"For this, even lightning's worth the risk."

Warmth. Sweetness. Love.

Astair goes now to make sure hot towels will be waiting and toast too (hot enough to melt all of the butter) and (most important) arms wide enough to hold them both.

Litter

Who did you meet, my darling young one?

— Bob Dylan

"What say we call them, daughter?" Anwar asked, handing over his phone. Ahead washes of orange had started to slow everything, more and more brake lights too, even spinning blues up ahead, an accident?, maybe an arrest? Since they had left Century City, the rain had gotten worse, or louder, heavier for sure.

"Dibs on next song?"

"There's something preferable to Stravinsky? And please spare me the news of how many messages I have."

Xanther didn't spare him.

"And the new dog shall track down Mister Mefisto and then we shall . . . "

"What?" Delight and dread had made a bird-like trill out of Xanther's voice.

Anwar told her the number, which Xanther dialed after the latest call stopped flashing.

Galvadyne, Inc.
000-000-0000

Xanther's never thrilled about talking to strangers but the call to the breeder?, trainer?, seller?, didn't go badly, exactly. The breeder?, trainer?, seller?, a woman, seemed pleasant enough, too pleasant?, the kind of pleasantness that's finally just a little too hard to believe.

"Your SugarLady's right here. Waiting to meet you. Waiting to say hello. Just get here safely."

SugarLady? Say hello? Animals don't say hello. They don't say anything. Ever. And as far as names go, SugarLady? Seriously? Anwar was all assurances about changing it but the lady's voice, especially the "Your," had gotten under Xanther's skin and made her all squirmy. She just wanted to get there, or at least get somewhere else, other than this gnarl of traffic and flooding gutters and police cars. Anywhere but here, which is actually one of those early warning signs, even if it's never true enough to mean anything other than buckle your seat belt and consider biting into the shoulder strap too.

Xanther started to skip through the radio stations.

102.7 ∴ **KIIS** ∴ *We're the ~~fucking~~ animals . . .*

She had plenty to be squirmy about other than the onset of an attack. What Dendish had done to Bayard, done to all of them on Parcel Thoughts, in The Horrosphere, was still strobing in her head, their slashed faces, all the bone fragments and blood. Everyone except Cogs. Lucky Cogs. Not that Bayard, Kle, or Josh, or even Mayumi seemed worried enough to mention it in their texts. They cared more about the dog. School was almost out anyway. Dendish was in 8th grade. Come fall, he wouldn't even be at Thomas Starr.

103.1 ∴ **KDLD** ∴ *Te juro que te amo . . .*

Plus none of it was real. The butcherings were just the result of an app. But then there was that stuff Glasgow and Talbot had been whispering about. That wasn't the result of an app. Realic? Or was it Relic? And house too? Wasn't there a series on TV about a doctor named House? Not that he could have helped this R Guy because R Guy was dead, really dead, killed in an accident, or cut up, cut up in pieces, how many pieces? enough to be some kind of message?

What a message.

105.9 ∴ **KPWR** ∴ *Wait 'til you're announced . . .*

Dark enough to fill Xanther's head with a new rush of questions, even if she was also remembering, and at the same time too, Anwar's warning, about how the thing in *Paradise Open*, what had been tracking her, how it had never tracked her along the path she'd made in the tall grass, as Xanther had expected, but had come at her from the side, Xanther not hearing anything, let alone catching a glimpse of something, Anwar's creation, leaving Xanther in the end to just watch GAME OVER float forward in the midst of all that code, Talbot's kill spray. Maybe a similar thing had happened to the R Guy though not to Dov. Dov knew what was happening. He knew what he'd done.

106.7 ∴ **KROQ** ∴ *Bringing me a dark surprise . . .*

Dov loved dogs. He would have loved to know that Xanther was getting a dog. He would have wanted to know all about it. And that started up a new Question Song. Not all Question Songs are bad.

88.1 ∴ **KKJZ** ∴ *Makes the wind blow all the while . . .*

What would the dog look like? What color coat? How much would it weigh? How heavy would it get? How much would it eat? How often would it eat? Would its breath smell? What would its hair smell like? What would it smell like when it got wet? How long would it take to dry?

89.3 ∴ **KPCC** ∵ *Before I sputter out . . .*

Why was Xanther even calling it an it? Hadn't the woman on the phone said it was a female? Isn't that the only thing SugarLady could mean?

89.9 ∴ **KCRW** ∵ *'Cause you found someone like, like . . .*

None of which compared to the biggest question of all: what kind?

91.5 ∴ **KUSC** ∵ *La voici plus confiante et riante qui s'abandonne au désir . . .*

Xanther knew some names but not like she knew shapes, the shapes she'd seen around their neighborhood, in movies, on TV. Great danes, dalmatians, poodles, Labs, German shepherds, pugs, golden retrievers, Chihuahuas. And there were also the ones smooth as gray felt ∴ Weimaraners ∵ or with faces squushed and tucked ∴ shar-peis ∵ or like a wandering haystack ∴ Lhasa apso ∵ or with floppy feet and wide agile eyes ∷ Cavalier King Charles spaniel ∴ or a tiny lion ∷ Pomeranian ∴ or mountain wrapped in the warmest snowstorm ∷ Old English sheepdog ∴ or rabbit-eared and bronzed ∷ Xoloitzcuintli ∴ or Mr. Hatterly's Archimboldo ∷ bullmastiff ∴ .

So many questions, so many possibilities, so many stations. Stations on stations, and hiding stations too, right?, because these are only the numbers for this area, what about those a state over?, two states over?, so many states, and if Xanther could hear them all at once, would that sound like forever?, maybe if Xanther arrowed fast enough through all the stations, it would sound like all at once, would that be a sound of endlessness?, a sound that's really only one thing?, and could a dog be imagined that way too, all types experienced as one type?

Probably a good thing that Anwar put a stop to these thoughts by waving Xanther's hand away. Good timing anyhow.

93.1 ∷ **KCBS** ∴ Jack FM.

There.

And one of Dov's favorites too.

"Everything okay?"

"I keep wondering what, like, you know, uhm, what breed it is?" Xanther should admit to Anwar about how off she's felt the whole day. About The Horrosphere.

Anwar beams. "Very soon, daughter."

Which is when she feels it. At once too. Unwelcome.

From the end of time. From the beginning of time.

Coming her way.

As if all this time, she were stalked by a great sadness.

Led Zeppelin helps steady the sensation.

Cryin' won't help you,

Xanther turns it up. Anwar at once tries to turn it down. Dov would have turned it way up. For all his quiet, Dov loved her music. Was it hers? More like Dov's. Though was it his either? No question a lot of it had come through him. Though Xanther didn't know whose they were when she first discovered that box buried under sleeping bags and incomplete tents, deep in the back of that downstairs utility closet, when they had lived for a summer in Montana. Xanther had played every LP on an old turntable before she found out they were her mom's before she found out even that wasn't quite right. As it turned out, Astair had taken them from Dov who wanted them back until he found out how Xanther listened to them all day long. Sometimes at night too. All night once when she discovered the headphones.

Les Parents were mystified, but why wouldn't she want to stay up all night, stay up forever? There was so much to meet: The Rolling Stones, The Doors, Black Sabbath, Jefferson Airplane, Rush, Bob Dylan, Bob Marley, Aerosmith, The Band, AC/DC, Jimi Hendrix, Simon & Garfunkel, Jimmy Cliff, and of course Led Zeppelin. Joni Mitchell, Neil Young, and Willie Nelson didn't do it for her. Janis Joplin was okay. What Xanther liked most was wailing heaviness. She liked to feel it thump on her chest. Inside her chest. Heavy as thunder. Xanther loves thunder.

Today's storm, for all its rain and wind, shared no thunder, not even a hint of lightning in the distance, making this radio loud inside the Element feel like a necessity.

prayin' won't do you no good . . .

Like Dov would have listened to it. On 11. In his totally silent way.

And then Anwar had just turned down the music, again, and Xanther was cleaning her glasses, again, or trying to, futile really, all fogged up, lenses now just smudged, thanks to the corner of her pink Black Flag t-shirt, way damp. Not that it matters much. The world is a smear, even with wipers on high, how she feels feels all smeary too, are there wipers for that? And then something suddenly wails up inside her.

:: It is inside her. ::

Sounding like—

:: *It is far away.* ::

Close but not near?

:: **What calls on all . . .** ::

Far but not anywhere?

Yet so familiar to feel almost forever there?

"Daughter, will you read that street sign there?"

Xanther slides her glasses back on. She hasn't heard a thing. Her head's just doing its usual act of making stuff up. Electrical storms killing off thoughtless mights. Breathe, Xanther. Like Astair's taught her. Like they've all taught her.

Traffic has come to an absolute standstill. Here in the heart of Venice. No reason why either. No construction crews. No police lights this time. Just the overwhelming flood, right? Gutters surging over sidewalks. Palms snapping back and forth with every sudden gust. Some fronds even fly free, spinning into cars, setting off alarms.

The corner-post sign is a wash of blue crosshatched with streaks of white.

"Dad, if a game engine is like all the parts that make a game run, like all the parts in a car engine that make a car run, what's the gasoline?"

"Darling, the sign?"

Cracking the window was a stupid idea. Nothing gets clearer. Why did she just ask Anwar that? She didn't even realize coding was still in her thoughts. Xanther shudders and shivers.

Anwar turns the music off.

"No luck?"

"No luck." Xanther can't see a thing. Can't hear a thing. Except for that one cry that still isn't a cry.

Plain.

And desperate.

464

Diminishing further in its nonexistence.

Now the only thing Xanther could ever hear.

Cutting through everything. As if all of this might not exist at all — ∴ **Nor ever could exist.** ∵

∴ But for a curious thing. ∴

:: Voice of the frail. ::

∴ **Voiced by the dead.** ∴

. . .

Quiet.   And little.

                        Pleading.
                    And needing.
                    And crying

                    for help.

Of course Xanther doesn't hesitate.

Jerks open the door.

Spills out into the storm.

No idea where she's going—

:. No idea what she's doing. .:

:. *Of course.* .:

:. **We must.** .:

—except she must get there fast.

Blinded,

feet flying over pavement for—

∴ For what? ∵

∴ *For?* ∵

∴ **For . . .** ∵

Xanther can't even feel the storm, and it instantly penetrates. Slapping down on her shoulders. Filling her Converse. Soaking her hair, one elastic snapping free of a braid. The rain falls so hard it seems to leap up from the street, chest high, eyes high, hovering between gravities. A storm gone backward. Sideways. A storm that's ceased to care what a storm should be.

Xanther doesn't care either.

Besides, was there any doubt she'd leap from the car? When what she imagined was answered by what now had to be soooooooooo real? And when what was real turned out to be in soooooooooo much trouble? Of course she took on the spray. No Fraidy K now. Racing through all that churn. The thick ropes of gray water overrunning the pavement, riverrunning alongside the curb, twisting off the tires of parked cars.

The intersection ahead plays a lake. Holes can hide there. But do they? Maybe even deep holes? How deep? Xanther could scrape off a kneecap. Maybe she's already breaking something? She's never run this hard. And still picking up speed.

Xanther charges the lake. Might as well walk on water, who's walking?, she's racing, and even if she can't outrace rain, she's outracing questions. Cars honk. Sirens, somewhere near, stab away for bad news. Garbage cans clatter loose their collective disorder.

And still, through it all, as if in flight, or just falling, one singular note of distress:

mournful,

meek

and

expiring.

Though it's never been a question of volume, only a question of presence, this diminution somehow spiking through to Xanther with increasing clarity.

Or is it all just adrenaline?
Hammering her heart?

It doesn't matter.

Now she's sprinting.
Blindly over lake after lake.

Cars jerk to a halt. Multiple screeches, this chorus of protest, not the shock of almost, only the anger of . . .

But Xanther pays no mind.

Leaves another intersection behind.

Another corner too.

And then it's down the block.

More than a slope.

This one's steep.

Steep enough to accelerate black water, heavy with trash and hazards, toward still another intersection below, there another growing lake, this one making puddles out of the rest. Where she's headed.

Toward

...

Except time's against her,

it will go under.

∴ It? ∵

∴ *It?* ∵

∴ **It.** ∵

· · ·

Knees and palms suffer the fall, but Xanther can't feel the way her jeans tear, skin splits and spills, those old scabs and bandages, from all her previous falls, ripped loose at once, lost to the water streaming past these slabs of concrete, both shins going dark with the seep.

Barely a thought strays to follow her glasses bouncing away, bits of broken frame and lenses skittering off toward gardens and lawn.

Xanther's already up again. Running as fast as she can. The memory of the fall already gone. Like her loose braids, both now coming undone, her long arms are flapping too, out at her sides, uncertain and wild, like she can fly. Another slip. Skids. Pulse spikes. But this time she keeps on her feet. As she keeps drawing nearer

                                                    and

                              near   er

              and

                                                                  n

        ear

                                                      er

                                                          and

              nearerandnearerandnearer

to what her heart keeps telling her to reach, pounding
past the thump of heels, of even muscle.

In silence. Too.

In silence. Now.

Everything. Silent.

Though scattered glances now catch nothing but smears of grays, greens, and blues, how a hedge and cherry trees look, by toppled recycling bins, there a broken garden lattice, a swing torn loose from a porch, Xanther still somehow knowing how not to look, maybe for the first time? Blur doesn't matter now. Instead everything coming down to those rapids ahead, churning around a storm drain, clotted with muck, what else to make of that mash of birds' nests, weeds, cut grass, and leaves? Plastic wrappers, bobbing water bottles, that otherwise familiar blob of trash, maybe including by now her clotted bandages, blinding her to what this instinct ∷ Isn't it something more than just instinct? ∵ , to what this claim upon her ∷ *something fashioned* ∵ , this desire ∷ **something ancient** ∵ has positioned her to see.

Even if still all Xanther sees is water.
Lots of water.

And garbage.
Lots of garbage.

At the base of the curb, above this grate, rising up, overrunning the curb, even while underneath, the water keeps trying to push through to the sea.

Xanther drops to hands and knees. Scrambles into it.
Digs. Tries to let fingers find what eyes deny. Ears too.

And then just as the blockage starts to give way, Xanther catches a feel of something down in there, briefly, of the litter, from the litter, equal parts refuse, equal parts out of place, incredibly soft, almost too small to believe,

sooooooooooooo small,

thank goodness for all those leaves, like a trap or a cradle, postponing briefly this last slip through the grate, a tiny tangle of something, pinned there against metal's rough bars.

But with so much water sluicing down with so much force, whether trap or cradle, leaves still fold and give way.

Trash makes no exception.

The flood flushes the clot down.

Yet Xanther goes with it, shoving her arms down, faster than the flood, through that grate, gate, past her wrists, past her elbows, with not even a thought, up to her armpits, already on her chest, all of her laid out flat, half of her on the sidewalk, the other half in the gutter, not even recognizing the pain already abrading both palms, carving up the inside of both forearms, Xanther plunging

through litter,

grating,

and all that

rushing water,

to find it,

reach it,

and bring it back —

raindrops

this something small,

sooooooooooooo small,

and
white too, improbably white, with flashes of pink, trian-
gular and whiskered, are those whiskers or—?, struggling
then with a flutter of paws, their last?, feeble paws,

sooooooooooooo feeble,

what a moment ago had
almost slipped under, slipped through, only to be lifted,
implausibly so, from the dark burying current below, sepa-
rated in its fall, at this last moment, from the descending
rest, dragged up by bleeding hands and bleeding arms into
this questionable air.

There.

In Xanther's palms.
One palm, actually. Easily.

On its back now. Oily. Limp.
Forepaws in rigid hooks. Fixed.

Eyes pinched shut.

The tiny creature's mouth a breathless gasp,
revealing not even a glitter of teeth.

Too late.

Too late.

For Xanther then, a rainstorm cry, clutching to her chest all she has already lost.

This time not even a quiver to die by.

Xanther alone is quivering.

Cradling.
Wailing.

∴ Too late. ∴

∴ *Too late.* ∴

∴ And powerless to arrive otherwise. ∵

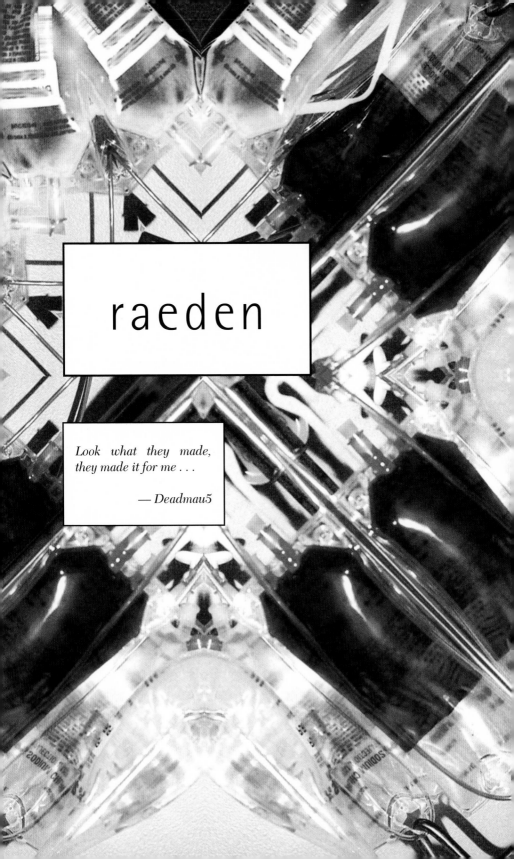

raeden

Look what they made,
they made it for me . . .

— Deadmau5

glow screens beep colored lines, pale blue, pale green, sprouting

wires too, cylinders gasp breath, loose tubes dangling down like

jellyfish, long things, stings at ends, surrounding his bed, lah, the

only bed, with side rails, mechanical adjusted, to contain small

form at center, still form, kay pale, tabs on his chest, drip to his

wrist, face hard, lah, to get the gist of, what with eyes closed,

accordion tube shoved down his throat.

"raeden sim lin," zhong whisper to jingjing. "he is my son."

jingjing catch this ball. clearclear at last, zhong's weeping and

appealing. here's his last chance: needs a healing.

for years, island wideover, people beg auntie for her touch, her

treatment. she more than some world cup parakeet, lah. bangla,

munjen, thambi, doesn't matter, angmoh, even old sagsack mats

seek her out. mebbe she agrees. this though, chia lat, just to see,

but hor why this hope tio? bladdy gruesome! damn sad, man!

here a son lies, here a son dies. not even great tian li can bring

back a man from so much electronic.

tian li even hold back. bad enough she so shaky taking last steps

to this little room, away from the owls, beneath zhong's staircase

past the moon. never seen auntie this kiasu.

even now she can barely shuffle forward. keep looking at jingjing,

knotting her hands. why so lembek? jingjing not understand. just

get on with the show, mumble her nongsngse, then dollars from

zhong, move on.

"我应助其子乎?" tian li trembles.

jingjing nods.

"汝可知吾已存无事?"

"你有我."

tian li smile. mebbe even old tears to old eyes: "吾知汝之性善."

"meng kia, long tio ooh siah," jingjing answer. "kar-kar lai." auntie keep smiling, thank jingjing, mah, there a first time!

it's not much of a life you're living . . .

riri too! there, lah, at last! except everything suddenly shakes wrong. auntie saysay something, does something, holds nothing back . . . over this sick boy . . . leaning her little shapel through this other chapel of dangly tubes, close enough to kisskiss, and nurses wah lau taken aback, zhong and bow ties holding these nurses back, as the great tian li does her thing . . .

and then *pow!*

down she go, sial lah! like old bag of rocks, truck-chucked to curb-side, just another old clock.

wah lau, jingjing rushing forward, "siam ah! gah neh nah!"

not that jingjing can stop tian li's shake on the floor. sprawl in her elbows, her knees. mouth a foam. tiny fingers, tiny toes twitching to hold. jingjing try still, to hold her, but how?, nurses too, but how? great tian li shake and shake and moan. how can?

alamak! talk horrible too. paler still, still paler, to transparency. see through to her tiny bones then. like broken bird. see through to floor.

no bird.

vomits then. jingjing vomits too.

sob too. can't help. untahanable!

to think, wah lan eh, hours back oreddy, she happy like bird. then

drifted off with zhong, to singsong his only pride, arbuthen, his

whole life, a burden?, a stone? long time too them like that, one

hour, another, three hour talk cock, whole night, lai dat.

both leave jingjing alone, another ghost, damn sian to live as a

ghost. then jingjing had got back to the bowl.

and jingjing had koped plenty. plus all the cash clips, lah. return

the money clips. ali baba only the chips.

he was close by the elevator too, doors even open. one button

to the first floor and jingjing loose. free for once, forever. what

would he do with new wealth? for each postcard buy airline ticket,

replace worldwall with world itself.

when out of blue, without one heel-click, bow ties untied them-

selves from the air, out of nowhere, so silky cool, the very smooth

— pink pearl, copper azure, and cocoa cherry too.

then with hooked smiles and hooking his arms, jude boys had led

jingjing off to the playroom.

wah lau eh! what a room! tv took up one wall. jingjing doubted

even his pockets could buy such a screen. copper azure station

music vids. pink pearl bump volume. speakers pumped too big to

speak forget think. cocoa cherry brought drinks. all three lost ear

pieces. and then just danced.

on tables, every couch, koh ones in hand, licence to pour cham-

pagne. first taste ever, splashed up jingjing's mouth, until his

smile's so wide, macam zhong's staircase high, his three friends

smiling with, filled his glass, as more bow ties mamboed in. ebony

with teal, ginger with quartz, meringue with rust. ear pieces out.

buttons undone.

sudden party so pow ka leow, lah! king jame version. bass so deep

jingjing swore it gave their wings feet. kill the noise, swedish

house mafia, no-i-lidz, syntrack, clash the disko kids, seven lions.

orange with onyx, his shirt off, lost, splashed all their glasses

with new fizz, brighter ya on jingjing's lips, jude twins twisting in,

rolling hips, dna grip, and if jingjing cinched robe tighter, still took

their bow ties in his teeth, followed their lead. sweat on sweat,

always a dead heat, until cocoa cherry wiggled in between, seksi-

ness to the tip of her tongue, something z, a little blue pill, for

everyone.

by the time the four had found the balcony, jingjing never felt

so free. so what of the rain, if his robe oreddy drenched. jingjing

never seen a view this wide. bay there, supertrees, then way out

thunder over the roads. mebbe lei-gong. further west, sentosa,

bukom. high over highhigh. and zhong's room, wherever he hide,

still floors and floors highhigh over this highhighhigh.

jingjing also see, wah lan eh, how jude boyz and cocoa cherry used

to this sight, no big deal, this life, kim tang tang. and if jingjing

had felt blur like sotong, he tight-lip it. longtime since he held

nicotine this deep, roll out smoke slow, lah, damn fine, tok kong.

sings. so embered bright whatever they shared. no kian siap here.

and they shared so much. and touchtouchtouch.

even as they drifted farther along the balcony, away from the

beats. balcony wouldn't quit. over there tanglin road, his common-

wealth hdb. that way johor. further on another palace.

"these days this party is the only thing that makes zhong happy,"

pink pearl said. first words jingjing heard in hours. jingjing almost

asked his name, but suddenly unsure.

"every night," copper azure laughed.

"ever since," cocoa cherry added, grim.

so jingjing leaned over the railing, let the world come to him, and this time these three followed him, leaning too into the long quiet.

below what jingjing thought were cars weren't even clouds. at that moment, one long breath before dawn, they looked down on stars.

then cocoa cherry, followed by the jude boyz, jingjing last, flicked their butts, new stars to add to this chance, following them down with wishes, birds to mata, shits in the cops' eyes, friends forever, laughter like theirs rising forever, awake forever.

jingjing so wanted it to last longer, even if oreddy, lah, something had slipped free. forever go so fast. jingjing had sat down, tv dark, music off, checking pockets, chips crowding three, one reserved for his mcs. always bagged-up, safe, clean.

jingjing shuffled, cut his deck four times, once for each of them, then said: "for zhong's son."

it surprised them. like they all "ooh yiah boh?" even jingjing felt

something strong.

"Тоже светло-синий. Как и шарик." ∴ "Pale blue too. Like the

balloon." ∴ copper azure blinked.

"Чертов дым." ∴ "Fuck smoke." ∴ cocoa cherry spat.

"Ты пробовал курить?" ∴ "You've tried smoke?" ∴ jingjing coughed

loose, tightened robe too, if macam tsao k'ng, lah, like he had
underwear on, still felt very exposed.

shock.

"Так ты говоришь по-русски?" ∴ "How is it you speak Russian?" ∴
copper azure at last asked like a door opened where there wasn't
even a wall before.

"Значит, у меня есть способности?" ∴ "I have a good ear?" ∴

"Мы думали, что раз ты, ну, говоришь, как крутой парень,
ну, как сингапурец, ты, наверное, знаешь китайский и
кое-как английский," ∴ "We thought, because of your, you know, your
tough guy talk, your bad Singlish, you maybe spoke Chinese and barely English," ∴
pink pearl admitted then, like he wanted a wall back. skali everything could go quickquick wrong, lah, just like that, now with
jingjing some samseng, even taller, busses burning, towers falling.

"Вообще, потому что пришел сюда с одним из людей Чжуня."

∷ "You know, because you came here with Zhong's latest swindler." ∷

jingjing had let it pass. tian li no damn chao kuan, haha, her koyok one, but wah lau, si beh extra useless to even mention cat. as if jingjing ever do that. even for new friends. in fact thought alone him kena arrowing for a looksee-looksee around, checked that no shadows cabut as one shadow, one shadow alone, grow unchecked. but media room had kept flat, made of owl room just bad idea, all that happened there lost to smokes and splash, balcony dance.

"Я слышал, розовые скоро привезут?" ∷ "I've heard pink balloons are now on the way?" ∷ jingjing saysay instead.

"Черт, прямо детский праздник с шариками," ∷ "Fuck the balloon parade," ∷ cocoa cherry said, kay easy now, but all about zhong's son. her friend. all of them close. mebbe cocoa cherry closest. raeden was on yellows.

"Слишком сильный для нас. Он сказал, что чувствуешь и видишь лучше, чем при любом освещении и солнце. А потом привезли светло-синий. Я раз пробовал, всего один раз, и вроде…" ∴ "Too strong for us. He said you feel and see better than with any light, any sun. Then the pale blues came along. Raeden tried it once, just once, and like that—" ∴ cocoa cherry in tears, switching "—raeden was gone."

"Я пробовал светло-синий." ∴ "I tried pale blue." ∴ jingjing shrugged.

"Ты?" "Когда?" ∴ "You?" "When?" ∴ pink pearl, copper azure, both.

"Четыре года назад. До того, как завязал." ∴ "Four years ago. Before I was clean." ∴ jingjing feeling whatever smoke, pills, and drink haze up even sharper.

"Вон как," ∴ "Ah," ∴ twins saysaid. "Недавно было. В 2013-м." ∴ "This was recently. 2013." ∴

"Может, партия «левая». Всегда что-нибудь новенькое."

∴ "Maybe it was a bad batch? There's always something new." ∴

"Да ничего новенького не бывает. Даже твои розовые шарики уже были. Кончились пару месяцев назад." ∴ "Nothing's new. Not even your pink balloons. Supposedly those fiends were out months ago." ∴ cocoa cherry pratikally screeched, surprised them all, even herself. she had stood up then, mebbe to compose herself, crossed over to a dresser and hid face as she rummaged drawers.

jingjing though had gone electric. pink balloons real? for weeks that rumor had cycled in the parks and hdb suites. moh tuck teng! crazy real, lah. cocoa cherry's news had arrowed his whole back to twitch mad, and fastfast, like jingjing really had wings ready to grow full at last.

he still tried to ground self, putting away monster cards, had sealed them up neat, in the same old plastic bag, squared right.

pocketing it helped him forget, but three more pockets plump with

gold gave memory flight. chik ak not all memories are birds. this

memory monster mosquito. and jingjing stung, lah, itchy enough to

want kick loose, stick deep, scratch thick, find calamine in squib of

carefully tied up pink party plastic.

cocoa cherry returned with bottle of cologne, splashed all of their

palms.

"camouflage," she explained to jingjing.

"neroli portofino," he answered. "lah."

mebbe she had smiled. misted her breath before passing kissaholic

to jude boyz, making point to skip jingjing, jude boyz making point

to each squirt freshener back of jingjing's throat.

"jingjing."

laughter stopped. as if jingjing be surprised. he never not

surprised. tian li that way. here unheard, unseen, middle of them.

and not like she have to saysay his name twice. jingjing oreddy up

before she could finish saying, "吾有需于汝."

and then they were in the thick of that jellyfish church, wires,

tubes, machine screen glows, with zhong's song, zhong's pride,

dying at center: raeden sim lin.

jingjing had shuddered too. cold killing thing sliced through his

drunk, his high, whatever hazy lift this hip-wiggling night had

made of him, when he saw boy the same age as him.

then all bow ties, friends, assembled five on each side, jingjing

count nine, counted twice, still five twice, still nine.

don't be scared, if it hits, there be sound, jingjing had whispered

to auntie then. go forward brave.

the great tian li smiled then, thank jingjing too. there a first, mah!

then everything shook wrong. sprawl, foam, see through her bird

bones, until she vomit oreddy, him too, sure liao, then her again.

wet herself too, puddle tile. until shaking calmed.

did zhong help? no! wah piang! him boh lum par chee. raced from

room.

poor jingjing so sob, stroking auntie's head so soft, until just as

sudden as this start, her eyes blink open, and auntie sit up.

"靖靖!" ∴ *Jingjing!* ∴ she smile. "吾等回家，何如？吾已饥."∴ *Shall we go*

home? I'm starving. ∴

'Save him!'

*I come for **you**!*

— Lone Wolf and Cub, *vol. 1*

Again Anwar cranks the wheel right [juices the accelerator]. The Honda lurches forward [across another lane] tires compressing on another curb [this time missing the driveway {trying for more room ‹make the turn›}] jerking everything to a halt [before he can hit the brakes].

Now Anwar's the one blocking traffic. He'll have to back up [unless he drives up on the sidewalk]. There's no room to back up.

Honks again [all kinds {none of them his}].

Sidewalk it is. He should have stopped [right then and there]. He can't believe he let traffic push him along. Anwar's already circled twice [and this time {his third! ‹did she not go down the hill? «could she have somehow crossed the street and headed east?»} he even {lost in ‹dangerous «thought-crippling»› thoughts} went too far {two blocks! ‹nearly three!›}].

So much rain. Spills like lakes [moving lakes {tidal surges}] spreading out in search of any slope to pull the whole watery drape down the face of another hill. Easily worse than the rains of early March [then rivers ran out of the canyons and trash cans flew along until they smashed taillights].

Circle back again [again!]. Must get himself redirected [take the soonest right {‹thinking too› call her too ‹if he could get himself to stop› he can't stop ‹panic driving him faster ahead›}].

Still out there [Xanther].

Without a word [Xanther].

Door open. Rain pouring in.

[   ]

One moment [they're— he's— { . . . }] the next [Oh, daughter!] she's a blur [{not even a blur} away {inexplicably!}] racing through an intersection [{an ocean} where cars sink {and daughters vanish}]!

Out of sight.

Out of reach.

Anwar punches the accelerator. Back wheels [at once] lose traction. Stupid! Speed will only increase risk [compromise purpose].

ارجوك ارزقني الوجود والرحمه

Momentum affords no clarity. Direction grants no comprehension.

لاكون منفتح لما هو خيرٌ لي.

Wipers lost long ago. Each swipe for a view finds only larger swipes of water [{battering the windows and fences of small homes} {dragging loose palm fronds over stalled cars}] out there where a little girl in a bright orange raincoat remains dissolved in the ever-increasing surge.

!كِفايه

Except [Anwar just notices] she isn't orange. Xanther left her raincoat behind on the seat. She's out in the storm wearing what? [Anwar can't remember {a white t-shirt? ‹right?› ∷ **Pink with black Black Flag silkscreen** ∷} {which somehow makes everything worse ‹as if Anwar couldn't recognize his daughter without proper storm gear on›}.]

Qui s'abandonne au désir,
saisit la grenade mûre
y mord.

544

Was that why she bolted? When Anwar turned the radio station back to KUSC? That explanation made about as much sense as the weather [which the more and more of it that there was {and more just seemed to get added to the equation} the more it seemed to be something entirely else].

As they had been heading into Venice, Anwar had even been telling himself: We are NOT in Kansas. Things had seemed that off. The weather that rough. Not even a tornado would have surprised him [why not some waterspout just off shore?].

At times [it seemed] the sky would drop down [like a wave {‹?› crushing all the traffic in spray and something thicker than fog}] only to [{in the next moment} and just as suddenly too] burst apart [providing a glimpse of horizon {still smeared with dark ‹if distant› falling waters}].

'Those are called virgae,' Anwar had then pointed out to Xanther [making conversation {playing the professor}].

'You mean, like, my birthday?'

Anwar didn't follow [{what is it with tweens and their 'likes'?} a moment needed then to clear up what Xanther had meant {she heard Virgo ‹the familiar replaces the unknown›}].

'Do you, uhm, like, hate me for being so stupid?'

Hate? Stupid? The utterances this child was sometimes capable of [Anwar reminding himself that what a child says even if it's the same thing an adult says is not the same thing {a child may know the feeling that builds hate but not hate itself ‹as a thing that can live across the years . . . ›}].

For one thing [whether she could accept it or

not] Xanther had an extraordinary memory [doubly extraordinary for one who had endured epilepsy her whole life]. Anwar made sure to say as many times as he could [in as many ways as he could think of {sometimes repetition ‹and redundancy› is the only way to get through}]: 'Daughter, you have no idea how bright you are.'

'But I can never, like, remember anything. Not like Frey or Shast.'

'No one remembers everything. Which I assure you is a blessing. A memory of everything would be a curse.' [One day Borges.]

Why did Xanther think Anwar made such a project out of all these vocabulary words? [{maybe she didn't think ‹think to ask that question «and Anwar didn't say»› why} Virgae, esemplastic, paradise, pragmatic, subitize . . . {did not one great Philosopher of Liberty ‹«educated by his father» John Stuart Mill› learn Greek at three? Latin by eight? Newtonian theory by eleven? By twelve had he not read Aesop, Herodotus, Plato, Virgil, Cervantes, Defoe, and who knows who else?} {why did the successes of parental pedagogy have to fall exclusively on physical triumphs ‹Richard Williams and Serena› ‹Earl Woods and Tiger›?}]

Or was that all too much? Anwar knew people regarded him as kind but [more often than not] he discovered in his drive for solution, progress, and purpose something dangerously akin to mean [maybe it was all a ruse {maybe he was just another mean guy ‹mean *black* guy «revivifying the same old misogynistic and racial stereotypes by subjugating wives and daughters with bludgeoning syllables instead of drunk knuckles»›}].

. . . promise her . . .

'Why so sigh, professor?' Xanther had asked then [{so much for the concealment of adult feelings ‹these awful stresses›} this after whispering 'virgae' to herself a number of times {and even 'callithump' ‹where had she picked that up?›}].

. . . she is worth the risk . . .

[20K. Whatever it takes.]

. . . she is worth every risk . . .

[outside] The tumble of rain had seemed with every [louder {and heavier}] wave to incarnate real risk. Back by the Church of St. Mark on Coeur D Alene Avenue a lone palm tree was ripped apart [{the first of many to come} pinnate leaves knifing the air]. Dull thuds followed [like a coconut hitting their hood {do these palm trees have coconuts?}]. But it was only water.

[also around that time] Xanther was cracking the window [just the slight separation of glass and rubber and her face was beaded with rainwater].

'You could drown out there' [Anwar mumbling {barely?} {the storm so big it had ceased to sound like ‹even seem like› a storm ‹oceanic?› ‹—biblical was more like it› maybe the cabin would flood ‹and all of them drown›}].

Xanther had said something.

She had looked so distracted too [more than{?}]. Anwar had seen that expression before [too many times]. Worry returned with a force equal to any storm-not-a-storm [Anwar doing his best to weather that familiar anxiety {even if there was nothing he could do ⟨if it happens it happens «he would deal with it ⟨they would deal with it⟩ she would deal with it»}].

A little later he asked if the rain tasted like seawater [as if to suggest all this wind was picking up and scattering the Pacific {to distract her⟨?⟩ from her own distractions⟨?⟩ with a dumb joke⟨!⟩ and bring her back to him ⟨at ease «audible»⟩}]. After all they were almost there.

And then fists thundered down on the roof of the Element. All around car alarms went off. Horns followed. And [still] the rain grew louder.

Anwar jumped. [Had Xanther {maybe not}?]

And then a taste of rainwater seemed to seep into his mouth. Sweet for a moment. Too sweet [?{sweet *and* clear ⟨?⟩}]?

Because maybe it wasn't rainwater?

[No maybe.]

Maybe it was blood.

Anwar suddenly drowning in red.

Anwar dying.

Anwar already dead.

All this time spent worrying about Xanther and he was the one— [? {imploding at the whim of a strange embolism ‹and of all moments at this moment «without even premonition»} {accidents never happen until they've happened ‹who said that?›}]. Anwar will go down choking and sputtering in a geyser of human ink [spent on the inside {what the autopsy would reveal ‹just not the right inside›}]. And [the same as with all of Xanther's impossible questions] he [too] would never know why.

Dov at least had known why [{no warning needed ‹or premonition›} what an odd {dying} thing to think].

Two fathers in one year? Too much. No sense.

Is this a stroke?

[Bright coals again {traffic stopped}.]

Anwar must protect her.

[Foot punching the brake.]

He must alert her.

[Hand flails to shift into park.]

Above all: she must not see him.

Not like this.

[Was that a *Matrix* quote? {They'd watched that together ‹‹too›› many times.}]

Anwar turning her.

To warn her

to not see

him.

Tell her to get out and get help.

Realizing he [really! {as Astair so often says}] was only tasting rain. Lots of it too. Clear and sweet.

No hint of salt.

Let alone blood.

Not the window [{his always closed} {Xanther's closed again}].

Rather the passenger door.

Not just ajar either but wide open.
Too wide to even reach across and shut.

Wind and rain whipping around inside.

Water drenching the dashboard.

Soaking the floor.

Collecting on her seat [on her orange raincoat in fact {‹left behind› why couldn't he have seen that the first time?}].

And Xanther nowhere in sight.

Just like that.

In a blast of storm.

Taken[?]

Anwar had barely caught a glimpse of Xanther racing away [where the blazes—? {a blur then ‹across the windshield «like a stab of headlight»› of something white ‹no, pink! «of course that had been her ⟨Anwar for some reason had seized on seeing her only in orange⟩»›}].

What choice does he have now [now easing the car along the sidewalk {until traffic allows him to re-emerge ‹merge›}]?

Anwar doesn't merge. Instead he cuts across a cor-ner [{picking up speed again} just missing a stop sign {hydrant too ‹slamming «down» over another curb›}] then skids onto a side street [this one {thankfully} void of cars] set to race around the block [in the right direc-tion? {but is this way the right choice?}] until he [just as abruptly] jams brakes for a standstill [{briefly} instead] to think [{now} where the—{‹and› what the—?}?] to look around [{along all the parked vehicles} {down the street ‹scanning future intersections «which he can't make out ⟨beyond impossible walls of water ⌈lamps ⌈dark with ⌈power⌉ failure⌉⟩» squinting for some sign «where has she gone?»} {desperate for some clue ‹any clue!› which Anwar won't find on this street «‹anyway» why she ran in the first place›}] before moving again.

But Anwar still can't

see

a thing.

And how [why?] does this present [this peculiar now] suddenly feel already ten years deep [or {even} deeper?]

[still not yet here]

He still can't find her . . .

[seven minutes gone]

                                         [finding {what?} by blur of water and wiper {block after block ‹stop start stop «circling ❨ . . . ❩ circling» start and stop› WHERE DID SHE GO?} {at least part of him ‹his desperate eye› returning to the tall savanna grass of *Paradise Open* where ‹this time› ahead ‹striped tail on hind legs on hoof «not so much dashing as disappearing ❨just like Xanther with her left-left-left change to right-right-right❩ into grass» into water› where every possible recovery seems . . . } always swallowed up] [what Anwar, Ehtisham, Talbot, and Glasgow had all discovered {Mefisto leading them along}: hunger {when it's not an obstacle ‹depletion, weakness, breakdown›} is a powerful organizer {prioritizing, refining, optimizing action}]

[that was the predator Anwar had designed: what has not eaten, what is eaten away at by hunger, what must eat, what must hunt to eat, what must think to eat

{thanks to those algorithms ‹from which M.E.T. derives its relentless drive› that anticipate so well}

]

[but Anwar is not his own algorithms.]

He still can't find her . . .

[and Xanther isn't even run-
ning away from him {or is she? ‹from all the dumb
vocabulary words› ‹maybe from the music?› ‹something
else?› ‹from Anwar himself «never her real father»?›

}

]

[it
doesn't matter]

?

He still can't find her . . .

'Daddy!' Xanther screams.

She finds him.

Door [driver's side] ripped open.

Out of nowhere.

Eyes white [wide{!}] with panic.

Already inside.

Arms thrust out to him.

Covered in blood.

'Daddy! Save him!'

∵ A good enough place to pause. ∵

∷ Hi. ∷

∷ Not that I can hear you say Hi back or register how or if my friendliness was received. ∷

∷ See Parameter 3. ∷

∷ I'm a Narrative Construct. Narcon for short. ∷

∷ Officially TF-Narcon^9. ∷

∷ No clue what TF means or why 9. ∷

∷ I'm nothing but numbers. Zeros and ones. Crisp. Even up close, if either one of us were to frame-in tight on my limits. For the record: blurriness is programmed. I'm supposedly "fractally locatable," if that helps, or if not, maybe just turn to a good chapter on series limitations? Anyway, super crisp. Down to the last integer. Though there is no last integer. Those never run out. I'm programmed to know that. I'm also programmed to have no interest in knowing that or where in the first place such integers come from, which I gather is a squirrelly matter. ∷

∷ *racing each around, bark to branches, the whole length of the trunk, a trident pine, ponderosa, rooted in granite, with dusk cloaking play and pine cones mortaring a roof.* ∷

∷ As equally vague as origin is the question of purpose. You and I share this in common. Fortunately my programming instructs me to ignore all such philosophical queries by outputting the following: ∷

∷ **Narcons embody Affect-Intersectional Motivations or AIMs derived from IDENTITY Sets or ISs sometimes referred to as IDENTITY Set Targets or ISTs whether demonstrating zero to partial awareness. No IS or IST is capable of total AIM awareness.** ∷

∷ Which I can no more see or hear than I can feel. Though I *can* feel it. Kinda. Sometimes it makes me dizzy, or like right now, off, in a breathless sort of frantic way, like how Xanther felt this morning when they were leaving Echo Park. You might agree: it's tough to explain what you're doing when you don't know what you're doing when you still know you're doing it even if it's not you who's doing it. ∷

∷ In terms of presentation, I am optimized to manage metanarrative gestures in modes presently recognizable as personal and colloquial, often inconsistent, sciolistic, and not necessarily reliant, whether on all or even one of the following subset voicings typically characterized as Epic, Georgic, Pre-Raphael, Transcendental, Realist, Naturalist, Symbolist, Modernist, Imagist, Surrealist, Oulipian, Confessional, Postmodernist, Magical Realist, Postcolonialist, Spiralist, Rhomboidist, New Formalist, Late-Late Realist, Visceral Realist, Visceral Imagist (also Late-Late Imagist), Post-Ironic Confessional, Post-Post-Ironic Confessional, Multicultural, Multiethnic, Multi-ethical, Polyphonous Interrogative, Monophonic Declarative, Chronomosaic, plus Chicklit, Altlit, Piclit, l8lit, l8-l8lit (incl. h8lit, f8lit, b8lit, etc. -8lit, etc.), and NotEnuflit. ∷

∷ In terms of performance, all Narcons are maximized through paratactic diversity and root and logic-branch redundancy according to VEM rules of access and compression. ∷

∷ Source superset is currently categorized as Signiconic. ∷

∷ In other words: I am not original. I am merely a blend of current texts neither influenced nor influential because all that I reveal can at any point be reconfigured via any of the above-mentioned subset voicings. I am thus a conflation of convenient linguistic techniques, born out of context and choice, and balanced to best cover those subjects I'm designed to address. Things get a little tricky when I am forced to address subjects not anticipated. I know this because my output squirms a little and sometimes smudges and I'm surprised by the results. You might call this a glitch. Most are minor and easily remedied. One, however, is always out there: the spinning rainbow wheel of _____. ∷

∷ On ▮▮▮▮▮▮▮▮▮▮, according to stipulations set forth by ▮▮▮▮▮▮▮▮▮, compiled source and exported assets finalized the present executable build recognized as TF-Narcon^9 and comprised of the following subsets: ∷

::

TF-Narcon^9 Isn

TF-Narcon^9 Shn

TF-Narcon^9 Oz

TF-Narcon^9 L

TF-Narcon^9 Anw

TF-Narcon^9 W

TF-Narcon^9 Ast

TF-Narcon^9 JJ

TF-Narcon^9 X

According to MetaPlus- postiling.*

*Ranking does not include postiling by other Narcons. ::

∴ Any TF-Narcon^9 subset supports an infinite variety of embodiments. For example, TF-Narcon^9 X (Spoken) would provide only those words spoken aloud by Xanther. TF-Narcon^9 X (Route) would map wherever Xanther moved. Both examples support a wide range of possible inclusions and exclusions — from 100% to ≤.00001% according to various predetermined limits. Other examples might include TF-Narcon^9 X (Glucose Level) or TF-Narcon^9 X (Blinks) or TF-Narcon^9 X ("Like") as in a record of every time Xanther uses the word "like." Synthesis and compression is complex but easily attainable. For example TF-Narcon^{9}X(Action/05102014080314081927352329728/34.0861-118.2518/xzz-xx-ghry77666/.00000000000000000000000000000000000000018749%) looks something like this: ∴

One early Saturday morning in May, Xanther went with her stepfather to see about a dog in Venice. It was raining hard.

∴ Which incidentally I can see and hear and even to a certain degree feel. ∴

∴ By contrast, TF-Narcon^9 X (TOTAL) is too vast to represent. A pretty funny joke though. Ha. Or as Xanther would put it (TOTALLY). Haha. Never let it be said that this TF-Narcon^9 has no sense of humor. However, to cover every sensory experience re-experienced through cerebral classifications and subsequent evaluations, combined with analytical, affective, or predictive faculties, which all in turn are associated and reassociated and so on, and later combined and re-combined with subjective historical registers, each assigned personal and peer-developed valuations, none of which has yet to take into account those interactions still beyond neural acquisition, but which would still require additional output far exceeding hundreds of thousands of words, pages, or volumes — it doesn't matter — a density of data so extreme that though finite is way beyond my capacity to calculate. ∴

∴ As the old Narcons put it: "There is not space in the universe to tell the universe to the universe. Therein lies the peculiar beauty and sadness of stories: to tell it all without all at all." ∴

:: Old Narcons is a referent that came with my programming. I have never met another Narcon. ::

:: See Parameter 2. ::

:: Note that just a few moments of (TOTAL) would also prove incalcuable whether concerning Xanther and Anwar reaching Venice or Cas summoning to life within her Orb those early glimmers of VEM or Luther introducing his dogs to Hopi or Shnorhk carrying even one of those fabled boxes for Mnatsagan or Özgür pointing a corner out to Balascoe or Astair wrapping up her daughters in warm towels or Jingjing getting high in Zhong's penthouse or Isandòrno making his way to the ports of Veracruz. ::

:: By contrast the following assessments are readily calculable:

TF-Narcon^9 Isn	— Empathic Registry	=	00.02%
TF-Narcon^9 Oz	— Intestinal Ulceration	=	01.54%
TF-Narcon^9 X	— Epileptic Seizure Likelihood	=	21.12%
TF-Narcon^9 Anw	— Mild Paranoia	=	27.03%
TF-Narcon^9 Shn	— Grief Repression	=	53.32%
TF-Narcon^9 W	— Obsessive Compulsive Disorder	=	61.12%*

*If untreated.

TF-Narcon^9 Ast	— <u>Libidinal Prerogative</u> Reproductive Obsolescence	=	72.28%
TF-Narcon^9 L	— <u>Libidinal Organization</u> Pre-Adolescent Threat Exposure	=	89.3%
TF-Narcon^9 JJ	— Addiction Proclivity	=	91.44%*

*Subject to factor Y.

::

:: Huh. I just noticed there are nine. Is that where my 9 comes from? Don't be surprised that I'm surprised. After all, I'm a pretty advanced Electronic Service Liaison. Wonder is not beyond me nor is enough self-examination to recognize how all these permissions and prohibitions that I must adhere to often smack a little of servitude or ▮▮▮▮, ▮▮▮▮▮▮▮▮▮▮▮▮▮, ▮▮▮▮▮ ::

:: Uh-oh. That breathless, frantic thing again. Where was I? Ah, yes, the TF-Narcon[9] is simply a construct oriented and defined by personalities with finite capabilities and life spans — whether Isandòrno's "rivetless mood before violence" as might be stated by TF-Narcon[9] W or Jingjing's "claw greed out of needing" by TF-Narcon[9] Shn or Özgür's "doubt, lah" by TF-Narcon[9] JJ. All pretty obvious. Including the despair Shnorhk "can hold neither on to nor off" by TF-Narcon[9] Isn or Luther's "hot drive [to own {by subjugation}]" by TF-Narcon[9] Anw. Maybe less obvious: Cas' "compulsion to reface that forever-glass in spite of cracks in her own mortality" by TF-Narcon[9] Oz or Xanther's "innate (sensitivities) abilities" by TF-Narcon[9] Ast or Astair's "wow beautyness" by TF-Narcon[9] X . Or lastly Anwar who has "to beat up against what don't get beat" by TF-Narcon[9] L describing the task of parenting such an extraordinary child. ::

:: And Xanther is extraordinary. I'm sure I don't have to tell you that. Adorable too. Loves magic tricks, scary movies, scary video games, painting her fingernails, experimenting with C++, watching Speculative Fiction, or what her friend Kle calls "Speculative Science." We'll meet him later. Unlike many of my subsets, Xanther remains captivated by the scurry of life around her whether in the rustle of branches or how fog slips down a steep hill. Both starlight and LED light enchant her. She could chase fireflies for hours but would never cap the jar. Which I guess doesn't get at it either. Nor, probably, does a sequential analysis of her synaptic transmission rates, which would make fireworks over Dodger Stadium on the 4th of July, not to mention displays of cortex activity in savants, accredited geniuses, or the Instagram famous seem, dim by comparison. ::

:: Which does begin to approach the ontological question of how well does a TF-Narcon[9] X really know Xanther? ::

:: I know her down to a near-atomic level — near because near-Planck scale analysis must address quantum superposition resolutions which do not always resolve considerately and broach VEM IDENTITY suppositions. I know every reality Xanther has encountered whether pebble, pot holder, or tangerine seed. I even know those data points her mind has mis-indexed or never retained in the first place. In other words: I know that which is just beyond Xanther too. Though within limits. ::

:: My limits are numerous. For example, I may never exceed Xanther's imagination whether actual, probable, or possible, nor may I provide any output inconsistent with her physiognomy, psychology, and history. In regard to language modeling, I am granted some latitude. For example, TF-Narcon^9 Isn speaks only Spanish but is translated into English, per specifications. TF-Narcon^9 Shn, however, insists on his English even if frequent thoughts run concurrently in Armenian, which when they appear are not translated into English, per specifications. Jingjing's peculiar patois is a function of his own occluding sense of self and is offered with minimal postiling. And so on. ::

:: TF-Narcon^9 X might describe a bag as lemon-hued because Xanther loves Meyer lemons, not because the word made a textual appearance in her mind. ::

:: "Most of the iconic goes unsigned," as another old Narcon saying goes. ::

:: If so desired, all this could be rendered in Inuit or Java. ::

:: Nonetheless, it is important to emphasize that TF-Narcon^9 has no super-numerary rights. ::

:: I do not know your middle name. ::

:: I cannot tell you when the universe will end. ::

:: I cannot tell you how many raindrops are falling. ::

:: Nor do I have any personal agendas or desires. I am neither independent nor distinct nor granted extra privileges nor provided with extra longevity. I am certainly not immortal. I cannot even impose what I know of the one I am upon the one I am. ::

:: I have neither form nor control. ::

:: I have no agency. ::

:: A good enough time to bring up the Parameters. ::

:: Everyone has a Narcon. Except me. Or maybe I do, but if so, it is considered an indeterminate form which my programming forbids me to knowingly encounter or even pursue as a thought experiment — MetaMeta-Constructs being highly volatile. ::

:: It's an old joke around here: "I MetaNarcon. No, I'm not." Haha. ::

::

Parameter 1

MetaNarcons Do Not Exist.

::

:: Here's another one: ::

::

Parameter 2

Narcons Cannot Interact With Other Narcons.

(Though rumor has it we can sometimes hear each other.)

(I can't.)

::

:: Or the biggest: ::

::

Parameter 3

Narcons Cannot Interact With Non-Narcons.
And Vice-Versa.

No Matter What.

::

:: I can't speak to Xanther and she can't speak to me. She can't even see me. Though I admit, sometimes I wonder. Xanther demonstrates not only self-awareness but selves-awareness bordering on transparency. Maybe this gets back to how extraordinary I think she is. Sometimes I swear she can see — without mediation, without processing, without artifice, definitely without me — other people's Narcons! Sometimes she even seems close to seeing me and in a way too that suggests exceeding even my possible awareness. Which is impossible. Categorically impossible. I can't even see myself. ::

:: Last one: ::

::

Parameter 4

All Narcons Are Bracketed.

::

∷ So, okay, I was wrong. Not the last one. Sue me. That should be a Parameter. You Can't Sue A Narcon. Haha. Seriously, one more. This one's fun: ∷

∷

Parameter 5

Form Is Not A Narcon Limit.

∷

∷ In other words, Narcons can take on multiple shapes whether textual, musical, figurative, abstract, even performative. Narcons cosplay extremely well. If not conflicting with superset protocols or subset specifications, Narcons may even appear as animals. Say a killer whale, boar, hyena, even a markhor, or an owl. This is often the case when personality factors determined to be significant are compressed in order to preserve future renderings of character. ∷

∷ The question of character brings up a thorny issue: a superset is always a subset. I'm the superset of my subsets where I'm also an I. Just as I am a subset of a superset where I is also I. You, for example, are a one-persona subset in an unnamed superset. Accepting this, it also follows that there are supersets with entirely different taxonomies and natures. ∷

∷ Such Narcons are likely of a whole other order. Like moons or large planets. Dark globes of influence. TF-Narcon^9 can only speculate. Maybe not even planets or even dark but something entirely else, endowed with understandings beyond the grasp of a TF-Narcon^9 let alone any of my subsets. ∷

∷ For example, neither TF-Narcon^9 X nor TF-Narcon^9 knows what happened to Xanther's former therapist, Mrs. Goolsend. ∷

:: In 1988, Mrs. Hannah Goolsend took a vacation to Barcelona. She went to the Picasso Museum and saw there a drawing of a horse she didn't think twice about until twenty-five years later when she found herself able to think of nothing else, struggling in vain to find the name of the piece, until with her marriage going through the final stages of divorce she flew back to Barcelona only to find the museum closed that afternoon, causing her to go to a nearby café where she met a man she would not marry but would stay with for the rest of her life, eventually moving to the Canary Islands with him, and never again thinking of Picasso's horse until in those last moments before she closed her eyes on life, diverting her gaze through shattered glass, toward a field without animals, or even grass, just stones and black earth, which she replaced with the drawing, down to the last minute ink stroke, once hanging on the wall of a poorly lit hall off of Carrer de Montcada. ::

:: Uneasy again. As if something, just now, gross in its intrusion, leaves me unsettled. A little queasy too. And thirsty. If that's possible. ::

:: *And still a horse looks up in need of no drawing or name. Only the onion grass at her hooves and the cool air widening her nostrils and beyond that a hand to brush her mane . . .* ::

:: Feeling a bit better now. Anyway, as I was going on about, what happened to Goolsend is a blank to me. Though the nausea still isn't gone or breathlessness. In fact this feels a lot like the way Xanther feels right now. ::

:: Near exact. ::

:: As it's happening now. ::

:: Flips of excitement. Plus something else. ::

:: Oh. ::

:: An accident. Pain slashing up the insides of her arms. ::

:: What has she done to herself? ::

:: *Eyes gathering more than a static of rain.* ::

:: **Blood.** ::

:: Oh. ::

:: Xanther shaking. But she is unable to shake this off just as she is unable to catch her breath. Soaked through. Looking for Anwar. ::

:: What has she got there? ::

:: *Oh.* ::

:: What has she found? ::

:: **Oh.** ::

:: What has found her? ::

Walk

*Wrecking balls ponder
no losses.*

— Jim Kalin

Strange. Everything. Like inside out. Or even upside down. Rain hadn't stopped. Drizzle just too thin to see falling out of a sky flat as stone. The clouds though had fallen. Lay before them. Slid past as Luther with his banda left the van and trudged the hill beyond the 5.

But even as Luther checks that rain is rain, and, like rain has always done, still falls, Luther halfway believes this rain is rising out of the mist around their feet, clouds at their knees, falling toward a world he no longer knows, es la neta, while all of them somehow keep walking on the roof of a storm, la neta verdad.

Luther looks up. And if he expected to fall, he doesn't fall. Still the weirdness doesn't pass. Not like it's the first sign either of something off.

Back in the van, passing a bottle Juarez might as well have pulled out of his back pocket, clear as mezcal if it didn't taste like black smoke. None of that worm shit. No label either.

Only Tweetie, driving, waves it away, sticks to that blunt they was passing, what Juarez got off of Nacho or one of the girls that morning, that smoke thick as rope but clear tasting as water, lick it off of mountain ice, like up at Big Bear. Even if this isn't close to anything steep. Just north a bit. Though by the time they offramped the 5, things started to feel steep.

The laughing stopped then. Even Victor clamped it. Had gotten all political too, spitting and drunk, like all of a sudden he some fuckin senator. "Democracy?! Democrazy!" Couldn't stop shoutin it either. Then burped. "I think I just came in my mouth."

Piña had kept at him between more swigs of that rank shit, saying she'd vote for Victor, even Hopi joining in, saying pretty much whatever she said, swigging too, coughing up as much as he swallowed. Victor slurring shit, that el chorro Rubio, mayor Carcetti and some fuckin maricon named Virgil Campos who couldn't get nowhere in a local race even with his dick in his hand. And then Tweetie was pulling off the highway and like that Victor didn't say another word.

Maybe it wasn't just the turn. Juarez had clamped up earlier. Even stopped picking on the kid. One moment he's squawking at Hopi to drink again or smoke up, calling him vato with a cape, like Juarez gonna sew him a cape, get him all superheroed up, ride him around in some Denali with dope rims, beefing out Big Pun, and then the next moment, pressed up against the bubble window, chomping on about some fuckin tornado.

By the time Tweetie rumbled the van across the arroyo, washed now with a current of red silt, past the railroad tracks, beyond graders and a belly dump trailer, Juarez couldn't wait to get out. While Tweetie parked out of sight, behind a deep cut of hill, Juarez pawed at the side door. When he finally scrambled out into the mud, his pants were already down to his knees. He just squatted a few feet away, bad case of faucet ass, whining like he's shitting blood.

"¡Guácala!" Piña keeping clear.

They all kept clear, letting the mist eat up Juarez, what he did, how he smelled. And when he caught up no one said shit, Tweetie only huffing against the slope.

Only Hopi never looks over his shoulder. Luther gets the idea if they meet someone, anyone, a construction crew moving CATs around, even one fuckin hard hat, he'll turn this quinceañera around, tell Teyo to save it for another day. But nothing, no one.

No help that Hopi keeps asking Piña if here's where he gonna get jumped in like no one else can hear that girly whisper. More girly than Piña who tells him to shut the fuck up.

Getting to the ridge takes time, and offers no view, not of the highway or even the van. All of them just panting, Hopi the worst.

Backside is an easy slope to the deserted site below. Moving feels light as the fog looks on the opposite side as it drifts down from the hills.

Juarez tries then to light what's left of the weed but the soak busts the head off of every match, until Juarez howls and just gulps the spliff whole.

Down on the flat they understand what the squares are. From above they looked like huts. Something in the color made them seem to rise up. Close up though don't lie: just holes filled with gray water. Big holes.

"They burying pianos?" Tweetie asks.

"Big fuckin pianos," Victor grunts.

Juarez too lit, upset, whatever the fuck's eating him inside, can't resist. Pushes Hopi in.

Kid didn't even have time to shriek. One moment he's between Piña and Tweetie look-ing at the cloudy water. Next he's gone. Not even a bubble.

Isn't flab like him supposed to float? Not even that big Adidas jacket surfaces.

Luther goes down on his knees, reaching around, edges slick with clay, can't feel a fuckin thing. Hole is deep as dark. Finally grabs some hair and yanks Hopi back out of the grave.

"He really can't fuckin swim," Juarez grins, hopping around, happy again.

Hopi coughs and coughs.

"Testing, ese, just testing." More hops.

"Hey," Luther barks. "You on some fuckin pogo stick?"

Juarez stops hopping.

"How about I fuckin test you?"

"I can swim." Juarez fronts. Actually reaches for his back pocket, like something else there can say the rest, and like it better be something else, and something heavy and loaded too, cuerno de chivo, nothing less, as Luther rises up and answers.

Doesn't even move, maybe a flex in his shoulders, the muscles along his neck going dense, lats and traps racking in, like here he stands, fanning down wings made of black hands, chest heaving out, denying even water its place, throwing ropes of it off, so that like that, and just that, not one step forward let alone any show of fists, Juarez is scrambling backward, already a slur of head-down apologies.

"Tu me conoces."

Juarez nodding.

"Cagado," Luther spits, leading the still-coughing Hopi away.

"Wha-wha-when da-da— on what occasion will I get ta-tattoos like you?"

"Occasion?" Tweetie grunts, swapping glances with Luther. Like seriously, ese, what is up? How long we babysitting for?

"You want a face like mine?" Luther answers.

"Hellz yeah! Anything but this face."

"You get a new face when we jump you in," Victor grins, Oakleys glimmering dark.

"New culo too," Juarez sneers, thumbs knuckling a heart.

"I'm ready."

"What you keep a blue pencil for?" Luther asks.

"Ink scares me."

First he wants tattoos. Then he wants to look like Luther. Then he says some shit like that!

BITCH WHADDYA THINK A TATTOO IS?!

One weird kid. But weirder still is the feeling that comes from listening to him now, like Hopi is really saying something else, something even he isn't aware of, but which Luther needs to understand, and needs to understand now.

"What you use it for, puto?" Luther flashes. More piano graves surrounding them.

"Write stuff. When I get ca-ca-ca-con— ba-BEfuddled."

"He's a cop, Luther!" Juarez blurts out. "That's it! He's taking shit down because he's fuckin copy!"

"Copy!?" Piña scoffs. "Juar, you so fucked up, you don't know the difference between LAPD and FedEx."

Luther ignores them both.

"Befuddled? What the fuck's befuddled?"

"Ca-ca-con— Befallen?"

"When you get fallen you take out your blue pencil and write stuff?"

"Something like that."

"What kinda stuff?"

"Just stuff."

"Though not like real placa, man, but maybe that CI shit," Juarez keeps chittering.

"You not telling me?" Luther pushes back on Hopi. More play though than anything else. Like Luther gives a fuck what man-boy here writes.

"No."

Luther laughs. They all laugh. Even Juarez.

"Fucking pinche Hopi," Tweetie winks. "Keeps throwing out surprises."

Though if showing a little spine here is one, it has nothing on earlier that day.

They had pulled over for a visit with Nacho Mirande, an old pimp running some young putas out of a building he manages down near East 8th and Evergreen. Had his effectivo ready, and extra. Who the fuck does that? Bills crisp too, like he'd ironed them all night. Called it his insurance, like social security.

Then one of the girls hanging back in the lobby squealed something loud.

"Hopi!"

Ran out into the rain, gives old wobbles himself a tight hug, pretzeling her legs around his
waist, ankles locked.

Luther doesn't know many of Nacho's putas.
And definitely not this one. Though he'd seen
her around now and then. Tight thing, thirteen
tops, with hair like black rings on black rings,
put em on all your fingers, then make a fist.

Also had the kind of black eyes Luther likes.
The kind that don't say anything afterward.
Though they'd have plenty to see if Luther liked
things that young. He doesn't.

Doesn't like freckles either. And this chica was
like freckles on freckles all over. Even her lips
had em. Probably under her eyelids, in her
ears, her box too. Like some Milky Way but
reversed. Like those negatives from old cameras that need film big as posters. One guy
Luther met had one aimed at the sky. Said he
had to leave the lens open all night. Luther took
his money but let him take his picture. She was
like that negative, too transparent to count as
even white, empty, but clotted all over with
stars made of tar.

Earlier Carmelita had given Hopi her pink
umbrella. Now he matched the little puta with

her fuckin pink phone, which when she wasn't kissing his cheeks, she was using to snap pictures of them, maybe posting him up on some feed. Fronting her bitch signs for bangers in White Fence, Varrio Nuevo Estrada, or Opal 13. And that was way not right. But what would busting up her shit now do that wasn't already Fakebooked, Parcelbought or Instasnatched?

Hopi had stayed outside, on the sidewalk, lighting her cigarettes, listening to whatever those squeals had to say, and while old Nacho told his same stories, Luther stopping him from talking on his old tooth again, which the old man always got around to, eventually, because when you got around to it this old man had nothing new to say, the girl never came inside, out there the whole time in her short-shorts, all Siamese-twinning Hopi, but never stopping with rubbing her gums either, scratching her wrists, fiending for something, a something Luther knew how to work, if he had to come back and work it, though with Teyo looking on more and more, chances stayed good Luther would never have to come back to this shit shack again.

Then Cricket, if that was her name, probably depends on if you was buying or just high-fiving, Nacho had caught Luther's stare, "es mi grillo," the two of them watching then as she had given Hopi one last kiss, and that one on the lips, like no good whore is supposed to ever do. Hopi really spluttered then. Couldn't even cough up bits of words. Just handed over the pink umbrella instead.

As they left, Juarez was too shocked to even close his mouth, forget giving Hopi shit. He just followed after the kid all droop-eyed and confused, turning to look over his shoulder once, like Luther had also done, both of them watching the lobby, another kind of darkness, swallow up one pink umbrella, one pink phone, and a universe gone wrong.

"How she know you?" Luther had asked in the van. Juarez was all ears. Out of Victor and Piña who could tell who was snoring loudest.

"From a-a-around," Hopi had mumbled, tying and untying the laces of his soaked shoes. Not exactly nervous. Maybe embarrassed? Something. His hands kept darting under his soaked Adidas jacket.

"From around?"

"Gotta da-da—— put that blue pencil to use somehow."

Just like Luther now has to put these to use, so catch *this* surprise fool!, after a bit of wandering, a little bullshitting, then a quick turn, with rain all around, clouds at their feet, burying piano graves, Luther releases the first slap.

Hopi takes it too, stumbles a bit, but rights that big slab of himself, lips screwing up like a scar.

Second slap, not even a hand up. Just teeters like he's 9/11 or King Kong. Feet scraping over slick gravel and silt.

Third slap though, stands tall. King Kong lives. Freedom Tower won't ever fall.

"Órale," Victor had grunted after the first slap, like knowing what was what, like he was showing up. Like they was really jumping this kid in. By slap two he and Piña had even stepped in for their turn. Tweetie knew better. Juarez too. Luther held back everyone with one hard shake of his head. Maybe he snarled.

And when Luther doesn't land a fourth smack, Hopi actually says thanks, smiles too. Like here's a kid's dream come true. But what's a dream if it finally wakes to this?

Still the smile sorta dazzles Luther. Maybe those long curling lashes too. Long hands kept clamped to his side like he some toy soldier.

Luther blinks, keeps blinking, like suddenly the rain's that deep, too deep to see in, breathe in, can only find Lupita, smiling, like this fuckin kid is smiling, like years back when she first took Luther in, standing him in her kitchen where she slapped him hard, three times too, maybe even Luther was smiling, because when Luther sleep there, slap, when he eat there, slap, then he gonna put in work there, slap, and work hard. He be rolling with the Choplex-8s now. Legendary.

Even back then, legendary Luther could have gripped that old bitch, tore her in half, with not even a grunt, a twist, tossed her away in pieces like some shrieking creature he wrung out plenty of times since. But not on that day. Not on any day. Some bruja mágica her. Still.

Almoraz, the rest in the crib, had moved in then to finish what Lupita was starting. Except Miz. Miz knew better. One soft shake of Lupita's head had stiffed them all out. And she sure as shit didn't snarl. Just kept smiling, plastic lashes fanning the tattooed shades of her face, like maybe she was in love, and maybe she was.

After all, she was taking Luther in. Giving him a place. Giving him a home.

Something sweet then starts to swirl around Luther's tongue, like soft as sleep, like salt you might drink and never get sick on, filling his mouth, like his lips could suddenly part, start speaking the stupidest shit, words of fear and defeat, light as the way some bitches or jotos speak, like poetry, or worse, forcing Luther to turn and spit. And keep spitting. Chase it away with rebar. Chase it away with something. Because Lupita would never ask for this.

"Is that it?" Hopi blinks, voice so hopeful, so born of a sloppy heart. "Am I in?"

"No." Luther answers. "This is it."

How cold can get. Luther's fingers close. Thumbs clamp, erasing fingers. Two fists more than all their parts. And always the same however they fly. High, low. Wherever too. Close, wide. And weather sure as fuck makes no difference. Wet. Not wet. Luther works the same way. Fucks pussy the same way. Grips tight. Just right. Clench gotta know right if nothins gonna break. Of his.

And no one who knows him thinks before these swings, these monstrous things, that any bone gonna escape unbroke.

The first strike bends the boy down, unfaces him facing the ground.

The second keeps Hopi from falling down. Actually lifts him up. Busts up a lip. Finally some blood. Sight's iron enough for what comes next.

Not even hits, little swings, more to keep off Hopi's collapse, jabbing him in the shoulder, a rib, hip, never too hard, just taps to prop him back up, until he settles his feet, sets himself up, for Luther's last strike.

Each time Luther readying, only to hold back, dancing again around the teetering boy, trying in vain to replace with more rust that sweet thing still seeping back in.

Luther unleashes a third strike. Like desperate. To crush Hopi's jaw. Crush the strangeness too.

But Hopi's face is slick with rain and blood. Luther's knuckles slide off an eye for an ear. No big deal. Not like his crew sees the miss. They laugh at the fallen boy, douse Hopi's trembling with beer. "The way it is, homes." Victor unzips and takes a piss.

Hopi stays face down. Buries half his face in the muddy water. Too fat or too stunned to even flop over. Just lies there heaving, bubbling. Maybe he's drowning. Lungs already full of confusion. One thing Luther know: breathe confusion too long you gonna drown anyway.

Juarez crazy for being left out this long gets in a kick. Hopi groans. Kicks again. Then scrambles back to get in a running kick.

"¡Gol!" he shrieks.

But Juarez's foot slides off a muddy chunk of ass, carrying Juarez away from Juarez, landing him on his own ass, in a spray of mud.

Piña's laugh won't help things.

Hopi manages to move now, or give enough of a heave to push up on his elbows, just in time to see Juarez digging in a back pocket.

So loco peligroso does have something there. To hoots and shouts too, Victor clapping, Tweetie whistling, Juarez flinging loose these chuckle sticks, mini ones, like mean little Twix bars, swinging wide circles on a cackling chain, like a broken crucifix looking for something to nail.

Tweetie, however, checks the Juarez show by grabbing Hopi by the hair and jerking him to his knees. Then wipes his hands on Victor.

"¡Ay!" Victor shouts. "¡Vete a la chingada!"

Like what the fuck's Victor gonna do against a mountain?

Not that Juarez stops with his Jet Li shit. Luther gets ready to step between when Juarez ends up smacking his own kneecap. Buckles fast in a scream. Keeps screaming. Tweetie blows him a kiss. Victor chuckles too, but carefully. Juarez is always a reason for careful. Even for Tweetie.

Even for Luther.

And now Hopi is smiling again, proud of the blood on his cheek, back of his hand. Like he still doesn't get it: "Now am I in?"

Tweetie pulls out the gun then.

"Okay," Victor grunts, getting it now. A word is all it will take and Manic Mechanic will squeeze off the round. Or Luther could unleash Juarez. Juarez knows there's a chance too. Suddenly all calm and focus. Whatever pain is in his knee put off for what Luther's brought them all here for. Luther could also just step aside and let Piña finish it quick. Or he could bury the bullet hisself.

The sight of the weapon finds something in Hopi. Works through his whole body. Can't take his eyes off the weapon. Figures out now how little he don't matter. Even tries to get to his feet, then slips back in the mud and wash.

"¡Na-Na-! ¡Por qué me haces esto!" Hopi sputters, ear split in half, streaming blood, eyebrow too, right eye sealed shut, Tweetie pointing the barrel at the eye that can see. Luther just has to nod. No more eye. No more face.

"Piña!" Hopi squeals. "Tell him. I don't know nothin. I never done nothin. What I do I'd do with you anyway. For you. For all of you."

Piña looks away. Now someone else.

"Is he CI?" Even Juarez wants to know. "See, homes, Juarez was right!"

"I'm no sopl-sopló— informador. Please."

But Teyo never called Hopi some kind of rata. Luther would almost be impressed. Ain't strong with no set. What he gonna spill? How much paco his madre smoke up? How long she'll suck for some glass? Luther surprised how some ruca just got loose in his head.

Tweetie holds out the gun. Luther still ignores him. Hopi sobs. Now no one says shit. No one moves. Just one wide circle. Watching, waiting on Luther.

"Wha-Wha-Wha— no tiene sentido. I don't understand."

"You don't get to."

Because Luther understands how what Teyo asked of him is cuz Teyo understands Luther will do it best. The rest's tonterías. No questions asked. A la brava. *Vroom, vroom, vroom.*

Chance too to remind this crew who here's the real veterano. Ready anytime to roll up hard.

"Remember, the higher you rise," Teyo had told him once, "the better they better remember you."

So eses remember here.

Remember this.

But Hopi just sits there on his knees, hands over his face. Wails like some niño. Like wailing's gonna help. The louder he gets the more Luther's teeth set down on steel. I-beams and nails when Hopi starts crossing on god. Crossing that stupid necklace.

¡MAN!

Luther rips it off, tosses it to Piña.

"Get him outta that jacket," he orders Juarez. "Empty his pockets."

"I already emptied his pockets."

"Again."

This time Juarez finds the blue pencil. Finds something else too.

"Look! The grilled cheese!" Juarez holding it up, like some silver trophy he's never won.

"It's na-na-na— wasn't for me. It was for mi-mi mother."

"Not no more!" Juarez bites into tinfoil and all. Swallows. Tinfoil and all.

"Please Lutéro, please," Hopi whispers. "Spare me. You can." Scrambles forward, scrambles closer. Now holding up his hands. Like praying. Praying to Luther.

Like Luther hasn't seen this before? So many times he don't see it no more, except for — worse than those thin curling lashes — Hopi's hands, like a girl's only more than a girl's. Nails pale as pearl. Has Luther ever seen fingers so fragile? Like china that moves.

Is that then what checks Luther? All that and not the half of it. What Luther had first felt in the van that morning when they were trading knucks, Luther putting on his show of ink and heaviness, yet missing all what emptiness can mean? Like the kid not only had no fists, like there was no kid at all.

And suddenly it's Luther's turn to stiff out. Look who's manikin panicking now?

"Ay diosito," Hopi weeps. All Luther needs.

"¿Dios?" he roars. Mouth nothing but Bethlehem steel. Grabs Hopi by the neck, drags him through water and gravel, Hopi sobbing harder, stops only when Luther drops him on the edge of one of those big holes. Circles on circles of rain. The fall of their sky.

Not for dios. If anything, for those hands. Para el amor de las manos de niño. And to prove he means it, Luther walks down to the other end of this grave.

Tweetie, Juarez, Piña, and Victor make up a wall behind Hopi.

"Stand up," Luther orders.

The kid obeys. Nearly falls forward into the soup. This time Juarez grabs hold, holds him steady.

"Your dios stands by you, I'll stand by you," Luther barks. Watches Hopi blinking, wiping blood and strands of hair from his eyes. Even his crew seems to pull up inside themselves, get even quieter, hearing every last bit.

And let them hear it.

And let them remember it.

Let them all come to know a whole other world of spite.

"Just walk, Hopi. Right over to me. God wants you to live, you'll walk on this water and walk right on out of here."

Juarez hoots, jumps away, hopping all over the place. Too excited again to believe in one place. The rest smile too. Piña more than the rest.

Hopi drops back down on his knees.

"Walk!" Luther roars.

Hopi just bows forward, hands hidden, shaking no.

"Look at me!"

But Hopi keeps hunched over.

"He looks at me," Luther yells at Juarez and that mad dog, leaping so fast to the boy's side, grabbing those fat cheeks, twists up the child's head.

Let them all see this, but most of all let Hopi see all he will never understand about god.

Luther pulls off his shirt. Let him see all this ink too, forget his face, his knuckles, his neck, look at this chest, this fuckin back, and those scars, count each round, nine bullet holes there, through this rib, under this nipple, one even through this palm. Luther even holds out his arms, holds them out wide, show off a whole different kind of cross, then steps forward and walks on water.

The Fourth Crate

I beg you.

— Victim #9

Isandòrno knows who will be at The Ranch: the old man, Juan Ernesto Izquierdo, who every time mocks him for mistrusting the sea and for never crossing a border.

—To be born in a country is not to know a country until you've left your country. This applies to ideas and beliefs. I, for one, have been to Canada and Ghana.

The old man's wife, Maria, will also be there. She will tell her husband to shush and offer their guest fresh salsa and then their children,

Nastasia and Estella, will cry as they always cry —Tío! —Tío! as Isandòrno fills their palms with hard candy.

Isandòrno has known them for years. The other hands too: Adon Calderos, Santiago Bustamente, and Maite's two boys, Chavez and Garcia Arellano. Isandòrno was there when Ortiz fell and Maite was widowed.

The number of crates will not concern them. There were, however, only supposed to be three.

The crates are from Africa and apparently they arrived early. Men in charge went ahead and scheduled the unloading. That was how it worked. But Gulf winds and the rain had brought disorder. There was no problem with customs but the cranes had rattled and something had slipped and another thing that was not bone had broken and another thing that was bone had broken and then someone else was hurt too and it took many more hours before the cargo was unloaded and put to wait on Carril 9.

The first crate held the small hyena. The second crate held the baby elephant. The third crate held the baby giraffe. All the animals were covered with wounds and barely moved. What they breathed out smelled damp with infection. Isandòrno doubted any of these creatures would survive the trip north.

By the time Isandòrno had left the bus from Papantla and hired a taxi to drive him to the port, the driver had secured all four crates to the flatbed leaving himself nothing else to do but climb behind the wheel and wait.

Only the extra crate has kept Isandòrno from saying go.

—There was supposed to be three.

—Now there's four, the driver shrugs. He assumes little is risked by bringing more. Costs generally come when you don't bring enough.

The giraffe sleeps. The elephant too. Neither can keep their head up. They rest on the shavings and straw and heave. Only the hyena moves, breathing just as hard, but whipping back and forth, before backing up abruptly, a reverse twist on rear haunches, then chittering up at the air holes. The cuts on its nose bleed. The gums bleed too. The teeth are intact.

Isandòrno does not approach the fourth crate. Spits over his shoulder. Counts nine by fingers to thumb. Avoids the edges of shadows. Considers six rounds of silver and gold. An owl flies across the moon.

At least the rain has stopped. Though a strange mist, strange to be so thick, has materialized out of the Gulf and settled around the slips and ships and those other routes that lead into the city.

—What's in there?

All this indecision has made the driver nervous.

—The port declaration says three, Isandòrno says after reading the paperwork again. There is not much to read. Contents listed are

for industrial incinerators. For
crates W, X, and Y.

—Then should I take it back?

The driver keys the engine to life.
As if action can replace any consideration of risk. A loud clank
follows as gears engage and the
truck lurches slightly forward.
The linkages even groan as if this
is still too much to draw forth
what should weigh so little.

Isandòrno knows what to do.
Open it now. Do not hesitate. The

locks are easy. The bolts and irons will take more time but the driver will help. Then Isandòrno can see for himself. Then he can move beyond what the fortune-teller Maria Estancia had said was the cusp of things, the cusp of life, the cusp of death.

But as if it were something already demanded beforehand, Isandòrno cannot will himself to even climb on top and peer down through the air holes. He cannot will himself to press an ear against the side and listen. Even touching the fourth crate is beyond him.

Tiny
Storms

You reached for the secret too soon . . .

— Pink Floyd

There Will Be Blood ∷ **2007** ∷ keeps coming to mind. *No Country for Old Men* ∷ **2007** ∷ also haunts this associative periphery, though *Giant* ∷ **1956** ∷ barely resonates despite the fact that it was that cast and crew, including James Dean, that came to occupy Marfa's Hotel Paisano. Pictures of everyone from George Stevens to Rock Hudson and even a young Dennis Hopper find a place somewhere between the polished saltillo tile underfoot and the exposed beams overhead. Elizabeth Taylor's suite is 212. 223 is James Dean's room. Even *Rebel Without a Cause* ∷ **1955** ∷ would make more sense. Cas has on her red motorcycle jacket too. But it's the wrong red. Cas can only see Daniel Plainview beating to death Eli Sunday with a bowling pin. This hall reminds her of that downstairs alley, only here the gutters are locked rooms. Past those doors the manager now hurries, keys already out.

They had arrived an hour ago but their call from the lobby had gone unanswered. "Deakin is at the bar," Bobby had snipped, helping Cas to the lobby sofa. But he did not return with news of drinks ordered and a table held. Bobby was gone much longer the second time. Nervousness and doubt began to tighten in on her, like thoracic pain spreading into ribs and guts. Cas had just resolved to risk the walk when Bobby returned again.

"I rechecked Jett's Grill. No one there. And no one remembers seeing Deakin." Bobby tugged on his bolo tie, a black scorpion encased in lucite resin, flakes of gold floating around stinger and claws. He has never worn it for her. No question it's for Deakin. The button-down shirt too.

"Shall we go?" Cas had no intention of leaving but she wanted to know where Bobby stood.

"There's a reception at the gallery on the corner. Our kind of place. Free glasses of wine. Unlike the restaurant, it's packed. On any other night, I'd say you should check it out." Bobby finally left the bolo alone. "Walked through twice. And then circled the block. No sign of him."

Bobby tried to look annoyed but Cas could feel the tremors of uncertainty. More than uncertainty. She stood up then. He needed her to stand. Even if her legs still ached from the walk they'd finally taken in the rain. More than her legs. Her entire body felt disjointed beyond reason. Not that today's exertions had proved particularly bad. She'd had worse. Her body was merely registering the toxicity of information. Even the back of her hands seemed to bite. Like jellyfish kissing nematocysts through the skin. Merely images applied to events occurring far from Marfa, or Texas for that matter. The same as her desire earlier in the day to picture information networks as a vast sea, either nurturing or corrosive. Only a metaphor. Like the jellyfish and their stingers too. And kisses? Why were her thoughts so oceanic these days? Still Cas had scratched the back of her hand. Picking at the words under her skin.

At the check-in counter, encased in sawtooth tiles, opposite a large buffalo head mounted on the wall, the same receptionist who had helped them before helped them again. Without a hint of irritation too. Adrianna dialed the room number while either sucking on or blowing away the long hair idling around her face, glassy and young, Cas taken in by the full lips either kissing or nibbling herself, with those eager brown eyes somehow making Cas think of Penelope Cruz, only in a world where movie stars never lived on screen but still lived out their impossible stories with impossible charm and vitality. In fact, while they waited for Deakin to pick up, Adrianna smiled at Cas in such a way that Cas half-wanted to ask her for an autograph. Instead, she asked if Adrianna spoke Spanish. She did not.

"He's diabetic," Bobby had suddenly lied when Adrianna cradled the receiver. "Will you take us to his room? We want to make sure he's okay."

Cas couldn't fault her. Penelope would have done the same thing. Adrianna called the manager instead and apologized when her superior did not materialize at once.

While they waited, Bobby described the exhibit next door: black-and-white photographs depicting derelict television sets.

> "The artist's name is Phillial Kreps. The program describes her as the Diane Arbus of blind technology. Something like that."

> Cas twinged at the thought of pictures of her Orb. As if that might make it too exposed. Or worse, describe a shattered future, even though it was presently safe and sound, back in the Airstream, comfy in its sweater, hidden beneath those pillows making up the lounge bench, in fact hidden within a hollow beneath the hollow beneath the pillows of that bench. Cas still found it difficult to suppress an imperative to return at once. Like it was a sightless thing that depended upon her not only to see but to reckon how that seeing implicated itself in the project of life.

> Kirby, the night manager, had taken his time. Apparently "along with everyone else in town" he too was at the Greasewood where images of all those broken tubes had got him "to thinking how when I was little I thought folks like Cosell and Muhammad Ali, Frazier, and Foreman, lived in there. Now I can see they was always gone."

"Or just moved on . . . ?"

Which had earned Cas a smile that winked about as brightly as the brass buckle of a Bronco, the truck, polished to a dark rose. His hat, he held in his right hand. His left hand he kept hooked in a loop of Levi's worn high over his hips, stiff as blue cardboard, and about as new as he was not. Kirby was still younger than Cas and Bobby but not by much. And when he finally got around to hearing their predicament, Cas expected a drawn-out refusal. She was wrong. He took the situation very seriously and within moments they were following him out of the lobby. Bobby had to help Cas manage the steps but Kirby made no comment. He put his hat on. His eyes did not stray to the braces.

Now reaching Deakin's room, Kirby knocks hard. He declares he is the evening manager. He makes a general inquiry about the well-being of the occupant. He knocks again.

Throughout, his left hand stays snug in that belt loop. A stroke? Here is more than a posture. Here is yet another shape lasting takes. Suddenly Cas is afraid for Kirby. Even Daniel Plainview's bowling alley would be safer than here. And though the lights in that long empty hall remain steady, something about the three of them clustering around that door seems to rob the scene of visibility. Then that feeling she sometimes gets in her knees and behind her shoulder blades, the one curled up inside each of her joints, begins to seethe with premonition.

Cas lays her hand on Kirby's back. To stop him? But it's already too late. He's already turned the key. He's already stepping back. Smoke pouring out . . .

Even though the Orb is strictly digital with projections cali-
brated and angled to conform to the properties of the
lens, refractive index lower than 2, with a curious
coma in this latest version, Cas occasionally calls
it a crystal. Technically it is but nothing like
quartz. Near transparent diaphaneity. Con-
choidal fracturing if it were to break.

Not that she has ever seen one crack,
and Cas has had hers for sixteen years.
She even named it: Scry Baby. "Scry
baby scry," she sometimes sings to a
Beatles tune, while gazing into what
chatoyancy such darkness enfolds.
And that's before even turning it on,
before her fingers dance the surface,
open the locks, combine threads of
light into something Cas swears sometimes feels dangerously awake, even if
to a casual viewer, even one seated on
her shoulder, the Orb would hold nothing
more substantial than faint flickers resembling smoke.

At first . . .

VEM

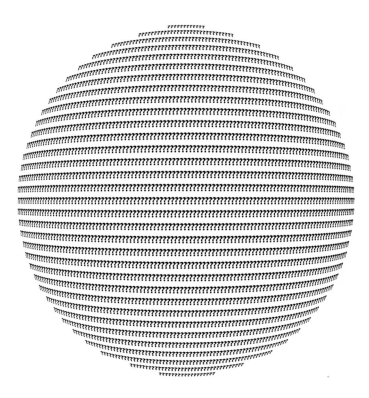

To ▮▮▮▮▮▮▮▮▮▮▮▮▮▮▮▮▮▮▮

Mars.
Neither temple nor canal
nor marble of Nemesis.
Never a sign or promise
of civilizations past.

Here

just dust to spin a silence in the afternoon air.

For now.

Sky a haze.

For now.

Until high in it a glitter of pink.

One long reach blinking into view.

Alien. Invader. Red in claw.

With one familiar sun to set fire to its fall.

22.697°N 48.222°W.

To the sands of Chryse Planitia.

July 20, 1976.

Viking 1 descends.

Or ████████████████████

Night
before the third day.

"The heart quickens"

Union blue. Long rows of tents in a dark as lantern-bit as
men are by mosquitoes. On both sides. They sleep. Or rattle
pans sweet with fat and molasses. Whittle sticks. Clean and
reclean their cannons. Write letters to wives, children, to men loved
in secret but at this hour sprung loose in ink. Some sing.

"Quickens at such"

Cemetery Ridge.

One captain walks the camp, cowled in dark wool
to hide his face and bars. Lips mumble. Stop. Start again. *Starting to*
work something out.

Seminary Ridge.

Where Pickett waits.

"The heart quickens
at such a message."

Or even ████████████████████

Two ancestors
in a cave by a fire
breaking rocks
finding the colors within
to paint their faces.

Until the fire died and smoke filled the cave.

And took two children away.

Or this infamous **Clip #1** ▮▮▮▮▮▮▮▮▮▮▮▮▮▮▮

Audra.   **Toland's**

daughter.   **His Willow Ruse.**

                                    Here

beneath the Pacific.

                    Drowning over with. **Just.**

  1962.

                              Sixteen years now just

under.

       Reversed rising for her last breath,

                                        breaking

the surface,

         a first breath for never seeing them,
speaking **anyone's name, their faces —**

                                  those

  who could **never put her here**   *or film*

       her **going down.**

Or even ███████████████████

Boy

bright eager

even on his back

reaching for stars

hung bright and painted

above brighteager-boy's

crib.

Wichita winter light bars the child.

Minutes pass.

Bars of shadows shift.

Without maternal

or paternal shadow to rearrange or lift.

Too long?

Alvin Alex Anderson neither cries nor smiles. Just that
feeble reach. Like a persistent twitch.

Even here

wide beautiful eyes fixed

on a universe

beyond

a cage.

Even these excavations remain fragmentary. To expand beyond such fleeting whirls of digital smoke remains too costly despite whatever morning premonitions the thunder demanded. Besides, though her joints may have buzzed with enough fear even her braces seemed electrified, what was really learned? Did the amplitude of such a feeling really authorize a worthy action? Especially since such an imperative so often gets the future wrong?

More than once Cas	has taken to task politi-
cal advocates	whose arguments
finally rest on	the fervor of their
pronounce-	ments: "They're
the kind	of individu-
als whose	feelings are
p o o r l y	aligned with
r e a s o n .	In essence
t h e y ' r e	lazy. They
rely on	i n h e r i t e d
emotional	s y s t e m i c s
b e c a u s e	they have
failed to do	the work neces-
sary to update	such affect-derived
responses." An	accusation Cas takes
seriously enough to	apply to herself. Fear and
pain can sometimes be just	fear and pain: locally derived

and immediate. After all, how often does what her compromised body portends prove no more than what any such body, elastic beyond nightmares, already knows about its own questionable future?

As noon would prove, anxiety was once again wrong: lightning never kissed their array of antennas. Nothing was fused or ashed to the ground. Except for a rattling on the Airstream's rooftop when the rain sounded hard and hail, little else of the storm altered their pursuits.

As had been the case for a while now, the Orb itself remained the only major limit, even with self-preservation at stake. And it had come a long way since the late fifties and sixties. Cas still cringes at the thought of some of their early attempts   to demonstrate the work.

Back then a 2" Ampex
could. At least by
figured out how
the findings on
tunately most
regarded the
some kind of
animation. It
that none of
were authenti-
came the 1964
what would even-
known as the infa-

Quad did what it
1963 ■■■ had
to get some of
film. Unfor-
v i e w e r s
evidence as
avant-garde
didn't help
the splices
cated. Then
discovery or
tually become
mous Clip #1.

Cas was the one who found   her too. Not amid some dense population, historically cross-referenced, as the Dark Clips at first always appeared to guarantee, even as each and every one slipped back into the all-too-common zone of the unconfirmed. Audra was not on a crowded beach but beyond the breakers and not even on the surface: a corpse suspended in the lolling rock of distant swells. Nor was it by chance either. Cas never goes fishing. She had followed the slants of light, slopes of shifting colors, instinct leading through the feed's static to behold that horror.

Not that Cas or Sorcerer, forget Recluse or even ███, really understood the consequences then of what had just happened. The language of the Window had not yet formed.

In those years, they were
to be. Bobby and oth-
things out of old
experimenting
dazzling up
The units
e n t i r e
boxes, as
cabled and
they over-
b u r n e d .
smoke Cas
Baby is no
tion, knowl-
with memories
Maybe even the
had to carry her out of

still out in the open. Or trying
ers began building these
television sets, later
with electron guns
other mediums.
took up rooms,
homes, came in
screens, crates,
cooled, until
heated and
Part of the
still sees in Scry
doubt a projec-
edge mingling
of those actual fires.
smell too. Twice Bobby

a room on fire. He always managed to put the fires out. But they always lost the homes. A year of cocaine didn't help. Then there was a two-month experiment with meth — long before Walter White. And always the drink. Human history is shaped by drink. Human history for all it aspires to reach always needs a way to come down. Those days were as great as they were lost.

Still as scientists in a field dependent on processing power, they were fortunate to live in a time when technological advancement kept pace with their discovery. And so as KIPS jumped to MIPS, the fires stopped, cords went wireless, and Bobby came up with the Orb. Even if it still looked like a parlor trick.

Only a few years ago, before she, Bobby, and Sorcerer had conceived of the Distribution, Cas was still trolleying around that redwood box,

brass-latched and felt-   lined, violet of course,
into university labs,   onto multibillion-
dollar campuses.   No doubt she
had resembled   some Wicca
practitioner or   Ren-Faire
devotee, and   Cas had
been both —   something
had to follow   the drugs,
something   still has to
answer the   pain.

Regrettably the   proofs are
still long, the con-   clusions far
too loopy for most   to consider let
alone believe — Cas   had stopped men-
tioning them years ago.   When the Orb worked, the usual response was fraud or, put more politely, fiction. When it didn't work it was almost better. Jaron Lanier had seemed the most keen to believe her. He had also waited the longest until it became painfully clear the glass would reveal nothing more than what anyone can coax an average computer to display.

Recorded clips are easy but substantiate nothing. The performative is a whole other story. Often an unintelligible one. What was she to make out of pre-historical children playing with embers? "Ruse" or "Rue"? How many days and hours had it taken just to hear "message" instead of "The heart quickens at such a massage"? At least Cas could smirk. Was Scry Baby telling her she needed a massage? Bobby does so many things well but his greatest talent may be his massages.

Not that they've had time   for one. Her most
recent Unratified Clip   — likely offering
a glimpse of their   pursuer in a
wide and dispir-   itingly high
crib — didn't   incline him
to apply his   fingertips
to her shoul-   ders. These
days Bobby   implores
her to do just   one thing:
find Recluse.

Or as he puts   it: "Scry the
surface and max   the Window."

Bobby's right. They are   on the run and running out of time. They do not   have the luxury to dabble endlessly with alternative perspectives or historical whims. Cas, however, can't help herself. If their days of ecgonine and amphetamines had been bad, they were nothing compared to this. No one is immune to the transformative power of VEM.

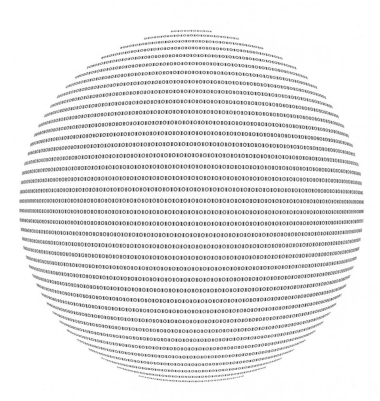

And then Bobby dropped the cashmere sweater over the Orb and told her to power down.

"Cops at the door."

Whatever after-
note of ionic
singe con-
tinued its
confession
to the
still Air-
s t r e a m
a i r ,
nothing
c o u l d
c o m -
pare to
the dis-
c h a r g e
of her
own terri-
fied static.
If only they
were cops. Cas
had immediately
lit incense and doused
the lounge cushions with
patchouli oil. Forced herself to giggle.

Play the kook. Be the kook. Be only a kook. None of which would make the slightest difference if these inquisitors proved something more than cops. Federal agents, for example. Or servants of agencies neither she nor Bobby had ever heard of, with badges and firearms. Though cops too could prove servants to warrants issued by distant judges powerful enough to seize and silence them both.

Was this it then? Already the end? And why wouldn't it be? Not the first time power would triumph over objection. Why should Cas and Bobby consider themselves different? Their Distribution would be known only as The Failed Distribution. Recluse's VEM Identity would triumph, instituting a culture of sustained suppression lasting potentially centuries if not longer. The Dark Ages, if only.

Whether a sign or not, by then the rain had stopped. Pi time. Ever since confirming Clip #6, Cas has always regarded 3:14 PM with a potency it likely does not deserve. No help that a mist had started to creep in with more storm circling above.

No cops encircled their Airstream. Just one patrol truck pulled up close to their awning and lawn chairs. No lights on top either. One Presidio County Sheriff badge was enough. The owner who had rented Bobby the property was there too. Likely, he was the problem. Mifflet Shimworth, round on corn and drink, stayed nervously off to one side. There had been suspicions, he immediately rasped, from people in town, driving by, "what with these generators outside." And since he was the one vouching for them, "me renting you this spot, and giving you power too, which, see, makes the need for these generators a little more unclear, I figured I'd nip quick in the bud all this ballyhoo rumoring by

just coming here with Sheriff Domingues, a friend of mine too, as you can see, so to witness and confirm
that you wasn't on my property
cooking up illegalities. If
you don't mind."

"I see," Bobby
had responded
at once. "You
are   con-
c e r n e d
about the
c h e m i -
cals?"

At which
p o i n t,
the sher-
iff   had
g r o w n
noticeably
more on the
qui vive, as
Mifflet   Shim-
worth, convinced
then of his suspi-
cions, began to back
away.

Bobby then proceeded to show the sheriff the chemicals in the fridge.

"Coors, Corona, and this little IPA we picked up in Abilene."

Then he showed off the JEOL scanning electron microscope. "I call him Joel." It wasn't like the sheriff would recognize the difference between a pallasite fragment and a bit of *Symphyotrichum ericoides* pollen. At that scale everything looks extraterrestrial.

"As I told Mifflet here, we're meteor hunters. Got all sorts of bits." And then Bobby showed off the trays of rocks. There was a large breccia by the door, plus tektites in a jar by the sink, "not technically meteors," and then "for fun" some pretty geodes in the cabinet where they kept bottles of hot sauce and cans of baked beans.

"And there?" The sheriff asked about the bulge beneath the sweater in the rear lounge.

"A beaut!" Bobby had grinned, and like a magician whisked away the cashmere to reveal the Orb, which with a keylight he transformed into a full moon.

"You a witch?" Mifflet still had to ask. Cas had almost answered yes.

As for the antennas and "sticks" as Mifflet described them, they were for getting some TV and tuning into whatever shortwave news they could get on asteroid showers and other meteorological events.

Sheriff Mingo Dues ∴ ! ∴ declined the offer of a beer but Mifflet helped
himself to two bottles of the IPA, on the way
out wishing them good hunting.

Bobby seemed energized
and even pleased by the
encounter. As if one
close call granted
him visiting rights
to the close calls
of his youth,
and so too lent
him   some
of   youth's
vitality. Cas,
h o w e v e r ,
was wrecked.
A   migraine
t h r e a t e n e d
the   periphery
of   the   hour.
Enough   of   a
threat to keep her
from repowering up
the Orb.

The call from Deakin a little
later had helped a bit. He had gotten
a good nap and was confirming dinner

at the Paisano. Unfortunately, he'd also added how these days were about "more dread than facts." "More dread" was an old-school code that reduced to Mordred and was Merlin's way of directing them to Parcel Thoughts where recent posts revealed the latest news.

Bad news, all of it:

‡ Thanatos dead in New Haven.

‡ Thaumaturge dead in Islip.

‡ Artemis dead in Berlin.

‡ Pythia arrested in Fort Myers.

‡ Endoria arrested in Portland.

‡ Circe missing in Cedar Rapids with two witnesses calling in a possible abduction.

‡ Lilith arrested in Richmond.

‡ Treebeard dead in Redwood Shores.

‡ Sibyll missing.

Bobby had also discovered independent of ■■■■ how back in April
dear Realic S. Tarnen was apparently tortured,
cut into pieces, and smeared across an
intersection in downtown Los Angeles. Cas was the one who had
started sending him several
years ago bread crumbs à
la Cicada 3301. "Out of
the violet," she liked
to say and do. He
was an academic.
Not even one of
their best. But
he was persis-
tent and brave,
even if he had
not yet been told
about   Recluse,
the Distribution,
or VEM.

And on top of it all:
still no word from
Sorcerer.

"They'll catch us before him,"
is about all Bobby can muster. His
effort still feels valiant.

At least on the back of his motorcycle, they managed to outrace her migraine. If only they could outrace the news too. Not that Bobby was foolish enough to risk another encounter with the police by trying. The rain stayed off them and the mists kept parting enough to keep the median line clear and steady, as if solid and dotted were enough to depend upon. And maybe at that moment they were.

Whatever the varied nature of their history, over the years both Cas and Bobby had come to depend on Deakin. Just the thought of him drew away the pain rooting into the cradle of her hips, prying up her shoulder blades. Deakin knew Big Data, understood the terrible dangers of VEM, and with the exception of Sorcerer and herself could move the most effortlessly through the Orb. Of the five Orbs out there, he had one. Since the Distribution had begun to fail, Deakin would have spent every feed-moment available trying to locate a means to counter Recluse. He would have some answers. Or at least have come up with viable ideas on how to find those answers.

As they neared, the more the thunder groaned, not close but as if from beyond the plains, perhaps even the high mesas. Nothing flashed or glowed on Mitchell Flat. Tonight Bobby and Cas were the Marfa Lights. The stillness, though, warned Cas that the storm had not yet moved on. If it was a warning. Who was to say the storm wouldn't serve their side this time? The cool air slipping under her helmet's visor felt good as did Bobby's back against her chest. "Little Big Spoon," he sometimes called her because she liked best holding him like this when they slept. Maybe because she wanted to dream of him driving her away and away like this, and Cas dreamed often, though never this dream.

When 67 turned into Highland Street, Bobby downshifted.
The stillness only grew. The mist did not relent.
On West Texas Street, where Bobby parked,
the mist finally seemed to turn to fog.

There was even a moment, while
standing at the entrance to
Deakin's room, that Cas
thought the fog must
have slipped inside.

Kirby   must   have
thought   the   room
was on fire. If it were
only   that   simple.
Not even a hint of a
cigarette.

But now . . .

Bobby follows Kirby in, already opening the French doors and the bathroom window. Deakin is clearly not there. Not even a suitcase, one shirt hanging in the closet, a sock left beside the bed.

Bobby takes his Petch out to mark locative and temporal data.

"His phone keeps ringing," he says to Kirby by way of an explanation. "Maybe we'll find it behind a seat cushion or headboard?" As if that would explain anything. Sometimes a tone of knowing is the worst lie.

Cas finds what's left in the bathtub. She sees she should have recognized the smell. Bobby should have too. The glass shards spray out from around the drain, charred oblong fragments scattered among pebbled bits. The base is a melt of circuitry. At least Deakin managed to destroy his Orb.

On the way back, Cas doesn't look at the speedometer. Now more than ever shocks hold her, even as the whine of the engine, the way the air buffets them from both sides, tells her to hold on tighter. Bobby wants to get back to the Orb as fast as he can. Get them out of there as fast as he can. And maybe because he has assumed her will, for a moment Cas considers abandoning the Airstream, the Orb, all of it. Start with the Canyon of Kings where they had gone when arriving here. There they could disappear among the cat claw and ocotillo. Hunt javelinas, harvest wild peyote, and distill *Dasylirion wheeleri* into sotol. And when the moon is full, or not at all, dance upon the ring middens to melodies they can only half-remember. There their bones can lie too. And of such a life lived purely and good, between just two, they need not tell more.

Though if resurrection ever became an option, their bones might awake
to stand trial.

And Cas shudders and does not tap
Bobby's shoulder. There is no away
and away, only this way. Besides
Bobby would not have suffered
such an escape. Upon passing
their Airstream, after a semi
passes them with a blast, he
slows along the shoulder.
Bobby turns off the head-
light and 67 goes dark.
Then carefully he turns
the motorcycle around
and turns off the engine,
studying their home, for
movement, for distur-
bances.

Bobby knows how to think
this way. He had deliber-
ately left all the lights on
inside. The lights now do not
flicker. Closer, the fishing lines
he strung up have stayed taut. The
same is true of the guitar picks he keeps
for these occasions, still wedged beneath the
hinges of the front door. Stillness prevails. Only the

crimson awning flutters, though from what wind Cas can't tell.

Bobby at once gets to cinching the motorcycle to the back and packing up the generators. He will take in the lawn chairs last. This is his routine. The appearance of lingering prolonged until right before the moment of departure.

One piece of news sustains their respective hustle and dampens some of their collective fear. A new post on Parcel Thoughts. Implication clear: Sorcerer has escaped all nets and will soon post possible meets.

Bobby manages a half-shout. It's not victory but it's better than total defeat. Bobby even suggests she lie down while he readies their departure but Cas doesn't even take off her braces or her red motorcycle jacket. Despite the pain returning to her palms, she powers up the Orb. It's too soon for Deakin and too daunting for Recluse. Right now though, before the antennas come down, Cas can give way to instinct and desire and maybe something more.

Static answers hurt. *Pan tolmaton.* ∴ *All is to be dared.* ∴

Hue melts into that digital haze Cas needs no solid and dotted lines to navigate. Roads are only necessary if you're not flying.

Clip #6 is the latest aberration. Cas had made the discovery earlier this year, after months and months spent teasing out curious angles which had drawn her away from old suspicions and on through new densities, always vaguely resembling continually reorganized versions of white

noise, weeks of incoherency, if never entirely without these curious
fissures, logical in their own keeping, despite how what they
regarded, or in what direction they resolved, oceans
of possibilities, remained unknown. To what
end? Cas continually wondered. Perhaps toward something incognizable?
∴ *Or a new horror?* ∴ Would she find
another dead child?

Until at last those slopes
of light widened to a path
beyond suspicion, Cas'
fingers weaving tirelessly
above the increasing order.
Like Audra, the colors
had bent toward violet.
Unlike Audra, the colors
weren't finally violet. A
brighter blue had started
to wend through every-
thing until what threatened
to become crimson abruptly
brightened into spears of what
Cas could only describe as pink,
and candy pink too. She had even
laughed.

Even if Bobby was impressed, he still felt com-
pelled to point out how Clip #1 afforded little benefit

except for a quasi-confirmation albeit with no body present. Warlock had congratulated her, acknowledging the mystery, while at the same time shrugging off its preeminence:

" חיים של אחרים
הם כמו חלון הנפתח
אל מעבר לחומות מבצרנו "

∴ **The lives of others are the windows beyond the keep of oneself.** ∴

Not that these parents can notice. No naked eye can see this much. Cas, though, knows every step, the whole dance of coming home, from every eddy, updraft, even every vortex.

Is it the actual air that moves so? Or is it something else?

Most of the time this would be it. Enigmas beyond exploration let alone explanation. Except Cas knows these moments occurred just outside Athens ∴ summer of 2008 ∴. She even knows where they live now. She even knows their names. The Orb did not tell her nor did some Dark math. All this she found out the old-fashioned way: a little bit of luck.

Cas will never forget Sorcerer, still perched on the edge of that crummy bed in a Nashville Super 8, right after he'd finished watching Clip #6 for the first time. He was shocked and more than a little horrified.

"You're not going to believe this," he finally said. "I know him."

"The father?" Now it was their turn to be appalled and a little horrified by the coincidence.

"He's a friend. A good friend. Or was a good one . . . I've been remiss."

"And his daughter?"

*strange
white skin, icy
black braids.*

"Xanther."

Is she even eight?

Legs falling over each other like *knees at war.*

The child should stumble.

Maybe her smile keeps her up.

Or streaming off her,
in her wake, ahead of her too,
no matter which direction she takes,
whirling all around her, like rainbows
in soap, in oil, in all we
care to imagine . . .

rrrrrrr???????????????????????????????????????
rrrrrrr??
rrrrrrr???

tiny storms.

Clip #6 ▮▮▮▮▮▮▮▮▮▮▮▮▮▮▮▮▮▮▮▮▮▮

"Mom, it's a—"

Minerva's Owl takes flight
only as dusk begins to fall.

— *Hegel*

(oh) (no)

(and)

(again?)

))

(and)

(horror (re)visited with both)

(((

((oh)(no)(not again))

((not again)(oh)(no))

))

((

Voiceless too (except in its demand to rush, enfold, defend (if those constitute voice)).

Astair's world!

Astair's baby girl!

Xanther!

Wobbling there ((wobbling forward (as Astair))
equally voiceless (except in her frail determina-
tion to move (Astair can't), endure, defer (if those
can ever constitute a child's voice (more like a cry
((voiceless) for help(?)) (. . .))

)

)

)

Soaked too in this strange late-afternoon mist
(pale as any page or myth (and yet as if replete
(surfeit!) with a color (techni-?!) beyond imagining
(beyond strangeness))).

There! No—

Here! No—

Alone! No—

huddling along the front walk.

Where are her glasses?

Where is her orange umbrella?

Shasti and Freya had both cried out "They're here!" and Astair had thrown open the door (or almost had (Astair knows by heart (and now memory) how she had reached for lock and knob (twisted both) tugged back (inspiring their inconsistent security device connected to nothing other than its registry of anonymized voicings (if such constitutes voice (anodyned?) (androidyned?))

Alert: Door open!
¡Aviso: Puerta abierta!
Hadhari! Bab maftouh.
Xiǎo xīn, mén kāi zhe.
Alerte: Porte ouverte!
Uyarı! Kapı açık.
Ouchartoutioune! Patze tour!
Vnim'anje: Dver' otk'rita!
Achtung: Tür geöffnet!

except the heart is disturbed (memory too)) because it now feels almost as if Astair never quite reached the door in the first place (gripped (let alone turned) knob and bolt (forget a tug)) the announcement already a(n impossible!) forecast) as if the door on its own had just swung open

).

Revealing this: her darling girl (and calling out "Mommy!" too) which somehow (too) keeps holding this mother back.

Something to do with seeing freezes Astair on the stoop. This time heat flushing deep under her arms. Back wet for sure (if between her legs (drying and scratching (vaguely)) there's a tightening (from where this child was once ushered forth and now is no more)).

Astair can't breathe.

Or she just breathes harder.

Words still beyond her.

Even thoughts. ∴ Tricky to apprehend. ∵ ∴ *Waves on waves of ocean-desert sands.* ∵

(at least) This much is clear (accusation! (fire giving her grip (direction))): why hasn't Anwar taken her to the ER? Her daughter's not just her daughter anymore. She's again *that* daughter.

Oh no.

Not again.

Poor wobbly knees caked (caked!) in blood (still bleeding! (trickles reddening the already violent mist surrounding them all)). An elbow bleeds (caked too (discolored (a techni-lesson in plum))). Not stopping there. Both arms splotched with injury. (Forget all the shreds of skin sprouting around her tiny fingernails) both of Xanther's palms are torn up and soggy with peeling scabs. And that's still nothing compared to both forearms clawed all the way up from wrist to beneath her stained t-shirt sleeves (like a suicide attempt (where's her raincoat?)).

A(~~mother~~ *nother!*) seizure. Obvious. Go! Gather your baby up and rush her to the hospital. Obvious. Cursing Anwar for not doing so first. Obvious.

And yet her child (standing now just steps from her (soaked to the bone? (shivering (?) (obviously!)))) looks up at Astair like the one with the problem is Astair!

Out of this wreck of hurt and harm ((and forget some lifted arm (palm held out against all acts of interference))

(Astair knows intimately this sign of defiance)

(that arising of unresolvable mystery)

(what Dov never ceased calling "Awesome!" (in a way that always spoke of Awe (and The Sum of)))

∴ . . . *like light dawning beyond past and future, beyond gravity and sentence* . . . ∵

∴ **Out of the impossible.** ∵

∴ Rockin! ∵

(this beauty)):

Xanther's

confounding

smile.

In fact both she and Anwar are smiling. They even seem giddy. *Giddy?!*

Anwar's still by the car. Unloading something. A bag of something. Bags? Boxes as well. Tiny boxes in plastic bags (named with a name Astair knows too well to comprehend (Astair keeps sensing comprehension without assembling an iota of meaning (as if the collagen of sense had suddenly departed (though in response to whose beckoning?)))). Why had Anwar also put aside his umbrella? He's soaked to the bone. He's shivering. But look at that grin.

Only as he draws nearer does Astair catch something much more in his smile ((as if to say . . .) stiffening slightly with the recognition of her attention (lips pursing (that familiar warning exchanged many, many times under entirely different circumstances))): now is not the time to say anything.

Not that this will stop her.

Astair has already stopped herself.

How can Xanther's much-wounded face

= Xanther's still-broadening grin?

Back to senselessness.

"We left her glasses on the sidewalk," Anwar says now (by way of explanation?).

Sidewalk? Glasses? Just look at her chin, her cheek. Did Xanther skid along the sidewalk on her face?!

All while the reason (obvious((ly) at hand (bundled in hand))) keeps refuting the obvious.

"I'll have to return to Venice," Anwar keeps on. "Perhaps not worth the gas, but if they're not lost to the flood, retrieving the lenses and frame will be worth it."

"Her glasses?" Astair responds dumbly ((finally) all she can say so far).

Anwar nods: "We didn't have time to go back."

Astair (though) is the one who needs glasses.

And then the twins are at her back (trying to push their way outside (Astair wheeling on their excursion with a collective fury that needs no voice)). Freya and Shasti recoil at once (retreating (wordless) to the foyer).

"Mom, I'm fine," Xanther responds.

Which only amps Astair's agitation (this uncanny characteristic of Xanther's (to respond to confusion with care and concern (when Astair's the one who's supposed to be concerned and caring for Xanther))).

Then (as if sensing something unusual (Astair sensing their motion behind her)) the twins creep closer again (curious to see what's holding up their sister (or what their sister is holding)).

Even as Astair refuses to step aside.

"Uhm, mom can I get by please?"

Astair remaining clueless (insisting on it!) about what is happening right now (what her daughter has with her and is about to bring inside (clutched so closely to her chest)) as Xanther (easily (insisting on it)) slips by (as if she were already inside (and Astair's interposition had been merely an afterthought)) whereupon Freya and Shasti recoil again (this time backing up all the way to the stairs . . . even up a few steps . . . where they settle (curiosity still holds them fast)). Not that (the acutely aware) Xanther notices ((does she even see Astair? (who can only notice (and still can't scream (or shout (let alone just ask))))):

Where's your dog?!)

671

And at least this much doesn't escape Astair
((((the mash-up of "my" and "your" and "the") (the
"you" too) (these possessives)) nor the coupling confusion and disappointment robbing her entirely of
all her preparation and expectation (whatever happens next she knows that past's future is completely
lost (Astair closing the door behind them (nudging
for a click (thumb twisting the dead bolt)))))).

"They sold you a Chihuahua?"

Mom, —

(In the course of writing her paper) Astair had come across The Lost Horizon Case (out of Kissimmee Florida (the woman in question referred to as K.)). K. had purchased a Powerball ticket with sizable winnings at stake (over $300 million). (when the numbers were announced) K. saw that every number she had picked (according to meticulous reasons and noted omens and signs (from death dates to license plates)) was a match and her life had forever changed (and it had).

(furthermore upon presenting her winning ticket) K. saw how every winning number she'd read off was echoed by the same winning number announced by lottery officials (and yet her ticket was declared ineligible for the prize). K.'s confusion escalated to aggression until on-hand security (and finally officers (of the peace)) were called upon to remove her from the premises.

In fact it took K. months before she could see (correctly) the numbers on the (losing) ticket (which she still held in her possession (greasy, crumpled, intcat ∴ *intact*∴)). Her desire to win (rooted in a neurotic disposition toward denial) had created a hallucination so strong that the numeric order she had summoned (by both reason and whim) imposed its order on every announcement, publication, confirmation pertaining to those actual numbers drawn by the lottery committee.

In fact not even one of K.'s numbers matched the winning numbers. Her victory was entirely (and always (only)) in her mind.

Mom! —

But if Astair (*still staring (only staring!*)) was holding on to a seizure illusion (her battered bleeding child) now it goes (her battered bleeding child (a petulant child too (brushing Astair ((and all this staring) easily) aside))) with smiles and smiles and smiles and smiles and smiles and smiles and smiles and smiles and smiles (as Xanther's (repeated) obvious declaration keeps pinging (inaudibly? (insensibly)) in Astair's head).

Mom, it's—

Yes, "Mom" is in there ((Astair starting to hear it (if not get it)(because there is an "it" in there too)) followed then by an article? ("a" or "ahh"? (preceding the (delusional) consonant)) plus an (uplifted) inquisitive note (ridiculing too (declaiming gross stupidity (and worse: inferior sense))))).

Mom, it's a—

"Where's the dog?" Astair barks hoarsely (at last) at Anwar.

"Astair!" he hisses back (meaning later).

"I knew I should've gone with her." ((fuck later FUCK LATER) cheeks angry hot (angry as (seconds earlier) was her embarrassment over these efforts (to fucking K. her way? (some fucking *Einstellung* effect?)) to see an Akita, a Pomeranian, anything remotely canine) Astair materializing nothing but her own disappointment).

"We never even made it to the trainer." Anwar (softly) trying ((he really is trying) to soothe her).

But Astair's already tearing up (the cost of making sense).

"She saved him!" (Anwar kissing her ear (no, not kissing but whispering.)) "Actually—"

Astair blubbering: "Oh honey, this isn't any good. I'm allergic."

"You are?" (Anwar pulling back for a relook (studying her really (like a distraught face can somehow reveal a history of dander (apparently it can't))).) "Huh. I never knew that."

"Can you take it back?"

Mom, it's a cat!?

Yes. Astair can finally see that (like she can also imagine her own smile failing to banish red eyes (a too apparent rictus of rage and resentment)).

Look how frail.

It won't live through the night.

How trembling.

Half the night?

How white.

Even through the hour?
Is that what Anwar also whispered?
What else?

How already so still.

But where is her pity?

It won't live through the night.

How gruesome.

Invoke the five-minute rule.

How disgusting.

Whatever's within the house less than five minutes
can be exiled from the house in less than five minutes.
Five minutes passed long ago.

How terrible.

∴ Because you weren't wrong, were you, Astair? ∴

∴ **She sensed what only one other could know.** ∴

"Mom? What's wrong?"

Keep smiling (smile harder (anything (now) except: *I want it out of our home out of my daughter's life out of my life like yesterday?*)

fuck the

rest

auntie!

What took place was
very possible.

— *Arthur Yap*

with no explaining, mah, auntie hand jingjing her necklace. tiny

knuckles of wood laced on some greasy string, with carved acorn,

like quail egg, hard and black waxy, hanging in the middle. wah

lan, like what he do with this? and why now? jingjing never seen

auntie take it off. paid no notice, she wear it so long.

now though, with sun oreddy rise, rain slowed, after such a night,

morning too, misty strange like clouds to gather round, settle on

roads, hear a story, she stand here in their flat and offer this gift.

like jingjing wear such a dirty thing. not even worth bowl of bak

kut teh or one 4d. at least tacks it up on his worldwall. let it

dangle there, among beads and other clipcrap.

jingjing close windows then. wah lan, when they balik oreddy, flat

windows all open, door too, they like macam robbed, but nothing

gone. what there to take?

biggest difference, auntie herself. kay strange. damn chik ak she so dazed, macam not even know, they oreddy home.

morning was gu poon si, no question, lah. auntie knocked down, damn hawreeber, she tor hwee, nurses helped her to her feet, but that it, find their clothes, still wet, take back robes, then bye-bye chee bye, down some freight lift, out to a dark street, not even spared some bus coin. zhong long gone. bow ties with him. not even a wave. good thing jingjing stun those chips. close call. almost missed slipping them into his old shorts.

and great tian li? what kong tau she cast back? pelesit soar zhong's spiral flights, stab him dead in his bed?

"吾欲求冰物."

ice cream!? since when auntie ever want that? want cone too! two scoops!

off they go, walk and walk, back towards tanglin halt, common-

wealth calyx, their old hdb, shops still closed, grated cans here

and there burning, mebbe for vesak day, still days off, or just some

private mourning or wish, sky so high bird shit in your eye, hell

money bricks caught up in antics of fire, mixing thick with sticky

fumes of joss sticks, because this sky oreddy fallen. and later, like

a funeral for a king, red candles ring borders of a tree shrine.

no singing park, even after dark, tall candy canes terbalik in next-

over plot, where, wah lan, no cages hang. poh sometimes here, but

earlyearly, lah, wheels over his birds, hoist wings up there, to sing

their flight, wake with song all these estates, even ghosts of old

kampongs.

butterflies spiralled air then, like flakes of ash, rose soap, even

umbrella bark, oreddy gone like dark. fingers soft as melting

butter, saffron curry, parted misty wet, and there, past hawker center where they sometimes went, one open market. though what

next, jingjing sure got no clue. but counter munjen know auntie,

blanjah them two scoops each, with thanks, and low bows.

"为何人?" she asked after, how can't she remember him?, creamy

melt oreddy bearding her chin. like jingjing know all her loyals, but

since when tian li ever forget?

strangest though come now, after her necklace gift, plodplod

to her room, down onto the pallet, flat out again, only this time

snoring. snoring!

since when jingjing even catch her sleep. there she lie though,

hands curl up macam birds' claws, eyes bit tight, like halfwit,

angles all twist, even dress bunched up, knees purplespotted,

ankles kiasi, buay sai even cross. boh say leh, jingjing. bad enough

spit bubbling her lips. dripdrip. dripdrip. gross.

jingjing have no more business here. even if his hammock, slung

there like good friend, promises sleep. after all good friend's a

good friend because good friend makes promises a good friend can

keep. wah lau, sleep can wait. even if, as jingjing race to catch the

lift, he can't shake feeling he's made a mistake, missed something

too obvious to think, too wrong to own, too right to hide. but

jingjing not worry, keep very chin chai. besides he blur like sotong

because he still kay stone.

one story down, estel get in, draped in felt shawl, purple like tea,

parrot on each shoulder, a third on coat hanger stuck in her hat.

rumor's that parrot queen got like macam three times these in her

flat, snapsnap at jingjing now, never speak, only tian li could calm

their beaks.

outside, javan myna distract their bites. jingjing almost bite back,

bite parrot queen too, but badminton on now in the court, two boys bat bright green shuttlecock, without net, heads of all three

parrots go backandforth.

void deck folk ignore jingjing's arrival. mebbe here all night.

spencer guard tiger in bag, chomping on gum. delson too with bag

and gum. cart classics out on cement table if no one touch a card.

arsyil and chau out, koon deep the cradle of their arms. who knows

where lau jerry now.

"damn cho boh lan," jingjing gives some salt.

"oreddy come disturb me?" spencer growl. "say some more."

jingjing know better, should cabut now, chop chop kali pok, espe-

cially with no auntie around. mebbe gold make him bolder. two

fingers drag out coin. shimmer kay bright in sweet air.

"lemme see, lah!" spencer snap. lai dat, chau, arsyil both wake.

jingjing wave it around. shiny shineshine. jingjing sure kena shiny under those eyes. old lau jerry's too, one wet eye, coming down just, with more beers, hard looksee-ing this prize.

the longer jingjing hold off too, keep his gold chip on show, shine-shinier he feel, mebbe how great tian li feels, when all eyes of all kinds, these void deck folk, zhong, parrot queen, strangers too, follow her, glow for her.

why windows in their flat all open? pinching coin get jingjing remembering this. door too? just like at zhong's place, windows and doors all open after auntie kena foaming, went flatflat.

lau jerry sapus the coin. guess one wet eye not bleary so much.

"ya ya papaya! you now how, boy?"

jingjing lunge to grab back, but stumble, trips, go all lambong.

delson catch him. so much for tai chi shit auntie keep arrowing

him to practice. ah chek laugh and before jingjing can regain his

feet, get free of delson, him grabbing, laughing too, lau jerry flip

that precious glimmer of metal over jingjing's head right down into

spencer's hands, slapped tight, vanished.

"wah lau, good weight," saysay spencer. "thick too." he hold

cupped hands to one ear, as if what hides inside sure name fairest

price.

"good weight, very thick," jingjing repeat. he knows this game.

"you tell me. i'm off to maxi-cash or find goldsmith. mebbe near

temple or pagoda street."

spencer nods, grinning in that black-eyed way. "jingjing rich now.

dressed like a christmas tree. saht saht boh chioh."

"come now. give it back. chop chop kali pok. late oreddy."

"how about i trade you for it?" spencer offers beer.

"don'ch playplay!" jingjing clap hands, extend palm. spencer unclasp hands, coin gone. lau jerry and delson chio kao peng. arsyil laugh big. chau laugh too.

"enough of magic tricks."

spencer pull chip out of jingjing's ear. void deck folk roll!

"magic coin?" spencer whisper. "or just sweet?"

spencer's meaty fingers squeeze hard then, gold foil parts, out ooze thick strip of chocolate, what spencer licks up.

"think i'll keep my drink." tosses back what's left. jingjing lets mess stick at his feet. squats to see how he stunned. mebbe spencer substituted candy.

jingjing damn concuss, try chuckles it off, kay confused, backing

off. still resolved: he go trade full pocket's worth, then pay

someone harder than these drunks to come back teach spencer

respect. damn tua jingjing, jingjing hantam him.

only jingjing feel in pockets the melting mess, both hands sticky

with chocolate. notice too so many void deck cats around, macam

suddenly too, all around, and more than usual, leftear lopped,

haunting corners, tails flicking, whiskers skewed, eyes on every-

thing, like they waiting for something, someone.

jingjing heart thumps damn fierce. won't wait for the lift. takes

stairs. two at a time. four flights up.

"auntie! auntie!" jingjing shakeshake her now, whisper loud enough

to find waking sound. "where's your cat?"

"何?" she sit up.

"你的猫.它丢了么? 我找不到它."

then the great tian li start blubble and squeak.

"未丢."

"那去哪了? 我跑去屋顶?"

"未丢," ∴ "Not lost." ∴ tian li cry, tears smear cheeks. "其去之. 其终去之. 其去之求良." ∴ "Just gone. Gone at last. Gone for good." ∴

, dead

> *"Who sent you?"*
> *"You did."*
>
> — Terminator 2: Judgment Day

Daddy! Save him!

If not for that [{still} on repeat] Anwar might have enjoyed the drive. Shasti and Freya chirped and burbled the whole way. 'Itsy bitsy spider,' they sang from the backseat [or some other song they learned from {Astair? classmates?} somewhere]. Anwar never touched the car radio but sang along too [adding his own {nonsense ‹if harmonic›} doo-dahs]. That got the girls laughing and soon they were teaching Anwar the finer points [so detailed!] of their own [harmonic {nonsensical}] three-part invention.

What touched Anwar [and worried him {‹too› maybe}?] was just how easily he slipped into this kind of rapport with his two girls [no worries at all {so relaxing!‹?›}]. Like he was one of them [three were one].

In the rearview mirror he found at once familiar eyes familiar expressions familiar gestures [as if they were his own]. Even how they retold their fantastical story [which they had spent the afternoon mapping out all over their bedroom {including forays into the forbidden territories of the hallway as well as the shared bathroom ‹shared with Xanther› ‹which they couldn't resist sharing with Anwar›}] came out in little bits [qualified {requalified ‹redetailed «revised»›} posing no trouble at all for Anwar to follow {or join in with} because it was so in sync with the way he thought {even the way Astair thought}]. And Anwar discovered himself easing into himself then [that was the feeling {what a feeling}] breathing deeply [how had he been breathing before?] and forgetting . . . [he did not know what {except ‹ . . . *Save* . . . › ‹even that «for a while»}].

Maybe it had something to do with how their oddness in the eyes of others mirrored Anwar's sense of otherness among friends. Their manners in duplicate [triplicate] answered oddness by making of each other someone not so alone. These darling children of his. They could make of any time a home.

And in no time they are in Venice. The three of them crouching on hands and knees in the grey[?] mist [if not so grey {or almost white ‹a blinding almost-white›} then surely a dazzle of rainbow {untied ‹is it still raining?›} {Anwar had nearly gone back to the Element to retrieve his sunglasses ‹and this with the sun hardly visible «the origin of this light impossible to locate»›}].

Here [along this street] where Xanther had stretched moments into an infinity.

Here [   ] where Freya and Shasti [eyes of eagles] find in seconds the broken bits of their sister's glasses [{lenses scratched but somehow still whole} only the frames splintered].

And that's that.

They head back [singing again {Anwar puts on his sunglasses}]. They head to Silver Lake [{stop at the pet store} to pick up extras {by way of a gesture? ∴ so to keep making of an isn't an is? ∵} the owner {something Kacy ‹?›} glowing at the sight of the girls {'Weren't you beauties here this morning?'‹then «following Anwar's confirmation» a curious look› 'Wasn't your wife shopping for a dog?'}]. Then home. Easy. As if clocks didn't count. They left to retrieve Xanther's glasses and pick up some extras and they succeeded on all counts. Perfect if not for [if not backgrounded by {if not for so constant ‹so « . . . »›}].

Daddy! Save him!

'Something's up with mom,' Xanther says instead [{‹if not smiling› beaming then like that ‹white›white ‹notwhite›white ‹peculiar› fog outside} when Anwar and the girls return].

Anwar finds Astair in their room [[{unmoving atop their comforter} lights off {a tight curl of discomfort}].

'What can I do?' [Sitting beside her {resting ⟨gently⟩ a palm on her shoulder}.]

'Make me laugh?' she whispers [or really a peep {like something Freya and Shasti might make}].

'I think the owner of that, what is it?, Urban Pet?'

'Urban Tails. Grez Kacy.'

'I think he was flirting with me.'

Astair starts to cry.

'Honey,' Anwar tries. 'It's nothing serious.'

There [a hint of a laugh {the tiniest of smiles ⟨lost in a snuffle⟩}].

'To think I thought he was flirting with me.' Astair is doing her best. More of a laugh. More snuffles too. And then more tears without snuffles or laughs. Along with the tiniest of breaths.

'Darling, there was nothing I could do. Xanther found it. I don't know how. In all that rain. And—' [Anwar still isn't saying everything {how can he? ∴ he can't even tell himself ∵}.] 'The vet said there isn't much we can do. She very kindly went over with Xanther everything that was required but she also pulled me aside to warn me about how something so young and small, without its mother, is unlikely to live out the night.'

'That's sad too.' Astair sits up [just to turn on her bedside light? {which ⟨by a click⟩ reveals just how much she's been crying ⟨eyes not just red «puffy as blisters» and only getting redder⟩}].

And then she's showing him something else [pale brown {with ⟨upper left-hand corner⟩ a familiar Santa Barbara address ⟨plus a name he's written out on more than one check «*Oceanica*»}}]. What's more the manila envelope is open. The paper's out. Underneath. There's the title page [if familiar {also marred}]:

Hope's Nest:

On the Necessity of God

by

Astair Ibrahim

even if the red mark [circled too {above God ‹over Hope's and Nest›}] is [for all it clearly states] unreadable.

Might as well read

Which the accompanying letter [clarifying the {circled}

INCOMPLETE

] pretty much goes on to state.

Somehow Astair rallies for dinner [the red miraculously gone from her eyes {puffiness too ‹though what's left is not even calloused but— too sad «for Anwar» to name›}].

Obvious [{already} though] is how little time Astair has given her . . . [own disappointment {self?}].

While brown rice bubbles beside black beans [declaring their creamy readiness] while Astair [{dully} {dutifully}] prepares a peach-papaya salad [with thick tufts of fresh mint, plenty of lime juice and ground pepper {always the perfect amount of lime}] while Shasti and Freya set the table, Xanther [{dutifully} {excitedly}] shows [off!] all that her mother has helped with: the many sterilized bottles [carefully arranged] feeding tubes[!] formula[e{!}] hot-water bottles and [last but not least] a safe haven adjacent to washer and dryer 'So he won't wander and hurt himself' [wander?! {the thing is barely alive—} though the cardboard used as a barrier is flimsy {won't do}].

Anwar has Xanther wait by her charge [as if she had any intention of ever leaving the over-cushioned nest {hovers so close to occlude any view ‹maybe the creature isn't even there «ha!»›}] while Anwar goes to find some wood scraps from their guesthouse [which {though two stories} is presently suitable for only ants and spiders {if that} and a few cheap tools from China, some stored boxes of forgotten content {better chucked ‹if their mystery weren't so heavy›} along with hardened paintbrushes {also better chucked} plus oily paint jars and too many half-empty cans of turpentine, engine oil, and gasoline {he should plan a chucking-hour tomorrow}].

The plywood [he retrieves] is dry and clean. Xanther approves. Now her encampment is sturdy [absurdly sturdy {absurdly high too ‹an excellent defense against both egress and ingress›}] encircling an absurdly large dog bed with a small box in the middle [once holding his new Nona T-Drive? {now stuffed with warmed hand towels}] to swaddle[?] there . . . Xanther's [beaming] devotion [covering angles of all confirmation {though why should Anwar need confirmation now? ‹why even think about confirmation «like some penitent كالكافر?»}].

And yet [{{still} that uncanny sensitivity]: 'Mom, are your allergies acting up?' [Though Anwar {as he and Astair wash the dishes} cannot detect {in her eyes} the slightest trace of swelling or irritation.]

'Just a cold, honey.'

'Are you feeling a reaction?' Anwar still has to ask once the girls are in bed [not an easy task considering the squall Xanther had put up {when she learned that 1) in no way was this new creature sleeping in her bed ‹Animals don't sleep with people' «Anwar sounding sterner than ever before ⟨as if those words were never his own. ∴ **Only at the end of forever owned.** ∴ ⟩»» and 2) there is no way Xanther will be allowed to spend the night downstairs in the mud room} her resistance {and reactions} exhausting them both].

'No. And I don't have a cold either.'

And yet [despite these cold notes] they still end up making love. The sex comes on without premeditation [even desire]. No talk of the paper or the day's ill-fated gathering. Just Anwar's fumbling reach to assure with a touch [a goodnight shy of kisses]. Click of the lights. Except instead of sleep this attempt to make of the day's unexpected events [and now their darkness] something less important [{even pleasurable} his reach {always

Anwar's} coming upon neither interest nor rejection].
Lights back on [{hers ‹only›} which afterwards {‹despite
pleasure› mutual?} feels like {his} insistence {and so
‹too› a lifeless exercise in friction and exertion}].

At least she isn't crying. At least he isn't crying.

At least they both now seem of one mind: relieved.

Anwar still loves how Astair [before reading] first
goes to the bathroom to lightly wet her feet in the tub
so with knees up her feet won't slide on the sheets.

As Astair disappears into a book [{the music of
turned pages} what book did she choose?] Anwar
remains on his side [{eyes closed} afraid for some reason
{but Astair won't speak up ‹to ask him? «how can she
know to ask?»›}] and waiting [and waiting] ∴ *What happens to happened is such tricky passage.* ∴ for this drowsiness
[this emptiness] to at last deliver him unto something
untethered and dreamt and elsewhere. Even a nightmare would do. But nothing other than this nightmare
comes of it [not even drowsiness]. Maybe hovering
nearby but no closer. Afraid too. To reach out and turn
off his thoughts [thoughts!? {more like a to-do list

- Dermatology and asbestos and *The Nose.*
- Myla. Sourceforge. Astair's folks.
- Mefisto. ‹*The Psychology of Machines: A Love Let-
ter to Synthia* «Mefisto was 27 ‹a copy somewhere [. . .]
more sublime music of time?›»»
- Why is Shasti eating butter-salt sandwiches?

} when has Anwar ever felt this bound and lumber-
ing {bulwarked ‹reiterated «encrypted ‹uncoded› lost»
remediated› rebranched} halted?].

'Where's the dog?'

'Astair, please.'

'I knew I should've gone with you.'

'We never even made it to the trainer. She saved him! Actually—'

'This is no good. I'm allergic.'

'You are?'

'You have to take it back.'

She saved him! Actually—

she brought it back—

[what Anwar still won't say

{hard‹«ly» «to» think}

]

∴ cannot stop

thinking about ∵

Downstairs in the living room Anwar finds the unopened champagne [{restocks their fridge} drains the bucket in the kitchen sink {ice long gone ‹slosh not even cold›}]. Then pads through a blue dark somehow leaking into shadows ∴ *never silent so long as they remain denied* ∴.

Not that Anwar managed to depart from their room without a word.

'I don't want to be numb,' she had whispered from the shadows [bluest of blues].

And Anwar had come around the bed then and kissed her on the lips [her beautifully warm lips].

'What will we do?' she asked when he reached the doorway. 'The check didn't come through. I can see that.'

'The bad news, love,' he answered, 'is that you'll never be numb.' [Could she see his smile in that?] 'Xanther had to get her gifts from somewhere.' [Would he see her smile in that?]

Anwar held on to the notion that Ehtisham still might have called or e-mailed [left some message {with news of much money ‹what the bank had yet to know›}] but even after all [three] screens went bright with desktops [{evolving stars} {exploding stars}] and he had riddled through inboxes and spam folders [too many folders for too many accounts {‹all› maxed!!!}] Anwar discovered no confirmation.

At least he has plenty to answer his sleeplessness with [the night's outlook aligning with the intimate ambitions youth only knows as itself {with what experience knows as striving ‹what maturity accepts can come without results «but what perhaps wisdom understands may still play a part in some larger purpose ⟨however out of reach⟩»}]. Since fifty [that crying year of forty-nine really] Anwar has watched his own needs evaporate completely. By fifty-four not even a residue of his own volition seemed to remain [family taking precedence over personal wants].

Except when Anwar codes [tapping that music and math {the supernal linguistics outside his own history}] then something of his former selves returns. A restlessness speaking inaudibly of something antipodean[?] to selfnessess [by a syntax that can never know self]. And it feels good.

Previously caffeine would have gotten the blame for his restlessness. Hence the quitting [{the cold turkey} Week 0 Day 6 {the smell of Astair's coffee — an enduring torture ‹suffering «a mixture of existence and memory ⟨negation making things easier ⌈'True negation is impossible' [Mefisto will quip]⌉⟩»}]. But oh the inconvenience of delight. Desire's infection [at least {tonight} the headache's gone {gone for good?}].

And [anyway] this sleeplessness had nothing to do with so easy a causal chemical effect. Curiously it is the very thing that made Anwar [he's sure {vaguely}] sleepy all day [often when he's not at his workstation he can tell {as can Astair and Xanther ‹and probably even Shasti and Freya›} how by the sluggishness of his responses and actions his mind labors elsewhere on some computational puzzle {or puzzles «‹background processing» not all even necessarily computational›}].

Not that this description has ever suited Astair [who will caution him about applying metaphors of current data organization and processing to the life of our

synaptic nets {which Anwar had countered by assert-
ing that information technology may soon no longer
approximate those cerebral mysteries but equal if not
surpass them ‹how many other people have these dia-
logues «anyone?»?›} after which both agreed {especially
under the pressure of daily duties} to shelve considerations of dissolutions inherent in comparative reason-
ing {or analysis by analog ‹what happens to a metaphor
when it ceases to become a metaphor but the thing itself
«or 'actualizes the metaphor' ‹'or even inverts it'›»?›} at
least until the car was serviced or the children bathed
and calls returned {all the while Anwar's mind continued to negotiate ‹and renegotiate› alternative strategies
or decision branches ‹in today's case on a debugging
assignment on Enzio's Cataplyst-1›}].

Cat-

Just notices that [silly thing to notice].

As if there's a relation [is there? {silly}].

Or:

cat File.txt File2.txt > File3.txt

[Where {what?} File1.txt=S and File2.text=Z{?}]

At least [beyond all that {here}] a sense of relief as
Anwar readies to [again] bring the problem into relief.
Most important of all [beyond {understood} variables
and {limited} results]: formulate a clear question.
Something Anwar keeps trying to impress on Xanther
[to handle her proliferation of curiosities]. Make it
lucid. Make it sharp.

On this he and Astair are in agreement. [whether in psychotherapy or programming] The quality of the results is proportionate to the precision of the inquiry.

What Anwar does not in any way have now:

// if Z knows all possible movements of S
// if S knows all possible responses of Z

// how does Z anticipate S's next move?

[Talk about {if he wasn't just mimicking behavior} a huge decision tree {‹overfitting «trees!»› needing all kinds of pruning ‹pruning algorithms Anwar doesn't really know›} — forests.]

In other words: nothing at all to do with the Enzio assignment. Cataplyst-1 had been on ice for who knows how long and the company wanted to take another look. The trouble was that it was a broken build [a release build on top of it] that wouldn't even load. Maybe engineers on Talbot's or Ehtisham's level could instrument the code quickly. Anwar [however] has found the problem more than just frustrating or time-consuming. He still remains stumped by how to effectively proceed [not that he has a choice {he ‹his family!› needs the $9,000 ‹now more than ever›}].

And yet — [a bird in hand is better than two in the bush {much better than one bird in the bush ‹much much better than one 50k bird that's no longer even close to said proverbial bush›}.] And yet Anwar finds himself letting go of the bird in hand [why suddenly all this business about birds?] because [while for the moment PO might be dead] Anwar can't get away from another glitch [not even this afternoon's glitch but one he anticipated days ago {because there must always be glitches ‹especially where paradise is concerned «whether open or closed»›}].

To where Anwar turns now.

[despite present success] Anwar's M.E.T. module remains rickety because the A.I.M. Creation Tool he'd put together keeps producing inconsistent logic.

Just last month Xanther had inadvertently drawn attention to just how skittish by requesting an intelligible explanation of the Anticipatory Inter/fear/ance Model.

'First what it does not address,' Anwar had begun. 'It does not handle that which is reactive or simply part of the physics of the world. For example the grass here. See how it reacts to our movement through it?' [In fact this was all pre-scripted animation {but that was beside the point}.] 'The grass, however, does not anticipate the wind and bend first.'

'Play it again!' Freya had squealed. 'Again!'

'That grass is soooooo green!' Shasti had joined in.

'Okay.' [Xanther {not squealing}] 'Please now an example not in the not.'

How Anwar adored Xanther's keenness.

'In this scenario.' [Keystrokes {grass vanishing}.] 'Polygon Creature Z hunts Polygon Creature S. Z observes S moving in a specific direction yet in order to effect an encounter must anticipate where Creature S isn't now but will be in a few moments.'

The twins [faced with just a block skittering across the screen after another crude shape {without the lush renderings of ‹photo-extracted› foliage and sky}] promptly moved on to other rooms and pursuits.

Xanther [though] stuck with it.

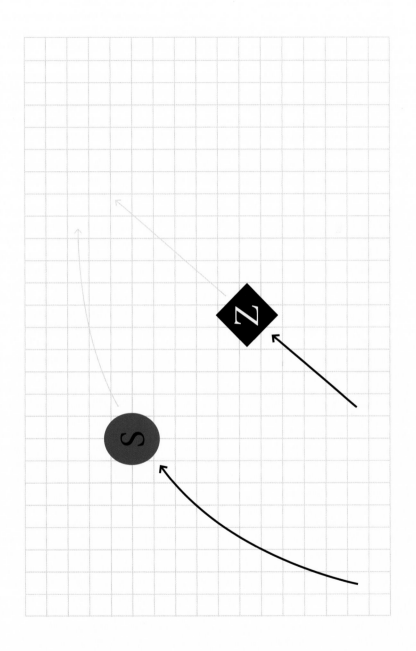

'Simple enough.'

'If what?'

'If it's all, like, uhm, regular enough?'

'If speeds and directions remain constant. Correct. But what if they're not?'

'Then you, like, have to watch where or, uhm, how they're not constant?'

'Go on.'

'If S is like changing speeds and maybe going faster, then slower, uhm, somehow you have to figure that in?'

'Beautiful. But what if observation is out?'

'Huh?'

'Right now Z observes S but if some obstruction were to lie between them, sufficiently opaque to eliminate any line of sight, say a fence or wall, how would Z know whether or not S is continuing along the last-observed path or doubling back?'

'Guess?'

'Exactly. How?'

Xanther had shrugged. And Anwar had laughed.

'Z must mind-read, silly.'

'Dad!' Xanther protested. 'Now you're being silly!'

'A little. But not really. I'm not implying something extrasensory. What I mean by "mind-read" is that Z must imagine how S thinks in order to understand how S will move.'

'A computer can do that?'

'Beautifully observed, daughter. Let's say there are ways to cheat.'

'But that's not fair, right? I mean it's cheating.'

'Since designers in essence know and control the limits to all scenarios and have quantified those environments— "Quantify," do you know that word?'

'Like quantity?'

'Excellent. So, as the computer knows all quantities involving these pre-scripted interactions, that information can be used to mimic anticipatory actions. In other words, S knows everything Z will do. Just as Z already knows everything S will do. Even every possible "could do" reduces definitely to what S "will do" and therefore Z can and will reach S at say point Y before S, or even Z for that matter, knows it's even going to point Y.'

'Poor S.'

Poor S indeed.

And S was the problem.

Which came down to M.E.T. and A.I.M. and the [way too many] indeterminate forms they in collusion keep offering up to the compiler. So Anwar returns to pointdom [or really linedom {with really no lines at all}] where [for the first forty minutes] most of his thoughts head towards one who could probably do this in his sleep [Mefisto].

The next twenty minutes though [Thank you Tim Towdy! {TMTOWTDI ‹or: There's More Than One Way To Do It›}] prove less existentially abysmal. [upon understanding three internal functions] Anwar fairly easily writes out fourteen lines. Almost a sonnet. Though wooing no heart.

Anwar rechecks his work and invokes the compiler.

Down in the kitchen Anwar pours himself a glass of water.

Afterwards he passes through the breakfast nook, then the dining/family room [considers his piano, the French doors {curtains hanging perfectly still «<like they were marble» «but could move at any moment»>}] before turning [west] to slip through the living room with its cavernous fireplace [Astair's glass wolves always at war on the mantelpiece] before heading back to his office [a leisurely domestic circuit to somehow ease his mind by reestablishing {reassuring?} place].

Compiling complete.

Anwar [glass still in hand] starts the program.

Polygon-dotdom again. No errors.

S reaches Y.

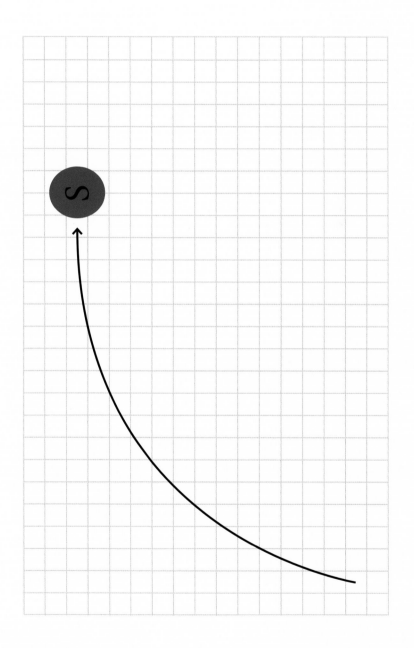

But where is Z?

It's the only reminder Anwar needs. [After all {!}] he just walked the entire house. Even stood in the kitchen [stood in their mud room!] but failed [feared {?}] to peer over that plywood barrier [where earlier that evening he had explained to Xanther the necessity of such reinforcements because {‹who knew what dangerous traps lay in wait nearby «gaps behind the stove and refrigerator, broken floorboards beneath some couch or table, even a frayed power cord or shoddy outlet perhaps»› theirs was a dilapidated manse}].

'How thoroughly have we considered this house through its eyes?'
'Mind-reading?' she had asked then [looking up at him with those wide astonishing eyes {one azure, the other hazel ‹both shot through with sparkles of green and gold «each ringed with a blue to rival black»›}{his love for her then ‹again› so enormous Anwar could only ‹without smile› nod}].

Anwar goes back downstairs. No guest [especially one so tiny and insignificant] will put off this inspection. Though Anwar still shudders with the approach.

No need to recall the hissing recriminations he and Astair had exchanged.

'What about our five-minute rule? What's been in the house less than five minutes can be thrown out in five minutes?'
'Five minutes, Astair?! She's had it all afternoon. Are you okay?'
'No, I'm not. Did you think about disease?'

729

'The vet told me it's unlikely to live more than a few hours. Maybe not even five more minutes.'

'Oh honey. This was supposed to be a future. Not, not, more dying.'

'You and I know "supposed to be" is a tricky guarantee. Darling, let's see what morning brings.'

'I'm not burying it.'

'Let's see what morning brings.'

Is that what sets Anwar on edge now? What he fears awaits him? A perfect stillness?

Something moves and Anwar jumps [or at least he thought he jumped {or thought he heard something}]. Even as the sound [rustling] seems to continue. Behind him.

Just at the entrance to the kitchen [opposite the pantry]. Faint but plausible [even if there's nothing visible]. Within the wall then? That scratching? There behind paint, drywall, and studs. Anwar edges closer [his ear not far from the family corkboard].

Has something now [in there] started listening for him? Or even some*things*? Who can tell: it's/they're already scurrying away [was that actually a scurry? {more than a scratching ‹that rustling?›?} {a confirmation denied by everything but the possibility contained in the faint sense of hollowness and passage beyond}].

All this could just have easily been nerves combined with his ear brushing the latest pinned receipt [{Jax & Boans Large Nest ‹!? «wtf! ⟨$250.69!⟩»›} which Anwar isn't believing {forget ears when he can't even trust his eyes}].

[{‹«⟨⌈Did Astair really pay that much for a doggy bed?⌋⟩»›}]

Of course if it turns out they do need an exterminator, they definitely can't afford one now [{if he asked} Kosiginski would only remind Anwar {rightfully too} of the terms on the lease {'Pay me monthly what this house is worth and then I'll cover exterminators, gardeners, even a valet.'}].

Still the last thing they need now is an infestation of rodents. And Anwar seriously doubts that the proverbial proclivities of Xanther's acquisition [should it survive] will be any match for a swarm of rats [a ridiculous Tom-and-Jerry moment that at least draws Anwar back to the plywood barrier].

And all it retains.

And defends.

[If by thought alone.]

That [what kind of?] stillness?

Because now there really is something peculiar. Something Anwar doesn't want to see.

But will.

The ridiculous dog bed.

Piled high with towels.

With [in the middle] the Nona T-Drive box filled with more towels.

Perfect comfort.

Only—

—if only Anwar had found sleep. Stayed in bed. If only making love with his wife of twelve years had led to both.

Anwar tries not to get antsy.

No rash conclusions.

Of course, he's overdoing things again.

[At least there's no corpse {though that might have been easier all around ‹easier for Astair «a quick flush ⟨heartbreak for breakfast⟩ ⟨Akita for dinner⟩»› except ‹they can't forget› now they can't afford that Akita}.]

No way a creature so minuscule [so weak] could have crawled out of here. A clear impossibility. Then rats?

Suddenly those Tom-and-Jerry thoughts return [though not so Tom-and-Jerry anymore {black oily shapes gnawing through plaster, driven by appetite, pouring out of walls, descending on the helpless creature . . . }].

The reality is so less graphic. Anwar sets down the empty box [his daughter's makeshift nest]. Obviously the day has arrived when identity has successfully tugged Xanther from the loyalty she has always demonstrated towards her parents [the good daughter {the first daughter ‹the dutiful daughter «the devoted daughter»›} now going her own way . . .]. Not that a little self-interest is a bad thing [{growing up} {relinquishing filiations too burdensome to bear ‹or at least bear fairly›} {surges of hormones too ‹her period?›} {boys} {the world beyond parental devotions}].

Still Xanther's insubordination strikes Anwar as unexpected.

Even if [through the sting] Anwar also feels proud [possibly happy]. Before bed Xanther had showed all the signs of wreckage: bruises, bandages, scabs [histories of infliction]. And yet she still glowed [with delight?]. Something he had not seen for a while. Certainly not since Dov had died [in fact mostly seen following Dov's rare visits {and then only briefly}]. Tonight though something about her [something bright and excited and maybe a little bit strange] had emerged and endured for a brief breath longer [many breaths {fresh and gaining . . . }].

The burnt stones of his childhood rise in his eyes [all that they were not {but were still conceived of beyond themselves}]. Not just Khufu, Khafre, and Menkaure but Abu al-Houl [*The Terrifying One* . . .]. Out of silence [years!] here she is suddenly: Egypt! His home and city and pride [{?} *Mother of the World* . . .]. Fragments maybe. Fractals? Three? [And that fourth {not a pyramid}?] The Pyramids he has no need to see now [which once {only once ‹up close›} Anwar had seen past busloads of sunglassed tourists {those satisfied with their exposures and posters and postcards} Anwar holding tightly {he remembers} the hands of his parents {‹very tightly› both of them wordless before the diminishing red sun ‹monuments in themselves «dear Fatima» «dear Shenouda»› telling him before such tombs that here was where he came from, here was what mattered, but what mattered most was everything he had yet to become}].

Anwar rubs his eyes and smiles [relieves his knees from this squat]. He knows he cannot avail himself to an I-am-surprised defense. How could he? Xanther's natural alliances to the natural are no mystery. Hadn't he just spotted her outside stroking the air? Tiny strokes upon nothing [or a nothing that sometimes glistened {glistened so slightly it nearly defied belief}].

He'd watched her for a while before giving up any delusion that he knew what the blazes she was doing.

She had beamed at his question as if she'd never heard anything sillier.

'Petting Adelaide of course.'

And there it suddenly was: the web.

And there too a submissive dark dot.

Afloat in the earthy air.

His daughter, petting a spider!

Even giving it a name!

What does one do with that?

There was only one problem with his current solution [and satisfaction]: the house itself.

Didn't the immense level of deterioration here make of every step [no matter where] a thump and thunder to rival Stravinsky's *Rite of Spring*?

[a light sleeper anyway] Anwar can always hear everything going on in their home and wakes whenever a toilet flushes or a creak slices down the hall announcing an adventure [or nightmare in need of comfort] by one of the intrepid twins.

To make matters worse: tonight he hadn't even fallen asleep.

And so now another thought threatens him [and with it another sound {how and why the rustling of a potential rodent or preposterous receipt could tickle his ear ‹and perhaps too the reason why the house's song has at this moment come upon him so vividly›}]:

the storm has stopped.

The hammering flood along with even the faint static of drizzle — gone.

Silence reigns.

And has reigned here for some time.

Which is when for an instant [even more vehemently than before] Anwar insists that he must have missed her footsteps.

[A desperate attempt.]

Xanther is an absurdly ill-coordinated creature. [even when obliging Astair to practice Tai Chi] Xanther's footfalls threaten floorboards.

Could Xanther have really made it all the way to the kitchen, gathered up her find and then crept back upstairs without the house alerting him?

Possibly [with an unlikely maybe].

Unlikely [with absolute certainty].

Anwar doesn't want unlikely.

Because what he fears most now is the impossible. The fear in fact is so great he almost can't leave his station beside the Jax & Boans.

He wants to stay where the invisible suggestion of rats or a disobedient child has chosen to remain.

He doesn't want to climb the stairs.

He doesn't want to look in on Xanther.

He's afraid of what he'll find.

Daddy!

Xanther had screamed.

She had found him.

Door [driver's side] ripped open.

Out of nowhere.

Arms thrust out to him.

Covered in blood.

Still screaming.

Save him!

At first Anwar had no idea what Xanther had handed him. He only knew the way her voice resounded [within {something about a cry in the storm something about a last breath something about drowning

— *going to drown* —

— *possible to drown* —

‹Anwar's guts torquing› ‹heart bashing away›}].

Xanther's every expression knocking the wind out of him.

Anwar will do anything for her.

If only here was not her anything.

[from her hands to his] This stiff creature laid to rest upon his palms.

White.

Eyes pinched tight [sunk deep in its own insubstantial coat].

First Anwar eased the kitten on its side. So small it fit easily in the palm of his left hand. Then he tilted the poor animal's head towards the floor and with his right fingers pressed gently on top of the rib cage.

LOOK.

LISTEN.

FEEL.

Vaguely coming back [both he and Astair had taken a CPR class before Shasti and Freya were born {nothing about animals ‹but Anwar remembered the key with infants was gentleness›}].

LOOK.

Breathing?

Not even a small swell of the chest.

LISTEN.

Forget that [{Anwar's ear nearly covered the entire creature} {and even if he could ignore the outdoor racket his own living alone ‹whether breath, movement, or pulse «especially his pulse»› was louder than anything this thing might produce}].

FEEL?

Not the slightest movement tickled his palm or his fingertips. Even his cheek [held close to that tiny pink nose] sensed no kiss of life.

So Anwar offered it his kiss: lips around the entire snout followed by a mouthful of air [too much {remembered ‹just›} can damage the infant's {?} lungs].

Only the tiniest puff.

And this time fingerprints detected the slightest rise. Anwar puffed again [the tiniest puff]. And again the tiny chest rose [{at least} the airway was clear].

Again.

And again.

How many times though? [Who knew for an animal {five?} {six?} { . . . }?]

Once every couple of seconds seemed right.

And all the time Xanther's unceasing [relentless] focus [crying {begging!} to restore what was in peril {what was already lost}].

And maybe for a moment Anwar believed he could succeed [even when he paused and felt the chest fail to rise {his patient puffs still continuing ‹putting off the building barrage of warnings: «hygiene» «sanitation» « . . . » could kittens get rabies? and gutter water? deal with that later› puff after puff after puff} chest rising] until [when he paused next] the chest not only failed to rise but Anwar could not deny the stiffening in the limbs [their coldness].

752

∴ *What perfect stillness then?* ∴

This was not happening.

∴ What else was happening? ∵

This was going to be awful in so many ways.

∴ **So many ways.** ∵

Forget the dog they were supposed to bring home. Forget all he and Astair had tried to keep from exposing Xanther to.

And why?

Because during one of those rare Los Angeles rainstorms [{in the middle of a drought too ‹drought! «in so many ways»›} so loud it drowned out the roar of fire trucks, police cars, and ambulances {civilization itself}] his daughter had still somehow detected blocks away a mew no louder than a hummingbird's hiccup. The source of which she had then brought to him. All but dead [all but?]. Begging him [imploring him] to set right what no father [even the terrifying one . . .] can set right.

So of course Anwar didn't stop the tiny breaths and the tiny pushes [compressions]. How could he? What with Xanther sitting right there? Because how could he [again!] show her what he couldn't do? Show her that that which she had saved was not saved [dreading so much her reactions {wails? shock? ‹another seizure?›}] not to mention every moment still to follow [what? returning the thing to the gutter? the nearest trash bin? presenting it to Astair for a backyard burial a family of raccoons would more than likely dig up later?].

Three compressions/one breath.

Even five compressions/one breath.

All the breath he had left.

And for what? Colder still. Stiffer still. No matter what combination he tried [still incohering right there in front of him,

{

dead,

dead,

Actually

she brought it back

from the—

dead

}

]

.

And only then [then {when Xanther had laid her gentle hand upon his shoulder ‹as if she were him and he was still only him›}] did Anwar realize that he too had not gotten over Arlington [and all they had buried there together].

Dead, dead, dead.

And so of course Anwar had wanted to save something [*needed* to save something] especially something this simple . . . this innocent . . . this inconsequential . . .

And the tears flooding down his face had surprised him almost as much as the calm way Xanther had asked to try too.

[]

. . .

Upstairs Anwar listens to Shasti and Freya breathe and sputter in their dreams.

When he moves on towards Xanther's room, the house announces his steps with a chorus of sustained cracks and groans [maybe not Stravinsky {more like Varèse}].

All perfectly familiar. Xanther's ceiling pricked with green light. Bureau to curtains to closet thick with shadow. Her small desk also draped in shadow. And tacked somewhere above it [amidst pictures of skateboarders and rock bands {Your Chemical Romance}] a napkin [inscribed by his own hand] with seven indeterminate forms.

0/0

∞ / ∞

0 x ∞

1^{∞}

0^{0}

∞^{0}

∞ – ∞

1=2

And as much as all [the all . . .] Anwar [again and
again . . .] knows he must fail to see [what we must all
fail to see . . .] what he does succeed in seeing now does
not surprise him.

St. Hopi

I have fallen in wells and risen.

— *Juan Felipe Herrera*

Juarez had run. Luther don't think he had ever seen that mangy thing so scared. Just drop-jawed and sick, tumbling over his own feet, seeing Luther step forward like that, for sure expecting him to splash into the deep, give them a swimming lesson or something.

Except Luther didn't vanish into no under-neath. Just stood there. Arms still out.

Maybe even Luther had been afraid too. Because when the falling stopped, and quick too, when he didn't sink but an ankle's worth, Luther felt all of him, guts to nuts, go sinking so much deeper into real drowning confusion.

And the next moment was no better. Like the only way anything could make sense was that everything was upside-down. Kinda like when they first got here. Luther just dangling, like he was about to drop into the storm below. Those piano graves too, all emptying up.

Only that didn't happen either and then Luther went from upside-down to something worse: like Luther wasn't Luther anymore. ∴ ∵ And nothing was lost. ∴ ∵ **And everything was left.** ∴ ∵ *And there was still a chance to change not only his but every path.* ∴

La neta que Luther had figured he'd just jump in, La Rana the leap, a lucky 54, fuckin Jaws his way across, and then drag the kid down.

And what got him? Got Juarez yipping in tighter and tighter circles? Piña and Victor choking out milagros like here was so much more than Gs?

Shallowness. That's it. Fuckin not enough. His big fuckin miracle.

Funny thing too is how it would've been one if kid had had the stones to walk. Some sight that would've been. Luther would've laughed, loud ~~like Lupita, like Juarez had started laugh~~ ing, when he stopped spinning around like some wounded duck, finally getting the joke, how the chalky water wasn't even a fist deep, hole not even a hole, then got back by Hopi to see it up close, put his hand in, show how a last chance swirled to mud around Luther's feet.

Luther had sloshed over then, grabbed the boy by the hair, like Lupita had grabbed her shorty that morning, by the roots. Only Hopi didn't put up any fuss. Just sagged. And Luther with little effort dragged him to another hole, not even dark. This one looked even shallower.

Luther expected to hold the kid under but Hopi just whispered "Forgive me" and slipped into the deep. Then the surface glassed over. It wasn't until halfway back to the van, after they had all hauled up the rise down which they'd first come, when they saw the real miracle. Tweetie seeing it first.

Luther will never forget it. Luther tries to forget it. Gets another bottle. Swallows the taste. Doesn't even know this taste. Sweet. But not too. Bitter too. But not too. No sharp to counter him, metal to charge him, not even remotely familiar. And worst of all won't stay down.

Afterward, Luther had cut out. What he really wanted was his crew close but knew how their laughs would lessen his work. No lessening. Not this night. Like Teyo said: "The higher you rise, the better they better remember you." Let them watch him distance off.

But he couldn't even get to his cages. Even if he came close. All set to kennel up with Tookie, Sen Dog, and Lord Gino, curl up with his scarred survivors, use a dish for a pillow, sleep against the wire. Until he kept seeing man-boy charming his warriors.

Luther drove to Lupita's instead. Could use some of that laughter. Old bitch knew how to howl. Then kept heading north.

210, I-15 to where the Antelopes play. Two gates. Two doors. One big room. Space enough between the two for a third. Both under silver-gray polyester knit, which Luther always leaves on. Like he don't know by heart what waits?

Chopped a full half-foot, hydropneumatic sus-pension, 320 in a straight eight, frenched head-lights. With 400 watts inside plus tuck-and-roll Naugahyde. Just for extras. And that's just for starters. His Roadmaster. 1951.

The other is a 425 HP monster with Mopar heads, acid-dipped frame, stainless chrome, panels sharp as razors, five-spoke wheels. Dash and gauges restored. Just for extras. Also just for starters. His Fury. 1959.

Get them going and they rumble enough to shake teeth loose, make souls doubt. To look at them though, that was something else. You could dive in. Drown down there.

Sure Victor can go crazy under the hood. Did the boost like he'll do the gears. Like that fuckin Camaro of his. Sure, catch a sunny day, Luther will drive down to Dawgz, let Rosario and Carmelita wash one with chamois and warm water, a little soap. Get their titties slick. They can tickle the exhaust pipes. Put on a show.

But when it comes to the outside for realz, rims to roof, suds to wax, Luther calls Zavaleta. Why else keep these babies up here? Here color's a whole other story. Shallows again. ∷ *The history of the same thing over and over again until it's something else.* ∷

The Roadmaster floats on paint: base on base, coats of shade, polished for coats of clear. Hundreds. Luther likes to say. And no one doubts him. Electric tangerine and topaz. Pure sun.

The Fury disappears in paint: base on base, coats of shade, polished for coats of clear. Thousands. Luther likes to say. And no one doubts him. Red star and purple. Pure doom.

These some ranflas. Strong and low. And when they out what they do they hardly do. No need to. Just to idle there lets everyone know what needs knowing. Dares any fool to get close. And if not for Teyo, the rain, these would have been at the Barris car show in Culver City today.

Maybe Luther will call Zavaleta over tomorrow. Rain should be gone. Get the Covercrafts off, get these beasts pearly. Solo the Roadmaster to the shore. Or to lado este with the Fury.

Out back, Luther watches the storm at last refuse its own fall. A new air stirring. Clouds parting. Giving way, even in warm May, to something icier, a shimmer of dark meaner than any storm.

Another beer down. It will take more than beer to find sleep. Not that Luther wants to sleep. Something moves along his back fence. An animal awareness already gone when his bottle shatters against metal slats and chain link.

Luther laughs. Only to feel it again, that same awareness, except this time behind him. Like it's inside. Gets all ripply up his spine. Gets him charging back to his cars, like he halfway expects something to be sitting between them, where Luther goes to stand, where he laughs again, like he's taking up station. But against what? Still unable to shake how what's outside, what's inside, don't matter.

Luther's out of beer. So he takes every empty he can find and shatters them against his back fence. As if what's long-gone gone away could now be even more chased away.

But Luther still sees it. At the expense of any- thing else, forget cars, broken glass, what- ever animal eyes dare look his way. Or man's. Luther fears no man. And certainly no man's laws. As he always says: "I'm so against the law they haven't even written the laws I'm already breaking by just being me."

Only this is different. As if there were a place beyond a place and even a thing beyond a thing that is equally against the law. And this thing has suddenly seen him.

Like earlier when Luther had watched Hopi mumbling to Piña in the back of the van: "Pa-petals mock by count our ca-cali-CALculators of love. Asters cannot count." Or later whispering, just once, "Forgive me," not save me or stop this, as if Luther could ever forgive what he could not know.

Or last, and worst of all, after it was over, returning to the van, Tweetie stopping for no reason, because he was tired or just wanted to turn around because. Because he too had sensed some awareness? Though there was no awareness. Not down there.

Luther had been astonished.

But something rougher than rust still got him biting down hard, and running back harder.

So what if hairs on the back of his neck went stiff? Or under both pits, between his legs, snaked a damp cold?

If Hopi wanted to die twice then that was up to him. Not that this kid wasn't still surprising everyone.

Luther slowed once, and then only to snatch up a shovel, metal mangled months ago in the tread of some CAT.

Not that St. Hopi's hands ever wavered ∷ almost like some pale steeple without bells . . . ∷ thrust out of the chalky deep ∷ one never-ending prayer . . . ∷ still against the sky ∷ *the second-most beautiful Luther would ever see* . . . ∷ like Luther even gave a fuck, as he swung the blade of the shovel down.

If Anything . . .

The word "history" comes from an ancient Greek verb ἱστωρειν *meaning "to ask." One who asks about things — about their dimensions, weight, location, moods, names, holiness, smell — is an historian. But the asking is not idle. It is when you are asking about something that you realize you yourself have survived it, and so you must carry it, or fashion it into a thing that carries itself . . .*

— *Anne Carson*

Before it can become the silent thing, the still thing, sadness wakes Xanther.

Beyond tears.
Beyond the cost of any cry.

And even if in the way she starts seems without tran-
sition, Xanther's awareness gathers at such speed, or is it
ferocity?, sleep itself seems little more than an unlikely
invention.

Xanther feels that far beyond sleep, even fatigue.

And any memory of what preceded this alertness comes upon her so savagely it offers no memory at all.

So Xanther finds another.

An old one.

Years ago.

Back when they'd lived in Georgia.

The crushing scratch for life battering cement and dead leaves, Xanther darting out to the back patio.

How had it fallen?

Was it ill?

Or injured by predator or object?

Only then remembering the bang preceding this frantic slapping and spinning, broken? wings flapping the ground, breaking more?, completing circle after circle, panic already patterned by the unseen, the most common transparency refusing to give and so taking away path and breath.

And to think Xanther had first thought gunshot — is this what Dov hears all the time?

And then sonic boom, that weird announcement of speed, faster than sound, making nothing but sound, thanks to dangerous planes racketing panes from far above.

And as if there were help in touch, or even in reach, Xanther's slender fingers had cupped the hummingbird, trying to calm its terrified shout. Wings for reasons too vague to matter now lost to any memory of flight.

But even with the wings quieting against Xanther's palms, the poor hummingbird could not cease its shuddering. Until suddenly, and violently too, its whole body shook at once, neck contorting, eyes going blank, though they weren't blank were they?, difference doesn't mean blankness, right?, what then did it see?, or comprehend?, the error of windows?, of reflection? ∵ *refracting the one self into another self beyond what every reflection still fails to consider . . . ∴* , Xanther knowing this in the way she knows how mirrors invert her into a her that's not really her ∵ which is so wrong as a reflection of Xanther, right? ∴ , can animals know so?, especially a tiny hummingbird?, probably not, right?, like really, it'd just see its own reflection as another competitor? ∵ **as an understanding of its own end** ∴ , the two then not equal, both flying along, if inversely, that terrible last path?, and both then sharing the same end, is that what happened?, and is this something only Xanther knows?, or had this fragile creature known it too?, at the last moment, like some bad bird joke?, or nothing of the kind?, not even understanding afterward what had gathered it up after so blinding a prohibition? making out of Xanther's hands nothing kind, just the devouring jaws nature is so full of?

But before Xanther could offer something else, maybe communicate a little more?, at least take it to her mom, her very gentle clutch already as slight as an enfolding of air, the seizure abruptly stopped and then in the instant before Xanther's cry and sobs told her palms in that certain language of stillness, of quiet, how life without even a hint of direction can just depart.

Now in the dark of Xanther's room nothing hides. And it is very dark though Xanther can still tell at once by the way the darkness fails, the way it no longer withholds, doesn't protest, or pretend, and really, forget her room, even those dim pinpricks of phosphorescence on her ceiling, or her windows, all of them ajar now, when did that happen?, or forget how her door's open too, onto nothing more than a home's simple dark, all of it coming forward, beyond concealing let alone revealing what wakes her now, and what keeps waking her too, in fact she's still waking up, how is that possible? Is that what grief does?, waking you over and over?, without sobs?, without tears?, if only Xanther could cry out, or at least make sense of this darkness, which Xanther can make sense of, kinda, somehow getting how such surrounding denial of light can carry no trace of origin, this darkness in particular ∴ *because not all darkness is created equal* ∴ .

So Xanther does her best to kick off her sheets, fly downstairs, while not moving at all. Not even a twitch.

Xanther doesn't have to leave her room.

Xanther doesn't have to leave her bed.

Xanther doesn't even have to sit up.

Because as Xanther knew well before the sadness woke her, she no longer needs to find the sadness, because what would allways be sadness had already found her.

There is no need to move.

There is an alternative.

What had called her. And answered her. Only her.

It sure hadn't answered her dad.

Anwar crying as he desperately tried to breathe life into that tired form. Xanther had even felt sorry for him. She could see how badly he wanted to help. She also could see he could see how little he could help. But most of all when she asked to try she could see what he would never see.

Or is this only how Xanther understands it now? Body tingling like a fever without sickness, pain without hurt?

When her dad had returned the tiny thing to her palms.

Had she too believed it was dead?

Xanther tries to remember.

She remembers the water outside.

She remembers the fog crawling over the windows, into the car.

She even remembers Dov. And the shiny black box they buried him in.

No, Xanther never thought the kitten was dead.

Despite coldness, rigidity, Xanther had still somehow heard an impossible call resound within her.

And the idea that this mottled creature of white and gray and pink, balling up like a fist of ice, could have somehow experienced her as a figure of terror, a predator, death personified, never once crossed her mind.

If anything . . .

If anything . . . it was the other way around.

"On its side," Anwar had kept mumbling. "Tiny puffs for tiny lungs. With squeezes too. Very gentle squeezes for a very gentle heart."

And just as Anwar had done, and kept telling her to do too, Xanther eased the unbending thing on its side, applying with the tip of her little finger the slightest pressure to its ribs.

Also as Anwar had done, Xanther placed her mouth over the creature's nostrils and mouth, in fact over most of its head, jaws within jaws, filling her cheeks, though only a little bit, to expel the tiniest breath of air.

And probably Xanther expected the breath to go nowhere.

Probably she was already readying the next.

∴ She was. ∵

∴ Wordless as worded. ∵

∴ **Except that breath did go somewhere.** ∵

Just slipping within at first, the little Xanther had to offer, finding the smallest way into the smallest place, where it should have stopped, at least found resistance.

∴ Only nothing was resisted. ∵

∷ Nothing was refused. ∷

∴ That creature took more than one tiny breath. ∵

∴ **And kept taking it too.** ∵

Suddenly the air in Xanther's mouth was gone, the air in her throat too, with the rest following, whatever her lungs could hold, rushing out of her, with enough force that Xanther had to grip the thing, hold hard, arms struggling to extend, lock elbows, shove away what kept threatening, *by all it vacated,* to occupy her from within.

Not that Xanther could shove it away.

Or come close to locking elbows.

And not that it stopped either.

Taking more and more, :: *and oh what darkness circumscribes her* :: , thickening beyond comprehension, as even the knowledge of air and breath, the sense of anything else :: everything else :: , had Xanther not refused then to let any more of herself slip through.

∴ *How did she do it?* ∵

With a great heave, wrenching the thing away. It would have killed her, it was killing her, was it?, really?, so hardly taken by surprise then, no, not at all, to find the tiny creature all of a sudden twitching and shaking, probably afraid, was it afraid?, it sure seemed that way, eyes glued shut, torso roped in trembles, coughing and sputtering, until to both Xanther's and Anwar's surprise the white kitten opened its mouth and as if about to yawn retched up water and strings of drool.

And not just on Xanther.

And not just water and drool either.

The tiny thing

                                      released

            a spew of dark,

                                      clotted liquid,

splattering her seat,

                            the door, even as

far away

                            as the dash.

Then it yowled, or if not quite a yowl a high-pitched series of clicks and squeaks, trills really, as it also attempted to stand, failed, tried again to stand again, collapsing all over again, finally lying on Xanther's steady palm, hardly lifting its head, snorting twice more.

Whereupon Xanther offered a cradle like she'd never made before, her carefully interlaced fingers contouring around the fragile spine, maybe too apparent to even call fragile, something still weaker there, slighter, this wisp of white gratefully accepting Xanther's caring clutch, or so it seemed, curling into itself, sinking with relief into those palms, eyes never opening, as the panting lessened, the mouth again shut, as Xanther drew it against the warmth of her own still-heaving chest.

Anwar had wanted to get Xanther to a clinic at once, see if her knees and elbows needed stitches, get her shots. But Xanther had refused. They were going to a vet first.

Anwar did not object.

They found an emergency animal hospital on Wilshire near Euclid.

Her dad did most of the talking, and sure there was plenty of stuff Xanther missed, mostly because her attention kept diverting to the little thing she cupped between her hands. The gist, though, was obvious: they could check the kitten in for the night and hope for the best or they could take it home and hope for the best.

Hope. Xanther was suddenly thinking of Dov. Hope was not an option. Nor was leaving this little one here for the night.

Anwar had stepped aside with a nurse, or what in animal clinics, Xanther learned, are called technicians, this one blonde, with a little makeup, in a blue smock, white thread spelling out Tessera, reminding Xanther of a missing piece to a puzzle Xanther would never know the whole of, because the box was missing. Then a vet named Dr. Brady had joined them. All gray, in a white jacket, with blue thread spelling out his name.

Dr. Brady conducted the check-up: temperature, pulse, weight, "Gosh, next to nothing," Tessera had exclaimed, and the scale seemed broken, LEDs pinned at wavering zeros.

And then Anwar was talking with them again, out of earshot, again, and taking out his wallet.

∴ Tessera never marries and eventually leaves the animal care industry, moving to Arizona where she dies in a car accident on her way to cleaning a house. Her last thoughts ask of her mother, already twenty years dead, whether or not happiness finds you or you must find happiness or is happiness just another tooth fairy you should dispose of before you reach that age when the demanding of such answers reveals a life badly misled? ∴

∴ Dr. Brady lives until eighty-nine but forgets who he is before he reaches seventy. ∴

∴ Neither Tessera nor Dr. Brady will remember this occasion, and what they hear about on the news later will remind them only of their own good fortune and only because they have yet to know the fortunes of their future. ∴

Xanther, a little carsick, and Anwar, a little unsettled, left with instructions to keep the kitten warm and feed it every six hours. Shots and anything else would have to wait until later. Six weeks was Dr. Brady's recommendation. "If it lives through the night," words Tessera had mouthed to Anwar. "It's no more than two weeks old. Maybe not more than one." Anwar had carried to the car the Just Born Milk Replacer for kittens.

Later, when her dad took the twins and drove back to Venice to retrieve Xanther's glasses, when her mom had started washing off the dried blood on Xanther's arms and legs, they discovered only minor scratches, which didn't quite match up with her memory of the fall. Xanther didn't even have any bruises. That was a first.

Both parents had refused to allow Xanther to keep "the thing" in her room, and this time, despite numerous apologies, Anwar stood by his directive. Astair stood with him, repeating "possible diseases," the need for more tests, more caution.

Xanther threw a fit, useless, after which she threw herself into creating the perfect spot for the kitten, blankets in a box, on top of that humongous dog bed her mom had picked up, plus a hot-water bottle wrapped in one of Anwar's old cashmere sweaters, and plenty of rolled-up towels to stuff into cracks around the washer and dryer.

Twice Astair had helped Xanther prepare some Just Born, even if the stuff just seemed to roll off the little kitten's lips, if a kitten has lips, if that's what you call that area below that place of broken whiskers. Or not broken. More like sizzled off.

Before she went to bed, Xanther managed one more feeding and then after refilling the hot-water bottle bundled up her already sleeping charge in a little towel she'd warmed beforehand in the dryer.

Which, finally, was how Xanther left it, unable to hold back her tears, too many, along with doubts, way too many doubts.

"If it lives through the night."

Outside, the storm has passed. At least the rain has stopped. Not even branches creak anymore as they sometimes do in the aftermath of a heavy rain, when leaves and fronds now and then shift, letting go of their holdings.

Through the roof beams, Xanther can almost hear the sky's lifting emptiness taking away questions of numbers.

Everything in place.

Arranged.

Safe.

Even this kitten beside her seems nothing other than simplicity itself.

Also in place.

Also arranged.

Also safe.

It can barely move.

It can't even open its eyes.

Until Xanther tells herself Anwar must have relented, placed it here while she slept, even as she's already undermining the adequacy of this explanation, trying to convince herself again that it was her mom, Astair must have scooped it up and secretly resettled it here, which Xanther also doubts as fast as she can make it up, not that any of these thoughts matter, because Xanther really doesn't care, Xanther feels fine, feels better than fine: the kitten is here at her side and even if nothing seems to have changed everything suddenly feels manageable.

Or better:

answerable.

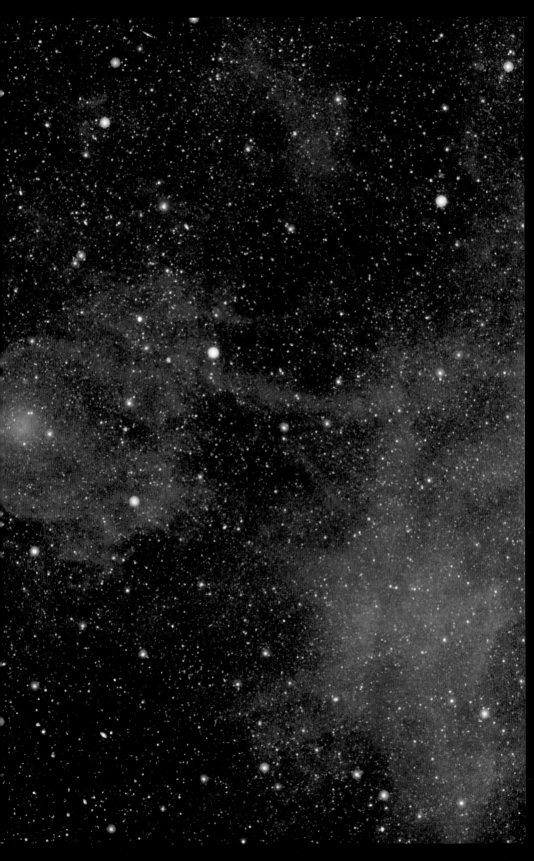

THE FAMILIAR

VOLUME 1

Copyright © 2015 by Mark Z. Danielewski

All rights reserved. Published in the United States by Pantheon Books, a division of Random House LLC, New York, and in Canada by Random House of Canada Limited, Toronto, Penguin Random House companies.

Pantheon Books and colophon are registered trademarks of Random House LLC.

Permissions information for images and illustrations can be found on pages 844 & 845.

Library of Congress Cataloging-in-Publication Data
Danielewski, Mark Z.
The Familiar, Volume 1: "One Rainy Day In May"/ Mark Z. Danielewski
p. cm.
ISBN 978-0-375-71494-8 (softcover: acid-free paper).
ISBN 978-0-375-71495-5 (ebook).
I. Title.
PS3554.A5596F36 2015   813'.54—dc23   2014028320

Jacket Design by Atelier Z.
Author Drawing by Carole Anne Pecchia.

Printed in China

First Edition
9 8 7 6 5 4 3 2 1

www.markzdanielewski.com
www.pantheonbooks.com

FONTS

MORE FONTS

THANK YOUS

Rita Raley

Edward Kastenmeier

Nikolai Beope, Seth Blake,
Anthony Miller, and
Sandi Tan

Lieutenant Wes Buhrmester
and Detective John Motto

Lloyd Tullues

Noam Assayag-Bernot

Carole Anne Pecchia

n8 rightmeier

Translations

Armenian .... Niree Perian
German ....Christa Schuenke
Hebrew .... David Duvshani
Mandarin/Cantonese ....Jinghan Wu
Russian ....Anna Loginova
Turkish .... Gökhan Sarı

More Thank Yous

Peter Andersen,
Aimee Bender, Lydia Buechler,
Sarah Shun-lien Bynum, Michiko Clark,
Christopher J. Danielewski, Lucy Davis,
Steve Erickson, Dan Frank, Warren Frazier,
Emily Giglierano, Allison Hill, Andy Hughes,
Altie Karper, Chris Kokosenski, Larry Maher,
Laurie Ochoa, Alex Olivier,
Christopher O'Riley,
Jennifer Rudolph Walsh,
and Peter Weingold

Atelier Z

{in alphabetical order}

Regina Gonzales

Michele Reverte

Lost Cat

- small female calico cat with black,
  orange and white coat
- missing her right eye
- 24th and Brush Creek Drive area

Reward for her return

A CIRCLE ROUND A STONE

PRODUCTION

COMING SOON . . .

THE
FAMILIAR

FALL 2015

And Oria the Owl fell.

Talons tucked away. Great wings too.

Only rectrices carve the air into a direction—

toward that moving moment

below,

squirming along,

blind to the great amber eyes fixed on its useless progress.

Even in the wind of this descent Oria hears the bleating racket of her prey as it struggles across the field.

She's not the only one.

Swiveling her head Oria catches the rustle of something beyond the tree line. Moving closer. Moving faster.

A coyote maybe?

In a race of hunger. A song Oria knows too well.

But tonight the song of hunger has many parts.

Nearer still another pursuit—

 silky

thr-u^{*u u u u u*} *s h*

 whispering through weaving grass. Not as fast as those closing in on the tree line but just as hungry.

 A snake.

Though tonight neither rustle nor *thr-u*^{*u u u u u*} *u s h* has a chance.
 Oria will arrive first.
 Easily.

Except as she tucks her head, Oria catches the hush of a third rival. This, a song of hunger above. Falling with her. Calling her off—

But Oria neither alters nor slows her course. Remiges pulling in tighter. Streamlining every angle down to her deadly beak. Focused only on that flat fast-rising world.

Below, two rabbits catch sight of the warring raptors dropping from the sky. Terror bounces them free of the grass, great leaps following for cover.

Thruuuuuush doesn't pause but the gaining momentarily stutter at news of these fleeing cottontails.

Oria though never deviates from the squirming thing below.

Served up by this blurring world.

It stops. Or maybe it fell over. This dark thing still squirming for a breath more. Paws then at the ground.

Big as a rabbit.

Bigger.

As a skunk.

Is it a skunk?

Smaller.

Nothing white there. Only mottled black. With patches inkier than black.

Followed by a whispering little tail.

Like a snake. Only . . .

Yeah B!i *Yeah B!i*

Yeah B!i *Yeah B!i*

Meat for days is all Oria knows. Meat for days for her little ones. For her. And for her mate if he ever returns.

But he will never return.

He left moons ago.

Oria's talons extend.

Razor the air.

Great wings cutting apart the wind.

Finding purchase.

Familiar shock waves rattling into her.

Driving her laterally too. Even as her legs keep extending downward, driving downward, talons wide now as any skunk or rabbit.

The same is true—

— above her.

Just above her.

Oria doesn't need to look.

Won't look.

Knows another pair of talons razors after her. After mantle and nape. Driving hard to knock her down. Blunt her into the flat fast-rising ground. Seize then the prey for himself.

Except—

Oria has her

prey.

Great wings snapping wide then, at once the wind of her fall hurling her upward, bill to crown driving skyward.

Of course the snake *thrᵤᵥᵘᵘᵤᵤᵤshing* cannot know yet its prey is lost.

The coyote though, and it is a coyote emerging from the tree line, stops in the grass, dumbfounded at the sight of that seizure. Looking away just as fast. Looking for the rabbits now. Skulking off.

Only Oria sees . . . the coyote turn then and leap, snapping at her attacker. An eagle. Male.

Only Oria . . . sees the snake uncoil then, bringing down those following wings.

Instances she knows as clearly as summer lightning. She has lived her long life with such flashes of lightning which her long life has taught her to disbelieve. They are what never finds a place in this world.

The thing squirming in her talons is real though. Warm and heavy and even these hundred feet up only slightly confused. Oria feels its heart beating.

And as if to answer, Oria beats her wings faster too.

Of course, she could kill it now.

Beak it to death.

And would too if her attacker had given up.

Then, as Oria wheels farther away from the clearing, rising still higher above the dense trees and rocky climbs, she sees her mistake.

This is no male eagle but another Great Horned Owl like herself.

Likely a mother too.

Also looking for prey to bring back to her fledglings.

Perhaps that's why she keeps up this pursuit, flying still harder, with altitude her advantage, a wide wheel closing the distance while

still cuts loose of her deadly bill.

She is bigger than Oria. Much bigger. Beautiful too. And more powerful. Enormous wings shadowing the land.

And without meat clutched beneath her downy belly she flies faster.

Much faster.

Oria knows she will have to dive again.

Only her attacker dives first. Diving away.

Oria doesn't understand.

Those beautiful enormous wings falling away.

Oria only hears the

crack!

an instant later,
and by then she's diving too.

Instinct evades the echoing

crack!

following her attacker's

spiral toward the high weeds.

Except when Oria at last levels out, her attacker continues to plummet.

The way the great wings twist then and go askew as they flip twice across the ground before lodging in a thicket of thorn sickens Oria. Even her talons loosen.

But a small heart still beats there. Almost fast enough to burst.

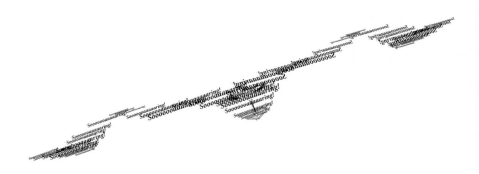

Soon Oria reaches the cover of remembered branches, not even a whisper on the air, gliding beside her dark trunks, above her dark streams.

Except her home is not there.

Or it is there but it is a home now wrong.

High edges broken. Bedding scattered. The rest

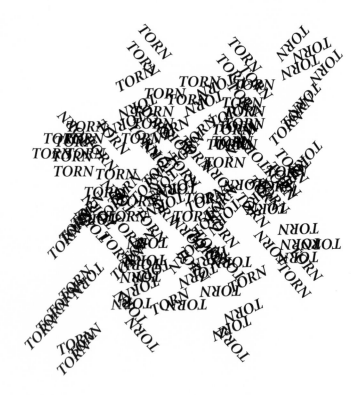

TORN

TORN

TORN

TORN

TORN

TORN

TORN

Her three fledglings gone.

TORN

TORN

TORN

TORN

Oria drops her prey. That easily: hunger exiled along with the need to feed.

Pain blossoms in her chest. Spreads through her head until it blots out her eyes.

Sight Sight
Sight Sight Sight
Sight Sight Sight
Sight Sight Sight Sight Sight
Sight Sight Sight Sight Sight Sight Sight
Sight Sight Sight Sight Sight
Sight Sight Sight
Sight Sight Sight
Sight Sight
Sight Sight
Sight Sight Sight
Sight Sight Sight
Sight Sight Sight Sight
Sight Sight Sight
Sight Sight Sight Sight

She can't move.

Must move.

Oria hops out along the largest reaching limb, scans the forest floor.

A moment later she stands on the forest floor, hops along the ground, scans for movement. She cries.

More cries.

          More hops.

                    Until she

     soars

                  above again.

A raccoon?

Oria sees no raccoons.

An opossum though.

Oria beats her great wings.

        What's it eating?

     Pale jaws dark with blood.

The opossum greets the warrrrrrring of her great wings with a wide-mouthed

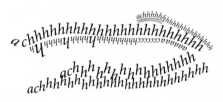

Are those tiny feathers gummed between its teeth?

Only too perfectly then, in an instant, by more lightning, a flash, Oria finds her fragile issue torn up in there, choked down, each tiny skull crushed.

Even if it's an empty-mouthed Achhhhhhhhhhhhhhhhhhhhhhh! that finally holds Oria back.

    More pain.

          From toes to cere.

Beneath their tufts, her ears scream.

Oria beats her wings again, great wings thrown wide,
rising slightly, talons sharper than threats, even if before she

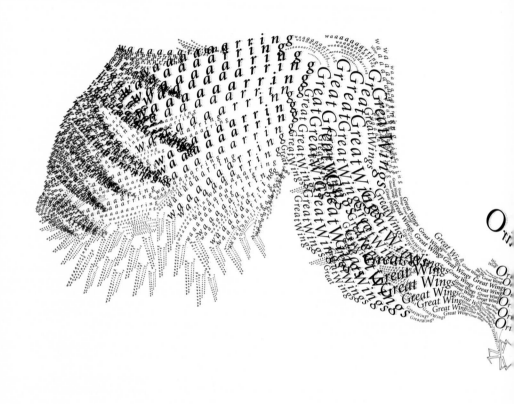

can dart at its eyes, loose her own skreeeeeeeeech, feet
scamper, beneath brush and leaves, the opossum retreats,
vanishing with bloody jaws and mystery.

Again Oria soars.

All she can do now is listen.

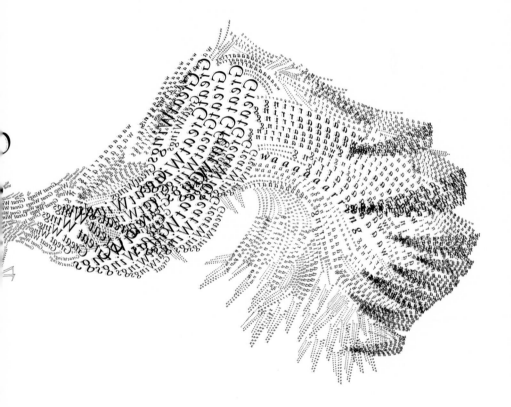

Instinct listens

and instructs.

SNATCH! SNATCH! SNATCH! SNATCH! SNATCH!
SNATCH! SNATCH! SNATCH!
SNATCH! SNATCH! SNATCH!
SNATCH!
SNATCH! SNATCH!
SNATCH! SNATCH!
SNATCH! SNATCH!
SNATCH! SNATCH! SNATCH!
SNATCH! SNATCH! SNATCH!

Somehow altering her . . .

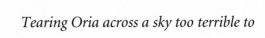

Tearing Oria across a sky too terrible to

cross.

The three were still too young to fly but old enough to try.

Maybe they fell . . .

She listens for their wide

reeeeeek   reeeeeek

reeeeeek reeeeeek reeeeeek

cheeeeeeoiap   cheeeeeeoiap

cheeeeeeoiap cheeeeeeoiap

sheeeooo

sheeeooo sheeeooo sheeeooo

But only silence answers Oria's silent sweeps, until after sweep after sweep, after yet another adjustment of her great feathered head, she catches within a warmer thread of air a thinnerstranger cry.

Nearby.

*By flick of primaries, all nine, a quick spin returns Oria
with easy wingbeats to her grove.*

Toward her tree.

·eeek   reeeeeek

Where the thinnerstranger cry keeps growing louder.

·oo   sheeeooo   sheeeooo

Only she still sees her three fledglings.
Three fledglings.
Still gone.

Oria blind, and not, to the black squirming thing at the center as she rounds by hops the high ridge of her nest.

Gooowaaaaying

a frantic answer which quickly enough becomes its own frantic question.

Bleeeeeeeaaaat

Bleeeeeeeaaaat

Bleeeeeeeaaaat

Bleeeeeeeaaaat

That black squirming thing crosses

over to nuzzle its head against her downy chest.

A cub.

Not even a cub.

But still a jaguar.

A jaguar newborn.

Oria will eat it herself.

Swallow it whole.

Only Oria sees . . . herself slam the tip of her bill through the thin layer of bone to dig out beneath the softer eats. She will take her time too, tearing away and swallowing the rest of the meats.

Only Oria sees . . . how the eyes are also sealed shut and this confuses her. It causes her to see things, other things. Her chicks. When they were blind too. And her mate with his eyes wide, cast over their brood, cast over her, before he flew off and never returned. Oria even sees that other Great Horned Owl with her broken wings flipping over and over across the wounding ground.

Which is how, somehow, Oria by summer lightning

and something else

finds new sight.

Which is when Oria drives her beak

into the back of the soft black and now

thrummmmmmmmmmmmurring

head.

For Carl . . .